Dear Glin

She'll not need
anyone else's love
if she has your Rose.

Aldonza Ramsey

Chapter 25 "a Red Rose"

Joseph M. Pugliese

GIRL WITH THE PURPLE RIBBON

GIRL WITH THE PURPLE RIBBON

Three childhood friends find themselves on separate sides of the Vietnam War. Coming of age in 1964 they learn that love, honor, and freedom cost more than they expect.

Joseph M. Puglia

Library of Congress Catalogue-in-Publishing Data is available

ISBN-13: 978-1533082176

Book design by Franchesca Liauw

Printed in the United States of America

Girl With The Purple Ribbon

For my girls: Sabine and Simone

Stay Gold,

Your Daddy, Joe

Acknowledgments

Before meeting Ofa Salome Petrosyan via Facebook, I had perused scores of names searching for the perfect forename for the perfect character. Thank you, Ofa for agreeing to lend your name. You gave Ofa Hawkins the life she needed. She couldn't help but become the heroine.

I fondly extend appreciation to the kids at Starbucks in La Canada, California. Your warm, welcoming smiles and the Earl Grey you poured kept me going. You were good company during the long and tedious process of creating my story.

I am especially grateful to Franchesca Liauw for designing the cover. You captured the dubious and complicated caricature of Ofa Hawkins, and you did it from England.

Raffi Alexander, I appreciate your can-do attitude as you perfected the cover. Spider Box Photography saved the day.

Jurgita Dargyte, your image made Ofa come to life. As a model, you defined her complex persona – beauty, brilliance, fragility, and grit. Thank you for believing in this project. Thank you for believing in me and for providing the resources, which propelled this book.

Luana Dutremble, my editor, thanks for your meticulous attention to detail. You made me look pretty darn good. I'll visit you and Grizz in the fall. Your cabin in Idaho will be a good place to push the sequel.

Jack Joy, you counted the edits and the re-writes – 37 no less. Thanks for doing the formatting and printing the hardcopy drafts.

A heartfelt thank you to the following whose names I used to define my key characters. Jerry Pollard, Gary Reynolds, Jim Burns, Butch Ragsdale, Steve Petit, Jimmy Messerschmitt, Fred Alexander, Gil Robinson, Matt Durney, and Dan Neremore. In 1969, we served together in the Marines, and you guys continue to define the ethos of our Corps.

Joe Quackenbush, you're no longer with us; I always admired you. Forever in my heart! In boot camp, you had the top bunk. Your memory will endure as the Communications Officer on the USS Midway.

Master Gunnery Sergeant Wood, you're the hard-ass of the Platoon. I think you were perfectly cast. With all due respect Master Guns.

My dear friend Buzz Baviello – Doc. You represent the Corpsman who saved my Marines' lives.

Sergeants R.S. Winston, Mothershed, Yanik, Poweda, and Crider my former Drill-Sergeants; I kept you true to character. Sir! Thank you, sir!

Ando Barsegyan, my former student, you took command of the 1st Squad and you truly were a credit to the Corps.

Lý Trúc Việt – Your story is remarkable. As a child, you escaped Vietnam by boat, and on a dream ship, you found America. Through your eyes, freedom is defined. I think you will like the character who carries your name.

Special thanks to Rick MaddogMike Flynn, a Marine from the fabled 1st Battalion 9th Marine Regiment. You left a year ago, but you will continue to live through your character, Rick MaddogMike Flynn – Carry on! Semper Fi...

Please note, a special acknowledgment to the First Battalion 9th Marine Regiment – Di Bo Chet. (The Walking Dead). I put my characters into your band of brothers.

Author Notes

I wrote *Girl with the Purple Ribbon* with no intention of reaching a particular audience. After I had written the first sentence, I wrote the next and kept going until I wrote the last. Perhaps somewhere, someone will need my story. Someone, who will somehow become a better person because of Ofa Hawkins, Seamus O'Grady, and Elijah Bravo. Perhaps my novel will give one a brave heart and give them the hope to believe – *nothing is impossible to a valiant heart*. But I suppose such perspective is our lament, and if that is so, then *Girl with the Purple Ribbon* is relevant to all.

Girl with the Purple Ribbon weaves between the nuances of fiction, historical fiction, and history. It was challenging to dance between these shadowy nuances of these genres. The battle of Hill 861 is history; however, I changed the circumstances and distorted the facts using poetic license to enhance the flow of the story – thus historical fiction. And, within the context of the Vietnam War, I've created the story – fiction. During the battle sequences, I attempted to use my knowledge as a former Marine Officer to illustrate tactical scenarios. I've taken the liberty to project the rationales of American and North Vietnamese strategies and their respective counter strategies. Subsequently, my account is both fact and fiction; however, I do not delineate between the difference.

The story does not happen sequentially. Although life events are; however, those events occurring in my novel, discover their own secession. I ask the reader to care more about the characters, and the unfolding events than sequential development. I ask that you pay attention to the time sequences depicted in the various subheadings, which are critical to the flow of occurring events. I trust the story will then be an unbroken thread of revelation – and as you go, you will see the Vietnam era and the lives of my characters in a greater context. Beginning in the middle of the story may enable one to understand the beginning and end of events.

I have placed an epigraph before the text of each chapter. I'd ask that you savor the words, look for its message, read it twice, and even a third time. These thoughts were carefully chosen, and sometimes you have to go deep and reflect to understand their significance to the chapter and overall story.

Throughout the chapters, I've used spacing that segment scenes and dialogue. Although spacing is slight, I trust the novel will be an easier read.

To add life to Ofa, Seamus, and Elijah, I attempted to write their dialogue in a Texas vernacular. Traveling though the Hill Country of South Central Texas, I studied the accent and mannerisms of the people. There are certain words and expressions, which I readily incorporated into the text. Over time their accents became subtle; however, when you're from Texas, you're always from Texas. Ofa Hawkins will carry many weapons, one of which is her Texas drawl.

There's some pretty rough language in my novel, and I apologize for that. Combat is surreal. There are no words in the English language that can effectively describe battle. Combat is not for the faint of heart; thus, the vernacular used remains true to form.

Painting the perception of both North and South Vietnamese soldiers and non-combatant Vietnamese was a dilemma; therefore, I decided to be blatantly honest. Throughout the war, it was common practice to dehumanize the enemy, a tendency that evolved from a very dark and primal place in the human psyche. Did not Achilles drag Hector's body along the walls of Troy? Vietnamese on both sides of the conflict were referenced in the vilest context. In the dialogue between Elijah Bravo and Lý Trúc Việt, Bravo explains, "To kill you; I must hate you." In war, hate and killing are synonymous and yet how can one readily kill another human being without dehumanizing them? Eventually, wars end, and if we are fortunate, we learn that all men share the same humanity. "We love. We laugh and hope for a better life for our children. How different are we?" Lý Trúc Việt expressed. The Vietnamese were indomitable, and the boat people came by the thousands and brought a spirit and a patriotic fervor that served America well. Recently, I visited a friend residing in Houston, Lý Trúc Việt. We went to a café, a Vietnamese enclave. Lý noted that many of the men sitting and drinking tea had fought and bled with Americans and after the U.S. had pulled out, they continued the fight; yet their children could not check the box noting that their dads were veterans. Yes, the Vietnamese were depicted in the vilest context, and I am sorry that my depictions referenced that dehumanization, but that was a long time ago during a circumstance the defiled rationale thought. Humanity is not perfect, yet we have evolved to believe that the Vietnamese were truly an indomitable people.

Preface

At 4:50 AM on 30 April 1975, Marine pilot Captain Gerald Berry, lands a CH-46 Sea Knight on the roof of the American Embassy in Saigon. Berry is under Presidential Order to evacuate Ambassador Graham Martin and the remaining American personnel who waited for some unfound miracle or a last-minute diplomatic reprieve. For the past 18-hours, Captain Berry had been flying evacuation missions. A Marine security guard then hands Ambassador Martin a neatly folded American flag that had flown proudly over the American embassy and had been the symbol of the American presence in Vietnam. Ambassador Martin boards the helicopter, the ramp closes, and Lady Ace 09 dusts off – and that was the end of it. American involvement in Vietnam had ended.

No one warrior, no protestor, no member of the silent majority walked away from the Vietnam War unscathed.

As a child, I listened to the stories of my surrogate grandfather, Denny A. Malvey whose exploits in France as a doughboy in 1917 stirred my imagination and I learned to dream of the nobility of battle and its glory thereof. I listened to the stories of how my father and the men of the village who raised me saved Europe and the Pacific during World War II. They were the greatest generation, and I was their son. In 1961, John F. Kennedy passed the torch to my generation. It was our turn, and we were summoned to go forth and carry freedom's banner.

So, I joined the Marines, and of course, I would go to Vietnam.

The Vietnam War was definitive in the lives of those who served. But those who made it home, never fully returned. My story was an attempt to find that part of me who remained in-country. Upon the story's completion, I realized the part I left behind, was perpetually lost.

I began to write my novel toward one particular direction – a fictionalized account of the Hill Fights occurring in April 1967. I wanted to write about heroes – ordinary people who make themselves extraordinary. I was blind to the myriad of themes that exist beyond the battle; subsequently, I found Seamus O'Grady and Elijah Bravo and built them as heroes. However, as I wrote, I learned that we are all heroes, we are all cowards, it just depends on the day. My story was in the doldrums, something more was needed. A softer touch! Subsequently, I created Ofa Hawkins, the pretty girl from the Hill Country of South Central Texas. She defined Dante's depiction of *La Vita Nuova*. So, I veered off the path. I veered again, and then again. Following a circuitous path, the story began to breathe and had no resemblance to its original intent. As the chapters came together, I began to see that my story was no longer about the Vietnam War but was a testament to Shakespeare's assertion of the nobility of the human condition: "what piece of work is man?"

Searching for a title became a compulsion, and then I found that the right words were simple words and Ofa Hawkins became – *Girl with the Purple Ribbon.* Her life became a vortex, and by living through her, I found themes of courage, loyalty hope, depression, patriotism, sacrifice, pacifism, devotion, hate, morality, righteousness, and friendship. As the chapters came together, the true nature of my novel evolved, and I found that the best story is a love story and we can always use another love story.

Love, which transcends all virtue, became the dominant theme of *Girl with the Purple Ribbon.* Ofa, Seamus, and Elijah would learn that love, honor, and freedom are worth fighting for. Throughout the story, they'd hold on to the mantra of an old man: *what's meant to be will find a way.*

Before I wrote my first word, I belabored to find the perfect home for my characters. A sense of place is crucial for character development. Place will define them and no matter where they go, they'll always be from somewhere. I chose Texas, and more specifically, I chose the Hill Country, west of Austin. Texas has a fabled history, and the Hill Country's rolling terrain dotted with oaks and cut by rivers burned a distinct and everlasting identity in their souls and also in mine. Ofa, Seamus, and Elijah would travel the rite of passage from Luchenbach, Texas.

Two years ago, I traveled to Luchenbach. I was searching for landmarks – idiosyncrasies – the deep hue of the Texas Bluebonnets – the sound of the South Grape Creek, and the smell of early morning dew clinging to swaying grass. I wanted to understand how the billowy clouds cast their shadows on the prairie and witness their extraordinary metamorphosis as they disappear into the distant evening horizon. I sat on the steps of the General Store exactly where Ofa, Seamus, and Elijah would sit. In 1965, the three would be giggling, eating pulled pork sandwiches, and drinking RC Cola. I tried to picture them, and if I were able to do so, perhaps I could add more life to their characters. I was lost in thought. And then I turned. There they were – sitting next to me. I saw them! They looked exactly how I pictured them. They were talking about big dreams yet were oblivious to the events, which waited. Only I knew their fate. Elijah was pullin' on brisket, and Ofa and Seamus were falling in love. Mere words are all I have to tell you that my characters are beautiful, but you'll have to decide this for yourself.

ONE

HILL-861

Out of one hundred men, ten shouldn't even be there, eighty are just targets, nine are the real fighters, and we are lucky to have them, for they make the battle. Ah, but the one, one is a warrior, and he'll bring the others back.

Heraclitus

24 April 1967 – Hill-861, South Vietnam

"Dang it – it's freaking hot," Lieutenant McGivens whispered. "I can understand Dante's journey through hell."

"Sir?" the Sergeant questioned.

"The *Inferno* – Dante travels through hell," the Lieutenant countered.

"Sure 'nough *El-tee* (Lieutenant), it's the kind'a heat that'd fry an egg in a chicken."

Staff Sergeant Seamus O'Grady took the green towel draped around his neck and handed it to his Platoon Commander. Lieutenant Calder McGivens wiped the beads of sweat that pooled on his forehead.

"El-tee, Vietnam is hell on earth."

The air was wet, and it was sultry. The silent heat pressing against the men moving through the elephant grass had its own sound, which the Marines would not forget. It was the kind of heat that drove men crazy, and where every breath was a struggle.

As he examined the lines on his Sergeant's face, the Lieutenant's eyes shone like a deer in the headlights. McGivens looked for reassurance but saw something he wished he hadn't.

The Sergeant whispered, "El-tee, everything's gonna be okay."

That's what the Lieutenant wanted to hear, and what the Sergeant wanted to say, but neither man believed it would be okay. Regardless, reassurance is crucial; it gives false hope, and in the *bush* (field), hope is often the difference between insanity and insanity. O'Grady was a seasoned veteran and knew what to say when the shit was about to hit the fan.

"Staff Sergeant, hell is not being able to love."

The Lieutenant attempted to mask the pending battle with the misplaced thought of Dostoyevsky, and yet O'Grady thought of a young girl he once knew. But her image quickly faded.

"El-tee, maybe you're right about love." He gave McGivens a look. "But Sir, don't over think it. It's just fucking hot."

It was the officer's first patrol, and it was O'Grady's job to ensure the Lieutenant survived. Silently, they waited in the elephant grass looking for the enemy and hoping they wouldn't find him. The officer turned toward the Sergeant and O'Grady anticipating needless conversation placed his finger to his lips.

"Quiet Sir."

The only sounds were the Lieutenant's shallow breathing, the mosquitoes buzzing overhead, and the heat, silently pressing against the men. McGivens had a bad feeling, typical of a 2nd Lieutenant. They hadn't earned the confidence to believe in a tomorrow.

O'Grady waited for Private Knap's signal to advance. Knap was the best point man in the Battalion. He had been sent ahead to find the enemy who waited in the hills surrounding the firebase at *Khe Sanh*, a strategic airfield, and base south of the *Demilitarized Zone* (DMZ) dividing North and South Vietnam. Knap was an outstanding bush Marine, but he disdained authority, which was why after three years in the Corps he remained a Private. But he'd walk into hell if Staff Sergeant O'Grady asked him to do so. Seamus had a way with the men.

O'Grady passed his canteen to the Lieutenant; McGivens turned the cap and drank the tepid water.

"Staff Sergeant, I'm glad you're here," he said.

"I'm not," O'Grady responded.

O'Grady had a cool head and had proven himself during his first tour in Vietnam, earning the Bronze Star in Operation Hastings. Regardless of the Lieutenant's apprehension, the Sergeant respected him. O'Grady believed the Lieutenant's nerves would temper his zeal and keep the Marines alive as they crawled up the southern slope of Hill-861.

The 1ˢᵗ Platoon was ordered to execute a *reconnaissance by force* and note enemy positions, strength, and engage. They were sent to scout for suspected caves, secure a defensive position, and find a suitable approach for the Battalion's inevitable assault. The hills overlooking Khe Sanh were too important to allow the enemy to occupy them. In 1954 the French were defeated by the *Viet Minh* at *Dien Bien Phu.* The Viet Minh was the nationalist movement of Vietnam, opposed to the colonialism and imperialism of the west. During the siege of Dien Ben Phu, the French bastion in Northern Vietnam, Viet Minh forces carved roads up steep mountainous terrain dragging field artillery to positions, which overlooked the French stronghold.

Hills-861 and *881-North* and *881-South* dominated the American combat base at Khe Sanh. The hills were critical to controlling the ingress of enemy forces into the south and vital in the bases' defense. The *North Vietnamese Army* (NVA) planned to occupy these hills and blast Khe Sanh during the upcoming siege. By controlling the high ground, the enemy would overlook American positions, which precipitated their victory against the French in 1954.

Knap moved through the elephant grass 30 meters ahead of the Lieutenant and the Sergeant. Each day Knap walked the razor's edge between insanity and insanity. He could smell the dried fish the enemy had for lunch. He was born and raised in the forests of the Natchez Trace of Tennessee. He was Chickasaw, a descendant of Tishomingo, their last War Chief. Knap lived by Indian tradition and moved like a spirit. As he moved, he silently prayed. "I walk with the spirits of my ancestors – I am weak – I ask for strength and wisdom. Look, they say – the lesson is written in the wind. Strength and wisdom are within – the nation walks beside you."

Knap's movements were slow and deliberate. He scanned the terrain from left to right and then right to left. If there were something wrong, he'd know it. He'd fixate on a sound – the sway of the grass – a distant flutter of wings. He could tell the time of the day by observing the dew on a leaf, and it was said that Knap could track an ant on the surface of a rock. The heat of a million suns shimmered from the ground and bounced off the triple canopy, which loomed above and created undulating waves blurring a man's vision. Knap, looking like a ghost, weaved his way forward through the rays of heat.

Suddenly, the Private crouched. His head jerked toward the right, his left arm shot upwards, and his hand formed a fist. He signaled, halt. He had found what the men had feared. Sergeant O'Grady pointed to the safety of McGivens' weapon and then flicked his. He then signaled the Marines waiting further down the trail. Quiet! Motionless! Waiting! The air was thick and laden with fear. The sun's rays were like golden knives whittling away at the nerves of the men of the 1st Platoon. The only sound was the heat tightening a noose around their necks and the tall grass swaying in a silent breeze.

Staff Sergeant O'Grady signaled *PFC* (Private First Class) Terry, the radio-man forward.

O'Grady whispered, "El-tee, let's get up there and have a-look-see."

O'Grady, McGivens, and Terry pulled themselves through the grass toward Knap. The point had found a bunker complex.

"El-tee, we need to fix their position, pull back, and call in an airstrike," O'Grady said.

The Lieutenant glanced at the Sergeant. McGivens was shaken, but he managed a nod. Things were real in Vietnam; it wasn't *Officer Candidate School* (OCS). McGivens meticulously plotted six digit coordinates on his *topographical map* (topo) and prepared a *fire mission* requesting *artillery* (arty) support. The men lay in the grass surrounded by hills formed by ancient volcanoes. Tiny trails used by the Hmong, the indigenous people of the Northern Provinces of Vietnam, crossed in diagonal patterns. They were soft trails etched by the bare feet of people who wanted only peace and simple harvests. They were jungle trails leading a traveler somewhere and yet nowhere. The triple canopy produced a blue hue as oxygen released from its tentacles collided with low hanging clouds filled with moisture. The Marine's next move would be definitive, but for the moment, they were content to lie and wait. The beauty of the hills juxtaposed the pending violence and created a surreal world. O'Grady noted the enemy's defensive positions, weapons, re-supply and escape routes. Lieutenant McGivens speculated on a plan hoping he would account for all eventualities. O'Grady understood that in battle, what could go wrong, would go wrong. The Lieutenant believed the tactics he learned in the classroom would be their salvation. But the lives of the men would depend on Seamus O'Grady's instincts and not on the Lieutenant's plan.

Knap rolled onto his back and observed the passing clouds. He was at peace. He wet his fingers with saliva, rubbed the red clay soil, and then painted his face. He whispered – "I ride swift and my lance is long. I face my enemy with thunder. Tishomingo! I have your warrior spirit. I am not afraid. Today is a good day to die."

"Sir, five gooks are moving our way," Knap whispered.

McGivens wondered how Knap knew of the approaching enemy while he was staring at the sky. Five enemy soldiers had left the bunker complex and were walking casually toward their position.

Sergeant O'Grady nudged the Lieutenant, "Sir, get that weapon off safety."

McGivens' hand shook as he made the adjustment. The Sergeant placed his hand on the Lieutenant's shoulder.

"You're okay El-tee."

Forcing a tentative smile, the Lieutenant quoted Isaiah, "In confidence and quietness shall be your strength."

Seamus O'Grady was a seasoned veteran; his faith was unshakable. The officer would draw his courage from the Sergeant. Suddenly, Knap rolled onto his stomach and stood as though he were taking a bathroom break at a Saturday matinée movie. He raised his weapon and fired point blank at the unsuspecting enemy. He stared at the dying soldiers. Knap appeared serene yet melancholy; it was as though he was taking account of what he had done. For a moment, the world remained still, floating on its oars. Quiet! Knap struggled to comprehend the violence he brought. You could hear the sounds of the Khe Sanh beetle buzzing over the bodies of the enemy soldiers. Knap then advanced toward the enemy bunkers and silenced the first emplacement. He screamed, "Tishomingo," and he ran toward the second bunker emptying a clip into their midst. He threw grenades into the third and was then cut down by automatic weapons. Knap's reaction saved the Lieutenant, the Sergeant, and the radioman but had cost him his life.

Exposing himself to enemy fire, Lieutenant McGivens stood and signaled the Platoon forward. The Marines were bound by tradition not to leave their dead and wounded on the battlefield. McGivens was determined to bring Knap home to the Chickasaw Nation.

Sergeant O'Grady shouted, "Lieutenant, we need to deploy the men in a defensive position."

O'Grady rushed forward cutting down two enemy soldiers who guarded two abandoned bunkers. It would be a good place for their last stand. Amid the bursts of automatic weapons, McGivens screamed into the radio, (*PRC-25*). "Contact! Contact!" He went to work as a seasoned veteran, but he wasn't a seasoned veteran, but if he survived the day, he would be. The Lieutenant reached for the handset of the PRC-25.

"Jackknife . . . Jackknife . . . This is Easy Rider . . . Over . . ."

The *fire direction center* (FDC) located at Khe Sanh, answered. The FDC received calls from the bush and *forward observers* (FO) requesting fire missions. He'd then pass the particulars of the mission to the gun batteries.

"Go ahead Easy Rider . . ."

It was the Lieutenant's first fire mission; carefully, he read the scribbled numbers.

"Fire Mission . . . Coordinates 728609 . . . I repeat, 728609 . . . Enemy all over the fricking hill . . . Bunkers, Spider holes . . . HE (high explosives) . . . *Fire for effect* . . ."

"El-tee, sure you don't wanna test a round for accuracy?" Sergeant O'Grady suggested.
"Sergeant, I got this."
"Very well El-tee."
A fire mission typically required numerous test rounds, which determined the accuracy of the final salvo. When the FO believed the coordinates were accurate, he'd then command: fire for effect.

The enemy understood the officer would be with the radio; consequently, they directed fire toward PFC Terry. Terry was hit in the chest and fell forward onto the red clay soil. The Lieutenant picked up the radio and continued to direct artillery trying to silence the mortars that blasted the Marines from *defilade* positions, situated on the reverse side of the hill out of the line of sight.

O'Grady screamed, "El-tee, there's cover in the bunkers."
The Sergeant fired to suppress the enemy.
"El-tee – move – now!"
McGivens grabbed the radio, but instead of running for cover, he ran toward Terry dragging him to the bunkers. Although McGivens was hit twice, he managed to pull Terry to safety.

"Terry – stay with me!" the Lieutenant pleaded. But it was too late.

"Big Daddy . . . This is Easy Rider . . . Over . . ."

McGivens frantically attempted to contact Captain Reynolds, Bravo Company Commander, provide a *situation report* (sit-rep), and ask for orders.

"Easy Rider . . . This is Big Daddy . . . Go ahead . . ."

"Captain – we're engaged by a superior enemy force . . ." McGivens screamed, ". . . waiting for orders . . ."

"Lieutenant McGivens, hold your position . . . I repeat . . . Hold your position . . . We'll hit 'em with airstrikes . . ."

Captain Reynolds believed 2nd Lieutenants didn't have the experience to estimate a situation and that McGivens was exaggerating the gravity of the circumstances they faced. Nevertheless, McGivens was ordered to fight. The 1st Platoon had found the enemy occupying the hills surrounding the firebase, and the first battle of Khe Sanh had begun.

The 1st Platoon was in a fight they didn't want. The enemy had the advantage; they chose when and where to engage and force the Marines to attack uphill. The enemy would commit forces if they believed they'd prevail or if they could inflict casualties on the Americans. Bravo, Charlie, and Delta companies of *1st Battalion, 9th Marine Regiment* (1/9) were in reserve at Camp Carol, an artillery base commanding the strategic *Highway 9 corridor* south of the Demilitarized Zone. The Highway 9 corridor ran east-west, south of the contested hills surrounding Khe Sanh. The road was vital to the NVA for moving supplies and men. The second and third Platoons of Alpha Company prepared to re-enforce the beleaguered Marines from Hill-558, adjacent to Hill-861.

NVA doctrine was to suck Americans uphill, ambush them, and inflict casualties. The NVA would then target likely helicopter *landing zones* (LZ) and wait for the Americans to reinforce. They, in turn, would reinforce from sanctuaries in Laos or along the DMZ and as we deployed more forces so would they. Although the NVA would sustain considerable losses, they'd inflict casualties and send Americans home for burial. They were willing to endure catastrophic losses to weaken America's resolve to continue the war.

Regardless of his wounds, McGivens manned the radio *bracketing* rounds, dropping them *danger close* to his position. He'd drop artillery behind and in front of the enemy, moving it closer and closer to their positions. He directed Huey gunships and pinpointed their 60mm machine guns (*M-60s*) and rockets on enemy emplacements. The choppers fired everything they had trying to save the beleaguered Marines struggling for a foothold on Hill-861.

"Corpsman up," O'Grady yelled.

Attempting to stop the bleeding, Buzz Baviello reached the Lieutenant and applied a tourniquet. Baviello, the Platoon Corpsman, was 20 years old; the men called him, Doc. The cries of Corpsman from other wounded Marines told Doc he could do no more for the Lieutenant. Doc grabbed his medical kit and disappeared into the fight.

"Corporal Wood, get Sergeant O'Grady up here," McGivens ordered.

"Sir, Doc says I got to stay here and hold this tourniquet to make sure you're okay."

"Wood, do it now," the Lieutenant ordered.

"Yes, sir."

Wood left the *command post* (CP) to search for O'Grady. With the Lieutenant down, O'Grady would command their last stand.

* * *

Seamus walked the perimeter of the 3rd Squad encouraging his Marines to conserve their ammo and not fire automatic. In a firefight, the men typically placed their weapons on automatic fire since they believed the increased firepower was their best chance to survive. But O'Grady was old-school and believed direct and accurate fire would increase their chances. If the Marines expended their rounds, they'd have nothing but the bayonet.

"Mark your target boys. Hit what you aim at," O'Grady ordered.

O'Grady reached the 3rd Squad's position on the perimeter's right flank. The North Vietnamese were attempting to flank the Squad, by hitting the right side of the Marine emplacement. If they were successful, they'd get behind the Platoon, and roll the defenders. O'Grady observed the terrain and the likely avenues of approach. If they were to survive, the 3rd Squad must hold the flank.

"Mother Fucker!" he screamed. "Elijah, you see that?"

Elijah Bravo was the 3rd Squad leader and O'Grady's best friend. They grew up together in the Hill Country of South Central Texas and joined the Marines on the buddy plan. Now they prepared to die together on Hill-861.

"Yeah Seamus, I'm gonna fuck 'em up," Bravo screamed. "I got claymores." Claymore mines fired hundreds of metal balls into a kill zone.

When Staff Sergeant Hadley was medevac'd Captain Reynolds promoted O'Grady to Platoon Sergeant over Bravo. Seamus was the obvious choice; he had both command presence and tactical ability. Although Elijah was a natural killer, Seamus had a way about him, and the men were confident in his presence.

"Elijah, get some guns on that approach," Seamus screamed.

Elijah didn't hear his best friend's warning.

"Sergeant O'Grady," Wood called out. "Lieutenant wants you at the CP. Now!"

"Wood, the gooks are trying to turn our flank."

The Marines were facing a Battalion of regular NVA soldiers. They were well supplied, well led, and determined to drive the Yankee aggressors off the hill or kill every last one of them. The 1st Platoon walked into a trap set by the strategy of Colonel Tran van Minh, the Commanding Officer (CO) of 810th Battalion of the 325th C-Division, of the *People's Army of Vietnam*, (PAVN). The Marine mission was to locate, close with, and destroy the enemy Battalion. American strategy was not to conquer North Vietnam or occupy territory in the south, but rather to ensure the survival of the South Vietnamese Government. Thus, General Westmoreland, the American commander waged a war of attrition. North Vietnam would lose if we killed enough of them; consequently, controlling territory was not in the equation for victory. The buzzword was *body count*. The number of dead enemy soldiers determined the measure of success. However, killing the enemy in sufficient numbers required close combat; consequently, Americans would also die. Ho Chi Minh, Chairman of the Central Committee of the communist Party of Vietnam, once said to the French, "You can kill ten of our men for everyone we kill of yours, but even at these odds you will lose, and we will win." At close combat men would die. The casualty rates of American sons would not be acceptable to the folks at home. The enemy was prepared to bleed; America was not. General Vo Nguyen Giap, the CO of the PAVN, realized support for the war would wane since the loss of American sons in a place most people never heard of would not be tolerated. The 1st Platoon was sent up Hill-861 to pave the way for a major assault so the Marines could kill enough of the enemy to show the politicians at home we were winning the war. But on 24 April 1967, the Marines were in a dogfight.

"Sergeant O'Grady, LT, wants you at the CP," Wood pleaded.

Seamus was hesitant to leave the beleaguered 3rd Squad. He moved forward and exposed himself to enemy snipers.

Lance Corporal Ashcraft screamed, "Get the fuck down, Seamus!"

But Staff Sergeant O'Grady had to warn Elijah about the right flank. The men of the 3rd Squad were teetering on the brink of disaster. Seamus stood; bullets screamed and peppered the ground around him.

O'Grady's cries went unheard. The men needed conspicuous leadership, and Staff Sergeant O'Grady would make that happen.

"Marines!" he screamed.

He saw his best friend leading a Fire Team, creating an *echelon*, (diagonal) defensive position that would block the enemy's advance.

"Guns up," Elijah ordered.

Two M-60 machine guns moved toward the front of the attack. The North Vietnamese were attempting to flank the Marines. Elijah waited until the last moment to counter their maneuver and thus inflict heavy casualties on their assault. The North Vietnamese ran into a wall of steel. The Marines were holding. As the NVA pulled back, Elijah moved to the front of his position setting claymore mines and preparing for their next assault.

Wood grabbed O'Grady. "Seamus! The Lieutenant!"

The Marines screamed, "Come get us you, motherfuckers."

Bullets buzzing, Seamus walked the 3rd Squad's perimeter.

"I'm a Staff Sergeant in the United States Marines Corps, and I'll crawl for no Viet Motherfucking Cong," he screamed.

The Marines cheered. Staff Sergeant Seamus O'Grady had given them hope and Sergeant Elijah Bravo, made it happen.

TWO

MESSAGE TO GARCIA

It is not book-learning young men need, nor instruction about this or that, but a stiffening of the vertebrae which will cause them to be loyal to a trust, to act promptly, concentrate their energies; do the thing, carry a message to Garcia.

Elbert Hubbard, *Message to Garcia*

24 April 1967 – Hill-861

Lieutenant McGivens had one hand on the tourniquet; the other held the handset of the PRC-25. The bleeding had stopped; McGivens had earned a one-way ticket back to the world on a *freedom bird,* the happiest plane ride out of Vietnam.

Seamus called a *medevac* to extract the wounded, and despite heavy mortar and small arms fire, the pilot hovered on a 30-degree slope above the white smoke, which Seamus had dropped. One skid touched the ground, the other hung a few feet from the hill's surface. Since the enemy had all the possible landing zones targeted, Seamus directed the chopper into an unlikely place to land.

"El-tee get on the chopper; I'll take it from here," Seamus said.

"No-can-do Seamus. Can't leave my men. Couldn't look at myself in the morning."

"Sir, if you leave now, you'll have a morning. You're a damn good officer; you've done your part. The Corps needs men like you; I take care of my Lieutenant. Let me do my job."

"Staff Sergeant O'Grady, I can say the same thing about you. The Corps would be better served if you were on that chopper."

The pilot leaned out the window. "Anyone else," he screamed?

Seamus gave him a thumbs-up.

The pilot shouted above the whining rotors, "Godspeed Sergeant; I'll be back."

He closed the window and dusted-off.

"Sergeant, Shakespeare said, 'a coward dies a thousand deaths; the valiant taste death but once.' How I can help?"

"El-tee, he also said, 'Discretion is the better part of valor.' Sir, the valiant may die once, but at the end of the day, they're dead."

"I didn't expect Shakespeare from a Texas Cowboy," McGivens replied.

On Hill-861 there would be many choices – choices that would determine life or death. Decisions made in split seconds would account for the fate of the 1st Platoon. Regardless of what happened, and for the rest of their lives, the Marines would recall the storm they walked into. But once the battle was over, those who survived would not remember the miracle that decided they should live.

"Sergeant, what's your plan?"

In a surprisingly calm voice, he answered, "Don't have one El-tee."

McGivens laughed "What the frick," he said.

Their cavalier attitude was not unusual. In the face of death, fear often buried. When you accept the inevitable, you get a *what the fuck attitude*. Ideological propaganda no longer mattered. It was Viet Fucking Nam. They were already dead. When they arrived in-country, they accepted their fate. The Marines were poised to fight to the last man. Seamus O'Grady was a Texan, and the Alamo ran through his blood.

"Sergeant, for a guy without a plan, you're sure holding it together."

"El-tee, don't mess with Texas. Sir, it's Bravo who's holding it together. He's got the right flank. Don't know how long, but for now, we're secure. If we get through this, I'm recommending Elijah for the Medal of Honor."

"Seamus, if we get off this fricking hill, I'm writing you up for the Medal of Honor."

McGivens never swore, and that was unusual for a Marine. Marines used the expletive "fucking" as an adjective. For example, a rifle is not merely a rifle; it's a fucking rifle. Lieutenant McGivens substituted the word "frick" for "fuck." He tried to be an example for his Marines. McGivens was a diamond, but he was a second Lieutenant. Until he promoted to first Lieutenant, he would remain a second-class citizen. McGivens attempted to make his Marines better people and to do that he tried to become the best version of himself. Sergeant Bravo believed McGivens was filled with college boy idealism; subsequently, he was insolent and refused to call McGivens sir. Instead, he called him Mr. McGivens or Lieutenant. But McGivens was a cherry. The Marines called him the *fucking new guy* (FNG). New guys were easy to spot. That clean helmet cover was the giveaway. A seasoned Marine's helmet might have a heavy rubber band encircling it, holding bug repellant and a well-used plastic spoon, but typically printed on the fabric covering of his steel pot was a message. The messages were written on camouflage covers stained by rain, dirt, and sweat. Those Marines with helmet covers awaiting a personal signature were known as the Fucking New Guy. In the *grunts* (infantry) the FNG is ignored until he proves himself. The Platoon placed a mythical quality on anyone who had seen combat. Regardless, the FNG was expected to live up to the same standard and would not be accepted until he made the cut.

23 April – Hill-558

The previous morning, Captain Reynolds, the CO of Bravo Company approached Staff Sergeant O'Grady. Reynolds was typically casual, and the men were seldom on edge in his presence. The CO was competent, and as a respected officer, he did not have to assert his rank.

"A-tennnn-hut," Wood screamed,

Except for Sergeant O'Grady, the men jumped to attention. Reynolds rolled his eyes and grimaced. In the field, there was little hierarchy between *NCOs (Non-Commissioned Officers)* and their officers. The NCOs, enlisted men, who were Corporals and above were the backbone of the Corps, and the officers respected them.

"As you were," the Captain replied. "This is "Lieutenant Calder McGivens, your new Platoon Commander."

Lieutenant McGivens extended his hand and Seamus followed suit. The new Lieutenant appeared like he was fresh out of college. He was quiet, and anxious, and didn't seem the type who always had an opinion.

"Lieutenant McGivens, do you need anything?" the Captain asked.

"No Sir, I'm good to go."

"Seamus, may I have a word?"

"Yes, Captain."

"Seamus, He seems okay to me; he's just out of *TBS* (The Basic School). If we've learned anything, it's not to judge a book by its cover."

"Sir, you never know 'bout a *butter bar* (2nd Lieutenant). Ask me when the shit hits the fan. That's when we'll see what he's made of."

"Seamus, I was once a 2nd Lieutenant. Go easy on him and show him the ropes, but hold off the NCOs. Those fuckers will bust his chops. Sergeant, may I remind you that it's your job to train an officer; how he goes is up to you."

"Captain, you're preaching to the choir. You're gonna have to speak to Elijah." Seamus grinned, indicating that a conversation with Elijah Bravo would not be an easy task. "But sir, I trained you."

"You trained me! Yeah right! And talking to Elijah is like talking to a wall. Carry on Staff Sergeant."

Lieutenant McGivens knew the Platoon's history and that Seamus was on his second combat tour. How could an FNG gain the respect of men who had gone toe to toe with the enemy? Regardless, McGivens had earned the right to wear the gold bars as a Lieutenant of Marines. The men understood this, but earning their respect was different and would be the most difficult part of command.

"Corporal Wood, please gather the men, I want a few words," McGivens requested.

"Sir, the men are filling sandbags on the perimeter. It's the Colonel's orders so may I suggest we have a formation later," Wood replied.

"Staff Sergeant O'Grady, where's the rest of the Squad leaders, the Sergeants?" the Lieutenant asked.

"Lieutenant, other than Lihue, Bravo, Wood, and Barsegyan that's it. We're *T.O.* (table of organization). All our command billets are filled; we have solid Corporals: Wood, Barsone, and Barlow. The NCOs have kept the Company together. You should do what you can to get them promoted. We need an officer for that."

"Staff Sergeant, can you write them up? I'll sign it."

"Lieutenant, with all due respect, I can't write for shit, you went to college; I'm sure you can write a whole lot better than me."

The Lieutenant laughed and attempted to minimize his education.

"We'll do it together; writing's not rocket science. One more thing, Staff Sergeant. Can you take me to the perimeter? If the men are filling sandbags, I should be filling sandbags with them. Sergeant – so should you and the rest of the NCOs."

"Sir, may I speak freely?"

The Lieutenant nodded.

"Lieutenant McGivens, you're an officer; the men aren't used to having rank do the shit work."

"Staff Sergeant O'Grady, I don't believe my rank makes me above the work of the men. I intend to participate fully. It's egalitarian; I believe in that. Do you understand? Staff Sergeant, my question was not meant to imply you're incapable of understanding. I mean no disrespect. But I want you to appreciate my philosophy of leadership."

"Sir, I understand egalitarian. Egalitarianism is a moral principle that all people should be equal. It's the mantra of the French Revolution – *liberté égalité fraternité*. We have the power to choose what we believe and what we believe is who we'll become. We can treat others with dignity, or we can decide not to."

Lieutenant McGivens smiled and realized Seamus O'Grady was a diamond.

"Ne te quaesiveris extra," McGivens replied.

"Yes, Sir, Emerson, do not seek outside yourself. That's my philosophy," the Sergeant countered.

I think I'm going to like this guy, O'Grady thought.

$$*\quad*\quad*$$

The evening before the hill fights, the NCOs of the 1st Platoon met to discuss their new Lieutenant.

"Ando, you believe the FNG?" Bravo questioned."

Corporal Andranik Barsegyan, a Fire Team leader, was an old salt who had learned his soldering in the Russian Army. He was an expatriate from Armenia and had spent ten years fighting the protracted wars of the Soviet Union. But his career ended when the KGB discovered he was a political dissident, a separatist, plotting the liberation of his homeland. He escaped from a gulag in Siberia and hired on as a seaman on a transport. When his ship docked in Baltimore, he deserted and joined the Marines. Although Seamus was reluctant to place him in a command billet, Ando had the soul of a warrior.

"Elijah," Ando said, "the FNG is gonna get us killed, I know it."

Second Lieutenants are 90-day wonders and after 90 days of *OCS*

(Officer Candidate School), and by an act of Congress, they gain the power of the Officer Corps and ultimately would decide the fate of men who had earned a place in a Marine Platoon.

"So, what did he say?" Corporal Wood asked.

"It ain't right," Ando said. "Get this guy. You know what he said? 'Make sure you give the men their dignity.'"

"We're fucked," the NCOs lamented.

Wood asked, "What the fuck does that mean? He must be a hippie."

"What does dignity have to do with killing?" Bravo interjected.

"Actually, he's a classist," Sergeant Alexander expressed.

"What the fuck is a classist?" Barsegyan asked."

"Ando, you of all people should know what a classist is; you're Russian."

"I'm Armenian," Ando curtly replied.

"The reference to give men their dignity comes from an Indian proverb, to give dignity to a man is above all things," Sergeant Alexander commented. "If you guys stop focusing on the fact that he's a butter bar, you'd see, he's the kind of officer who'll give the Sergeants freedom to run the Platoon. It's egalitarian. He talks to us as equals, respects us, and at the same time maintains his position. McGivens doesn't fake it. The guy isn't that bad."

"I agree with Alexander. We ought 'a give the Lieutenant a chance. So far, he's been fair," Sergeant Lihue added. "Seamus, you've not said a word. What do you think?"

Seamus paused and thought for a moment.

"I agree with Alexander. We're NCOs. It's our job to shape the officers. McGivens told me we'd run the Platoon and not because he doesn't know what the fuck he's doing, but because he understands his place. Listen, we joined the Marines to serve, but there ain't one of us who's not here to fight. That's why I'm here. But not, McGivens. He's not like us. He joined the Marines to make the world a better place and believes that making the world a better place begins with making his Marines better people."

Alexander interjected, "I just heard him say, 'I'm here for freedom.' I didn't say a thing, but it was the most stupid remark I've heard. He actually believes that."

"Freedom, what the fuck is he thinking?" Wood replied.

Elijah interrupted, "He believes that? He's a lot like you, Seamus. You guys believe we're defending freedom in Vietnam. Other than killin' gooks, why we here?'"

"What a man believes has nothing to do with his competence in the field," Seamus replied. "Regardless, we need to respect him and just because he's a geeky FNG and believes Vietnam is a just cause doesn't mean we shouldn't give him a chance. And you Elijah – It would do you well if you showed some respect and referred to McGivens as sir."

"We'll see how he does when the shit goes down," Elijah commented.

"Elijah, that's true of all of us, Captain Reynolds was once a butter bar," Wood commented.

"I can't believe Reynolds was a second Lieutenant," Elijah added.

The NCOs would give McGivens the benefit of the doubt, but if he didn't perform in combat, he'd be gone.

$$* \quad * \quad *$$

That evening, Lieutenant McGivens visited his men in their fighting holes.

"How's it going Marines? Need anything?"

The men responded, "Sir, good to go."

They were trying to send McGivens on his way. The FNG had not earned the right to speak with combat veterans.

"You boys hear from home?"

McGivens had touched the heartstrings of the men. Regardless of being an FNG, they wanted to talk about home. The Marines would take letters from their packs and read a sentence about a son's first words, a love note from a girlfriend, or a funny comment from a dad. Nothing was more important than a letter. Talking about home brought them peace and each man found peace differently. Some prayed, others wrote letters, or carried that special something. Some read the Bible; others covered themselves with their *poncho liner* (blanket). How they wrapped themselves would determine their survival during the night.

In the evening, Sergeant Lihue would wait for the Battalion OCS (intelligence officer's) analysis of the expected danger. If there were imminent danger, Lihue ordered 100% alert. If contact were not imminent, he'd order 50% or 25% alert. Lihue would then gaze at the North Star and whisper, "Good night Anna." His gaze would linger as though he expected a reply.

That same evening, Lieutenant McGivens had found Lihue in such a moment.

"Lieutenant, when I left, my wife and I promised to look at the North Star each night. We knew that at some point during the day we'd be staring at the same star, and each of us would make a vow of love. She's 10,000 miles away. But I can see her."

24 April – Hill-861

McGivens and O'Grady watched Private Carney run a zigzag pattern toward the CP. By some unforeseen miracle, he slid into the CP unscathed.

"Sir, Sergeant Bravo wants the claymores," Carney said.

Seamus handed Carney a canvass bag with three claymore mines. The 2nd Squad opened up with suppressive fire. Carney took a deep breath and ran back to 3rd Squad.

"El-tee, hand me the radio. I'm gonna unleash hell on the bastards."

"Jackknife . . . This is Buckaroo . . . Over . . ."

"Go ahead Buckaroo . . ."

"Jackknife . . . request fire mission . . ."

"Buckaroo . . . what's your situation . . .?"

"Jackknife . . . gooks are all over us. We're pinned down. They're waitin' for us to reinforce so they can kill the choppers in the LZs. Adjust fire to 720600 . . ."

"Buckaroo . . . I repeat. What's your situation . . .?"

"Jesus H. Christ! I just told you. We're about to be overrun. Just get me the rounds . . ."

"Buckaroo... you're talking to an officer . . ."

"I don't give a flyin' fuck who you are. Give me the fuckin' rounds, or I'll come back from the dead and shove your head up your ass, you *REMF* . . ." (rear echelon motherfucker)

The Marines in the rear often felt guilty they weren't with the forward grunts. Although every Marine was trained as an infantryman, it was the luck of the draw that some were in the rear. But when called upon, the rear echelon motherfuckers did their best

18

to keep their brothers alive.

"Go ahead Buckaroo; I copy . . ."

"Sir, I want you to walk *HE* (high explosive) from coordinates 720400 toward my position 760-break-800 . . . I'll correct . . ."

"No can-do Buckaroo . . . Too close to your position . . ."

"Sir, just give me the rounds, or we're dead . . ."

"Buckaroo, don't blame me if I blow the shit out of you . . . Godspeed Marine . . . I'm on the hook (Radio) for your adjustments . . ."

Moments later the 12th-artillery Regiment began dropping rounds in the rear of the enemy. The NVA knew someone had their number, and all the enemy guns fired on Staff Sergeant Seamus O'Grady's position. He walked the rounds toward his perimeter adjusting with each barrage. Regardless, the enemy began their assault.

Seamus screamed into the handset, "Fire for effect . . .!"

The gun line responded and dropped a tight ring of steel around the besieged Platoon. The enemy's attack stalled, but they would reinforce and attack again.

Seamus left the Lieutenant at the CP and ran to check on Sergeant Lihue's position.

"Sergeant Barsegyan, where's Sergeant Lihue."
Ando didn't answer. He appeared shaken.
"Ando, pull yourself together. Where the fuck is Sergeant Lihue?"
Ando lowered his head, signed the cross, and whispered: "Axberes moise ashxar gnadez," (my brother has gone to the other world). Seamus knew the fate of his friend.
"Where is he, Ando?"
Seamus found Lihue lying with his right arm extended outward. Death on the battlefield was unforgiving. The contortions of men's bodies or what remained of them were ghastly. Where was the glory, they were promised? The foolishness of boys! Lihue was dead and lying with his right arm extending from his poncho liner.
The nature of battle had not changed. It's hard, close, brutal, mortal, and decisive. The tools and circumstances may change, but

the primordial truths do not. The Vikings understood this and established a special tribute for those that mix fire, iron, blood, and courage in the gilded cup of combat. They call it Valhalla. It's where warriors go when they're gone.

Seamus knelt beside his friend, touched his forehead, signed the cross, and then took Lihue's arm and placed it under the poncho.

"Sergeant Barsegyan, assume command of the Squad," Seamus ordered. "Ando, don't disappoint me."

"Semper Fi, Seamus," Ando replied.

Ando was a former officer in Russian Special Operations, the Spetsnaz Army. He was awarded The Order Virtuti Militari for service in the French Indochina War. Sergeant Andranik Barsegyan had been to Vietnam before, but the last time he fought for the other side.

Semper Fidelis was the motto of the Marine Corps, Always Faithful. It was a promise to remain true. Loyal to the end. To fight until there was no fight left, and if necessary, give your life for your brother. Andranik Barsegyan was Russian, and for a Russian, death on the battlefield was understood. Regardless, he would be faithful to the end.

"Carry-on Sergeant Barsegyan."

*   *   *

"El-tee, Lihue is dead," O'Grady said.

"Why Seamus?"

O'Grady didn't answer.

"Who decides who lives or dies? Now, this – Sergeant Lihue dead. Staff Sergeant O'Grady, I am turning command over to you. Get my Marines off this hill. *Message to Garcia,"* McGivens said.

Seamus appeared confused.

"Sergeant, the book."

"Sir, What book?"

"*Message to Garcia,*" the Lieutenant repeated.

"Ah yes, *Message to Garcia,*"

Seamus remembered the book Lieutenant McGivens distributed to his NCO's. "Read it," he said.

"Sorry El-tee, I didn't read it. I'll read it first chance I get."

The Lieutenant hoped the inspirational essay would inspire his NCOs.

"It's about you, Seamus. It's a story about a soldier in the

Spanish-American War. He's given an impossible mission of finding the Cuban Guerrilla fighter, General Garcia and deliver the message that America is invading Cuba. Rowan does his job and loyal to the trust given him. The man who does his job is the hero. It's you. You're the warrior. You inspire us."

"El-tee we're all doing our job."

"Staff Sergeant, it's up to you to deliver the message to Garcia. Keep my men alive. I can't have them die like this, and there's nothing I can do."

Seamus spent his whole life doing what was right, but now he could no longer count on tomorrow.

"Sir, I can bring in a chopper; I want you on it."

"Sergeant O'Grady, it doesn't matter. How can I give a frick about my life when today, Sergeant Lihue's wife will speak to him in the North Star?"

"Sir – how do we live with that?" Seamus asked.

THREE

HILL COUNTRY WEST OF AUSTIN

Being a boy is the best story ever told.

Charles Dickens

September 1964 – Luckenbach, Texas

Elijah **learned from his daddy Angel, who was half Comanche and half Mexican that to get fishin' worms, you slap the ground with your hand.** But you have to do it ten times. If you don't do it ten times, it don't work. The worms think it's rainin' and come to the surface.

Seamus grabbed one of the slimy critters that came for the promise of rain and impaled the worm on the fishhook. He was careful to weave it through the barb three times so it wouldn't fall off when he cast into the South Grape Creek, which ran through Luchenbach, Texas. It was a typical fishin' Friday morning. Since the boys was old enough to ride horses, every Friday, Seamus O'Grady, and his best friend Elijah Bravo played hooky from school and headed to the Hill Country. There was just too much to do to waste a Friday in school. Even sittin' next to Ofa Hawkins wasn't enough to keep Seamus at Fredericksburg High School. Well, it was almost enough.

The Hill Country spread across South Central Texas with Austin to the east, San Antonio to the south, and Luchenbach in the center. It's a wonderland of limestone knolls, live oaks, cypress-lined creeks, and pin-dot towns. It's a land that time forgot and like no other under the big Texas sky.

Their favorite fishin' tackle was a long, strong line tied to the thin end of a pole. But to fasten the line correctly, they'd use their knife to cut a notch on the top of the pole, and then affix the line with three half-hitches. Not two or four, but three. Fishin' was an exact science. At the end of the line, they tied a weight and two fishhooks. When it came to fishin' and foolery, they were meticulous boys, so they made sure the hooks were individually tied 12 inches apart on the main line. Two feet from the hooks the boys fastened a cork from a wine bottle. I don't rightly understand why the cork had to be from a bottle of wine, but those were the peculiarities of Seamus and Elijah. They'd search for a wine bottle, and if they were fortunate to find a bottle with a few swigs remaining, they'd drink the wine, keep the cork, and throw away the bottle. The pole had to come from a leafy willow tree so it could bend without breakin'. The boys stuck the pole upright into the ground and fixed a small bell to the top, so if they'd catch a fish, the bell would ring. There was a lot to fishin'; hundreds of decisions to make. Live worms, or dead worms! Where to cast? How far into the crick? Fishin' gave them hope; it was something they were supposed to do.

They'd fish all morning; catch an old boot, and maybe some bluegill. They'd throw the boot back and keep the bluegill – and I'll be damned if they didn't catch the same boot the following Friday. The boys were the Tom Sawyer and Huck Finn of South Central Texas. Charles Dickens said, "Being a boy is the best story ever told." And Seamus and Elijah were writing their story, adventuring among the Texas live oaks that dotted the horizons and lined the rivers, which cut the canyons of the Hill Country.

They knew every gully and stream, where the catfish bit, and where they didn't, the best swimming holes, and which tree gave the best shade for an afternoon nap. They knew the sounds and smells of the land, the dewy mornings, the blazing hot afternoons, and understood the folklore of the hills. Their granddaddies rode with the Texas Rangers. They were Texas boys. If you don't know where you're from, you don't know who you are. Their internal compass pulled them into the land, and the land became their roadmap. Texas gave them a sense of place and big dreams.

On Friday afternoons, they'd lay under the shade of an oak and dangle a blade of grass between the tip of their tongue and their lower lip. It had to be perfect, one that had gone to seed. They were longer and sturdier and would last through the fantasies the boys created while watching cloud formations floating overhead. They'd gaze into the sky, and with their hands clasped behind their heads, they dream of being heroes. In Texas, heroes are important. It had something to do with the Alamo and one thing for certain, a Texas boy always remembers the Alamo. In the heat of the afternoon, they'd listen to the sounds of the landscape, the insects, the breeze, and watch as the shadows of the prairie disappear into the sunset. There was a soft whisper – a question floating in the wind. It was always the same. "Who are you?" The answer waited on the other side of their journey through their rite of passage. They weren't yet ready to crossover; they had some growin' to do. They'd eventually learn, that finding the answer to the question was not a matter of words; it was a matter of actions.

*   *   *

Elijah called out, "Seamus, some good ol' boys mus' a been drinkin'. Lookie here – by the tree. There's a bottle cap."

The boys had found a treasure trove of empty beer bottles that would bring a five-cent deposit on each bottle at the general store.

"Let's get 'em Elijah, and get on into town. We'll get some Coke and Life Savers and catch Ofa coming from school."

"Let's get some Moon Pies too," Elijah added.

The boys would spend hours square squatting in front of the general store, waiting for Ofa Hawkins. Each Friday after school, Ofa would stop to fetch an ice cream. She'd wear a pretty dress, scuffed-up boots, and broad brim hat. She tried everything to get Seamus' attention: sit next to him, twirl her hair, bat her eyes, and sometimes she'd even bite her lip. She learned to do that from the books she read. There were only so many things she could do and still keep her dignity to get the attention of the boy she liked. But when it came to girls, Seamus O'Grady was dumber than a doornail.

Ofa Hawkins – why she was the prettiest girl both east and west of the Brazos River. She was tall, had long legs, a rosy red complexion, full lips, deep-set green eyes, and long curly blond hair. She was also the brightest girl in the whole school and maybe just as far as the eye could see on the Texas prairie, and Texas is a big state. Well, just last year, Ofa could throw a ball, climb a tree, bait a hook, and ride a horse as good as any boy in Luckenbach. But when she turned 17, she was no longer one of the boys. She stopped wearing her hair in pigtails and traded her crayons for perfume. She wasn't the same Ofa anymore. She was more like, Ophelia. But the hometown folk still called her Ofa.

Seamus O'Grady, I wouldn't say he was cute, but I wouldn't say he wasn't. I'll never understand why the girls of Gillespie County called him a heartthrob. The boy rarely combed his hair. He was devilishly shy and maybe a bit charming. Mrs. Bone, the town busybody, said, "Seamus O'Grady had a face only a mother could love." But that was just one woman's opinion.

No one – absolutely no one understood why Ofa was crazy about Seamus O'Grady. But she was. In 1964, a girl would never tell a boy she liked him. That was the boy's job. Ofa would wait a long time for Seamus, but she was willin' to do so. He was just a hayseed cowboy and just as crazy about Ofa, but he didn't know it. Nevertheless, he wrote her name on his arm and promised one day he'd get a real tattoo with just three letters – O F A.

Each time they'd meet he'd try to show his affection. He'd put his head down and with his hands in his pockets; he'd shuffle his feet and say something stupid. But no matter what he said and how he said it, Ofa would laugh and think it was the funniest thing in the whole wide world. You might say he was socially awkward. But his momma loved her blue-eyed boy, and you know how some mommas are – they want their baby boys to stay babies.

"Ofa, y'all want a Lifesaver?"

"A Lifesaver?" she responded.

Ofa had a puzzled expression; Seamus was awkward as usual.

"Seamus O'Grady, is that all you have to say to a girl? You know the answer to that question. Sure 'nough, I most definitely want a Lifesaver, and that's especially true if it comes from you."

Seamus pulled out a roll of Lifesavers and with a grin as wide as the Pedernales River; he'd extend his arm and opened his hand. It was his way of proclaiming his undying love for Ofa Hawkins.

"Ofa if you don't see the color you want, you can pick through till you find the right one."

Her favorite color was purple.

At one point during their conversation, things became awkward, and Seamus would have nothing to say.

"Seamus, you missed school today," she'd exclaim.

She could have pinched herself for sayin' what she said. She didn't want to be like the others who'd chastised the boys for playin' hooky. But if she didn't say something, Seamus would just stare at the ground.

"I'll help you with your homework if you want," she'd ask.

Seamus took a deep breath and went for the ace of diamonds.

"Well, Ofa Hawkins, I just might take you up on that."

There were times when Seamus could actually put an entire sentence together.

They'd sit in the general store, and Seamus would pretend he didn't understand algebra. It was just an act, and she knew it was, but she played along. It was a romantic dance. However, Seamus didn't know how to dance, but Ofa did. He was a bright boy but hated school, but I'll bet he had more common sense than anyone at Fredericksburg High School. If you gave him a problem, he'd find ten solutions.

But he loved ridin' horses, fishin', and huntin'. She loved his spirit – wild, free, and fearless. She loved his confidence, his bravery, his sense of right and wrong, how he cared for his granddaddy, his best friend Elijah, and sticking up for people. But when it came to girls, and this was especially true of Ofa – Seamus was a chicken.

Ofa asked Seamus to accompany her across Main Street to the post office. I'm not sure you'd call Main Street a street. It was just a dirt road. But it was a girl's ploy to spend time with the boy she liked. But he didn't understand that Ophelia Hawkins was becoming a woman and no longer the tomboy she was a year ago. That was exactly his problem. The girl had begun to change and time was running out before he was expected to make a similar change.

"Sure Ofa, I'd love to walk you, let me get Elijah."

"Why do you always have to get Elijah?" she asked.

"Ofa, I couldn't leave him behind. He's my best buddy. We're blood brothers. Blood brothers don't leave each other."

"Seamus, you and I are blood brothers too. Sometimes a girl wants to be alone with a boy. Can't you leave your blood brother behind for ten minutes? He's my blood brother too. It's downright possible I just might like you."

She opened her big eyes, and when she smiled, she lit up the Texas sky.

"Ofa Hawkins, you flirtin' with me?" he asked.

"You are a precocious boy. Don't ever think I'm one of those silly girls who thinks you're even the slightest bit cute. Seamus, some girls don't care if a boy is cute. What makes you attractive is who you are."

Seamus and Elijah were blood brothers. They were inseparable. If Ofa were going to spend time with Seamus, she'd have to take

Elijah as well.

Elijah bought three bottles of Coke, six Moon Pies, and two packs of LifeSavers. The boys made a fortune redeeming the bottles and were happy to share their bounty with Ofa Hawkins, the prettiest girl both east and west of the Brazos River.

Seamus was tempted to hold Ofa's hand. It wasn't the first time he felt that way. Ever since ninth grade when he first laid eyes on her, he had a hankering to do so. But for now, they walked to the post office side by side. Her shoulder brushed against his. She noticed, but he didn't. But he did notice her curly blond hair. And when she walked barefoot on the dusty Luckenbach roads – well, there just was no way to describe it. But holding Ofa's hand would take more courage than Seamus had.

Ofa was expecting a package from the Book of the Month Club. Each month she'd find the latest adventure waiting at the post office. Books took her away from Luckenbach, and she traveled the world on a magic carpet of words. Her teacher, Mrs. Harris, said if she maintained straight A's, she could attend any college in the country. She had big dreams and hoped to be a Doctor, but girls growing up in the 60's rarely became doctors. But it was just like Ofa to defy the odds. Yeah, she was different all right; she was no longer the third musketeer.

The boys opened the post office door. The old oak floor creaked as Ofa ran to see if her package had arrived.

"Mr. Ignacio, do I have a package?"

The old man peeked above his spectacles. "Now let me see Missy."

He went to the dusty shelf and pretended to read the addresses.

"Sorry, Missy, I don't see one for you."

"But Mr. Ignacio," she pleaded, "could you please look again?"

The old man raised an eyebrow and said, "For you Ofa darlin', of course."

He walked back to the shelf and then shook his head.

"Wait a minute. I didn't see this one. Well, I'll be doggone; it's for Ophelia Hawkins, 7 Travis Street, Luckenbach, Texas."

She opened the cover and walked toward the potbelly stove and sat and read for a spell. Pops, along with the usual suspects were sittin' next to the stove pulling on a jug. It was a typical afternoon at Ignacio's where the old men of Luchenbach sat around playin' checkers and talkin' about when they was young. It's a funny thing what old men do – goin' back to the past tryin' to catch a glimpse of when they was soldiers in the First War. Eventually, they'd realize they were old men sittin' around an ol' stove and tellin' yarns. And Ofa sat among the old men reading a book about future dreams.

Ofa doted on Pops, and the old man thought the sun rose and set on the pretty girl.

"Hey darlin'," Pops called out.

Pops was Seamus' granddaddy. In the 60's it was okay to call a girl darlin'; the women's movement hadn't reached Luckenbach.

Pops was a sturdy man, a bit lanky and even muscular. He was a Texas Ranger. He had a way about him. You knew he had done time in the saddle. He was 15 when he joined the Army and fought battles against a band of Mexican renegades led by Poncho Villa. The O'Grady family traced their heritage to the Alamo. Pops' great-grandfather, Finbar O'Grady died with Colonel Travis at the west wall. Colonel Travis was a Texas hero. Every town in Texas had a street named, Travis. The last lines that Colonel Travis penned were no less than heroic and addressed: to the people of Texas and all Americans, "I shall never surrender or retreat: victory or death." Such thoughts were the ethos of the O'Grady boys; they were Texas Rangers, riding for Texas.

Texas is a state of mind with a fabled history. It's a big state with a strong sense of unity. If you're from Texas, you're from Texas. Seamus and Elijah grew up listenin' to Pops' stories of the Alamo and life on the prairie fightin' the Comanche, horse thieves, cattle rustlers, and Mexican banditos. They were the same stories that Seamus' great granddaddy, Finbar O'Grady told his son Ennis O'Grady, who then told his son McCauley and McCauley told his son, Liam, who was Seamus' daddy, who then told Seamus.

The stories of Texas are bigger than the sky. They're stories of great deeds and bravery. At the Alamo, with no hope of success, the Texans crossed the line in the sand and chose to die instead of surrender. They were all slaughtered, but people still shout, "Remember the Alamo." Those stories shaped the character of Seamus and Elijah.

"Ofa Hawkins, you're the prettiest girl this side of the Brazos River. My grandson is an idiot for not sweepin' you off your feet," Pops exclaimed.

Ofa threw her arms around the old man and gave 'im a big ol' kiss.

"Pops, I thought I was the prettiest girl east and west of the Brazos River. That's what I am – I guess. People been tellin' me that since I was two – maybe even younger. Pops, I wanna be smart. I'm tired of being called, Pretty Girl. I like to think there's more to me."

"Well darlin' girl, there ain't nothing wrong with being pretty. But you know what's really appealin'? It's being a woman; it's being an honorable woman, someone who believes in some'in. Like standin' up for big ol' ideas, bigger than you. Like, doin' for somebody else."

"Pops you're a wise man. That's exactly what I wanna to do. I wanna stand up for some'in meaningful."

"So, when is Seamus going to ditch Elijah and take you to the movies?"

She paused and reflected carefully on her words.

"Seamus and I are just friends, and that's exactly how I like him. And besides, he's just a poor hayseed cowboy who ain't got a field to hoe and who don't care about nutin' 'xcept fishin', ridin' horses, and playin' hooky from school."

Pops smiled, took a puff on a cigar, pulled on a whiskey bottle, and made the next move on the checkerboard. Ofa Hawkins had just confirmed his suspicions. She was smitten over his grandson, Seamus.

"So, what's all the excitement about Pretty Girl?"

He called her Pretty Girl, and she loved the attention.

"I just got a new book," she said.

"It must be a darn good book," Pops laughed. "Darlin' what's the name?"

"It's *Deliver Us from Evil: The Story of Vietnam's Flight to Freedom*. Dr. Tom Dooley wrote it," She replied.

"Girl, I don't suppose I ever heard of Dr. Tom Dooley."

"Dr. Dooley was a humanitarian who helped children in Southeast Asia," she explained.

"Ain't they a bunch of Commies over there?" he asked.

"That's the point Pops, Dr. Dooley helped stop communism by caring for the people. He was a great man, and I admire him. I'm fixin' to be a doctor just like him."

"Where's Vietnam, Pretty Girl?"

Ofa knew the geography, politics, and history of the region. She was unlike most girls who were content to flirt with boys.

"Vietnam is east of Cambodia and Laos and west of the Gulf of

Tonkin and the South China Sea. We have soldiers fightin' there tryin' to stop communism. It's the Domino Theory," she said.

The Domino Theory was the political theory President Johnson inherited from John Kennedy and who inherited it from President Eisenhower.

She explained, "Vietnam is two countries, North and South; we're helping the South drive out the communists and become a free nation."

"Two countries – What do you mean two countries?" Pops asked.

"After World War II, the Viet Minh, led by Ho Chi Minh, established a communist nation in Hanoi. In 1949, non-communist Vietnamese politicians, with our help, formed a rival government in the South with the capitol in Saigon. The '54 Geneva Conference divided the country into communist and non-communist."

"Ofa, what's this Domino Theory you talk about?"

"Mrs. Harris told us President Eisenhower said, you have a big ol' row of dominoes. You knock over the first one, and sure 'nuff what will happen to the last one is the certainty that it will go over very quickly. If Vietnam becomes communist, then the countries around it will become communist. It's like dominoes. If they're next to each other when one falls the rest fall."

"Why should we care if Vietnam becomes communist? Hells bells, I bet no one other than you and Mrs. Harris knows where Vietnam is."

Pops called the boys who were busy looking at the list of the most wanted criminals that hung on the post office wall.

"Boys, you know where Vietnam is?" Pops asked. Seamus and Elijah appeared confused.

"Pops, I've no idea, but I think it's in China."

Pops laughed and said, "Seamus, I can't tell you the difference between Vietnam and New York City."

"Pretty Girl, how y'all know so much," Pops asked?

"We learned about Vietnam in school last Friday. But Seamus and Elijah don't attend school on Fridays, cause they's out fishin' at the South Grape Creek."

FOUR

DULCE ET DECORUM EST

My friend, you would not tell with such high zest to children
ardent for some desperate glory, the old lie; it is sweet and right to
die for your country.

Wilfred Owen, *Dulce Et Decorum Est*

February 1965 – Luckenbach

"**My daddy says the war in Vietnam is wrong, and we got
no business meddlin' in the affairs of Southeast Asia!**"

Ofa Hawkins said exactly that. It was though she was lecturin' to
children. She learned that from her daddy. The old men playin'
checkers around the pot-bellied stove smiled. She was just a child,
but they didn't appreciate her condescendin' ways. Regardless, the
men indulged the pretty girl.

Ofa's daddy, Professor Asa Hawkins, taught theology at the
Austin Presbyterian Theological Seminary. He was a preacher man,
and when her daddy would preach, Ofa went along. Asa was an
honorable man in thought and deed, yet contemplative. He carried
the world on his shoulders. Such men were never content. They'd see
the shortcomings of life and try to fix things according to what they
believed. To Asa, the cup was always half empty. And he'd find fault
with that part, which remained in the cup. If you asked Asa a
question, he seldom gave a quick response. He'd gaze into your eyes,
take off his glasses, and then place one of the stems in his mouth. In
his Texas drawl, he'd comment, "You need to define your terms."
And if that weren't confusing enough, he'd complicate your thoughts
by asking, "What in heavens do you mean?" Attempting to shed
some light on the nature of your question, he'd quote the classics,
history, philosophy, and psychology. Then he'd question you until

you answered your own question. By the time he finished answering your question, the answer he had given had no resemblance to the question you had asked. If you asked Asa for the time of day, he'd tell you how to build a clock.

The old men didn't take kindly to a young girl speakin' against the Vietnam War. They were not accustomed to being challenged. They were ol'-school and had earned the right to sit around a pot-bellied stove, playin' checkers, smokin' cigars, shootin' whiskey, and havin' an opinion. But Ofa was a brazen girl, and she spoke her mind. She was like her daddy but a bit more gracious. She learned grace from her momma, Scarlett.

There's something about old men and war. They were soldiers in the first war, but now they were willin' to send young men to kill and be killed. It was the next generation's turn, their rite of passage. A man had to be a man, and he had to do his duty. It didn't matter whether it was right or wrong.

*　　*　　*

"Ofa darlin', don't ya think there're things in life worth fightin' for?" Pops asked. "What kind of world would it be if we didn't stand against hatred?"

"Pops, you can't beat hatred with hatred. In Buddhism, peace is possible when human rights are respected, where people are fed, and where individuals and nations are free to be what they choose to be. True peace with oneself and with the world can only happen through internal peace. That ain't happenin' in Vietnam. We're imposin' our views on others."

"Ofa, why's a pretty girl talking about Buddhism?" Pops asked.

"Pops, being pretty has nothing to do with a girl havin' an opinion. Would you hear me out?" she asked.

"Pops, there's an ancient wisdom more powerful than anything you and I might know. The Buddhists call it, *Wisdom of the Ages.* They believe in it, and so do I. It's the only way we can overcome hatred. When you love your neighbor even when your neighbor hates you, it works. It's non-violence. That's eternal wisdom."

"Pretty Girl, I wish you was right," Pops said.

Ofa inherited Asa's courage of conviction and wasn't afraid of confrontation. She was glib, could think on her feet and had an understandin' of history and politics that exceeded most adults. The old men were no match for this child of the '60s. Regardless, she was a respectful child who'd let them off easy. She didn't learn that from her daddy. Asa was a bully.

"Pops, my daddy's a man of peace. He's a pacifist and objects to takin' another man's life. He says the movies glorify war and sure 'nuff, It's an outright crime. Movies don't show the sufferin' of families. Mothers don't raise their sons to die 10,000 miles from home for the corrupt government of South Vietnam. Pops, ain't you afraid Seamus and Elijah will fight this war? They're boys, and boys are gullible. They think there's glory in fightin'. There's no glory in fightin' and sure ain't no glory in dyin'.'"

"Ofa, if we didn't fight in Europe and the Pacific, what a horrible world this would be. War keeps men free. It's horrible, but it ain't the worst thing. Thinkin' that nothing is worth fightin' for is far worse. A war to protect people against evil and to protect right from wrong is just. If you have nothin' to fight for, then you ain't worth a lick. The only chance those people got to bein' free is for other men to do their fightin' for them. There's evil in the world, and there must be men to stand up to it."

"But Pops, there ain't never been a war fought between people who were certain they was right. The really dangerous people believe they're doin' whatever they're doin' because it's without question the right thing to do. If that ain't President Johnson, then I don't know who. All men are divine and created in the image of God," she expressed. "We have the Lord's light in our soul and yearn to love and be loved. Love is our reason for livin'. It's worth dyin' for. If I had a choice of how I was to die, I'd die for love."

"Well, Pretty Girl, I think you should live for love. I wish it was true, but my view of the world is different from yours. I've seen the worst of men, the horrible things they do to each other."

"Pops, you've seen the best in men: bravery, sacrifice, and love. That's the spark that makes man "Deevine," the image of God, and is in all men. 'What piece of work is man,' Shakespeare said. He's telling us that we are "Deevine.""

When she spoke, she melted the hearts of the old men. But Ofa couldn't see the reality of the world through a pragmatic lens.

"Darlin, I want my grandson to be a soldier and do what the O'Grady's have done since the Alamo. That's what a man does."

"I don't see it that way Pops, it's not a man's duty to soldier. The duty of man is to serve others. Pops, the Texans were all killed at the Alamo. Do men have to die to prove they're men?"

33

"But they died bravely," Pops said, "to save Texas."

"Oh, Pops, they died for land. Greed! Man has a determinin' spirit. The determinin' spirit goes against the nature of the universe. The world has harmony – the natural order of things is perfect. And it's the determinin' spirit of man that changes the harmony of the universe, and that's why we have war and killin'."

"Pretty Girl, I don't know nothin' about that, but at the Alamo, the Texans died for freedom. At Bellow Wood, I would have gladly died for my country. I would expect the same from Seamus. Anyway, where'd you get all them ideas?"

"It's Indian Mythology: *Black Elk Speaks*."

The old men never heard such nonsense.

Ofa knew Seamus would fight in Vietnam and carry the banner of the ill-fated crusade. He was idealistic and brave but foolhardy. The government would manipulate a boy like that.

Ofa, said in a sassy voice, "Horace, a Roman poet wrote, Dulce Et Decorum Est, it means, it's sweet and right." Sometimes the pretty girl could be downright righteous. "Politicians say this when young men die in war. They say it's glorious to die for your country. Pops, there ain't no glory in dyin'."

There was sadness in the old men's eyes.

"Dulce ET Decorum Est," she said. "My friend, you would not tell with such high zest to children ardent for some desperate glory, it is sweet and right to die for your country."

Ofa darlin' had those men listening; that was just her way.

FIVE

DON'T MEAN NUTHIN

The most desperate time in battle is when you no longer care.

Seamus O'Grady

24 April 1967 – Hill-861

"**S**ergeant Barsegyan, give me the flag," Seamus ordered.

"Platoon Sergeant, we can't fly the flag," Ando countered. "What if the gooks get it?"

"If they get it we'll all be dead so what the fuck does it matter?"

Sergeant Barsegyan would not argue with his Platoon Sergeant when they were on the verge of being overrun by a determined enemy.

Seamus stuffed the colors of 1/9 (1st Battalion 9th Marine Regiment) into his pack and ran back to the CP.

Enemy fire had intensified; they were tightening the vise on the Marines holding on to Hill-861. Seamus searched his bag of tricks, hoping to find a miracle. If only he had read *Message to Garcia*.

Lieutenant McGivens was a man of 'letters' and believed the answers to dilemma were found between the covers of books. The Sergeant was not. The miracles he'd find would come from him. Regardless of *Message to Garcia*, life and death was depended on Seamus O'Grady.

"Seamus, the CO wants us to hold and wait for re-enforcements," McGivens said. "Says Battalion's afraid they'll control the hills and bring arty from the high points surrounding Khe Sanh. They don't want another Diem Bien Pho."

"El-tee, same old shit; this thinkin' is fucked. We ain't overrun cause arty fucked 'em up, and Elijah stopped them with claymores.

Bravo just reported Corporal Engstrom and Private Fields are *KIA* (killed in action). I don't see a plan to get us out of this. We kill the enemy, and we bleed too. This hill ain't worth the loss of life it'll take to win this fight today."

It was typical Marine Corps doctrine: hold a position, make contact, close with, then kill the enemy with overwhelming firepower. The tactic was to kill more of them than they killed of us. It was called body count. But, close combat in the jungle with 100 meters separating adversaries assured Marines would also die. Lihue, Terry, Knap, Engstrom, and Fields were dead, and seven men were *WIA* (wounded in action).

Twenty miles away, at Camp Carol, Colonel Shelby made decisions with little knowledge of the tactical situation. Hold, he ordered, but the enemy had numeric superiority, terrain advantage, camouflaged and fortified bunkers, supplies, and reinforcements. The only chance the Marines had was to withdraw.

"Big Daddy . . . This is Buckaroo . . . Over . . ."

"Go ahead Buckaroo . . . Big Daddy here . . ."

"Captain, got 5 KIA, 7 WIA, 28 effective . . . We're up against a reinforced Company they're forming for an assault . . ."

"Buckaroo, hold your position. You'll have 'em in the open. Got F-4's on station; we'll blow the fuck out of 'em. Shelby wants to bring in firepower . . . You're the bait . . . Out."

The 500 pound bombs the Phantoms dropped had no effect on killing the enemy. When the aircraft were on station, the enemy hunkered down in bunkers protected by six layers of logs and dirt. But Shelby smelled a kill and was convinced Seamus would give it to him. Seamus had a plan and if he got his way and with a little luck, he might get them out.

"Corporal Barsone, hoist the Battalion flag here. This is the CP; the Lieutenant's here, this is where we'll make our stand."

"Yes Sir," Corporal Barsone screamed. "But what if we can't hold, and they get the flag?"

"Barsone, what the fuck's wrong with you guys? It's the same bullshit. This is not a time to be chained to tradition. The enemy knows how we think; they understand whatever we do, we do accordin' to a stupid doctrine established 191 years ago. We're gonna fool 'em; do the opposite of what we'd normally do."

"Seamus, how you gonna explain losing the colors?"

"Don't know. We'll know tonight, and when tomorrow mornin' comes whether we live or die, it'll be over, and it won't fuckin' matter."

"Yes Sir," Barsone replied.

Referring to Sergeant O'Grady as sir was a sign of respect. Barsone was a tough kid from the Bronx: complicated, conniving, and angry. Red took the flag tied it to a beam and using sandbags as leverage hoisted the colors of 1/9. The flag swayed in the afternoon breeze. Seamus told the enemy the Marines would remain and be ready to fight.

"Come get us, motherfuckers," Barsone screamed.

Seamus wanted to send that exact message. If the enemy saw the Americans raise their colors, they might think the Marines were reinforcing and would fight to the end. Seamus believed that seeing the flag would make them hesitate and buy the beleaguered Marines valuable time to find their miracle.

Seamus needed to see Elijah and maybe for the last time. They had only the moment and if they were lucky, the moment after.

"Seamus, you look like something the cat dragged in," Elijah said.

"I love you too, Sergeant Bravo."

"Seamus, y'all think we'd wind up like this? I keep thinkin' of Ofa warning us 'bout the war. It's all for nothing. She's right, panyo. We lost five good men today. For what? For Viet, Fucking Nam!"

Elijah called his best friend panyo; it was the deepest term of endearment. There was nothing else he could say when they were about to die.

"Elijah, something good has to come from this. I don't know what, but something. We have to believe that. I can't accept this sufferin's for nothin'. It can't end this way. It's time we have faith."

There was little hope, but Seamus held on. It was his nature to be loyal to a cause even if it were a cause he didn't understand. Losing hope was losing everything.

"Seamus – it don't mean nuthin," Elijah said.

Elijah's comment had sealed his fate. There was no hope remaining. Everything was lost. So, life itself meant nothing. *The most desperate time in battle is when you no longer care*, Seamus thought.

Did Seamus hear Elijah correctly? "It don't mean nuthin."

Elijah had endured more than he could. He'd seen his friends' lifeless bodies. He'd lost his soul. And, all he could say was, "it don't mean nuthing."

Seamus refused to believe that Elijah had lost hope and was resigned to die. But they were already dead. The only way for Elijah to accept his destiny was to convince himself that, it don't mean nuthin. But what Elijah meant was life meant everything and he was about to lose it.

"Seamus, we ain't dyin' for Viet Fucking Nam. We're dyin' for each other. We're together; I'll never leave you, Seamus. The Battalion flag you hoisted over the CP – I'll die for that but I ain't dyin' for this fuckin' hole. For me, it's never been about Vietnam. I'm a Marine; I'll do my duty, and when they come, I'll prove I'm the better man."

"Elijah, it ain't gonna end here. I'll get us out. Promise me, no hero shit."

"Listen up Bravo; they're gonna hit us at dusk. I'll bring a wall of steel in our front. Hold the flank as long as you can. The secondary position is the CP. If we're forced to retreat, we'll make our stand at the CP. I want a *hedgehog defense*. We'll break up into smaller mutually supporting positions. Each position will coordinate interlocking fire. They'll have to split their forces to engage us. It might tie 'em up."

For the moment, Elijah's position was stable. The claymores were set, the 60s were in place, and the right flank was ready.

Elijah pulled a silver flask from his pack. He poured some *hooch*, (whiskey) into his canteen cup and handed it to Seamus.

"Staff Sergeant O'Grady – here's to us and those like us –"

"Damn few left," they shouted.

"Elijah Bravo, I will see you after the fight."

"Aye-aye Platoon Sergeant."

"Elijah, if you get out of this, and I don't – tell, Ofa I loved her. I always loved her."

"Hey, Seamus, you stupid Irish fuck, tell her yourself."

SIX

IT'S MY CALL

The majority merely disagreed with other people's proposals, and, as so often happens in these disasters, the best course always seemed the one for which it was now too late.

Tacitus

24 April – Hill-861

"Sergeant Bravo, my weapon's jammed!"

"Carney! Pull the bolt back," Elijah screamed.

"Sergeant! It's still jammed!"

"Ram the cleaning rod down the muzzle."

"Staff Sergeant, there's no cleaning rod with this weapon."

"Jesus H. Christ Carney, listen up. When you eject that round take your magazine out; try to re-seat your rounds. The magazines are fucked up – springs are weak. Don't fill 'em with 20 rounds, put 17. It should work," Sergeant Bravo said.

Carney released his magazine from the chamber and tapped it twice on his helmet pushing the rounds to the front of the magazine.

"This fucking piece of shit!" Carney screamed.

Something was wrong with the M-16 rifle (*16*). The weapons of three other Marines were also jammed. In 1967, the 16 became the standard rifle in Vietnam and replaced the M-14 rifle (*14*). Early models malfunctioned. The 16 failed to eject the spent cartridge. In the early stages of the war, men died because their rifle failed. The 16s of dead Marines were found broken down lying next to them. The Army failed to ensure the weapon and ammunition worked together, failed to train the troops in maintenance, and neglected to issue enough cleaning equipment.

The Sergeant grabbed the radio.

"Cowboy (Elijah) . . . This is Buckaroo (Seamus) . . . Over."

"Go ahead, Buckaroo . . ."

"Got any problems with the 16 . . .?" Seamus asked.

"I got two down . . ."

"Push a cleaning rod down the muzzle; force the cartridge out . . ."

"Seamus, I don't mean to be an asshole, but if everyone had a cleaning rod, we'd do that . . . Out."

"El-tee," Seamus complained. "Some weapons are jamming. They send us to war, and you'd think they'd give us weapons that work. I don't believe this cluster-fuck."

Seamus' orders were to hold the position at all costs, but the Platoon Sergeant had four 16s down. The Marines had lost confidence in their equipment. It was imperative they apprise Captain Reynolds of the situation.

"Big Daddy . . . This is Buckaroo . . . Over."

"Go ahead, Buckaroo . . ."

"Got four 16s down; maybe more to go. Request we pull back. The enemy is regrouping; they'll hit us at dusk . . . The 500 pound bombs aren't shit; their bunkers are heavily fortified . . . Sir, there's no way we can hold this position . . ."

"We'll reinforce from Camp Carol . . . Hold . . ." The Captain ordered.

"Sir, that's what the gooks want us to do. The LZs are targeted. We'll take heavy casualties coming in. When we reinforce, they will too. They got terrain advantage, and they'll shoot the shit out of us. Once we close with them, they'll leave the battlefield and take their casualties with them . . . Sir, tell Battalion . . ."

"Seamus, stay on the hook; I'll be back . . ."

Captain Reynolds believed that if O'Grady couldn't hold the position, it couldn't be held.

"Buckaroo, Battalion wants the position held. Regiment won't re-enforce till tomorrow . . . I told 'em the LZs are targeted and moving the Battalion late in the afternoon is risky . . . The Colonel's worried the situation is affecting your judgment . . ." Reynolds said.

"Jesus H. Christ, Captain!" Seamus screamed. "If Shelby thinks I'm callin' this wrong let him get his ass down here and see for himself! Tell him exactly what I said . . ."

"Buckaroo, wait one . . ."

"Buckaroo . . . Big Daddy here . . . Over."

"Seamus, these are your orders. It's your call. If you withdraw, pull back to coordinates; I *shackle* – Yankee – Dodger – Bridge – Houston – Ford – Baseball. That's my CP . . . You copy . . .?"

"Big Daddy . . . Roger . . . Out."

Seamus noted the shackle code taped to the prick. He hoped he had copied it correctly.

Seamus used a lull in the battle and called a meeting with his Squad leaders to plan their tactical withdrawal.

"Gentlemen, what's your situation? Ando, you first."

"Staff Sergeant, we've got the left flank. We have one KIA, two WIA, eight effective. The enemy has no avenues of approach to flank us. We have 0 claymores, 2,400 rounds for two 60s. Each man has an average of 10 magazines and four grenades."

"Ando, send one of your 60's to Elijah with 1,000 rounds," Seamus ordered.

"Alexander, go."

"Staff Sergeant, we've got the CP, one KIA, two WIA, nine Effective, no Claymores, two 60s with 1,200 rounds, average two grenades, and eight magazines. Interlocking fields of fire with the first and third Squad."

Seamus thought carefully. His decisions would mean life and death for the beleaguered Marines.

"Okay, Alexander, this is what I want you to do. Move one of your Fire Teams with a 60 on echelon and interlock with the forward 60s of the third Squad. Use your other 60 to provide cover fire if 1st and 2nd Squads withdraw."

"Got it," Alexander answered.

"Elijah!"

"I got three 60s includin' Ando's, 2,200 rounds, three Claymores, nine effective, four magazines per man, average two grenades, three WIA's, and three KIA."

"Elijah, you gotta hold. Ando is sendin' you a Fire Team. There's no magic bullet here. It's time we find that miracle Pops told us 'bout."

"This is the situation," Seamus said. "We have been ordered to hold this position. Battalion thinks they can mass enough firepower to cripple them. They believe we can lure them into the open. Whether we hold or withdraw, it's my call. We fucked them up with arty, and Elijah hit 'em up with claymores, but they're regroupin'."

"How you gonna make that decision," Elijah asked?

"*Intel*, (intelligence)" Seamus said. "Carney and me will sneak around their perimeter; we'll check their numbers. Wood will be actin' Platoon Commander. Anything happens to me, you take command and Wood takes the 3rd Squad."

"Seamus, I'll go instead," Elijah said. "If you go down, we lose our Platoon Commander."

"Elijah, you'd have no problem taking over. Wood takes 3rd Squad."

"Seamus, Joe Buck and me will go. You know no one can do this better than us."

SEVEN

LEAVING THE WIRE

If a man were to know the end of this day's business 'ere it come.
But it suffices that the day will end, and then the end be known.
And if we meet again, well then, we'll smile. And if not, then this
parting was well made.

Shakespeare, *Julius Caesar*

24 April – Hill-861

"Sergeant Bravo, *cammy-up* (camouflage)."
Corporal Joe Buck was as gutsy as he was salty; he would've been more effective if he had common sense to temper his fearlessness. The men thought he was an arrogant son of a bitch. He acted as though he was from the Ol' Corps, one who knew the ropes and had served his time in hell. Buck did know the ropes, and he did serve his time in hell, but he rubbed it in everyone's face. Bravo and Buck had been together since boot camp and had not always been friends. The night the Texas boys left for Paris Island, they almost came to blows at Austin Station. A Sergeant stepped in, noted Joe Buck's cocky attitude and gave him the nickname 'John Wayne.' But time brought the boys together, and they learned to respect what they saw in each other. Buck swore Sergeant Bravo was the best Squad leader in the Marine Corps and Sergeant Bravo thought Corporal Buck was the best field Marine in the Battalion. Buck favored the jargon of the Ol' Breed, used by the Marines of the Pacific War whose heroics assured that the Corps would be remembered for a thousand years. "Cammy-up" was the ritual of putting on camouflage.

"Jesus H. Christ, Buck, we don't need any of that shit. I can sneak up those motherfuckers and scratch their balls before they know it."

The Comanche of South Texas brought Bravo into their spirit world. He had their blood, and they taught him their skills. From the tribal Shamans living on the *reservation* (Rez), he learned the sacred teaching of the medicine wheel and became one with the earth. Elijah believed that everything in nature is connected and has spirit. It's a life force, which lives and breathes with purpose, fulfilling the mandate of the great circle of life. At fifteen-years-old, he experienced a vision quest, a spiritual adventure into nature and himself. The vision quest took a boy from the distractions of life and immersed him into the wonders of the Creator. It's a sacred time of change, a rite of passage into a new and a deeper level of spirituality. A vision quest connects man with the four sacred directions: North, South, East, and West, and also with all creatures and entities of the universe: trees, stones, sky, stars, and wind. Everything has spirit and has a life of its own. He learned to see, to understand, and learned about his power. Each of the directions has spiritual power, and he learned its ways and Elijah was filled with the wonders of the great mystery. Elijah fasted and hallucinated for three days and then discovered his animal sign. He was the Eagle and could see life from a distance, and with his penetrating eyes, he could understand its complexities. He could become a vapor and slip in and out of this world. He could assume the spirit of any form of nature and become that entity. Elijah was a spirit. He believed he was invisible and all he had to do was will it. Whether he was or he wasn't, it didn't matter, because since he believed he was, he was.

"Corporal Buck, remember, *Celer – Silens – Mortalis*."
"Sergeant Bravo, what the fuck you talking about?"
"Swift, Silent, Deadly – Let's go."

"Hey Buckaroo, you okay?" Elijah said to his best friend as he prepared to leave the perimeter.
"Yeah fuckhead, I am sending my best friend on a suicide mission. Of course, I'm okay," Seamus sarcastically commented.
Seamus was shaken but had no choice. Elijah and John Wayne were best suited for the task. To make the right call, he needed intel.
"Seamus, do somethin' for me, would ya? Send Ofa a letter."
"Elijah, for someone who played around with every floozy in Texas, I didn't think you'd be so sentimental."
"There's much y'all don't know about me, Buckaroo. One day I'll

44

tell you my secrets."

Elijah smiled; it was difficult to speak.

"Seamus – I'll see you in the North Star."

"I'll be watching for you, Cowboy."

Sergeant Bravo turned toward the Lieutenant. He wanted McGivens to know he respected him and regardless of being an FNG, McGivens was his Platoon Commander.

"Sir, if I may say, you were brilliant today. Any words?"

McGivens smiled and hoped he deserved the sentiment.

"Yeah, I do Sergeant Bravo, "if a man were to know the end of this day's business 'ere it come. But it suffices that the day will end and then the end, be known. And if we meet again, well then, we'll smile. And if not, then this parting was well made."

"Carry on Sergeant Bravo."

"Sir!"

"Joe, move out."

And Seamus watched his best friend disappear into the elephant grass.

"Ell-tee, you holdin' up?" Seamus asked.

"Yeah – I've never felt like an officer until this moment. Respect coming from a man like Sergeant Bravo defines every notion I've had about being a Marine Officer."

"Seamus, what's the situation?" the Lieutenant asked.

"Elijah's gonna snoop and poop around the enemy's right flank and see what they got; see if we can handle 'em. Lieutenant, it's my call whether we hold or abandon this position."

"Seamus, I have a good feeling about you. I'm recommending you for OCS."

"Sir, may I speak freely?"

"Go ahead, Sergeant."

"Lieutenant, I don't want to be an officer. I'm enlisted – from the men. Sir, a Sergeant, is the backbone of the Corps."

"Sergeant O'Grady, I agree with you. But being an officer is a good career move."

"El-tee, I didn't join the Marines to plot my way up the chain of command. I joined to be a Marine. No disrespect intended but being a Marine is defined as a Sergeant."

McGivens believed leadership was egalitarian and evolved from the ranks of the men. He didn't respect the command and control of the Marine Corps hierarchy. Rising to the position of leadership among one's peers was the path of the Sergeant. The Congressional Appointment to the Officer Corps that McGivens received did not define the essence of what it meant to be a Marine.

Seamus stared at the PRC-25. A faint and garbled voice broke its silence.

"Buckaroo, Cowboy here . . . Do not respond . . . Click the receiver twice to acknowledge my transmission . . . Over . . ."

Elijah was close to the enemy and didn't want the noise of a radio transmission to give away his position. The radio cracked; Seamus listened.

"There's at least three companies of regulars. They're staging for an assault. Their mortar positions are entrenched about 75% effective . . . waiting for our choppers to land then they'll fire . . . Raising the Battalion flag worked. They're deliberate; you got 'em blinking. Seamus, it'll be a mess. They've taken heavy casualties but reinforcing from Highway 9. We can't hold . . . I repeat . . . We can't hold . . . Get the fuck out of there. Leave the 60s I set on 3rd Squad's flank. It's perfect cover fire. That's where they'll come. Third Squad will cover your retreat. Acknowledge with two clicks. Don't wait for me, Buckaroo. I'll get back. I am the jungle . . . Out."

The situation on Hill-861was deteriorating. The PRC-25 cracked again.

He thought of Ofa, the beautiful girl he left behind. He thought of Elijah and the pledge he made never to leave, but he was leaving.

"For he today that sheds his blood with me shall be my brother," McGivens said quoting Shakespeare's *Henry V*. "I'll stay back and man the net. I can bring arty down on a dime. You go. I'll call in the *FPF* (final protective fire)."

"I can't do that El-tee; I gotta wait for Elijah. I promised. Sir, you're my Lieutenant; I'm responsible for you. I'm getting you out. You gave me command of the Platoon. Now let me command."

"I am giving you an order, Sergeant. You are to leave with the third Squad. We'll need you for tomorrow's attack."

"Sir!"

Seamus took the radio handset from McGivens. The Lieutenant understood.

"Seamus," McGivens said. "*Caedite eos. Novit enim Dominus qui sunt eius*" (Kill them all… the Lord knows who are his.).

"Big Daddy . . . This is Buckaroo . . . Over.

"Go ahead Buckaroo . . ."

"Sent scouts. Situation hopeless . . . We're getting the fuck out of Dodge . . . Out."

Seamus gathered the Squad leaders for their final orders.

"Sergeant Barsegyan, move out in five minutes. Swing south of my position. You got the Lieutenant. Alexander, you'll cover Ando's withdraw. On my direction, you'll follow him out. Corporal Wood, third Squad's yours. Send half your men with Alexander. You and your remaining Marines will provide cover fire for third Squad's withdrawal. Pull back, on my direction."

"Seamus," the Lieutenant interjected.

"El-tee, we've had that conversation. No need Sir. Sir, I got this."

"Gentlemen," Seamus said "by Elijah's direction, we leave 3rd Squad's forward position in place. We're leaving the 60s. He set good fields of fire; it'll slow 'em up. They'll blink. He'll make a break when we're out of their kill zone."

"Platoon Sergeant we're leaving Elijah and Joe Buck?" Wood questioned.

Seamus remembered the promise he made at the South Grape Creek when they vowed never to leave each other, but Hill-861 changed everything.

"I will wait for Elijah and John Wayne," Seamus said. "Any questions?"

Suddenly, the NVA began firing. They were coming. The Squad leaders had their orders. It was time to execute and see if 'adapt and overcome' would work for the beleaguered 1st Platoon.

"Squad leaders, take charge of your men. Execute." Seamus commanded.

The Corps stressed small unit leadership, and regardless of rank, the Squad leaders would step up. Marines train to command. During the Vietnam War, it wasn't unusual to have 19-year-old boys commanding a Marine Platoon.

"Get those weapons off automatic fire; Conserve your ammo. We're marksmen," Wood ordered. "Ashcraft, move your Fire Team into the forward positions, lay down cover fire. The rest of the Squad follow second Squad out."

Five Marines remained to cover the flank. Ashcraft placed his guns on the extreme right to provide fire down the center of the enemy's attack.

"Buckaroo, this is 3rd Squad . . . Over."

"Go ahead, Wood . . ."

"We've enough rounds for 10 minutes; Sir, your orders . . ."

"Hold them for five minutes. Then get the fuck out . . . The rest of the ammo is for Elijah and John Wayne . . ."

"Roger Buckaroo . . . Out."

Ashcraft directed fire on the enemy's advance. The NVA's attack stalled; however, they used spotters to detect who was responsible for directing the accurate fire.

"Ashcraft, get the fuck down," Wood screamed.

Corporal Ashcraft ignored his plea. Ashcraft was hit and fell forward.

"Corpsman up," Wood cried.

Doc Baviello ran, but Ashcraft was dead. Lance Corporal Barlow took command of the Fire Team and continued the fight. Seamus monitored the net and waited to hear from Elijah.

"Wood, get the rest of your Squad out of there. Do it now!" screamed Seamus.

"Platoon Sergeant," request permission to pull the 60s."

"Denied," Seamus countered.

"But Sergeant O'Grady, they'll get the guns."

"Corporal Wood, I'm giving you a direct order. Abandon your position and leave the 60s. When Elijah gets there, he'll buy us time."

"Seamus, it's a world of shit up here. No one can get through the enemy's line. Elijah and John Wayne didn't make it."

The receiver dropped from Seamus' hand; he tried to speak. He whispered, "Just do what I say, Bob."

The last of the 3rd Squad moved through the CP. Seamus decided he would man one of the guns. There'd be no life without Elijah Bravo.

"Platoon Sergeant, shall I strike the flag?" Wood asked.

"No, we fly the flag as long as Elijah and John Wayne are out there. They'll think we're here; and be more cautious."

"Seamus, I'm sorry about Elijah. But you're leading this Platoon;

we need you thinking rationally. They didn't make it."

The PRC-25 cracked.

"Buckaroo . . . Seamus, you there? . . . Over . . ."

"I'll be dipped in shit, where the fuck you been?" Seamus asked.

"Long story panyo . . . John Wayne and me are in place. The gooks are movin" slow. Getting ready to assault . . . I see the flag; I knew y'all fly her as long as we were out. It worked buddy; they think we're still here and we've reinforced . . ."

"Cowboy, get their heads down, blow the claymores, and get the fuck out. I am gonna drop another steel curtain . . ."

"Seamus, I got great fields of fire. Gonna kill 'em all . . ."

"Elijah, please! I'll wait at the CP when I see you and Buck getting' out; I'll strike the flag..."

"My brother, if we both die, it's for nothing. You gotta make it home. Promise me, Seamus. Promise me you'll live. Seamus, if you make it, then I've made that difference . . . Out."

EIGHT

PROMISE AT THE SOUTH GRAPE CREEK

Ultima Ratio Regum

King Louis XIV

24 April – Hill-861

"**C**owboy! Pick up…"

Seamus held the receiver tightly; he was holding on to his best friend. His head dropped into his hands, and he covered his eyes. He didn't want to see the inevitable. One more moment. One more word. He never had the chance to say goodbye. He never told Elijah, he loved him. But their casual farewell would be the best way to let go. Elijah understood, but Seamus didn't. A spontaneous joke and a fake smile were all that remained for the boys who fished at the South Grape Creek. They joined the Marines to find glory but not to die on Hill-861.

Seamus knelt on the red clay dirt clutching the receiver of the PRC-25. He thought of Ofa's warning. He and Elijah were two crazed teenage boys who were eager to prove themselves and fight the battles of a misguided country. How sweet it is to die for your country. Her words were a cruel reminder of the naiveté of young men. Dying for your country on Hill-861 didn't seem so sweet.

"Elijah," he called out. The sounds of incoming mortars overpowered his grief.

"Staff Sergeant O'Grady," Corporal Wood screamed. "What do we do? We need you. Dammit Seamus, get your head in the game. What are your orders Platoon Sergeant?"

The North Vietnamese were attacking in force and exercising *fire and maneuver* against an enemy that had abandoned the field. They moved cautiously, moving their units one at a time with each firing to cover the advance of the other. But the Marines were gone. The enemy believed the Marines were making a stand and rallying around the flag that flew over the makeshift command post.

"Platoon Sergeant, what are your orders? Wood again screamed."

"Corporal, lead the Platoon toward the Company CP, Hill-558. I'm gonna look for Elijah and John Wayne."

"No Seamus, we need you to lead us."

The words of his best friend were haunting – "If we both get killed, it's for nothing. You have to live."

"Wood, I'll call the steel curtain and blow these motherfuckers to fuck and back. My orders are – establish a defensive perimeter on this spot on the map and wait for the 1st Battalion to reinforce. I will meet you there."

"Seamus, I'll wait for you," Wood said.

"Wood, do it now goddammit!"

Seamus grabbed the radio, threw it over his shoulder, picked up his 16, ran toward the bunker, and disappeared into the smoke.

"Jackknife . . . This is Buckaroo . . . Over . . ."

"Buckaroo . . . Jackknife . . . Go ahead . . ."

"Fire Mission . . ."

"You sure it's 728607? That's your position . . ."

"*Ultima Ratio Regum* . . ." Seamus shouted.

"Repeat your last . . ." Jackknife requested.

"The final argument of kings. Affirmative . . . Out."

Louis XIV of France believed that war was the final answer and artillery was the king of the final answer. Subsequently, he had the words *Ultima Ratio Regum* cast on the cannons of his armies. It became the motto of the 1st Battalion 11th Marines. Artillery was the final solution.

The gates of hell opened, and the ground trembled sending shock waves throughout the hill. Clouds of dirt billowed. Armageddon! It was the reaper taking souls and sending them to hell. Trees splintered and crashed into the oncoming North Vietnamese. Elijah and Joe Buck had moved into position and prepared to make a stand with the 60s. The North Vietnamese were swarming. Then the distinct sounds of claymores exploded sending hundreds of steel balls into the enemy.

Seamus monitored the net hoping he'd hear of their escape. And then a transmission broke. It was Elijah and John Wayne. They were singing the Marine Corps Hymn and fighting to the death.

> From the halls of Montezuma to the shores of Tripoli. We will fight our countries battles in the air on land and sea. First to fight for right and freedom and to keep our honor clean, we are proud to claim...

The transmission stopped. The guns ceased, and within moments, North Vietnamese assault troops came through the perimeter of the 3rd Squad.

"Elijah!" Seamus cried.

"Jackknife . . ." Seamus called. – "Fire for effect . . ."

A shower of steel fell. Seamus fired at three NVA soldiers killing them moments before they overwhelmed him. A soldier ran through the artillery blasts, screaming with a fixed bayonet. Seamus aimed his 16, pulled the trigger, the weapon jammed. He pulled his 45 and shot him point blank. He stood over the enemy's lifeless body and emptied his clip into his head. "For Elijah and John Wayne," he said. He looked at the Battalion flag flying over the command post. Enemy gunners were peppering every inch of the CP. He had no choice. Seamus ran leaving his best friend and the Battalion flag behind.

NINE

SEARCHING FOR THE HOLY GRAIL

For where thy treasure is, there also will thy heart be.

Matthew, *6:21*

March 1965 – Luckenbach, Texas

"Why Seamus O'Grady, you jealous of Tommy Tucker? It was just a little ol' innocent kiss on the lips. I can see you bein' jealous if I was your girl, but you ain't ever asked me to be your girl, so you have no right to pout like a little baby."

Ofa was playing Maria in the school play, *Westside Story* and Tommy Tucker played Tony, her love interest. There was a kissin' moment, and if you ask me, it was a bit too racy for Luckenbach. But Tommy kissed Ofa, and I bet that changed Tommy Tucker's life. During the spring of 1965, Seamus saw every performance. He sat in the front row and watched Tommy Tucker kiss Ophelia Hawkins five times in one weekend. It was more than he could take.

The girl was changing; she was tired of being a tomboy. To most boys, girls were a burden, but Ofa Hawkins was not like most girls. Why she could fish all day without the slightest complaint. One minute she was drinkin' Dr. Pepper and makin' it come out of her nose. And now, she was paintin' her fingernails. She was evolvin' into a beautiful young woman. It was the way she moved and the sensuous glance she gave the boys, that showed she had come of age. Asa was worried sick about his little girl and hoped that the Christian principles he taught her would keep her away from the passions of men.

"Ofa Hawkins, if I asked you to be my girl, what would you say?

That's a hypothetical question. But let's say I did ask."

"Hypothetical! You even know what that means? Well – how would you ask me, Seamus? You know it matters how you ask a girl to go steady."

"Well I don't rightly know," he said. "I'd just ask ya."

"Seamus, y'all don't even know how to flirt. A girl likes it when a boy flirts. A girl wants to be swept off her feet. Romance! Sure 'nough, askin' ain't good enough. I want the moon, heaven, and shootin' stars. But you ain't answerin' my question. Close your eyes Seamus; just pretend."

"Dang Ofa, this is silly. But I'd say some'in like, Ofa would you be my girl?"

"Seamus I'd have to say, no. Absolutely not!"

"Well, why wouldn't you Miss Stuck-up?"

Seamus looked at her with his puppy-dog eyes. She was playin' a game, but he wasn't. Ofa, hurt his feelin's. She wished she had a do-over, but all she could do was give him a sweet smile.

"Seamus, you have no clue, do ya?"

"Dang Ofa, I do too have a clue. A Clue 'bout what?"

"See, you don't even know what I'm talkin' 'bout. You don't ask someone to be their girl when you ain't never asked them to go to a movie."

"Ofa Hawkins, just because you're the prettiest girl in Texas and the smartest that don't mean you know everything 'bout romance."

"Oh, Prince Charmin', I supposed you do."

"I know more than you think I know," he said.

"Well, I think you know nothin' Seamus. So, what do you know?"

"Ofa, I know that I'm . . . I'm . . ." He hesitated and then lowered his head.

"You're what Seamus? What you fixin' to say?" she asked.

"Ofa, in the past four years, we've seen every movie that's come to Luckenbach. So, what on earth are you sayin'?"

"Seamus, You're such a silly boy. Askin' a girl on a date to a movie, or invitin' a girl to the parlor for an ice cream is different than square squatting in front of the general store. And each time we went to the movie Elijah was with us. Seamus O'Grady, you never even said you like me. I think you'd rather be with Elijah than with me."

"Well, that's not true Pretty Girl. You're both my best friends, and I want to be with both of you."

"Well, that's exactly the problem. There comes a time when a boy and a girl become more than buddies. Seamus, the fact that you don't get it means you don't get it. So, what were you going to say?"

Ofa took a deep breath and waited for Seamus to tell her what she hoped to hear. Did Seamus see her as a desirable woman that a boy wanted to be with?

"Seamus O'Grady are you or are you not jealous of Tommy Tucker kissin' me?" Ofa asked.

"Pretty Girl you sound like a lawyer."

"If I'm a lawyer, then answer my goddamn question, Seamus."

"Ofa, you're throwin' a hissy fit? What's come over you?"

"Seamus, yes or no?"

He hadn't seen this side of her. She put him in a corner with no way out. Seamus couldn't look her in the eye.

"No, I ain't jealous of you kissin' Tommy Tucker. Well, I don't rightly know, maybe I am."

"Seamus O'Grady, y'all can't turn a no, into a yes, with a maybe in between." And that was all she said.

Somethin' in Seamus' eyes told her not to leave but to wait till he was ready. But she was tired of waiting. She wanted more than the boy could offer, so Ofa turned and walked away. He wanted to tell her that he was insanely jealous of Tommy Tucker and that he was insanely crazy about her, but Seamus didn't have the courage. When it came to romancing a girl, doing nuthin' ain't an option.

April 1965

In the spring of 1965, life changed for Seamus, Elijah, and Ofa. It was their senior year, and the boys had neither the grades nor the inclination to attend college. Ofa had straight A's, a perfect SAT score and was a national merit scholar. The boys were goin' nowhere. And to make matters worse, Seamus insisted he wasn't jealous of Tommy kissin' Ofa, so she kept her distance. She believed he didn't care, and he believed she didn't care. The boys continued to play hooky every Friday at the South Grape Creek, but instead of ridin' horses, they drove a truck, drank beer instead of Coke, and smoked cigarettes instead of eatin' Moon Pies. And Elijah, he was a shit kicker, wild, and reckless. If he wasn't fishin' or fightin', he was makin' love to an older woman. With his black hair hangin' below his waist, his tall, muscular body, and his olive complexion, he was something else with the ladies.

*   *   *

"Elijah, I should have told her I like her. I should have told her I was jealous of that fuckin' Tommy Tucker kissin' her."

"That's water under the bridge, Seamus. She's moved on, fixin' to attend Dartmouth and be a doctor. Where the fuck we goin'? Nowhere! You gotta move on buddy," Elijah said. "She's not the same Ofa anymore, she's a woman, and we're just cowboys."

"Elijah, you got so many girls that like you. I wish I had Ofa."

"Seamus, what I have's empty. There ain't no meanin' in playing around. Do somethin' about your feelin's for Ofa. Just don't go around and wish. Remember what Pops said, 'If if's and but's were candy and nuts, every day be Christmas.'"

"What the hell he mean by that?" Seamus asked.

"I don't rightly know, but I think it has some'in to do with the notion that to get some'in y'all gotta stop making excuses and do some'in 'bout it."

"Elijah, I think it's too late."

"Well, that's up to you to think that way, and that's a pretty fucked up attitude. You ain't gonna get nowhere thinkin' like that. But if I was you, I'd let her know."

The boys were looking for a purpose. Many of their classmates were goin' to college, joining the service, getting married, and hiring on as cowboys. Seamus and Elijah didn't want the ordinary. Not having a purpose left a hole in their hearts.

"Buckaroo, I don't want to be a ranch hand. There's gotta be more to life than that. Where's our Holy Grail?"

"What the hell's a Holy Grail? Y'all ain't goin' all Jesus on me like Asa?" Seamus asked."

"Seamus, didn't you ever read King Arthur and the Knights of the Round Table? Well, King Arthur has this desire to find the Holy Grail; it's the chalice that Jesus used to drink wine durin' the Last Supper. It's a metaphor 'bout findin' meaning in life."

"Elijah, I get it. Sure 'nuff we're like the Knights of the Round Table, searchin' for the Holy Grail. I kind'a like that."

"We'd never get into college, but I still want to be somebody and make a difference. Life's that shit that happens when you're waiting around for somethin' that never comes. Seamus, ol' buddy – the trick is not to wait. We got to do some'in 'bout it."

"Well, I'll be dipped in shit Elijah, we can do that, but not in college. I wish there was a sign from God to tell us what to do," Seamus said. "Elijah, you believe in God?"

"I suppose I do. Not sure, though. It's hard to believe in some'in' I ain't never seen. Y'all could claim anything is real if the only basis for believin' is that nobody proved it don't exist."

"Elijah, that's what faith's for. When you got faith, you believe in some'in' you ain't ever seen. Maybe the answer is to take up religion. That's the secret of havin' purpose. Just look at Ofa and Asa. They don't question life; they're intent on servin' God. It's the will of the Lord. That's what they call it."

"But Asa's a fuckin' lunatic. I'd feel a lot more comfortable with an arrow pointin' us to our future," Elijah exclaimed. "Our granddaddies was Texas Rangers; they was trackers. We should be able to 'find sign.' Seamus, I can sure use a fishin' Friday."

"Well, Cowboy we gotta first get through Monday, Tuesday, Wednesday, and Thursday before we get to Friday.

May 1965 – Luckenbach Career Day

Seamus beamed when he saw Ofa filing into the auditorium. "Hey Pretty Girl," he called out. He was workin' on finding the nerve to tell her how jealous he was of Tommy.

She ignored him, but she really didn't.

Career Day would give the seniors an idea of what the future had in store. There were nurses, lawyers, engineers, policemen, firemen, ranchers, and the military ready to make their pitch.

"Stop starin' at her Seamus," Elijah exclaimed. "You're actin' like a hurt little puppy; you gotta have some pride. You want her to respect ya, don't cha?"

Ofa put a knife in Seamus' heart as she smiled and sat next to Tommy Tucker. She turned the blade when she touched his hand. The courage that took weeks for Seamus to muster disappeared.

At Career Day, each occupation gave a presentation. Only one remained, the military. The Army went first. A soldier in a baggy uniform spoke about the wonderful opportunities the Army offered. The Air Force spoke about finishing a college degree at the Community College of the Air Force. The Navy told the seniors that if they joined, they'd see the world. Then a tall man impeccably dressed in a Marine Dress Blue uniform appeared on stage. He wore an insignia with three stripes and two rockers and four rows of battle ribbons. He was a Gunnery Sergeant. He had broad shoulders, a narrow waist, and a chiseled face. Briskly he walked to center stage. He came to an abrupt halt, faced left, and came to a position the military calls parade rest. The class of '65 waited on the edge of their seats for this rock hard Marine to speak.

"Good afternoon ladies and gentlemen," he said. Please excuse me if I address my comments to the young men here today. My name is Gunnery Sergeant R.S. Winston. I am here on behalf of the United States Marine Corps."

Ofa was shootin' glances from the other side of the auditorium, but Seamus was fixated on the Gunnery Sergeant. Even Ofa Hawkins was no match for this Marine god.

"Class of '65," the Sergeant bellowed. Today you've heard the presentations of these fine services. Regardless of which service, you join; you will serve your country." The Marine stared into the souls of the boys sitting before him. "I will make you one promise – If you join the United States Marine Corps, you will have the chance to fight for your country."

Sergeant Winston came to attention, made a left face, and briskly walked off the stage.

Elijah turned toward Seamus, "Buckaroo, there's our sign."

TEN

BEGINNING THE JOURNEY

Conviction is worthless unless it is converted into conduct.

Thomas Carlyle

June 1965 - Luckenbach

"Seamus, my daddy taught me never tell a lie. It's the Golden Rule. I'm tired of y'all bein' such a boy."

"Ofa, that makes me mad cause I ain't no liar. I don't know why you'd say that."

"It's not my problem that y'all don't understand. You're not a big ol' liar in the real sense of the word, but sure 'nuff you ain't honest 'bout your feelin's. It's the same thing like you was tellin' an outright fib. I saw you checkin' me out at the career assembly. Well, that was at least till that Marine came on the stage. Y'all want to be with me, but you live a lie when you deny your feelin's. Seamus, you have to have the courage of your convictions, and if you don't, then you're dishonest. When you saw me at the assembly, y'all were jealous of Tommy Tucker. I touched his hand on purpose. When I saw you starin' at me with that look on your face, you told me what I wanted to know."

"I wasn't jealous I was mad as all get out," Seamus blurted.

"Seamus, bein' mad and bein' jealous are the same. Jealousy – it'll make ya crazy. If you was honest with your feelin's things between us would be different, and you wouldn't be jealous, and if you weren't jealous, y'all wouldn't be mad. When two people like each other, a relationship shouldn't be that complicated."

"Dang, Ofa Hawkins, you're the most confusin' girl in Texas. I'm not jealous. You know how much I like you. I just need time to figure things out."

"Seamus, that's the thing about being honest, you don't need time to figure things out."

Seamus was a sweet boy, but he could be stubborn as a mule. Ofa had placed him in a corner, and a corner was not a place for Seamus O'Grady.

"Someone asked me to the prom," she asserted.

It was her way of tellin' him that she was moving on.

"Who?"

"You know who Seamus. That's what I mean. You're hidin' your feelin's."

"So, what ya tell him Pretty Girl?"

"Enough of that 'pretty girl' shit. When you'd called me Pretty Girl, it meant the world to me, not anymore. So then, what's it to ya what I told Tommy? If you don't care, then why would you ask? Y'all want to be with me, but you don't want to do any of the work. We don't put a lot of value on what we get cheaply. You're always dancin' around my feelin's. How you treat me, it ain't right. I'm not one of the boys. And you need to learn what that means."

Seamus pretended he didn't understand. Ignoring Ofa was his way of dealin' with a frightening situation.

"Seamus," she screamed. "Is bein' a bitch the only way to get your attention?"

Seamus had deep-set blue eyes, and they were soft and gentle. She wanted that in a man. But he was a just a boy, and she would walk away.

"Ofa, I do care. Sure 'nuff I really do. I just don't care the way you need me to," he blurted.

"Why would I want to be with a boy who doesn't care for me the way I think he should? You don't even understand the meanin' behind your words. I don't need you to care; I want you to care. You won't be the kind of man you could be if you don't care. Seamus – any woman, would worship you if you'd be the person she sees in you."

"My daddy told me that life is like cultivatin' a ga'den: you have to water it, turn the soil, plant seeds, and pull the weeds. You don't have a ga'den without doin' the work. What would come of it?"

"Ofa, carin' for you ain't never been a problem. It's just..."

He hesitated.

"What Seamus? Why can't you complete a thought?"

Seamus had something to tell Ofa, but fate stole the moment.

Elijah drove up in his '55 Chevy truck and tossed him a beer.

"Get in," he said. "We gotta get to Austin and meet the Gunny."

"Seamus, what did you do?" Ofa screamed."

"Ofa, I gotta run. I'm joinin' the Marines."

"Seamus, don't do it! Don't join."

Elijah popped the clutch, flipped a bitch, and the boys drove off to find their Holy Grail. Ofa began to cry, and Seamus watched her from the side mirror of the truck, and she watched him.

The boys left Ofa sobbing on Main Street in front of the general store. And there's nothing more to say about that.

ELEVEN

LOVING OFA HAWKINS

I think I first fell in love when I was in fifth grade with this boy
who kept his glass ruler in the sunlight and made rainbows on my
desk with it.

Saiber, *Stardust and Sheets*

June 1965 – Marine Recruiting, Austin, Texas

The Gunnery Sergeant walked into the recruiting office
looking for the cowboys eager to join his Marine Corps. In
one hand, he held their school records, the other, a cup of steaming
coffee. Inscribed on the cup were the words: "death before
dishonor." That caught the boys' attention. They were Texans. They
understood honor, but neither had given much thought to death.
Gunnery Sergeant R.S. Winston had told them, if they joined the
Marines, they would fight for their country. Seamus and Elijah had
come to take him up on his promise.

Winston inspected the boys; he was not pleased. If it were up to
him, he wouldn't have let them through the door. He had the
discriminating eye of the Ol' Corps, and by the looks of the boys,
they wouldn't live up to his image of a Marine. But the Corps needed
bodies to fight the yellow man in Indo-China, and the cowboys
would have to do.

*   *   *

"So, you two-hayseed cowboys want to be Marines," Winston
said.

"Yeah, we do," replied Elijah.

"Listen, Cowboy," Winston said. "Never use the word yeah in the presence of a non-commissioned officer. You're lucky I don't put my foot up your ass."

Gunnery Sergeant R. S. Winston didn't intimidate Elijah Bravo. The boy with the long black hair stood his ground and stared into the Sergeant's eyes. Regardless of this imposing man, Elijah was determined to become a Marine.

Winston studied their high school transcripts and noticed their truancy. He put the papers down and peered at the boys above his reading glasses.

"Why do you both cut school every Friday?"

"Fridays are fishin' Fridays Gunnery Sergeant," Seamus confessed

"Have you done this all through high school?" the Gunnery Sergeant asked with a look of disbelief.

"Yes sir," Seamus replied. He was interrupted by the gruff Sergeant.

"Listen, son, don't ever refer to me as sir," Winston barked. "I'm enlisted, a non-commissioned officer. I earned my rank. You will refer to me as Gunnery Sergeant."

"Hey Gunny," Elijah interjected, "We're here to join the Marines; we don't need a lesson in manners; maybe you can save the tough guy act for boot camp."

"You fucking puke," Winston screamed, "I should kick you out of my office, but you're just a number, and I've got to fill my quota for the week. Mr. Bravo, you have a lot to learn about respect. Being a Marine is about being a man, having character, and measuring up. It's loyalty to your brothers. It's Semper Fi," he shouted. "I bet you've no idea what that means. Listen, cowboy, I don't doubt you'll make your mark as a Marine, but your insolence will destroy you."

Elijah felt the wrath of the Sergeant. He understood the nature of respect, but since his daddy, Angel left to chase whores in Juarez, Mexico, Elijah's life hadn't gone well. Angel was a son of a bitch, with no redeeming qualities as a father. It was Elijah's mama who taught him the difference between right and wrong, and she taught him well.

"Mr. O'Grady, I'm still waiting for an answer to my question. Why did you guys play hooky every Friday?"

"Well, Gunnery Sergeant, me and Elijah go fishin' every Friday at the South Grape Crick near Luckenbach."

"You ever miss?" the Gunny asked.

Seamus shook his head slowly. "No, never!"

"Well, I'll be dipped in shit," Winston said.

Elijah laughed.

"Gunny, I'm sorry 'bout before, but I ain't laughin' at you. I'm laughin' cause me, and Seamus says the same thing."

The Gunny looked at both teens and said, "Well boys, I'll be dipped in shit."

"Do you boys have a MOS preference?"

"Gunnery Sergeant, what's a MOS?" Elijah asked.

"It's your military occupational specialty; it's your job."

"We want to fight," Elijah said. "Be in the infantry."

"Be careful what you wish for boys. I can send you to boot camp on the buddy system, and if you graduate together, you'll be assigned to the infantry and serve in the same unit."

"Where do we sign Gunny?" Elijah asked.

"Guys, let's do this right. Complete the paperwork and bring it back on Friday."

"Gunny," Seamus said. "We go fishin' on Friday."

Winston shook his head. "Are you serious?"

Seamus nodded.

The Gunny stared at the boys and said, "Well I'll be dipped in shit. See you Monday morning boys."

Austin Presbyterian Theological Seminary

Asa Hawkins loved his little girl. The sun rose and set on his darlin' Ofa. But he indulged the child. She was spoiled, but not in a bad way. Regardless, the circle of love that surrounded her gave her the confidence that many took for being a brat. She'd often visit her daddy, a renowned philosophy and theology professor at Austin Presbyterian Theological Seminary. She idolized Asa, and when she heard him speak, she felt his power.

She opened the old oak door of the professor's class; the door creaked as she closed it. Ofa crept into the room and sat in the back. Whoever came in late caught the professor's attention and would receive a stern glare from Dr. Asa Hawkins. But instead, he beamed when he saw his girl.

As she crossed her legs, she caught more than Asa's attention. The boys sitting in the lecture hall watched her calculated moves, and that didn't sit well with her father. Although she appeared innocent, there was incipient sexuality.

Asa was speaking about the Vietnam War and its moral

implications.

"You have to walk the walk," he told his class. "You can't say you're opposed to war and then do nothing. You have to be accountable to change – to peace. Go beyond the confines of this institution and influence others to believe as you believe. The apostles of Christ were paralyzed by fear, just as you are. They hid behind closed doors." Remember what John F. Kennedy's Inaugural Address, "Here on earth, God's work must truly be our own."

The boy in the first row raised his hand.

"Yes, Paul."

"Professor, it's like the lyrics of Paul Simon's, "I am a Rock."

Ofa gave the boy an approving smile. He appeared smug, but she had noticed him, and he noticed her.

"Paul, I see your point, but please elaborate on your idea. You've given me an analysis without a rationale I want to know, why?"

That was just like Asa.

"Dr. Hawkins it appears that it's the habit of man to make comments about the state of affairs of the world to make himself look good. Everyone wants to make a positive change in the world, and when they talk about doing so, it makes them appear righteous in the eyes of others. So, in the lyrics we are told not to talk about love but instead do something about it. If we don't, then love becomes dormant since it "sleeps in our memory." One must go out and do something about the ills of the world and not just talk about it."

Dr. Hawkins was pleased.

"That's right, Paul. It's like the businessman who clings to morality and then says – first I'll make my million, and then after that, I'll go for the real things in life.' So, what are you going to do about the ills of the world? I challenge this class not to just talk about changing the world, but to do something about it."

Paul again turned toward Ophelia, but he had a different smile. She was becoming aware of her beauty and the pull she had on the boy.

Asa Hawkins was a powerful speaker. He commanded his class with eloquence and diction. He was inspirational, and his presence influenced the initiatives of his students.

"Who's joining my daughter and me at the protest rally this afternoon?"

General Store – Luckenbach

Seamus and Elijah arrived in town at dusk. They were one step closer to joining the Marines and were filled with nonsensical thoughts of battle and glory. Elijah parked his truck in front of the post office, and the blinking red light hanging in the intersection of Main and Alamo bounced its colors into his eyes.

"Hey, Buckaroo, I'll buy you a pop."

"Get one for Ofa too," Seamus said.

"Seamus, I don't see her. What makes you think she'd be here? Wishful thinkin' don't make things happen. If you want some'in' to happen, you have to make it happen."

"Elijah, since when are you a philosopher? I just thought she'd be here. She was upset as all get out 'bout us joinin' up. I'm sure she's comin'. You think she feels sorry for us?" Seamus asked.

"Are you shittin' me? She thinks we're the biggest fuckin' idiots in all of Texas. Seamus, goddammit! She ain't here, and she ain't gonna be here, and it's your fault, Buckaroo. You've both liked each other forever, and she did everything a girl could do to get you to make some kind'a gesture. Seamus, you're my best buddy, but I got to be honest, y'all suck at romance."

"Hey, Cowboy, why did you buy that extra bottle of pop if you was certain she ain't gonna show up?" Seamus asked.

"Cause it'd make you happy, ya dumb shit!"

Austin Presbyterian Theological Seminary

After class, Professor Hawkins announced, "I'll see you at the peace march."

Dr. Asa Hawkins was a charismatic man, a brilliant teacher, and popular with the ladies. His grayish black hair neatly knit in a ponytail extended down the middle of his back. His jeans, an old blue ranch shirt, and his scuffed boots set a juxtaposed persona. Here was a laureate in his field who was comfortable in his own skin. As the young college girls approached his desk, he peered over the wire-rim spectacles that sat at the end of his nose and answered their seemingly ridiculous questions. It was just an excuse to talk to the Professor. Once the daily gaggle was done, Ofa approached him.

"Daddy, I'm with you. I want to dedicate my life to peace. I'm ready," she said.

She was thinking of the boys and wanted to do whatever she could to stop the war. In her mind, she was saving their lives.

66

Asa was pleased his daughter had embraced his life's work. Knowing that he had swayed her toward his way of looking at the world fed his characteristic arrogance.

"Paul, I want you to meet my daughter, Ophelia. Paul is one of my best students."

"Hello Ophelia, your dad told me much about you. I am pleased to meet you." Paul extended his hand.

"I am pleased to meet you too," she said.

She was flirtatious, a bit sexy, and that was a dangerous combination. She barely understood her power; regardless, she toyed with the boy's emotions as she used her long eyelashes as weapons. She was vying for the attention of a college boy.

Asa was a calculating man. He was tired of his daughter pining away for Seamus O'Grady. Ofa was beautiful, a scholar, and had been awarded a scholarship to Dartmouth. He didn't want his daughter to waste her life on a cowboy from the Hill Country. Paul Bannister was part of the Professor's scheme. The boy was from a well-to-do Boston family, bright, handsome, and personable. He would be a perfect match for his daughter.

"Ophelia," Paul said. "Can I walk to the peace rally with you? After we can get barbecue."

She could tell by the look in his eye that he found her attractive, and she liked the idea.

General Store – Luckenbach, Texas

The extra bottle of pop had lost its fizzle. Ofa hadn't shown. The boys were leaving for the Marines and Ofa for Dartmouth. Maybe Elijah was right; she was moving on. The future had finally arrived, and life was complicated for a boy who had little experience living it.

"Elijah, you want to drink this pop?"

"Jesus, Seamus, it's warm."

Seamus threw the bottle into the trashcan. It was his way of dealing with the problem of Ofa Hawkins.

State Capitol – Austin, Texas

There were hundreds of students circling the capital building in Austin. The peace march was the largest anti-war demonstration the country had seen. Ophelia and Paul walked together singing, "Where Have All the Flowers Gone." The flowers were for the graves of young men who would be killed in Vietnam but were not yet dead. Ofa and Paul's encounter was heightened by the fervor of adolescence, and it brought them together. Neither could tell what was real or attributed to circumstance. Nevertheless, Paul Bannister was smitten, and Ofa was interested.

After the march, Paul took Ofa to Franklin's for the best barbecue in Austin. It was an official date. A boy had asked her to dinner. She wasn't eating Moon Pies and drinking Coke on the steps of the general store. Paul held the chair, and she sat.

"What would you like?" he asked. She wasn't accustomed to having a boy ask what she wanted for dinner. Normally Elijah handed her a bag of fries and a pulled pork sandwich. And Seamus would offer a pack of Lifesavers. She wanted more from a boy.

"Ophelia, your dad mentioned you want to attend medical school. Why a doctor? Those are amazing goals."

She appeared serious as though she was piecing together the rest of her life. A handsome boy had asked her a question that required some thought.

"Paul, the scriptures say we are our brothers' kee'pa. "In James 2:14-17 it says, 'What good is it if someone says he has faith but does not have works? Can that faith save him? If a brother or sister is poorly clothed and lacking in food, and one of you says to them, go in peace without givin' them the things needed for the body, what good is that?' Paul, faith without works is meaningless."

Paul responded, "Galatians 6:2: 'Bearing another's burdens, and so fulfill the law of Christ.'"

"Since I learned 'bout Dr. Tom Dooley, I have a-hankerin' to be a missionary and tend the people in Southeast Asia."

"It's dangerous there," he responded, "You must have a big heart to want to do that," Paul replied.

"I believe we have a moral mandate to help others."

Paul thought of what she had said. He was not as adventurous.

"I'll be an attorney and practice in Boston. My family's there. My grandfather and father have a firm; I'll practice with them."

They spoke until the waiter flipped the sign from open to closed. Ofa had never spoken to a boy at such length; no one before had ever listened to her thoughts or asked her about her dreams. But it was late, and she needed to be home by midnight.

"Ophelia, I'll take you back. I had a great time tonight. Can I see you again? I'd love to take you to the promotion dance in two weeks.

Would you go with me? Please say yes."

"Paul, you're a great guy, and I had a great time. But, I have feelin's for another boy." I just don't know.

Paul lowered his eyes. "Ophelia, we have a connection; we should see if it's real."

"I want to be friends. I'm confused," she said.

"I'd like to get to know you, but you in love with this guy?"

"I don't rightly know," she said.

TWELVE

THE RED BLINKING LIGHT

When a man is in despair, it means he still believes in something.

Thomas Carlyle

June 1965 – General Store, Luckenbach

"Well, I'll be dipped in shit," Elijah whispered. The boys stared at the red Corvette driving down Main Street heading toward the red blinking light in front of the general store. They'd never seen such a fancy car. But it wasn't the car that got their attention; it was the blond in the white dress sitting in the passenger seat. Seamus watched as the Corvette approach the light.

Was it a nightmare? Would he wake? What he saw didn't make sense. He closed his eyes then slowly opened them. He hoped that what he had seen would only be the red light's reflection in the post office window.

He shook his head and whispered: "Ofa."

The Corvette stopped at the light. Ofa turned from Paul. She glanced at the steps in front of the general store. She hoped what she saw was only a nightmare. Would she wake? She closed her eyes then slowly opened them. She hoped she would only see the red light's reflection in the general store window.

"Seamus," she whispered.

Their eyes met, and for a moment they held each other's hearts. Ofa was in a car with another boy, and Seamus was sitting where he always sat on the general store steps with Elijah.

It was the worst of pains; more than anything he could imagine. All he could do was wipe the tear that ran down his cheek.

She noticed every line in Seamus' face and watched the tear glide down the side of his cheek, and she saw how he caught it with the back of his hand.

Ofa stared at Seamus staring at her. But she had been his sidekick and nothing more. She had done everything a girl could do to get him to notice her. Paul made her feel special; he made her feel like a woman. Although Seamus had her heart, he didn't understand that love is fueled by deeds.

The Corvette lingered at the light. Paul wondered why Ophelia had tears in her eyes.

"Just go. Please! Let's just go," she said.

"Ophelia, you okay?" Silence. "You okay Ophelia?" He repeated.

"Can you just take me home!" she blurted.

The tone of her voice caused him to look at the general store. He saw the desperate boy, and he knew who he was.

Paul wanted to hold her. Be her Lancelot and save his Guinevere. Paul was falling for her at the red blinking light in front of the general store.

He put the Corvette in first gear and crossed Alamo and continued down Main Street. Seamus didn't move. He watched the turn signal. The Corvette made a right on Travis and disappeared. The blinking light bounced off the post office window reflecting in the helpless eyes of a distraught boy.

"Holy shit Seamus! You okay Buckaroo?" Elijah asked.

"It hurts. Ofa! Why? What did I do? I think I love her."

"Buddy, when it comes to love, you don't think. You either do, or you don't. If you think you love Ofa, you don't love Ofa," Elijah said. "Are you fuckin' crazy? You're asking what you did? You need to ask yourself what you didn't do. When people break up, it ain't because someone did something to the other. They break up because of something they didn't do to the other. You gotta be together to break up and sure 'nuff I never seen you two together."

"It's too late. She was with a college boy," Seamus said. "You see that fancy car? I ain't no match for him. He looked like he knew what he was doing."

"Seamus – you don't know that. And Ofa – She ain't the type of girl who'd like a boy cause he's got a fancy car. You're my best friend in the whole wide world, and I hate to see you sad. I'd die for you buddy. But you gotta get Ofa out of your mind. You don't know what fate's gonna bring. Remember what Pops says, 'What's meant to be will find a way.'"

THIRTEEN

TAKING THE TORCH

You still stand watch, O human star, burning without a flicker, perfect flame, bright and resourceful spirit. Each of your rays a great idea. O torch which passes from hand to hand, from age to age, world without end.

Karel Capek

June 1965 – Luckenbach

Seamus opened the book his granddaddy gave him and turned to the dog-eared page. It chronicled the great American speeches of the 20th Century. He was looking for a special page that he had read a thousand times, and after today, it would be a thousand and one. It wasn't motivation he was after; it was reassurance.

He wanted to understand the sentiments of a man who had compelled the youth of the nation to serve their country. He was tired of being a cowboy, so he stood at a crossroad and sought the wisdom of the man who changed a generation.

He searched for the underlined words. "Ask not what your country can do for you, ask what you can do for your country." Seamus understood the connection of John F. Kennedy's sentiments. The O'Grady's believed every word the president said, but in 1963 Kennedy's life was cut short by a bullet and they were left without their hero.

In 1961, Kennedy offered young Americans a chance to make a difference in the world.

> Let the word go forth from this time and place to friend and foe alike that the torch has been passed to a new generation of Americans... born in this century, tempered

by war, disciplined by a hard and bitter peace, proud of our ancient heritage, and unwilling to witness or permit the slow undoing of those human rights to which this nation has always been committed, and to which we are committed today at home and around the world.

He offered Seamus the chance to be a knight and carry the torch of freedom. It was a chance to sacrifice even life itself, and that spoke to wanderlust of the boy.

Seamus was an Irish Catholic, but he was not religious. He was righteous and held firmly to a defined sense of morality and justice. He did what was right not because of the presence of a Divine Being but because it was right thing to do. John Kennedy's words would exploit a boy like Seamus O'Grady.

With a good conscience our only sure reward, with history the final judge of our deeds, let us go forth to lead the land we love, asking His blessing and His help but knowing that here on earth God's work must truly be our own.

Seamus wanted to do God's work. But his idea of God's work was different than Ofa Hawkins'. He and Elijah would carry the sword of retribution and righteousness, and Ofa would carry an olive branch.

Seamus heard two blasts of the horn. He closed the book, grabbed his Stetson, jumped into the truck, and headed to Austin to join the Marines. He closed the door behind him and left his childhood in Luckenbach, and he didn't look back.

Marine Recruiting Center – Austin, Texas

"Raise your right hand," Gunnery Sergeant Winston bellowed.

His command mimicked the sound of a preacher man at a Sunday afternoon revival. Since Winston liked the boys, he wore his dress blues.

"O'Grady, you look like a deer caught in the headlights. You okay boy?"

"I'm fine Gunnery Sergeant; just nervous. I hope I measure up."

"Boy if you are going to get through boot camp, you gotta look like Bravo."

Elijah had ice in his veins. He was cool, confident, and ready for anything the Marine Corps would throw at him. Seamus was pensive – a thinker. He saw all the potential problems waiting. Elijah didn't need to reflect to cure his anxieties. He didn't give a shit. He was a bull-headed boy who'd put his head down and plow through any wall.

"Repeat after me," the Gunny said as he prepared to administer the Oath of Enlistment.

I do solemnly swear that I will support and defend the Constitution of the United States against all enemies, foreign and domestic; that I will bear true faith and allegiance to the same; and that I will obey the orders of the President of the United States and the orders of the officers appointed over me, according to regulations and the Uniform Code of Military Justice. So, help me, God.

"Welcome to my Marine Corps," the Gunnery Sergeant said.

"Gunny, I've always wanted to be a Marine. All my life," Elijah interjected.

"Mr. Bravo, do not call yourself a Marine until you've made it through Parris Island and boy, that ain't no joke."

"Gunny, I'm gonna make it through boot camp, and you're gonna hear 'bout me."

Sergeant Winston heard a lot of talk from the cowboys who came through his office. But, it wasn't what Elijah said that made him believable. It was how he said it.

Winston found Bravo insolent, insubordinate, and arrogant; nevertheless, he liked the boy. However, the drill instructors would cut Bravo in half to see what he was made of. Yet Winston believed Bravo was an unusual young man. The boys would ship out the evening of their high school graduation, Friday, June 18, 1965.

"Remember, we ain't Marines until we get through boot camp, Elijah said."

"Elijah, I just wish Ofa would be proud of me. I hate to think she's become a peacenik. She's against everything we'd fight for."

"I don't see it that way," Elijah answered. "She's a peacenik because she don't want us to die in a war she believes is immoral. But I don't give a flying fuck what Ofa thinks, and that goes for her righteous son of a bitch father. How she believes has nothing to do with what I believe. Who's to say Ofa has the truth. We don't know the truth but sure 'nuff, she don't know it either. The truth is separate from what each of us believes. She and Asa sit in Luckenbach and pontificate 'bout how the war is wrong. And we defend the war. All of us believes our view of the world is true. Well, buckaroo, we're goin' to Vietnam to find out the real truth. We ain't just goin' to bullshit from an ivory tower."

Luckenbach

The boys arrived in town, walked into the post office, and saw the usual cast of characters sitting in front of the potbelly stove. The old men were soldiers of the first war and were not easily impressed with the young cowboys.

"Hey pops," Seamus said. "Me and Elijah just done joined the Marines."

Pops stared at the boys like he was gut-shot.

"Well, I'll be dipped in shit Seamus, you did what?"

"We joined the Marines, Pops."

"Yeah, I heard you the first time. You're just boys. You guys haven't even begun to live, and now you're goin' to Vietnam and get your asses shot up. Why did you do that?" Pops asked.

"Pops we're goin' to be Marines; we're gonna defend our country like you guys did in France," Elijah blurted.

"That's different," Billy Bone said. "We was fightin' to save Europe and not some stupid country in Asia that most people have no idea 'bout. You, boys, are apt to get yourselves kilt."

"There ain't nothin' more stupid than a young man wantin' to go to war," Pops added. "It's like you fell off the stupid tree and hit every branch on the way down."

"Look who's talkin'," Johnny said laughing.

Elijah was disappointed that the old men didn't see them as heroes. Since they were children, all they ever heard was that a man had to defend his country. After they joined up, the old men thought they were dumber than doornails.

Pops then put a knife in his grandson's heart

"Seamus, what you gonna do about that Ofa? She and Asa are peace freaks and they ain't gonna think too kindly of you for joinin' up."

"Granddaddy, me and Ofa don't hang out no more. She's goin' to college in New Hampshire and gonna be a doctor. I just may never see her again, and I don't care one doggone bit if I do. I'm goin' to be a Marine, and Ofa Hawkins has nuthin' to do with that. And if she and her daddy are against the Marines and the war, then I don't give a rat's ass."

"Son, you ought to think before you shoot your mouth off like that. I hate to think you mean that 'bout Ofa. I thought you and she would wind up together, and now you don't care if you see her again. That's too bad Seamus."

Joining the Marines was something Seamus had to do. It was his rite of passage. Pops understood this, but too many of his friends were killed in France. He knew that war was a young boy's foolishness. In 1917, he left with Black Jack Pershing to fight the Germans. Seamus would do the same. He wanted to be the hero of his story, so he'd follow the footsteps of his grandfather.

"Son, you need to go see Ofa and get things straight with her. You don't want to run off to the Marines and leave things unsettled."

"Pops, she's got a boyfriend, Seamus lamented. "I saw her drivin' down Main Street with a guy in a red Corvette. Elijah says, 'She's moved on,' and I don't think . . ."

"Stop!" Pops interrupted. "Just don't think. The more you think, the more you imagine things that may or may not be true. You don't know if the boy you saw is her boyfriend. Maybe he just gave her a ride home, or maybe he is her boyfriend. But if you care about her, you need to tell her. A girl like her wants to be with someone who cares. Son, don't hide behind your feelin's; that's for cowards, and you ain't never been a coward."

*   *   *

"Elijah, I'm gonna ask Ofa to prom. I don't think she's goin' with Tommy Tucker."

"I can't possibly believe Ofa Hawkins ain't goin' to the prom," Elijah commented. "Maybe she was asked and said no cause she's waitin' for you to ask her. But Asa don't like you. What the fuck you gonna do about that? And he's really gonna hate you when he finds you joined the Marines. You'd better do it today since the prom is Saturday."

"Elijah, you goin' to the prom?"

"Ya dumb fuck, you think a 34-year-old married woman would go to a high school prom?"

Seamus would reach deep to find the courage to ask Ofa to the prom, and if she'd be his girl. He was leaving for Parris Island in two weeks and then to Vietnam. He needed to tempt the hand of fate.

Seamus ran from the general store to ask Ofa to the high school prom. He turned the corner at Travis Street and saw a red Corvette sitting in her driveway.

FOURTEEN

BELIEVING IS SEEING

You need to believe in something before you see it.

Seamus O'Grady

24 April 1967 – Hill-558

Elijah's last words – make a difference, haunted Seamus. In Elijah's last defiant act, he made the difference he spoke of. Elijah Bravo saved the Platoon and his best friend. But he was gone, and Seamus was running away. "You have to live for both of us. Tell Ofa you love her." Elijah was a dreamer. Love her! Seamus hadn't seen or heard from her in two years. Elijah's mind was on the moon; it always was. "Go home. Live." How could he? No one walks away from war. The living go with the dead. Seamus would live with the guilt of deserting his best friend and for leaving the Battalion flag, which would be torn down and trampled by a ruthless enemy.

The Regiment's strategy of massing heavy guns and airpower on a well dug-in enemy, hadn't work. The first Platoon was used as bait to lure the NVA into the open, so that American firepower could kill them. It was the same strategy, which the North Vietnamese understood. Make contact, close with the enemy, and hold on to him long enough to destroy him. This time, fortune didn't follow the Marines up the hill. The Platoon suffered seven KIA, two missing and seven WIA. Seamus was broken.

The Platoon made it back to Bravo Company. However, at first light, the Battalion would return, and the enemy would be waiting. The Marines would take the hill; then abandon the ground they bleed for.

*   *   *

"Staff Sergeant O'Grady, Captain Reynolds wants to see you ASAP," Corporal Wood said. "Sergeant O'Grady, you Okay?" he asked. "Jesus H. Christ, you brought us the fuck out Seamus. I didn't think we'd make it."

"I'm sorry about Elijah; I don't know what to say."

Seamus acknowledged Wood's sentiment and gave a solemn nod.

"Seamus, what Elijah did – he gave his life for us."

Seamus raised his head. His eyes were unexpectedly lucent and focused.

"Corporal Wood, Elijah is still alive. He's out there waitin' for me. Tomorrow we're gonna get him."

Sergeant O'Grady said exactly that, and he said it as though he was asking Mr. Ramirez for a roll of LifeSavers.

Wood heard it before. Men lived in denial and refused to accept the death of a friend. Denial eased their pain. But Seamus had to lead the Platoon and Wood couldn't have him delusional.

"Elijah – alive – impossible – 300 gooks overran his position," Wood said. "They fired the 60s as long as they could. Then we heard those explosions, and the guns stopped."

Elijah's death was inevitable, but Seamus didn't believe what was real. He was certain Elijah was waiting for him on Hill-861.

"Bobby, those explosions in their position were the claymores. Elijah set 'em before the final assault. If they weren't the claymores, they blew the guns in place to prevent the gooks from getting 'em."

"Maybe you're right Seamus."

But Wood knew there was no chance.

"Bobby, your Squad okay?" Seamus asked.

"Yes, Staff Sergeant."

Seamus grabbed a cup of coffee and left for the Company CP.

Alpha Company CP

"Captain Reynolds, you wanted to see me?"

"Seamus, you brought 'em back. Lieutenant McGivens is recommending you for the Navy Cross."

Captain Reynolds fumbled with random papers; he couldn't express his feelings. "I'm sorry about Elijah." The Captain's head fell, and he whispered, "So sorry Seamus – I read the Squad leaders' *after-action* reports. Each report gave the same account. The overwhelming onslaught of the NVA – it's a miracle that any of you made it out. You made the right call; I knew you would."

"Captain – big decisions are easy when there's no other options."

"Sir, Sergeant Bravo deserves the medal. He protected the right flank; set the kill zone, set the guns, scouted the enemy, and set the claymores. Captain, he and John Wayne stayed behind and covered our withdrawal. I'm writin' him up for the Medal of Honor and John Wayne for the Navy Cross."

"Very well then Seamus, you and McGivens will write the reports, and I'll make sure Elijah and John Wayne get their just due. Stand down for a few hours; I'll call you for a briefing at 2000 hours. You know we're going back tomorrow. Regiment wants that hill and the bastards holding it. We got to get our dead. Don't worry Seamus; we'll bring his body back."

"Sir, how's the Lieutenant? You know, he refused to be medevac'd."

"He didn't say anything about that Seamus, but he's good. He's at the *MASH* station at Regiment, recovering from his wounds. I think he'll be going home. Get some rest."

"Sir – Elijah is alive."

"Sergeant – what did you say?"

The Captain was not sure he heard O'Grady correctly. "What did you say," Reynolds repeated.

"Elijah Bravo is alive. Request permission to go back and get him."

"Seamus, I don't know how to tell you this, but Elijah didn't make it. I spoke to everyone; they said it was impossible. Let it go Sergeant; it'll eat you up. He died a hero. He gave his life for you – for you and the Platoon."

"Captain Reynolds, Sergeant Bravo is half Comanche. You don't understand – his animal spirit, the Eagle, protects him. I believe that Sir. I can't leave him and John Wayne. I have to get them."

"Sergeant, it all sounds reasonable tonight, but wait until tomorrow."

Seamus wouldn't listen to reason.

"Staff Sergeant O'Grady, 1st Battalion is going back in force tomorrow. We'll pay the motherfuckers back for Elijah and the rest of the men. But I can't let you go. Not tomorrow. I'm sorry Seamus. Get some rest."

When a soldier loses a friend on the battlefield, his Commanding

Officer keeps a close eye on how he copes. If his judgment is affected, he is relieved from combat so one loss, doesn't lead to more.

"One more thing Sergeant. I'm putting 1st Platoon in reserve."

"Captain, the Platoon doesn't want to be in reserve. We want to be in the assault."

"Sergeant O'Grady, I understand how you feel, but did you ask your men if they'd do it again? They've been through hell and putting them in the assault wouldn't be right."

"I'll do that sir, and I'll be back at 2000 for the briefin' and tomorrow morning you'll follow me up that fuckin' hill."

"Captain Reynolds – Sir – you need to believe in something before you see it."

FIFTEEN

MAKING GOOD ON THE PROMISE

Our doubts are traitors, and make us lose the good we oft might win, by fearing to attempt.

William Shakespeare, *Measure for Measure*

24 April 1967 – Hill-861

"**John Wayne, you're gonna be okay, ol' buddy?** Got ya all patched up. Before you know it, you'll be pissin' vinegar and crapping thunder. Sure 'nuff – Seamus – he'll be back for us in the mornin'. Let's get through the night," Elijah said.

"Why you so sure Seamus will come for us? No one thinks we're alive," said Joe Buck. "If you was Seamus would you think we survived considerin' what we've been through?"

"Jesus H. Christ, Joe – Seamus – he'll find a way. He knows that angels protect fools and Elijah Bravo. My story ain't gonna end on this fuckin' hill. I was born in the sign of the Eagle. I'm half Comanche, and they were some kickass motherfuckers. I'm protected by my spirit animal."

"Don't pull that injun shit on me, Cowboy. Captain Reynolds will have Seamus sit out the assault. Not even Seamus can endure comin' back and doin' it all over again."

"Joe – he'll be here in the mornin'. Seamus and me made a pledge on our last fishin' Friday. We promised never to leave each other. He'll keep that promise."

"Elijah, a lot of people, make promises. Some people don't understand the promises they're makin' when they make 'em. They're just words. It's easy to make a promise with a fishin' pole in your hand. But this is different. What's said in Texas and what's happening here are two different things."

Elijah changed the bandage on Joe's leg and gave him a pull from his canteen. A Marine never leaves a buddy. That was a promise John Wayne could take to the grave. They would make it through the night, and Seamus would come for them in the morning. He promised, and Elijah knew that when Seamus O'Grady made a promise, he would keep it.

Even though the men were wounded by friendly fire, the artillery had saved their lives. After the enemy's assault, Bravo and Buck blew the guns and abandoned their positions. Elijah attempted to carry John Wayne down the hill, but he had lost too much blood and collapsed in the middle of the elephant grass. Seamus dragged John Wayne into the remnants of a bunker, destroyed by a 105mm round. They'd spend the night with four dead enemy soldiers and one wounded NVA officer.

"Sergeant, you da Lone Ranger; we fucked them up with those claymores. You blew the claymores right when the motherfuckers cleared the elephant grass. Boom to the Chakalaka! Boom! Boom! Like they was here one second and gone the next. You're the reincarnation of Chesty Puller.

"Chesty Puller," Seamus sarcastically remarked.

"Well – I'm more like Chesty than you. You're like Poncho Villa," Buck added.

"I never thought Chesty Puller was what he was cracked up to be, Elijah commented. "He was too tough for the Marine Corps, but he got a lot of men killed with all that gung-ho shit. How many Marines had to die so he could be the hero? Generals don't die on the battlefield; they die in bed."

Elijah set the claymores on opposite sides of the enemy's approach. He waited until they were in the kill zone then blasted them. After the explosions, the enemy retreated giving Elijah and Joe enough time to drag two dead enemy soldiers into their gun pits. They detonated incendiary grenades destroyed the guns and burned the soldiers beyond recognition. The NVA believed that US artillery killed the Marines who manned the guns.

"If anyone's a hero, its Seamus," Elijah commented. "You don't point the finger at the guy who steps up. You cheapen his deeds. Men step up because it's who they are. We make them heroes because they did something we couldn't do. We regret we couldn't do it and maybe we feel some shame. Joe, sometimes being a hero is a simple pat on the back. We're all the same, Joe. We're all heroes. We're all cowards. It just depends on the day. Get some rest; we're gonna need it. We'll stand watch, three on and three off. It's 20-hundred hours (8-PM). I'll wake you at 23-hundred," Seamus said.

Bravo Company CP – Hill-558

The time was 20-hundred hours. Captain Reynolds was known for his timely briefings. The meeting was at a makeshift CP on the southern slope of Hill-558.

"Gentlemen, take out your notebooks, Reynolds said."

The Captain began his briefings with a joke. He used humor to soften the reality of Vietnam. He told Little Johnny Jokes, which were an ol' Marine tradition. Although the Platoon had seven KIA, nine if you counted Elijah and John Wayne, Reynolds believed humor would soften what they were going through.

"Have you heard the one about little Johnny and the teacher?" he asked. The men had heard it a thousand times, but regardless, the Captain wanted to tell it.

"No sir, we didn't hear it," they replied.

"Well, Little Johnny was sitting in class one day when all of a sudden, he needs to go to the bathroom. He yells, 'Miss Jones, I need to take a piss,'" Reynolds explained. "The teacher replied, 'Now, Johnny, that's not the proper word to use in this situation. The correct word you want to use is, urinate. Please use the word urinate in a sentence correctly, and I will allow you to go.' So, Little Johnny thinks for a bit; then says, 'you're an eight, but if you had bigger tits, you'd be a ten.'"

There were a few smiles and then the juxtaposition of mixing humor and fear along with the fact that the Marines had heard the joke since they were in boot camp caused a moment of hilarity. Those who think they are about to die will laugh at anything. There was more to Captain Reynolds than tactics.

Everyone laughed except Seamus O'Grady. He interrupted the moment.

"Captain Reynolds, my Platoon wants the lead tomorrow, and Sir, with all due respect, I will not accept no for an answer."

The Captain couldn't look Seamus in the eye and tell him what he was thinking. He lowered his head. No one believed Elijah and John Wayne were alive. But O'Grady believed his best friend was out there

84

and was waiting for him to come. People want to believe, and they fill the unknown with gods, tales, and superstitions. The first Platoon had been through hell, but they were willing to go back for two men they were convinced had died in the enemy assault. Seamus believed so the Captain couldn't say no.

"Sergeant O'Grady" – the Captain looked squarely at the determined Sergeant. "I want you to lead Alpha Company up Hill-861 tomorrow and kill every motherfucking gook on that hill."

"Aye-aye Sir," Staff Sergeant O'Grady said.

"Gentlemen – take out your notebooks – copy my orders," the Captain commanded.

Reynolds was a meticulous man and would account for every detail in the plan to take the hill.

"Situation – Elements of the 325-C Division, approximately 350 men, are dug in on Hill-861. They have small arms, automatic weapons, rocket-propelled grenades, and mortars. Colonel Tran van Minh commands them; he's tough in a fight and considered a tactical genius. He's not one of those fanatical NVA officers who'll risk the lives of his men to make Americans bleed. The guy's educated in America. He has a Master's Degree from Yale. If we can get him, he'd be a prize."

Reynolds distributed a picture of the Vietnamese Colonel.

"He's tall for a gook," Wood commented. "Looks like some Oriental movie star from a James Bond movie."

Seamus took the picture and passed it on. He wasn't going up 861 to capture a North Vietnamese Colonel.

"Mission – First Platoon will lead. Seamus, you've been there, and I expect you to know the best way up. Minh will defend the least likely approach. He'll think that's the one we'll take. But you will take the straightest way to the top. I think we'll get a pass on this one. You are to make contact with the enemy and create a convex defensive position. Once their attack commences, you will conduct a tactical withdrawal. Bravo Company will envelop from the right rear flank and Charlie will envelope from the left rear flank. Look out for Colonel Minh. If we can get him, we'll break the back of their command structure. Seamus, you're to make contact and close with the enemy. I want you to provoke a fight; get him engaged."

"Second Platoon, you're on the left flank and third Platoon you'll deploy on the right flank. Seamus, you're down 17 men, but you got the middle. Gentlemen, we're 1/9; the Walking Dead. Except for

Minh, clear the battlefield – no prisoners.

In 1966, the Song Nu Yi River Valley, 15 miles south of Da Nang was a Viet Cong stronghold. The Japanese and French armies could not pacify the area. That changed when 1/9 was sent to establish a base on Hill-55. The Marines called the sector 'Arizona' because it was reminiscent of the Wild West. When 1/9 arrived, they took the battle to the enemy. They perfected the tactic, search and destroy. Because of Marine tactics, the Viet Cong became incensed and captured and tortured a Marine. From that day forward any sense of humanity ended. The sweeps through the valley became vicious and subsequently caught the attention of Ho Chi Minh. To describe the Marines, he coined the phrase, *di bo chet,* (the walking dead). He said 1/9 was already dead and had not yet been buried. General Vo Nguyen Giap, their commander in chief and tactical guru, vowed he would liberate the valley and wipe out the Marines. He sent Colonel Tran van Minh to accomplish this mission, but 1/9 defeated Colonel Minh. The propaganda war heightened when enemy disc jockey and radio personality, *Hanoi Hanna* played Martha and the Vandellas Nowhere to Run *Nowhere to Hide* and then dedicated it to the 1st Battalion 9th Marine Regiment.

"Gentlemen, are there any questions?" Captain Reynolds asked.

Silence sounded like fear. Seamus gathered his notes, map, and compass and placed them in his pack. There was no fear in his eyes.

"Sergeant O'Grady, you okay about tomorrow?"

"Why yes sir, I am."

"Remember Seamus, you fight with your head, not with your heart," Reynolds said.

"I got it. It's never been clearer to me. I'm goin' up there with both my head and my heart. I'm gonna get Elijah and John Wayne; I'm gonna get our Battalion flag, and I am gonna kill every motherfuckin' gook on that hill. And Sir, I'm gonna run my bayonet through Colonel Minh's heart."

SIXTEEN

SEE YOU IN THE NORTH STAR

Hope in reality is the worst of all evils because it prolongs the torments of man.

Friedrich Nietzsche

25 April 1967 – Hill-558

Seamus drifted in and out of restless sleep and crippling fear. But what he feared most was if his premonition was wrong. He was dreaming of home and fishing with Elijah at the South Grape Creek. His dreams were both escape and punishment. He remembered the promise they made, never to leave each other. Seamus broke that promise on Hill-861. He opened his eyes; it was time. He tried to relax, and slip back into that peaceful normal. But reality was the new normal. It was time for payback. During the middle of the night, he'd flash his light on the newspaper clipping from the Austin American-Statesman. "What's the use?" he whispered. "Ofa was with another man." There wasn't much left of the clipping; nevertheless, he carefully folded the newspaper and placed it in between two pieces of cardboard cut from a C-ration box. He then rewrapped the cardboard in plastic. He thought, *would Ofa even care if he died in the morning*?

*   *   *

"Staff Sergeant O'Grady, it's 4 AM," Corporal Wood noted, "here's a cup of Joe, black the way you like it."

"We get a replacement for the Lieutenant?" Seamus asked.

"No – McGivens doesn't want to be medevacked. He wants to stay."

Wood rolled his eyes. Calder McGivens was out of his mind. Who'd want to stay in Vietnam?

"Seamus, it's no longer McGivens' command. It's your Platoon. Captain Reynolds wants you as the Platoon Commander until McGivens comes back. You're the head honcho."

"Son of a bitch, Bobby!"

Seamus didn't like the idea of having operational command over an officer, even if the officer was a 2nd Lieutenant.

"You sure that's what the Captain wants?" Seamus exclaimed.

"He told me himself."

"Well, lucky me, Bobby."

Seamus scowled. "Head honcho!"

He laced his boots, folded his poncho liner, took his coffee, and sat on the edge of the perimeter looking at the sky. He needed a moment to clear his head. As a boy, he found comfort in the stars, ancient points of light that were once suns. Some stars had burned out eons ago, yet their light still traveled the universe. "It's a beautiful mystery," Seamus whispered. But the mystery of why men kill each other was more perplexing. *These stars have been in the sky for millions of years, and whether I live or die, they'll be there for millions more*, he thought.

"Sir," the new replacement called out. "Sir, I'm Private Flynn. Where do you want me, sir?"

Being referred to as sir, especially by a *boot* from the states didn't sit well with Staff Sergeant O'Grady.

"I'm sorry, what's your name?"

"Private Flynn sir!"

"Flynn, you're first name."

"I'm Rick MaddogMike."

Most men wanted to remain impersonal, but not Seamus; he wanted to know a man's first name before he ordered him to do something that could end his life. Knowing their names and hearing of their families made him work hard to keep them alive.

"What kind of a name is that? Rick MaddogMike Flynn."

"It's just my name Sir."

"How old are you Maddog?"

"Sir, I just turned 17."

"How'd that happen?" Seamus inquired.

"I joined the Corps at 16 – forged my birth certificate. I ain't in any trouble, am I?"

"Just don't go shootin' your mouth off to any of the brass!"

"How'd ya get a name like Maddog?" Seamus inquired.

"Sir, in high school I got into a lot of fights and got my ass kicked. But they said I fought like a mad dog."

Seamus nodded and turned his attention toward the hot coffee. He wondered what was wrong with a guy who lost all his fights. He wasn't sure how Maddog would fit into his Marine Corps.

"Okay, I'm putting you with the Platoon Sergeant – Corporal Wood. He's a damn good Marine so don't fuck up."

"Sir, how comes the Platoon Sergeant ain't a Sergeant?"

Seamus didn't answer.

"One more thing Maddog, I'm a Staff Sergeant. You'll call me Staff Sergeant O'Grady. Do you understand that?"

"Aye-aye Staff Sergeant."

"Staff Sergeant O'Grady, don't worry; we'll get your men back."

Maddog was the only one besides Seamus who believed Bravo and Buck were still alive. But Rick MaddogMike Flynn wasn't at the battle and didn't see the hordes of enemy soldiers overrunning Bravo and Buck's position. Nevertheless, Seamus thought it was a good sign that someone other than himself believed. Maybe the FNG would bring some luck.

"Maddog, you think they're still alive?"

"If you say they are Sir, then I believe they are. The men say you walk on water, and that's good enough for me. If they're alive, we'll get 'em."

Seamus gave Maddog a tight smile and nodded.

"Flynn, that's exactly what I'm gonna do, and you're goin' to help me do it."

"Staff Sergeant, can I say something else?"

"Sure."

"It's about today; I don't think I'm gonna make it. I don't have a good feeling. I'm a boot, and boots get *waxed* (killed). I mean – I'm not really scared, but just thinking about it."

"Maddog, I'm scared too. It's normal to think that way. Let me tell you what works for me. I say a prayer. I don't rightly know if I pray to survive or if I pray for the sake of prayer. Because if your time's up, nothin's gonna change that. So, you might as well go through the day bein' brave. Just do your duty and try not to think 'bout it. I ask God's help that I will do my best. I don't want to get up there and be so scared I can't function. Bein' a Marine is important to me. And if I die, I die like a Marine facin' the enemy. Maddog, if you do your job right and listen to Wood, you'll make it."

"Thanks, Sergeant. The men said you saved the Platoon yesterday."

"Flynn that ain't the facts. Elijah Bravo and Joe Buck saved us. After we get 'em, I'll tell ya what they did. Don't want to do it now; it's bad luck. Private Flynn, I got a good feeling 'bout you, don't do anything stupid."

"How do I know what's stupid?" Flynn asked.

"Flynn, if we only knew the answer to that question. Stick next to Wood; he's a fuckin' killer."

Seamus picked up his rifle and glanced at the North Star. His friendship with Elijah was like a Star, eternal. The star twinkled, and he could see Elijah Bravo in its light.

"I'm comin' Cowboy; I'd never leave ya."

The Marines were writing letters to moms, dads, girlfriends, wives, and children. It was a macabre ritual and done just in case. For some, it would be their final words. Seamus reached into his pack; this time, he found a pen and paper.

25 April 1967

Dear Pretty Girl,

I don't know where to begin or what to say. It's been two years, and you've never left my mind. I carry a picture of you. I am in Vietnam. I's crazy, but I still believe in freedom. Elijah doesn't. He ever did. We're moving out in a few. I'm a Staff Sergeant and the acting Platoon Commander. Elijah is missing! I know he's out there; I saw him in the North Star. He saved our lives yesterday. Don't worry; I'll bring him back. We promised each other we would. Enough of the war. Remember we'd talk to each other through the North Star? I've looked up a few *times, but I don't see you there. I know you've moved on. I wish I can relive those days in Luckenbach sitting on the steps of Ramirez's store. I'd like to relive a lot of those moments. But I can't. If I could, I'd ask you to be my girl. Did I ever screw up! I realize it would take more than a big ol' red rose to get you to believe that I really did care. I always cared Ofa. I just didn't know how. Is it too late? If not, write me. If it is, I understand. You have a good life. You're gonna be a great doctor. I hope that guy you're dating treats you like the pretty girl you are.*

Love always,
Seamus

Seamus addressed an envelope to Miss Ofa Hawkins; 7 Travis Street; Luckenbach, Texas, and threw it into the mailbag. The Company executive officer would place it on the next outgoing chopper. But it was just his luck the chopper would not make it back to Regiment.

"Squad leaders we move out in two," Seamus ordered.

SEVENTEEN

METAMORPHOSIS

Whoever lives for the sake of combating an enemy has an interest in the enemy's staying alive.

Friedrich Nietzsche

25 April 1967 – Hill 861

John Wayne struggled to breathe, but he would make it. It was the million-dollar wound, and a ticket home on a freedom bird, the happiest plane ride out of Vietnam. However, if he were back in the world, he'd leave his John Wayne persona and enter a world of regulations and spit and polish.

Buck liked the smell of gunpowder, and would not sit out the war in some cushy job in the States. In the meantime, he held on to the illusion that Seamus would come in the morning. Since the enemy was convinced the Marines were killed, Elijah and Joe Buck were given a precarious reprieve, so they clung to the darkness of a destroyed bunker.

The light of a full moon bounced off the ancient hills, and the trees shimmered in the moonlight, which exaggerated enemy movements. The sounds of shovels and men laughing were maniacal indications of what the morning would bring. The North Vietnamese were digging in, cleaning weapons, preparing kill zones, camouflaging, and waiting for the Marines. The moonlight oozing through the slits of the bunker cast a ghoulish light on the four dead Vietnamese soldiers. Death never happens as one imagines. There's no grim reaper, no angels, or demons. It was death: silent, and unimaginable. The war was over for them, but those who remained would continue to suffer. The yellow glow of the moon cast a macabre aura on the dead of Hill-861. Marines! Vietnamese! The angel of death is impartial. Each of those boys had been some mother's son. The moon keeps to its course and gently influences. It pulls an entire ocean toward the shore. The moon is faithful to its nature, and when it sets in the morning, more men will die.

Elijah hadn't awakened John Wayne for his shift. Instead, he remained awake throughout the night. Buck's heavy breathing, the moaning of the wounded NVA officer, the digging, and the din of enemy voices were constant and yet they were almost soothing. Bravo took a deep breath and found a moment he hadn't known since the South Grape Creek. He would talk to God. His momma said: "God listens even to sinners."

He rifled through the packs of the dead soldiers. They were no longer the enemy. He wiped a tear from his eye. Were they not men? Did they not feel joy, love, and sorrow? Did they not laugh? His best friend had killed these boys. He remembered Ofa's pleas — no more war. But only the dead would see the end of war.

He found pictures, letters, and prayer books with dog-eared pages and underlined sentences. Two of the soldiers wore wedding bands. There were photographs of small children, fathers holding them tightly. Was it their last embrace? "How could I have hated so much?" He whispered.

*   *   *

"Sergeant," the captured NVA officer called out. "Your tears, they say much about you. I have no tears left for this war. It has taken everything."

"You speak English," Elijah exclaimed. "Where?"

"We Vietnamese are not as illiterate as you Americans think. Mission School — I am Catholic. All communists are not atheists. I had American Missionary Sisters."

Seamus nodded to acknowledge the enemy prisoner.

"Sergeant, may I have some water?"

Elijah passed the Lieutenant his canteen.

"There's little left, Sergeant. You sure?"

"Drink it," Elijah said.

"Your name, Sergeant?"

"Elijah Bravo — yours Lieutenant?"

"Ly Truc-Viet! I see your sorrow over my dead soldiers. This tells me you are a good man. I think, why do I hate you? You are a man; I am a man."

Elijah listened, the Lieutenant wanted to talk.

"Sergeant, why did you come to Vietnam? You kill our people so we must kill your people. America brought this misery. We want to live without foreigners. You have caused us to hate each other. You see us not as humans but as beasts that hate America. This war would not have happened had the Vietnamese been treated justly. You have taken our humanity, and you have made us monsters."

"Lieutenant, I'm a Marine, and I do my duty, and I don't ask why. I've been told I must kill you."

"And Sergeant, I must kill you so I must hate you. How can men do the things we do to each other and not hate?"

Sergeant Bravo, you must know the difference between right and wrong. We fight for our freedom like your George Washington. We fought the Chinese, French, the Japanese, and the French again, and now the Americans. We have fought invaders for centuries. Why do you come here? We want to be left alone. I walked for six months traveling to the south to fight you. You call our road, Ho Chi Minh trail; we call it – *Troung Sun Trail* – the road of iron will. You Americans do not respect us. You bomb us, shoot us but we kept walking to the south. We are born in the north to die in the south."

"Lieutenant Viet, why do you come to the south and take the freedom of the South Vietnamese?" Elijah asked.

"Vietnam was one country until you Americans split us making north and south. The government in the south is evil. I will die Sergeant, but your country will lose this war. America is a great country, but your President Johnson misleads you. I learned in school that the ideals of America are worth life itself. We want the same rights that you have, but you don't allow us. Your president calls you, 'the keepers of peace.' He says America will endure with the support of the country and that you will prevail. Irony! Sergeant Bravo, how can you not see it? You will not have the support of your country."

"I need to change your bandage Lieutenant. Get some rest. You will need it to survive what may happen to you tomorrow."

The Marines were John F. Kennedy's knights. He told the world Americans would go anywhere, pay any price, and bear any burden to defend freedom. Knap, Lihue, Fields, Stoa, Ashcraft, Terry, Engstrom, and Johnny Luna were the down payment on that costly contract. But the man who wrote the contract was not there when the Marines fulfilled his promise. John Kennedy waited for them on a hill in Arlington National Cemetery. Eventually, they would come by the thousands and fill the slopes with white marble crosses and would ask Kennedy if that was the future he envisioned.

Elijah did not believe America was in the right. But he came to Vietnam, killed the enemy, and stayed alive. He told Ofa, "My country right or wrong, my country." Ofa answered, "But not if the country's wrong."

It was 0500 hours. The sun would rise in the eastern sky and bring the new day.

Elijah peeked through the cracks of the bunker. He noted the concentrations of troops and avenues of ingress and egress. The enemy's scheme of battle began to make sense. They would lie silent, waiting for the Marines to approach and when they were at arms' length, the NVA would unleash hell. Bravo needed to warn Seamus of the danger.

He looked in the direction of the Platoon's CP, where Seamus had called in the artillery. He could vaguely see the lifeless body of Corporal Terry. Ten thousand miles away, his fiancée would be planning their wedding. In the coming days, a chaplain would knock on her door, and another future would be destroyed.

Slowly, the jungle came to life. Elijah began to see shapes, Terry's M-16, his hand clutching his helmet, the Battalion flag, and a small square object. What is it? Elijah had not slept. He was weak. He wanted to surrender, never wake up, end the misery, his senseless suffering. He closed his eyes; he was out for 10 minutes. He awoke.

"Well, I'll be dipped in shit," he said. The square object leaning against the bunker was a PRC-25. Seamus had left the radio.

He hadn't the strength, but he had to get the radio and warn the advancing Marines of the enemy's ambush.

"Sergeant Bravo, you don't look too good. Why didn't you wake me the fuck up for my turn at watch?" John Wayne asked.

"Joe, Seamus left the radio at the CP, must'a called in arty – left the Prick, and got the fuck out of Dodge."

"Elijah, I'll get it."

"John Wayne, you always wanted to be the hero. That pisses me off. It's like you planned this."

"Elijah, I am the hero. I was the Platoon guide. I can do it. I can get the radio. You won't make it Sergeant. As your former Platoon guide, I order you to stay the fuck where you are and leave this to a real Marine."

The darkness would give him cover, but he must be quick. He took an AK-47 from one of the dead North Vietnamese soldiers. John Wayne inched his way toward the radio. He could hear the chatter of the enemy and see their silhouettes moving between their spider holes. He'd move a couple of feet, stop, and bury his head in grass. Then he'd crawl three more feet. Eventually, he reached the radio, strapped it on his back, and returned to the bunker.

Suddenly artillery rounds dropped from the sky. Seamus was coming.

EIGHTEEN

LOOKING FOR BRAVO

Throughout history – the romances and the grim civic monuments of Europe tell us – that we should never count the price when one needs rescue.

25 April 1967 – Hill 861

John Wayne flicked the switch and the radio powered up. He turned the squelch dial used to suppress the channel noise emitted when receiving and transmitting.

"I'll be damned, it's working." He called out to Bravo.

For the Marines moving up the hill, communication would determine life and death.

"Elijah, Seamus must have changed the frequency," Joe Buck said.

"Jesus H. Christ, if he didn't change it and the VC got the radio, they'd be able to monitor the net," Elijah replied.

Marine Phantoms began dropping 1,000-pound bombs. The 500-pounders dropped the previous day barely made a dent on enemy positions. The ground shook, and dust and debris filled the bunker making it difficult to breathe. Bravo and Buck hoped the pilots would overlook their position. The ground assault would follow the bombardment.

Elijah had to warn the Marines advancing up Hill-861 not to take the alternative approach but to follow the ridgeline from Hill-558. The enemy worked through the night fortifying the not so obvious. Elijah noted a hidden trail, not shown on the map; it was undefended. He had to warn Seamus.

"The fucking tuner is loose. I can't switch the frequency," Elijah said.

"You're a farmhand, you can fix anything," John Wayne replied.

Elijah frowned. "I'm a cowboy, not a farmhand. You boys from Uncertain are farmhands – It's the wingnut on the tuner; it needs tightening."

He reached into his pocket and pulled out the Swiss Army knife Seamus had given him on his 12th birthday. He was careful not to strip the nut as he turned the pliers.

"The radio is damaged, but we gotta go for it. Bet they'll be in range right 'bout now. Not sure how long it's gonna last. It's now or never," Elijah said.

Elijah grabbed the handset, flipped the power switch, turned the freak to 2500. He then signed the cross, kissed his fingertips and touched his heart.

"Buckaroo . . . This is Cowboy . . . Come in . . . Over . . ."

There was no response.

"Buckaroo . . . Cowboy . . . Can you copy . . ."

"Damn!" he screamed. He tried again.

"Cowboy . . . Buckaroo . . . Over . . ."

Silence!

The 1st Platoon moved along the ridge that connected the hills overlooking the firebase at Khe Sanh. The sun peeked over an eastern sky highlighting a line of green zombies moving toward battle. Seamus refused to walk in the middle of the column; instead, he walked with the point. Although Wood was junior to Sergeant Alexander and Barsegyan, Seamus selected Corporal Wood for the job, as the Platoon Sergeant. He thought it best not to upset the chemistry of the Squads. He gambled and placed Corporal Barlow as acting third Squad leader. Barlow had come a long way since being the screw up of Platoon 6586.

Wood was skeptical about the FNG, Private Rick MaddogMike Flynn. The kid was too gung-ho. FNGs were typically killed during the initial moments of combat. Regardless, Seamus made Maddog the Platoon runner and assigned him to Wood knowing that he would temper the cherry.

Red Barsone *humped* (carried) the radio. As the Platoon Commander's secretary, it was imperative that the radio operator be competent. Barsone was carrying 14 magazines of ammo, six grenades, an M-16, and two light-anti-armor weapons (*LAWS*). He was moving slowly, but Seamus knew he'd perform.

"Lance Corporal Barsone, I'll hump the radio for you," Private Flynn said. Trying to hide his fear, Maddog appeared confident for an FNG.

"Hey, boot, Wood gave this to me, and I'll carry it. What the fuck do you know about the PRC anyway?"

"I carried it in ITR (Infantry Training Regiment). I was a fuck-up, so they made me hump the extra 25 pounds."

"Flynn, what the fuck are you two blabbering about? We are in a tactical situation," Wood scolded.

"Corporal Wood, let me take the radio from Barsone, he's carrying a lot of shit."

"You know the PRC?"

"Like the back of my hand Corporal Wood."

Wood noted the gear Barsone carried. Since Barsone was an expert with the bunker buster, he'd be more efficient without the added weight of the radio. If Seamus needed comm, Barsone would be slow getting to the front of the column.

"Red, if the boot wants to carry the radio, give it to him."

"Corporal Wood, I won't let you down," Flynn promised.

Maddog moved along the ridge toward Hill-861 with the combat veterans of the 1st Platoon. If he survived the day, he would be one of them.

The Platoon moved in a tight formation and Wood worried that one grenade would take out five men. Private Guess, a woodsman from the Ozark Mountains of Missouri, walked point. Seamus and Flynn followed close behind. Guess was capable but he was not Knap.

Step, step, wait, listen, look, then Guess would do it again. The 1st Platoon inched their way toward the summit of the hill.

Elijah continued to try to make contact with the advancing Marines.

"Buckaroo . . . this is Cowboy . . . Over . . ."

Private Flynn heard the broken and barely audible transmission from someone named Cowboy. He turned the squelch hoping to make sense of a call sign he didn't understand. He checked the list of designations affixed to the radio. There were none with the names Buckaroo or Cowboy.

"Staff Sergeant O'Grady," Flynn called out.

Seamus turned. "Jesus H. Christ Flynn, we are in a tactical situation. You don't yell. Do you want to get me killed? Don't make me tell you again."

"Sorry Sir," Flynn replied. "Staff Sergeant, you need to hear this," he said in a whisper.

"Get up here, Flynn," the Sergeant ordered.

"Staff Sergeant, I'm receiving transmissions with calls signs that are not registered at Battalion. Someone is fucking with the net. There's a Cowboy calling for Buckaroo."

Seamus dropped to a knee and signed the cross.

"Tell me one more time Maddog. What did you hear?"

"Staff Sergeant, I heard Cowboy calling for Buckaroo – Sir – is that Elijah?"

Seamus grabbed the handset from Flynn.

"Cowboy . . . this is Buckaroo . . . Over . . ."

"Well, I'll be dipped in shit Seamus . . . I knew you'd come; there's a God in heaven . . . I found the radio you left . . . There's little time on the battery . . ."

"Elijah . . ."

"I know Seamus. I knew you was comin' . . ."

"Elijah, it don't end for us on 861 . . ."

"Seamus, Change your approach. At the saddle, make a hard left and go about 20 yards, you'll find an old *Hmong* trail. It'll give you cover and bring you to where the elephant grass ends. Pick a fight from there . . . Artillery's overshootin'. Change to coordinates: Eight . . . Niner . . . Seven . . . break . . . Six . . . Six . . . Four . . . This will put your rounds on top of 'em . . . Hit 'em with *Willie Pete* (White Phosphorus). *HE* (High Explosive) ain't working. They're dug in deep along the ridge . . . They've got two crew-served 50s (*50-Caliber automatic weapons*) about 25 meters from where the ridge trail meets the grass. The Hmong trail will take you left of those guns. When you get to that point, you'll be in a draw. The guns are on a 17-degree *azimuth* (compass bearing) on the other side. Got to take 'em both out . . ."

"Elijah, you sure about that bearing . . ."

"Seamus, I shot it myself . . . I'm staring at the map . . ."

"Okay pard, got it," Seamus said. "You okay buddy . . . How's John Wayne . . ."

"A little shot up, but he's still a fuckin' pain in the ass . . ."

The radio went silent. Seamus handed the receiver back to Flynn.

"Maddog, call Captain Reynolds. Tell him our boys are alive. Pass the word down the line. Good job PFC Flynn."

"Sergeant O'Grady, you promotin' me?"

"Fuck yeah, I am. Tell Wood you're now a PFC, but you're still a FNG. I want you to call in a fire mission. Think you can do that? These are the coordinates. I want Willie Pete."

"Aye-aye Sir," Flynn said. "And Sir, thanks for the promotion."

Seamus signaled Private Guess. The 1st Platoon changed course and headed for the Hmong trail.

"Wood," Seamus whispered, "there's the elephant grass. Two 50s are 30 meters from the trail. Shoot an azimuth of 17 degrees from this point. They're over that rise along that trajectory. Take em out, Corporal."

"Aye-aye, Staff Sergeant."

"Corporal Wood, I want to go with you," Flynn asked.

"Boot, you're a real fucking pain in the ass. You want to do everything. You're carrying the radio," Wood smirked.

"Corporal, someone else can carry the radio; I want to go."

"Seamus," Wood whispered. "I'm taking Flynn. The kid has piss and vinegar. Let's see how he does facing the elephant."

"Barlow, your Squad supports the assault," Wood directed. "We'll follow the depression up to the rise and go from there. The 60 should draw their fire, and with a little luck, we'll be on them before they see us. Anything you don't understand?"

"Got it, but what if there's a Squad there?" Barlow asked.

"I'll kill em all," Flynn interjected.

The veterans didn't appreciate the FNG and were not pleased that Wood was bringing him along.

The Marines followed the draw hidden by a ridge, which ran parallel to the enemy's gun position. Wood sent Lance Corporal Quinn up the hill for a fix on the enemy's 50s. Quinn turned toward Wood, nodded, extended two fingers and pointed below. Wood checked his watch. "Get ready! In three minutes!"

The men clutched their weapons and crawled toward the crest of the ridge. The M-60 commenced firing, and the battle to take Hill-

861 had begun.

Barlow laid down cover fire; subsequently, the enemy turned their attention toward his position giving Wood valuable time to prepare the assault. There was a Squad supporting their position.

"Flynn, go tell Seamus we need reinforcements."

Flynn either didn't hear Wood, or he ignored him. He stood, pulled the receiver of his weapon, and locked in a round. He then ran down the hill screaming and firing. He surprised the enemy and gunned down eight soldiers and silenced their guns.

Wood called Seamus to provide a sit-rep.

"Buckaroo this is hard ass . . . Over . . ."

"Go ahead . . . Hard-Ass . . ."

"We got 'em, Seamus . . ."

"How'd the Boot do . . ." Seamus asked.

"He's a fucking killer . . ." Wood replied.

NINETEEN

FINAL POINT OF DEPARTURE

And Caesar's spirit, raging for revenge, with Ate by his side come hot from hell, shall in these confines with a monarch's voice, Cry 'Havoc,' and let slip the dogs of war.

William Shakespeare, *Julius Caesar*

25 April 1967 – Bunker on Hill-861

Elijah used parachute cord to tie Lieutenant Ly-Truc-Viet to a post that supported the roof of the bunker. Although Lieutenant Viet was wounded, he was a soldier in the North Vietnamese Army and would fight to the end.

"Sergeant Bravo, kill me," Viet said. "Your puppet Vietnamese will torture me, and I die painful death. If you have mercy – kill me."

"Elijah, if you don't cut his fuckin throat, I'll do it. Let's waste him."

"Listen John Wayne we're not gonna kill him. If we survive, so will he. Make sure those AKs are ready and distribute what ammo's left."

*　　*　　*

The first Platoon followed the ridge toward Hill-861, and two companies of Marines followed. Attack – it was always the same tactic. Attack, even in defense. In attacking men are brave; in defending men are fearful, and after a battle, the brass will thump their chest and exclaim, how heroic. Regardless, Marines will die.

Elijah warned Seamus of the enemy defenses. They would lure the Marines into their kill zones and hit them with point-blank fire. They built a concave defensive position with the opening facing the advancing Marines. When the Marines were in the kill zone, the NVA would *hug* the Americans, and because of their proximity, it would make close air support useless. The enemy had learned a lesson from the battle in the A Shau Valley that to avoid the intense artillery and air power of the Americans they would fight close-up. The patient enemy hoped the Marines would take the bait.

"John Wayne, take that weapon off auto. I want one round at a time. We make every shot count."

"Elijah, you sound like Seamus. I want to go out in a blaze of glory and take all these slopes with me. Damn, I love the 47 (AK-47). How we get so lucky with the 16? The 47 has been laying in the dirt, and it'll fire like a champ."

"John Wayne – here's the plan. The Marines are following a trail parallel to the ridgeline coming from 558. They'll pass through this perimeter. When I see Seamus coming through the draw, we'll engage the fuckers in the trees. If we take out their snipers, it'll be a lot easier for our boys to maneuver. That should break the ambush."

"Yeah Sure, Elijah, it's going to get hot when Seamus lights up this position."

Indian Country

"Boys – this is the final point of departure. When we go over that rise, we're in Indian country. Here's what's going down. We've got two Platoons behind us. Second Platoon will move to our right flank and third to our left. Our mission is to break the ambush, get Elijah and John Wayne, close with the bastards, and blow the shit out of them." Seamus pointed, "We're 20 meters from our final point of departure. From that point, we'll be in the line of sight of Elijah and also the enemy.

"Once we're on the ridge, we'll see their position. We need to get our boys out of the kill zone before air assets bomb this place into the stone age. They gotta be there; that's the only way they'd have a line of sight to the enemy's 50s. We'll advance online. Flynn, you're with me. Wood, take third Squad and help Barlow secure the bunkers. Ando and Wood, you'll lay down suppressive fire while third Squad gets our boys. It's 2nd Squad's original position. Gentlemen, we're the tip of the spear. We get our boys, start a fight, call in the guns, and withdraw. Easy day! Listen to your Squad leaders other than that; you know what to do."

Seamus bowed his head, "Let's touch God boys – Let's touch God. Barlow, would you say some words?"

Lance Corporal Charles Barlow had evolved and had learned to trust himself; subsequently, he earned the trust of his fellow Marines. Barlow bowed his head and cited, Revelation 6:8.

> And I looked, and behold a pale horse: and his name that sat on him was Death, and Hell followed with him. And power was given unto them over the fourth part of the earth, to kill with sword, and with hunger, and with death, and with the beasts of the earth.

Barlow paused, wiped a tear, and looked toward Seamus. "I owe you my life." And, he continued.

> Let us find our strength in the Lord; our cause is righteous.
> Let us find our strength in each other, for we are brothers.
> Let us find our strength in ourselves, we are Marines. If we perish on the field, we die facing the enemy.

"Platoon Sergeant, what if Elijah and John Wayne ain't there?" Flynn interjected. "What do we do if the NVA are waiting for us?"

"Jesus Christ Maddog, Elijah's there. I left the radio 30 meters from that position. He's there."

Ando nodded. Seamus had always been right, and he trusted that he would be right again.

"Staff Sergeant, where are you and the FNG going to be," Wood asked.

"Me and Boot are goin' after the Battalion flag; it should be 'bout 30 meters from Elijah's position – where I left the radio. Barsone hoisted it in front of the bunkers. Remember, they'll hold their fire trying to suck us into the kill zones. Let's do a feint; make 'em think we're fallin' for it. We get our boys, start a fight, we pull back and unleash hell. Are there any questions? We move out in five."

"Hey Boot," Seamus said. "I'm putting you in for the Bronze Star for knocking out those 50s. Were you serious, when you said you were scared?"

"Sir, I said a prayer just like you advised; I think it worked."

"Maddog, you're having a good day. Wood can't figure out how the hell you managed to do what you did."

"Staff Sergeant I disobeyed Corporal Wood's orders. He wanted to wait for reinforcements. After I said a prayer, I saw everything clearly. I knew I could take 'em out. Please don't bust me; I ain't been a PFC much more than an hour."

"Do me a favor Maddog; The angels are protectin' you today. Say another prayer and stay close to me."

Seamus grabbed the handset of the PRC from Flynn.

"Big Daddy, this is Buckaroo . . . Over . . ."

"Go ahead Buckaroo. . ."

"Moving out . . ."

"Godspeed Seamus. Out."

"Corporal Wood, let's get our boys."

TWENTY

LIEUTENANT LY TRUC VIET

One day we shall meet again – we will have tea, and talk about the old days when we were soldiers.

Lieutenant Ly Truc Viet

25 April – Hill-861

"**John Fucking Wayne – well here we are, the gunfight at the OK Corral.** You always wanted to be the hero; looks like ya got your wish. We're the Earp brothers."

"Earp brothers?" Joe Buck questioned. "If you'd listen to the VC Lieutenant, you'd think we're the Clanton's. Elijah, he's convinced we're the bad guys."

Elijah grimaced, "It's more like Custer's last stand."

The two men stared at each other – each with a nervous grin.

"Elijah, I want you to know how much it meant to me when you let me keep the guidon in boot camp. You kicked my ass; the guidon should've been yours."

"Listen, Joe; you were our honor man. You earned it. You brought us through boot camp, the hell of Staff Sergeant Mothershed – you led us through that."

"Till I became a Marine, I was nothing. But when my daddy saw I was the Platoon honor man, it was the first time he was proud. If I die, I lived my dream, and it was because of you, Elijah."

"Listen, fuckhead," Elijah said, "nobody's dying on my watch. Seamus is coming, and we're getting the fuck out of here."

"You're out of your fucking mind Elijah. We got 300 gooks in front of us, and you want us to take 'em on. And then you say we're gonna get through this. But if you say we can, I guess we can."

"Joe, you're better off thinkin' you can do some'in than not thinkin' you can do it. If you believe you can, then you might pull it off. That thinkin' always worked for me."

"Sergeant Bravo, I didn't know you were a philosopher."

"Joe, there's a lot you don't know 'bout me. We're Marines, and we're badass motherfuckers. That's how we're gonna get through this."

"You Americans are arrogant," Lieutenant Viet said. "That is why you will lose this war. You underestimate us. You think because we are the yellow man we are inferior. We are more determined. You invaded our country. You are the foreigner. You are on our soil. It is you who is hubris. You think you are stronger than God. You're are blind, and you don't see it. Sergeant Bravo, when one is troubled by the realities of the world, it can be comforting to consider other possibilities. But America has a narrow vision; you think you must defeat us, and now you are trapped in a prison of your own doing."

"Shut the fuck up you commie bastard," John Wayne commanded. "I swear I'm gonna fuckin' waste you."

"Do it Marine. Kill me! You do me favor."

"Knock it off Joe. The Lieutenant is trying to get into your head. Now's not the time to lose it. Focus on what you have to do. Listen – as soon as we see Marines coming over that rise; we start picking off the NVA in the trees. The center point is that tree." Elijah pointed. You fire, center to right, I'll fire center to the left. We're marksman. Concentrate. It's trigger squeeze, slow and steady."

To cover the advancing Marines Wood placed a 60 at the crest of the rise. This time they would shape the battle.

"Fire that gun on my command. They'll engage when enough of our advance is in their sights," Wood said.

Bob Wood had found his calling. He had stepped up as the Platoon Sergeant and commanded his Marines with confidence and skill.

"Flynn, what the fuck you doing with me? You're with Staff Sergeant O'Grady. Move out."

Corporal Wood, I'd rather be with you; I wanna be in the fight.

"Jesus H. Christ Maddog, you wanna carry the PRC, and then you don't. Then you want to go with me to take out the 50s, you disobey an order, and now you don't want to be with Staff Sergeant O'Grady. Do you think this is your show? You will report to Staff Sergeant O'Grady. Now!"

"Yes, Platoon Sergeant."

Rick MaddogMike Flynn walked away like a hurt child who didn't get his way.

As the Marines crossed the final point of departure, sporadic sniper fire erupted. Barlow ordered 3rd Squad into the craters, made the previous day by the 500-pound bombs.

"Buckaroo . . . this is Hard Ass (Wood) . . . Over . . ."

Hard Ass was the perfect call sign for Corporal Wood.

"Go ahead Bob . . ."

"Where's that fire coming from? Sounds like well-aimed shots, slow and steady . . ."

"Bobby, look for muzzle flashes then suppress but keep moving. We gotta get our boys . . . Out."

Wood searched for the red tracer rounds coming down range toward the Marines, but there were none.

Seamus adjusted his field glasses and scanned the tree line 350 meters to his front. He saw two enemy soldiers drop from the trees.

"Well, I'll be dipped in shit. It's Elijah."

Seamus grabbed the handset of the radio.

"Bobby move on those bunkers, the fire's coming from Elijah; that's where our boys are . . . Get 'em, Bobby... Out."

Enemy counter-fire exploded, but It wasn't directed toward the advancing Marines. It was directed 250 meters in front of Wood's Squad.

The 60 opened up raking the enemy positions. Seamus called for mortar fire into the center of the spider holes. However, the return fire coming from the enemy proved that they were in the fight.

Barlow's Squad leapfrogged toward the objective. The Marines ran ten yards, hit the deck, and then ran ten more. The 1st and 2nd Squads provided cover fire. Two men were down, and Doc Baviello ran to the action to care for his Marines. They were 20 meters away. One more Marine down.

"Corpsman up," Barlow cried.

One more rush they'd be there.

Barlow screamed, "Let's go Marines!" They stormed into the bunker.

Elijah turned, and with a big Texas grin said, "Knock three times and say Joe sent ya why don't ya."

"Seamus was right; you're alive. It's good to see you guys. Let's get you boys outta here," Wood said.

"Seamus – where's Seamus?" Elijah questioned.

"Sergeant O'Grady is getting the colors. He's okay."

"Can you walk," Corporal Wood asked.

"Yeah, it'd take more than the 105s you dropped on my ass to slow down this Texas cowboy."

"Those dead gooks have any intel on them?" Wood asked.

"No, I checked them out."

"Let's get out of here before Seamus lights this place up," Wood said.

"Bobby, I left something in the bunker. I'll be a second," Elijah said.

Elijah returned to the bunker. There was something he had to do. Lieutenant Ly-Truc-Viet boldly stared at him and awaited his fate.

Elijah pulled his bayonet then shook his head. "There's been too much killin' – No more." He cut the ropes that bound the Lieutenant's wrists.

"Lieutenant Viet – wait three minutes then get the hell out. Your Battalion is doomed. We're gonna light this hill up. Go west. You'll be safe."

"Sergeant Bravo, you spare my life – I would not spare yours. You are the better man; It was as you said."

"Lieutenant, no more. We are soldiers. You have served your country well. You must not die; you must continue to live. The world will depend on men like us. We're enemies, but maybe one day we'll see that we are just men. Lieutenant, there is a God – so you will live."

"Sergeant, your mercy is a sign from God. Maybe the world will be filled with people willing to sit down and talk about their differences. There would be no problem good men could not solve. Elijah Bravo, I will always be in your debt."

Lieutenant Viet shook off the ropes then raised his hand as if to say goodbye.

"One day we will meet again – we will have tea, and talk about the old days when we were soldiers," the Vietnamese officer said.

Elijah smiled, threw him his canteen, turned, and left.

Wood attempted to reach Seamus on the radio.

"Buckaroo . . . This is Hard Ass . . . Over . . ."

"Seamus ain't picking up," Wood said.
"Try again," Elijah pleaded.

"Buckaroo . . . This is Hard Ass . . . Come in . . ."

"Hard Ass . . . Buckaroo here . . . You got my boys . . .?"

"Affirmative . . ." Wood said. "They're shot to pieces, but okay... Medevac coming . . . We got six wounded including the boys . . . Seamus, what's your orders . . .?"

"Pull back below the rise . . . Get Elijah and Buck out of there . . . get our dead and the wounded on that chopper . . . maintain a position below the crest . . . I'm calling the steel curtain . . ."

"Seamus . . . you get the colors . . .?"

"No . . . The motherfuckers took em . . . Out."

Seamus knelt on the ruins of the bunkers. It had to be there. He glanced at the lifeless body of three NVA soldiers he killed the previous day. Barsone had raised the flag on that spot. He saw the staff used to fly the flag lying broken.
"This can't happen!" Seamus exclaimed.
"Platoon Sergeant, you okay?" Maddog inquired.
Seamus didn't answer. "Sir, is everything Okay?"
"Jesus H. Christ Boot! Don't refer to me as sir."
Seamus gave the Boot a hard look; the young Marine was hurt by his Sergeant's reaction.
"Maddog, sorry. It ain't you. They have our flag. I flew it on this beam. The flag's gone. They took everything —spent cartridges, C-rat cans – everything. It's a disgrace to lose your colors," Elijah said.
"Platoon Sergeant, we can get another flag. You got Elijah and Joe Buck; you brought the Marines out."
"Maddog, you don't lose your colors. Especially us. We're 1/9, the Walking Dead. They hate us; now they have our colors. The colors are the Esprit de Corps of the unit. Victories and defeats are determined by colors being lost or captured."
Flynn didn't understand the gravity of his Sergeant's feelings.
"Sir, let's get out of here."
"Boot, I'm not a sir."
"Goddammit Staff Sergeant O'Grady, I don't call you sir because of a rank. I call you sir because I respect you."

Seamus looked at the young Private and managed a nod.

"Get on the hook, check on Bravo and John Wayne. I want to make sure the chopper got out to the Sanctuary," Seamus ordered.

"Staff Sergeant O'Grady – Captain Reynolds for you," Maddog said.

"Sir... O'Grady here . . ."

"Seamus, damn good job. Elijah and John Wayne are okay. Medevac'd to the Sanctuary. We're pulling you to the rear. Bravo and Charlie Companies are pushing through your position. Get back and help me coordinate fire support . . . We'll have the hill by noon . . . you get the colors . . .?"

"Sir . . . I did not . . ."

"No biggie Staff Sergeant . . . Out."

Hill-558

"Staff Sergeant, the Captain wants you at headquarters. Maybe he's gonna make you a Gunny," Maddog exclaimed.

"Yeah sure. He's gonna bust me to a fuckin' boot like you for losin' the colors."

"Excuse me Staff Sergeant, but if he does that, I'll outrank you."

"How's that," Seamus asked.

"You forget you promoted me to Lance Corporal?"

"I did that? I don't remember promotin' you." Seamus said. "I must of been out of my mind. What I meant to do was promote you to Private First Class. Flynn, you're comin' with me. From now on you work directly for me. Havin' you around just might keep me alive. Get on the hook, tell Barlow, Ando, and Alexander to withdraw toward 558."

"Aye-aye Sir."

Captain Reynolds recommended Seamus for the Silver Star. He designed the tactics, which held 300 enemy soldiers at bay. He brought his men off the hill only to return the following day. Reynolds recommended Elijah for the Navy Cross. He held off a superior force, evaded capture, saved Joe Buck, warned of the impending trap, and then broke the enemy's ambush. Elijah was a hero and kept his promise to Gunnery Sergeant Winston. Joe Buck got the Silver Star.

The hill fights continued for three days. The Marines would move toward the summit while the enemy waited in ambush. Marines rushed to aid their wounded only to be killed or wounded themselves. The Marines would fix the enemy; pull back, and call for air support. The North Vietnamese expected the Americans to attack uphill. It was General Westmoreland's war of attrition. The enemy would occupy a hill and use it as bait. After inflicting casualties on American forces, they'd slip away and follow pre-determined escape routes. The Americans would then abandon the hill and move toward another. Westmoreland's search and destroy strategy was a failure. Body count was a weak determinant of success. Regardless, of the number of enemy killed; their losses would be replaced.

During the early morning of the third day, the enemy disappeared into the jungles of Laos and took their dead with them. The Marines took the best the NVA could throw at them and beat them hands down; however, it was not without cost, 155 Marines were lost in some of the bitterest fighting of the war. The enemy lost over 900 men. The enemy showed the American public that North Vietnam was willing to sustain heavy casualties to kill Americans. There were 155 coffins sent home. The Marines abandoned the hill, and the enemy returned. The evening news would highlight the horror of the battle and the number of dead Marines. On the nightly news Walter Cronkite would comment: *after capturing Hills-861, 881-North, and 881-South and enduring 155 casualties, the Marines abandoned the hill only to re-take it another day.*

In January 1968, The Marines would do it again.

TWENTY-ONE

LAST RIDE OUT'TA DIS PLACE

You think the right thing is blame yourself for this man's death.
There is violence in Vietnam; it visits us all. You are alive; this
man made that possible. Do something with the life he gave you.

Nguyen Lu

25 April 1967 – USS Sanctuary, Gulf of Tonkin

The rotors of an incoming chopper make a distinct sound.
They don't have the high-pitch whine of an outgoing bird, but
instead a dull whop, whop, whop that is accentuated by a dense
jungle canopy. The Marines could tell the difference between an
incoming and an outgoing. Both were welcome. Incoming choppers
brought supplies, reinforcements, and rescue. Outgoing choppers
extracted the wounded, took the dead home, and brought the living
out of Dodge.

The chopper was coming in fast, nose down, and hugging the
trees. There was an added dimension – desperation. The Pilot
brought the bird down exactly on the white smoke that Corporal
Wood had dropped. The man in the doorway kicked food, water, and
ammunition onto the red clay soil. Wood watched as the boxes
bounce off the skids and tumble onto the ground.

The 3rd Squad approached the chopper's doorway carrying
ponchos holding the bodies the dead Marines. They used the weight
of the bodies to swing them until they had enough momentum to get
the dead-on board. The man in the opening dragged the dead across
the deck and piled them into the corner. Blood pooled next to the
door. Earlier they were living breathing human beings; now they
were lifeless stacks of wood. The wounded then ambled on the
chopper.

Wood made eye contact with the door gunner. *He's going, but I'm staying to continue the fight,* Wood thought. But the man at the door would return. The gunner stared at Corporal Wood, gave him a thumbs-up, and grinned. The Captain gunned the engine, and the blades of the Huey turned faster and faster. Time was not on Feldman's side. He'd been shot in the chest attempting to rescue Elijah Bravo and John Wayne.

The chopper began to lift, and with nose down, it barely cleared the ground. With seven dead, six wounded, and the crew, the bird, was heavier than it should've been. Too much weight Elijah thought. As the bird fought for altitude, it was vulnerable to enemy fire. John Wayne looked for a sign from the Crew Chief as to what would happen. He looked at the pilot, but neither gave a clue, yet they appeared calm. It was just a smokescreen. The rotors spun faster and faster. The chopper struggled for altitude. "Lift – Lift," the Captain shouted. He gunned the engine, and the whine of the blades gave the Marines on board a feeling they wouldn't make it to the hospital ship that floated in the Gulf of Tonkin. But the chopper rose, picked up speed, and headed east. The door gunner turned the dial of a boom box duck taped to the cabin above the door. He casually tied his harness and hung-out the doorway with both his arms draped over the M-60 machine gun. They would make it.

Elijah and John Wayne were silent and stared at lifeless forms wrapped in green ponchos: Lihue, Knap, Terry, Ashcraft, Fields, Engstrom, and, Johnny Luna. It was the color of death. The steady shaking of the rotors moved the bodies in a subtle macabre rhythm. And yet it was visible even to the naked eye. It would be the poor bastards last lift – their last extraction. The crew-chief adjusted the IV and stared at Johnny Feldman. He wiped the dirt from his bloody face and held his hand. Feldman opened his eyes and whispered, "Mother." It was often the last word of a dying soldier. The door gunner gently touched a wet cloth to his lips. "You'll be okay," the crew-chief said. "Stay with me." The chief moved to the doorway and halfway hanging out, draped his arms around the mounted 60 searching for movement below. He began firing. Elijah peered out the window and wasn't sure the shapes on the ground were enemy soldiers. The man in the doorway was just a boy.

The treetops below the speeding chopper appeared and disappeared, and the music from the boom box bounced off the cabin walls. It was Eric Burdon and the Animals: "We Got to Get

115

Out of This Place." The music played and the dying lay dying, and the dead were dead, and the wounded were silent, and the music played. Leaving Vietnam was everyone's dream, but the dead never planned to leave, lying stacked on the floor of a helicopter. The music told of lost hope, and those on board wondered – if it was worth it.

"How much longer?" Elijah asked.

"Lance Corporal, How much longer?" Elijah screamed.

"What's that?" the door gunner questioned.

"How much longer?"

The music continued and told they would be dead before their time was due.

The chief scanned the horizon and saw the Gulf of Tonkin.

"Sergeant, It's 20 minutes. You okay," he yelled over the sounds of the chopper.

"I'm not worried about me; it's him. He gonna make it? He got hit trying to rescue me. It just ain't right."

"I don't know if he'll make it Sergeant. You can't blame yourself. None of us has any control over who lives or dies. It's one big crapshoot."

The wounded Marine extended his arm toward the crew-chief. His breathing was shallow, and it appeared something had caught his attention. Elijah looked but didn't see anything. Feldman tried to speak but was fading. The boy at the door cradled him and began to cry. Feldman reached for the silver cross hanging around the gunner's neck and then a blank stare, "I'm sorry," the chief said. And Elijah looked out the window; everything was blue; over the Gulf of Tonkin – and the Sanctuary loomed ahead. And the music continued to speak and the dead were leaving, and it was their last ride, and they were going home. Sergeant Lihue, Private Knap, Private First-Class Terry, Lance Corporal Engstrom, Lance Corporal Fields, Corporal Ashcraft, Corporal Feldman, and Johnny Luna, and were getting out of dis place, and it was the last thing they ever did.

The chopper came in fast landing into the wind. Doctors and nurses ran to extract the wounded.

"I can help," Elijah said.

A woman with dark hair and a darker stare ordered, "Help me with this man."

"He didn't make it," the Sergeant replied.

The woman showed little emotion; she had seen this before.

She pointed to Elijah and John Wayne, "Wait here; I will care for you shortly."

"Sergeant Bravo, I think I'm gonna like it here. She's got round eye in her. She's so hot you can fry and egg off of her," Joe Buck commented.

The woman moved down the gangway, and her long hair barely concealed a curvaceous body.

Moments later, the woman returned.

Elijah and Joe Buck remained on deck with their fallen brothers. They wouldn't leave them.

"Miss," Elijah said. What's going to happen to them?"

"Don't worry Sergeant; we'll take care of them." There's a higher power watching over you. If your wounds had been different, you too would not have made it."

Elijah signed the cross then brought his fingers to his lips.

"Sergeant, you are religious?"

"No ma'am, but I believe."

"I'm Sergeant Elijah Bravo."

"Nurse Nguyen Lu," she said.

"Sergeant Elijah, was this man, Feldman your Marine?"

She clutched the dead Marine's dog tag to make sure it matched the one tied to his boot.

"He was in my Platoon; he was killed rescuing me. I don't know how I can live with this."

"Sergeant, you think the right thing is to blame yourself for this man's death. There is violence in Vietnam; it visits us all. You are alive; this man has made that possible. Do something with the life he gave you. Let this go and be thankful for his sacrifice. You would have sacrificed for him."

The woman nodded in the direction of John Wayne and said, "Sergeant Bravo wait here, I will take care of the Corporal. Come with me please."

John Wayne winked at Elijah as he walked through the door and down the hatch toward medical. Nguyen followed and moved like a swan. She turned, smiled at Bravo and disappeared through the bulkhead.

TWENTY-TWO

SERENDIPITOUS CONNECTION

He moved on . . . yet tried to forget a girl he couldn't forget. But she was real and she existed without him and she belonged to someone else, and that someone was not him.

June 1967 – Camp Carroll, Vietnam

Seamus crumpled the paper and tossed it onto the ground. He sat on an ammo crate attempting to find the right words to explain the heroic deeds of his men. He couldn't express what Elijah Bravo, John Wayne, Bob Wood, Lieutenant McGivens, and Rick MaddogMike Flynn had done. There were five discarded papers laying on the red clay soil.

"Wood, sure 'nough, I should of paid attention in English class. Maybe I'd be able to write these commendations."

"Seamus, Elijah tells a little different story. He says you guys never went to school."

"Like you did, fuckhead," Seamus remarked. "If we had education we wouldn't be in Vietnam. We'd be in dental school."

"Yeah, Seamus, the only place you'd be is Viet Fucking Nam cause that's where the fight in's is."

"Staff Sergeant O'Grady, Lieutenant McGivens refuses to be medevac'd," Maddog exclaimed. Get this – he told the CO he wants to stay with his men."

"He said that?" Wood commented.

Maddog turned toward Corporal Wood. "What the fuck's wrong with the Lieutenant? He'd rather stay in this shit-hole than go home. Hell – don't he know we got this?"

Wood smirked, looked at O'Grady and laughed, "Doesn't Maddog know he's a fucking new guy? And he don't got shit."

"Sir," Rick MaddogMike Flynn interjected, "Have you promoted me to Lance Corporal yet?"

"Listen, boot, I told ya I was gonna do it, didn't I? But what the fuck do you mean? Lance Corporal."

"Sergeant Bravo, you do remember you said, Lance Corporal."

"I did? I made a mistake Maddog; you gotta become a PFC before you make Lance Corporal. Listen, I got a lot of letters to write and eight of them ain't good. Don't bother me. One more thing, the El-tee is still here so you'd better watch that sir crap. There's one 'sir' in this Platoon and it ain't me."

Mash Unit — Hue City

Lieutenant McGivens placed the book on the table adjacent to his hospital bed. It was the third time he had read *Le Morte d' Arthur* by Sir Thomas Mallory.

"Staff Sergeant O'Grady, listen to this."

Yet some men say in many parts of England that King Arthur is not dead but had by the will of our Lord Jesus gone into another place, and men say that he shall come again, and he shall win the holy cross.

Calder McGivens believed in fairy tales and knights and kings. He saw himself as the reincarnation of King Arthur and Seamus as one of his knights.

"Et-tee, what did you study in college? I'd like to go to college one day."

"Majored in the classics, at Dartmouth," McGivens said.

"Sir, did you say Dartmouth?"

McGivens nodded.

"Sir, did you happen to know an Ofa? – Ofa Hawkins."

"I didn't know an Ofa, but I sure knew an Ophelia Hawkins. Actually, I knew her very well. She a friend of yours?"

"We grew up together in Luckenbach, Texas."

Seamus stared into the cup and hoped his thoughts would be absorbed by the black coffee. He had moved on and tried to forget a girl he couldn't forget, yet he knew that she existed without him and that she belonged to someone else, and that someone was not him.

He raised his head and tried to suppress his next thought. His instincts told him not to continue the conversation, but the coffee hadn't work.

"How is she, Sir?"

Lieutenant McGivens smiled.

"Sergeant O'Grady – you're Seamus O'Grady. I didn't get the connection. Now it's clear. She told me about you. I remember you were friends in high school. It's a small world. She had some nice things to say."

Seamus wasn't sure he wanted to hear those nice things.

"She's beautiful, has a boyfriend, Paul Bannister. Can't say I like the guy. She had feelings for you, didn't she? She never said so, but I could tell she liked you. It was just her mannerism when your name came up. She became an anti-war activist and marched for peace all over the country. I've seen her on TV, magazines, and newspapers," McGivens commented.

Yeah, Girl with the Purple Ribbon," Seamus said.

"She's hardcore. Belonged to the Students for a Democratic Society, but no more. She's against the war but supports the troops. She traveled all over the attending the funerals of soldiers, and still managed to get A's. She knew I was going into the Corps, but it never bothered her," McGivens said.

"El-tee, can I ask you a question?"

"Sir, what's wrong with her boyfriend?"

"I can't put my finger on it. I meet him a few times. I don't think he's a heads-up guy. Hey – she loves him; that's all that matters – right? But she never seems very happy. I hate to say it, but the war devastated her. Seems like she carries that weight in her heart. People at school call her the Ice Queen."

"Staff Sergeant, may I ask a question? You ever date?"

"I had feelings for her, but to tell you the truth; I can't say for sure we ever went on a date."

TWENTY-THREE

CLASS VALEDICTORIAN 1965

In every age, it has been the tyrant, the oppressor, and the exploiter who has wrapped himself in the cloak of patriotism, or religion, or both to deceive and overawe the People.

Eugene Victor Debs

June 18, 1965 – Fredericksburg High School

"What's wrong Ofa darlin'? You can tell me," Asa pleaded.

"Daddy, I'm okay; really I am." Cross my heart and hope to die."

Trying to fool her father, Ofa gazed out the window; she didn't want him to see the tears in her eyes. She was worried about the boys and hadn't spoken to them in two days. That was not typical of a one-horse town like Luckenbach. She wanted to explain, that Paul was only giving her a ride home. It was just a simple ride, nothing more than that. He didn't even try to kiss her. But she wondered why he hadn't. Seamus never tried either. *Was there something wrong*, she thought. She gave Seamus a thousand chances to steal her heart. Regardless, she couldn't forget the look on his face when Paul stopped at the blinking light. It was a painful way to learn he cared.

"Daddy, the boys are late for graduation."

"Those boys don't care about nothing except what they want to do. They're irresponsible and have no concern for anybody. Sweetheart, Paul's here; he cares about you. Forget about that Seamus boy; he'll never amount to anything."

"But daddy, they're leaving for the Marines on the 10 o'clock train from Austin. I'd feel awful if I didn't see them before they go."

"Ofa, he doesn't want to see you; that's what he's telling you by not coming to graduation. He doesn't have the guts to tell you in person. He's not the boy you thought. Sweetheart, enjoy graduation. You're summa cum laude. It's your day."

"Daddy, you're right. Thanks for making me feel better."

But Ofa didn't feel better. She was lying for the second time that morning.

As the graduates filed into the auditorium foyer, the class of 1965 anticipated becoming adults. The girls wore white gowns with red mortarboards, and the boys wore black gowns with black mortarboards. By the time the girls were 20, many of them would marry and have children. Some would go to college, and some would take menial jobs at the Five and Dime. Some of the boys would join the military, wind up in Vietnam, and be dead within the year. Most of the girls would take subservient roles and become the victims of a society that wasn't ready to give them a place at the table.

Ofa would go her own way and use her intellect and charm to forge a path that she chooses. As class valedictorian, she wore a wreath of red roses and would lead the procession. The townsfolk were anxious to hear what the pretty girl had to say.

Mrs. Bone, the high school secretary, inspected each girl to make sure they secured their mortarboards properly with a bobby pin.

"Ofa, you look prettier than a picture," Mrs. Bone remarked." "You ready for your speech?"

"Why yes, I am, ma'am" Ofa answered. "Mrs. Bone, would you happen to have some purple ribbon?"

Mrs. Bone had a special fondness for the girl. When Ofa's momma left, she promised Scarlett Hawkins to watch out for her daughter.

"Dear, I'll go backstage and check; I'll find some ribbon."

Mrs. Bone tied the ribbon around her wavy blond hair.

"I'm wearin' this ribbon to respect the memory of the soldiers who died and who will die in Vietnam," Ofa exclaimed.

"Ofa Hawkins, it's just like you to always have something on your mind."

Moments before the ceremony, Ofa appeared nervous.

"Ophelia don't be nervous," Principal, Hopkins said. "You're a good speaker, and everybody admires you."

"We're missin' Seamus and Elijah. I'm sure they're comin' – Mrs.

Hopkins, shouldn't we wait for 'em?"

"Ophelia. I've dealt with those knuckleheads for four years, and frankly, I am tired of their lack of concern for others."

Ofa pleaded with the principal to wait. She wasn't anxious about giving the graduation speech; she was worried about her best friends.

"Ophelia, in a few minutes I'll give you the sign, and when I do, I want you to walk down the center aisle just like we practiced."

"But Ma'am – it wouldn't be right if they ain't here."

"Ophelia, you know what day of the week it is? It's Friday. For the past four years, every Friday those knuckleheads fish the South Grape Creek. I bet that's exactly where they are."

Ofa smiled. That's what she loved about the boys. They were running wild and free, through the Texas Hill Country.

"Mrs. Hopkins, I'm ready now."

South Grape Creek – Luckenbach

"Seamus, stop thinkin' 'bout Ofa. Ain't no good. We're gonna be Marines, and we gotta job to do. Ain't no time to be thinkin' 'bout a girl. Girls will just mess you up; you won't be able to concentrate."

"You know it all, don't ya Elijah. I ain't thinkin' 'bout Ofa. I'm fixin' to catch a big ol' catfish and fry it up for lunch," Seamus said.

Elijah smirked, "It ain't gonna do you no good to live in denial. I'm gonna kick your ass if you don't stop being stupid."

"Yeah, It's easy for you Elijah. You don't got the problems I got." Seamus spoke without thinking.

"Sorry Cowboy, I didn't mean that."

Elijah's alcoholic father, Angel Bravo, beat him. If it weren't for his mother, Elijah would not have had a good story. Faviola Bright-Eye, his momma, was the beauty of the Rez (reservation), the queen of the Corn Harvest. She left a promising career as an actress to marry Angel, a guerilla fighter who fought with Mexican revolutionary, Rubén Jaramillo. Life with Angel was hell, but he gave her three daughters. However, Faviola prayed for a son. The priest suggested she pray to the prophet Elijah, the wonder worker of the Northern Kingdom of Israel. On the feast of Saint Elijah, Faviola gave birth to a baby boy.

"Hey, Buckaroo I'm sorry 'bout your situation with Ofa. But you're lookin' at it the wrong way. It's ain't a problem; it's an experience. Experiences ain't problems but only if you make 'em so.

It's your attitude. You both created this, and there ain't no simple solution. You gotta cowboy up: Bronco Billy!"

The boys lay barefoot under the oak on the east bank of the creek. Their poles formed a shadow pointing west and west was the direction they'd be heading. One last time they cast into the center of the channel.

"Seamus, we'll I'll be dipped in shit, we're missin' graduation."

"Cowboy, suppose we are. But I wouldn't miss fishin' with you for all the tea in China. Elijah, when we go to Vietnam, and we ever get to fightin', and you get in a jam, I'll never leave you."

"Jesus H. Christ Seamus, you don't have to tell me that; it's understood."

There are things in life between men that need little affirmation. It's the fiber of their stuff; it's what they're made of that determines if what they say is true or if they can be held accountable to a trust. Seamus O'Grady and Elijah Bravo were cut from the same mold, and when they made a promise, you'd best believe they'd keep it.

Fredericksburg High School

Paul Bannister watched Ophelia lead the procession for the class of 1965.

"Professor Hawkins, why is Ophelia wearing a purple ribbon in her hair?" Paul asked.

"She's doing that, isn't she? I haven't seen her wear a ribbon since she was a little girl," Asa said.

"Maybe it's a girly thing – girls and ribbons. Professor, she's amazing. She'll put a stop to those baby killers in Vietnam."

Asa was surprised by Paul's reference to American soldiers as baby killers. The professor was an ardent advocate of peace, opposed to war, and not sympathetic to the soldiers who fought, but he never referred to American soldiers as baby killers.

"Paul, she believes they're tools of American imperialism, but not baby killers."

"But Professor, imperialism kills innocent women and children."

Asa Hawkins seemed annoyed by Paul's reference, but not enough to chastise his favorite student.

Ofa was not happy about the boys missing graduation. It wouldn't be the same without them. She sat in the first chair of the first row and hoped Seamus would come to hear her speak. She unfolded the paper containing an outline of her speech. She stared at the first line that her father had written. "America is an imperialist nation." She crumpled the paper and dropped it on the floor. She would address the graduates from her heart.

Mrs. Hopkins bellowed, "Graduates, Ladies, and Gentlemen, I'm proud to introduce our class valedictorian, Ophelia Penelope Hawkins, summa cum laude for the class of 1965."

Ofa was everybody's girl. The folks sitting in the hot auditorium gave her a Texas cheer that Fredericksburg High School had never quite heard before. She walked to the podium, stared into the crowd, and took a deep breath. She remembered what Asa said – "smile." But she didn't smile.

My fellow graduates . . ."

Ofa paused and scanned the auditorium hoping Seamus and Elijah would turn up.

John Fitzgerald Kennedy said in his inaugural address, 'Let every nation know, whether it wishes us well or ill that we shall pay any price, bear any burden, meet any hardship, support any friend, oppose any foe to assure the survival and the success of liberty.'

President Kennedy's words were eloquent, but what have they brought us? We are mired in a war in Vietnam 10,000 miles away from Luckenbach. Our young men are bein' killed and maimed, and our young men are killin' and maimin' other young men. And as a citizen in a democracy, I am appalled how the president of these United States would decide to commit American soldiers to this immoral war without a declaration from Congress. 'We the people,' the first words of our beloved *Declaration of Independence* mandates that the power to determine the fate of the United States rests with us. George Washington said:

'The Constitution vests the power of declarin' war in Congress; therefore, no offensive expedition of importance can be undertaken until after they shall have deliberated upon the subject and authorized such a measure.'

War! – The mere concept of war is a concern of gravitas. Should an act of war be so whimsical that it can be decided without the most severe forms of deliberation? This war is unconstitutional. I am the people. I evolved from *We the People*, and I am opposed to the Vietnam War. I fear for the class of '65, not only here at Frederiksberg, but every high school class throughout the nation. The class of 1965 will bear the burden of this war."

The audience was not ready for a politically charged speech. She was speaking to Texans, and they still remembered the Alamo. Many of the men were cowboys who didn't take a liking to speaking against America. They were patriotic and proud of their country. Most of the men were part of the greatest generation that liberated Europe and the Pacific during World War II. But Ofa stared them down and continued to speak.

We're payin' an installment with American lives fightin' a foe who ain't unlike ourselves when we was fighting the English in our War for Independence. President Kennedy said, 'Pay any price...' Sure 'nuff those words will seal the fate of countless Americans, and those Americans will join him on the hills of Arlington, Va' gin'ya.

What is patriotism? What does lovin' your country mean? I love my country, and because I do, I speak against her when she's wrong. And the United States is wrong. It's with great pain that I have become a dissentient. The notion that a radical such as me hates their country is naïve. Eugene Victor Debs said, 'In every age, it has been the tyrant, the oppressor and the exploiter who has wrapped himself in the cloak of patriotism, religion or both to deceive the People.' My dear graduates, y'all should never underestimate your ability to change society because your courage can be contagious. I challenge you to take up the cross for this beloved land and heed the words of John Kennedy. He told us that 'Here on earth God's work must truly be our own.'

So, don't ask what your country can do for you, but what you can do for your country. And what you can do for your country is not support this war in Vietnam.

My dear classmates when everything around you is lackin' in integrity, y'all must find integrity in yourself. Then you can change the world right from where you're standin'.

She gave her fellow graduates a flirtatious glance and aware of the uncomfortable stares she received, Ofa took her seat.

TWENTY-FOUR

LAST FISHING TRIP

There are good ships, and there are the ships that sail the sea. The best ships are friendship and may they always be wood ships, and there are good ships but the best ships of all are friendships.

Irish Proverb

June 18, 1965 – South Grape Creek

"Seamus ol' buddy, we come here since we was boys and over the years, we've gone through lots a changes. This place is sacred, and the river here knows the future. Comin' here has been the best part of growin' up. When I go fishin', I touch God, and the river assures me that regardless of what happens, the world remains. It makes me feel secure and I feel one with the world."

"Elijah, if I knew what you was talkin 'bout, I'd suppose I'd agree with you. But I thought we've been coming here to catch Ol' Joe. We've been fishin' the crick four years and we ain't ever so much as seen 'em."

"Well, I'm not so sure 'bout that. I think that big ol' log floatin' down the creek last week wasn't a log. I think it was Ol' Joe," Elijah answered.

Seamus' daddy Liam and Liam's daddy McCauley had been talkin' about catchin' Ol' Joe ever since the boys was young. Ol' Joe was a legendary catfish. Some of the old men sittin' around the Potbelly stove told stories 'bout seein' him swimmin' upstream when they was boys. Swimmin' upstream is unusual for a catfish. But Ol' Joe swam just as though he owned the whole damn South Grape Crick. Some even said Ol' Joe could talk. Everyone wanted to catch him, but nobody did. It's not like they was goin' to gut him and fry 'em up. Ol' Joe had earned a lot of respect. And that was understandable for a catfish that was over one hundred years old.

"There ain't no more catfish in the Crick, so I suppose Ol' Joe's moved on to the Brazos," Seamus said. "This spot been fished out years ago. Well shit, I don't even know why we come here all those fishin' Fridays. It sure wasn't to catch Ol' Joe," Seamus said. "Maybe we should 'a gone to school."

Elijah grinned. "I don't think even if we tried we'd get more than a C."

"Hey, Pard, you're wrong about Ol' Joe. Sure 'nough he still swims these waters. He's out there, and still, the biggest and meanest catfish that ever lived in a river. But ain't it strange that only Pops, my daddy, and the old codgers that hang around the potbelly stove have seen 'em. Billy Bone said he was out fishin' just the other night when he heard the bell ring, and by the time he got to his pole, it was dragged down the crick by some monster fish. He said it was Ol' Joe. He was sure of it," Seamus remarked.

"Seamus, it don't matter if we catch any fish, and it don't matter if we ever see Ol' Joe. Being here with you every Friday was the best part of bein' a kid. But it's time we put up these fishin' poles for a spell. It's time we growed up."

The boys pulled on a bottle of Sweet Lucy Wine.

"To us, and those like us. Damn few left." Elijah said.

And with one voice they chimed – "There are good ships and there are the ships that sail the sea. The best ships are friendships and may they always be wood ships, and they are good ships, but the best ships of all are friendships."

"Elijah, I ain't sure I want to grow up."

"Well, I'll be dipped in shit Seamus. We missed graduation, and sure 'nough if that ain't a sign that we ain't growed up, I don't know what is."

"I feel kind a bad about not showin'," Seamus said. But don't get me wrong. Today's a fishin' Friday, and even if I were getting' married to Ofa, I'd be here fishin' with you."

"I don't give a shit 'bout graduation," Elijah interjected. "I see us when we was freshmen, throwin' our lines in the crick. It was the most fun we ever had. And then over the years, it got less and less fun. Fishin' the crick don't seem like it's enough."

"Maybe that's what's botherin' me, Elijah. I didn't get to hear Ofa's speech – she bein' the class valedictorian. We should've been there to support her. I think what she had to say might of been more important than fishin'."

"Seamus, we weren't there, and we can't change that. She's moved on, and you gotta do the same. It's just a speech and knowin' Ofa; she's gonna bad mouth everything we believe in."

"Well, the problem is – Elijah, I don't know what I believe in. I don't believe like Ofa. I don't know if I've moved on. It's like the growin' up thing. Movin' on is leavin' Ofa and the people I grew up with. I ain't ready – I'm scared. I ain't scared of goin' into the Marines or fightin'. I can do that. I'm scared of leavin' home and the people I care 'bout. Thinkin' 'bout all the rough times you had growin' up, how can you be so damn sure of yourself?"

"Seamus, I don't believe anyone is ever ready to grow up. It just happens. A lot of people grow up but they ain't adults. I don't rightly know what makes an adult, but whatever it is, we ain't got it. When we was kids, we never thought 'bout the future. We was fancy-free from responsibility and worry. That began to change senior year. The day we fret about the future is the day we leave our childhood behind. My momma gave me more love than there are stars in the sky and because of her, I learned my place in the world, and I can see things – maybe I can see things that you don't see."

"Elijah, you always had a different take on things," Seamus replied. "I guess we've been growin' up for some time, and we didn't even know we was growin' up."

"We ain't gonna be different. It means we're gonna do different things," Elijah said. "I'll never stop lovin' fishin' at the Crick with you or hangin' out at the general store and shootin' the shit with Ofa and talkin' to Pops. But a part of growin' up is expandin' our world and the way we look at things. We never thought of our future, and now our future is here."

"Elijah, let's renew our blood brother promise. We'll bury something new."

There was an old Indian ceremony that to become a blood brother, each boy would cut himself and draw blood. They would rub their blood together and recite the blood brother promise: "I promise to be loyal and true to my blood brother." Each boy would then bury something of value.

"Let's bury these fishin' poles; they ain't gonna do us no good no more. When we get out of the Corps, we'll dig em up and go fishin' just like the old days," Elijah said.

Elijah knew when Seamus said something it came from the heart. He didn't say things because they sounded good. So, when Seamus said, he'd never leave him, he meant it. The boys buried their fishin' poles underneath the old oak tree that had shaded them every fishin' Friday afternoon. They dug the hole right next to where they and Ofa buried their class pins when they first became blood brothers and promised to be friends forever.

"We're leavin' from Austin in three hours, Seamus. Let's get on down the road."

"Elijah I'm gonna see Pops at the Post Office; I'll meet you at the bus stop."

Post Office

"How's my favorite grandson doing," the old man asked?

"I'm your only grandson."

"Don't matter Seamus; you're still my favorite. No good-byes. It's I'll see ya later."

"Yeah Pops, I just wanna say – I don't rightly have the words – I wanna say thanks for bein' the best granddaddy a guy could have."

"Seamus, I'm the only grandfather you got, so there's nuthin' to compare me with."

"Pops, even if I had ten granddaddies, you'd be my favorite."

"Thanks for bein' the greatest grandson an old man can have. You understand respect. You're a good boy, Seamus, and you'll make a great Marine. Mark my word son; you'll be a leader one day. You got character and that's the mark of leadership."

"I just wanna' make it through boot camp – never mind 'bout being a leader," Seamus remarked.

"Boy, the best leaders don't seek it, they become leaders because of who they are. Don't take that lightly because character is the only gift you give to yourself. You're gonna go to war, but you'll be okay. Trust yourself. You have a good head on your shoulders, and you got brass balls. Stay close to Elijah; he's a killer," Pops commented.

"Thanks, Pops. I don't feel that way. I don't think I'm the toughest guy. Elijah is."

"Seamus, bein' a leader ain't bein' the toughest. The men want a man to lead them who is a man of honor. You're a man of honor. Remember, a leader doesn't concern himself with doin' things right a leader does the right thing. And to do the right thing takes honor and courage."

"Seamus, maybe now ain't the time to tell you this, but you really messed things up between you and Ofa. She gave you so many chances tryin' to get you to see her as a girl and not as a buddy. Well – you let her walk right out of your life."

"Yeah, I know Pops. I'm sick over it. But we're goin in different directions. I'm goin' to the Marines, and then I'm headin' to Vietnam. Ofa's goin' to Dartmouth. She's gonna be a Doctor. I ain't in her league and to make matters worse; she's a hippy."

"Son! That's nonsense. You're a good and honorable man and a woman like her wants a man like you. Just because you ain't goin' to college don't mean you ain't in the same league. You callin' her a hippy! Well, I've heard all the lame excuses. Son, I'm an old man, but watchin' you throw away the possibility of loving a girl like Ofa hasn't been easy. You gotta let her know you care for her before you leave. Do something. Tempt the hand of fate, and if that fate ain't in your favor, you gotta try and change it. The slightest things we do can change the direction of our life. But it's gotta come from you. I know you have feelin's for her and tonight might be your last chance."

"Seamus, let me tell you a story; it happened long ago. I had feelin's for a girl, but they came at the wrong time. I was shippin' out with the 5th Marines heading to France to fight the Germans. It was 1917. This girl was on my mind, but I never told her I even liked her. I couldn't leave her and face the possibility of dyin' in combat without tellin' her how I felt. We was shippin' out from Austin, heading to New York City to take one of those liberty ships across the ocean. I picked a rose from the courthouse ga'den and before I left, I took that rose over to her house. You see, I was gonna give it to her, but she wasn't home. So, I left it on her doorstep. I wanted to write her a note, but I had no paper, so I just left it, just like that – no note. Just dropped it by the door. Well, she got the rose, and she waited for me. That girl was your grandmother, and I ain't never forget the time I was in love."

"You go, boy. Get a rose and take it to Ofa and then you get on that bus and give 'em hell. Seamus, remember – always be a man. And regardless of what becomes of you and Ofa, you'll never wonder, what if."

TWENTY-FIVE

A RED ROSE

She'll not need anyone else's love if she has your rose.

Aldonza Ramirez

June 18, 1965 – Ramirez General Store

It was 6:30 P.M. The bus to Austin, would leave in thirty minutes. Seamus didn't have much money, and he hoped a rose wouldn't cost more than a dollar. Besides, he only had a dollar. But if he had a hundred dollars, he'd spend every penny on that girl. He wouldn't need money where he was going. The Marines would pay for everything. It was a good deal for Uncle Sam – a few dollars a day for the bodies and souls of the class of '65.

"How much for the white roses?" Seamus asked.

Mr. Ramirez wasn't there. It was graduation, and he was attending a celebration for his daughter, Carmella. Seamus had never seen the strange woman.

"Son, those roses are three dollars a dozen. We've been selling so many. It might be all that's left."

Seamus fidgeted, and with his hands in his pockets, it was as though he was buying a diamond ring. Whether it was diamonds or roses, it was all the same to the cowboy.

"Who are they for?" she asked.

"For a girl Miss," Seamus said.

"It's Aldonza – Aldonza Ramirez; I'm the mother."

"Oh – It's a pleasure to meet you, Mrs. Ramirez. I – a – I didn't know."

"So why are you going to give a rose to a girl?" the old woman asked.

"I like her." Seamus stuttered. He had never expressed his feelings about Ofa to anyone but Elijah.

"I mean – Mrs. Ramirez, I really like her – and I'm leavin' for the Marines tonight – and I want her to know – I really like her," he blurted.

He had kept his feelings for Ofa hidden, and now he was exploding like a volcano.

"Young man, these white roses won't do. You need a red rose. I believe I have one."

"But Mrs. Ramirez, I want to give her a dozen roses, not just one rose."

"Young man, when you like a girl, you give her a red rose. El rojo es para el amor (red is the color of love). She'll not need anyone else's love if she has your rose."

The woman returned with a red rose.

"I suggest you take it."

"What can I pay you for this?"

"Son, I hope you find the love you seek. No hay ningún cambio para el amor (there's no charge for love)."

The woman became somber as she wrapped the rose with tiny white flowers. She had lost her oldest son on Iwo Jima. War is the hate of mothers.

"Mrs. Ramirez. Thank you. Thank you so much."

"Now you give that rose to her young man."

Seamus ran from the store, and Mrs. Ramirez signed the cross "Que Dios te acompañe joven," (God keep him) she said.

A young man's love is magical. The world turns for young lovers. There was something genuine about Seamus. To be in love and to be loved, is the moon and the sky.

He ran down Main Street and turned on Travis. He wished he had worn a better shirt or combed his hair. But it wouldn't matter where he was going. What would he say?

"Ofa, I love you."

No – That wouldn't work. Too much too soon.

"Ofa, wait for me."

That wouldn't work either, too much drama. He would tell her his heart. Something simple and something true. "That's it," he mumbled. "I'll ask her to be my girl."

Every young man needs a girl to wait for him. But he was a boy and didn't understand the pain of waiting when a loved one was off at war.

"Ofa, please be my girl."

He practiced, took a deep breath, and knocked on the door. There was no answer. He knocked again. No answer. Again! Again! No answer.

"Ofa, you home? It's Seamus. I'm here to say goodbye. Please Ofa, answer the door. I want you to be my girl."

It was 6:55 PM. His feeling for Ofa Hawkins had come full circle. He had professed his love to an empty house. He was free. Seamus stopped knocking. He searched for a pencil and paper but had none. Then he placed the rose on the doorstep of the girl he loved. He turned, didn't look back, ran to the bus, and left for the Marines.

*   *   *

Later that evening, Asa drove down Main Street in a black Coupe de Ville. He stopped at the red blinking light at the intersection of Alamo and Main. Asa had a virtuous soul but a pretentious heart. Such a car suited this conflicted preacher man. They stayed late at the dinner that honored Ofa's achievements. The clock on the '53 Caddy read 8:30 P.M. Ofa was tired, and she was tired of pretending to be happy.

It had been a busy day, filled with accolades, but none of it mattered. *Seamus never came to say goodbye. How could he not care?* She thought. They had promised to be friends forever, sealed it with their blood, and then buried their senior pins under the oak tree at the South Grape Creek. A blood brother promise lasts forever. But now there was Paul. She had to forget Seamus. There was Dartmouth, then medical school. Paul was everything Seamus wasn't. Tonight, she would close a chapter and would move on without Seamus O'Grady.

Her father interrupted. "Darlin'," he said in a kindly tone. "I hope you had a good time this evening; it was a beautiful celebration. I'm proud of you. But something's bothering me; you've not smiled all day. If there were something wrong, you'd tell me, wouldn't you?"

"Daddy, thanks for the fun night. I was a bit overwhelmed. Too much attention."

"Ofa, you're gonna do great things, just you wait. Follow God's will and accept His challenges."

Asa thought it was strange that his little girl would be overwhelmed by attention. The sun rose and set on Ofa Hawkins.

Asa began to speak but hesitated. He wasn't sure how she'd react to his next comment.

"Paul's coming over and wants to take you for a drive."

"Sure Dad," she said. "I'd like that."

Asa pressed the accelerator and drove through the signal on Alamo and Main.

She walked up the brick path toward the front door. Something lying on the step had caught her attention. Ofa moved closer; she saw a rose lit by a full Texas moon. It was a red rose.

"Daddy!" she screamed. Give me the keys to the car."

"Ofa, what's wrong darlin'?"

"Give me the keys! Just give me the keys."

"But!" Asa protested.

Then in a calm yet assertive voice, she said, "Don't ask Daddy. Just give me the goddamn keys."

Holding the rose, Ofa grabbed the keys, jumped into the car, and headed 72-miles east on Highway 290 toward Austin.

"That sweet darlin' boy," she whispered. "He gave me a red rose. He loves me, and I love him."

In her daddy's black Coupe de Ville, she drove like a demon to say goodbye to the boy she loved.

TWENTY-SIX

A BANKRUPT SOUL

Nothing is easier than self-deceit. For what every man wishes, that
he also believes to be true.

Demosthenes

June 18, 1965 – Luckenbach

Paul Bannister sat in the parlor, a formal room reminiscent of
the Victorian era where guests were greeted. The house at 7
Travis Street was a traditional southern mansion. It appeared somber
and stately, yet it represented the sensibilities of a man like Asa
Hawkins.

As the two men waited for Ofa, Paul's knee bounced with a
steady beat as if to suppress the anxious timbre of the room. Asa
couldn't explain why his daughter left in a frenzy; she had found
something on the doorstep. Whatever it was, she picked it up,
demanded the car keys, and sped out of town in the direction of
Austin. Neither man talked about why she ran off. But they both
knew why she did. They feared she'd find Seamus. Paul hadn't met
the boy, yet he feared him. He feared the power he had over her. But
mostly; he feared the power Seamus had over him. How could a
cowboy with no future and who barely graduated high school attract
a girl like Ophelia Hawkins? Paul was jealous of every thought she
had about the boy and wanted to rip Seamus from her mind. Paul
was intent on courting her, and of course, Asa was hoping he would
do just that. But Seamus O'Grady, this nothing of a boy, was in the
way.

"Professor Hawkins, don't you agree that a virtuous life should be a man's goal? The Greeks believed that virtue is essential for civilization."

Paul's attempt at breaking the silence between the men worked. The professor was impressed, but their conversation was a smoke screen for what they were thinking.

"Paul, would you consider yourself a religious man or a righteous man?" The professor asked.

Paul carefully answered the question as he was unsure what the professor wanted to hear.

"Professor, I'm a righteous man. I live my life with honor and integrity. But religion is important because it gives us the foundation to live righteously."

"Paul, you are a good man. You'll bring honor to law."

Austin Station – 9 P.M.

The Marine recruits came from all over Texas and gathered at track eight for the 10 o'clock train to South Carolina. There were ranch hands from Amarillo; cowboys from Pipe Creek, farmers from Muleshoe; fishermen from Galveston, scoundrels from Uncertain, and hayseed plowboys from Luckenbach. The boys waited on the platform anticipating their transformation from boys to men. But they were there for another reason. The Texas boys wanted to fight. It was their rite of passage, a strange way to become a man. Some of them would be dead within the year.

Carrying brown paper bags, Seamus and Elijah sat on a wooden bench.

"Hey Buckaroo, it's time to put up or shut up. No more bullshit 'bout wantin' to be a Marine. This is the real thing," Elijah said.

"Cowboy, we're either gonna do this, or we're gonna die."

Elijah looked at his best buddy and said, "Why are you so dramatic. I've heard Pops' stories all my life. That man lived on a grand stage, fightin' Poncho Villa in Mexico, the Hun in France, and bein' a Texas Ranger on the prairie. Well it's our turn now, and we're gonna have stories of our own," Elijah remarked. "Seamus bein' a Marine ain't about dyin', it's about livin' the values of the Corps – courage, honor, and commitment."

Seamus answered, "What stories we gonna have? We're goin' to boot camp and not become a character in a Sergeant Rock comic book."

"Seamus, you don't seem like a scaredy-cat no more."
"Elijah, I ain't. I ain't scart one bit."

Ofa was eight miles outside of Austin; it was 9:40 p.m. She was traveling faster than the road would allow. She would make it, but what would she say to Seamus? I love you. No, it'd be too much for him to handle; he wouldn't understand. I'll wait for you. No, that wouldn't do – too dramatic. She would say what was in her heart. Seamus O'Grady, I'm your girl. I've always been your girl.

Track 8 – Austin Station

"Seamus, don't look but that guy next to the post over there is so full of shit shootin' off his big mouth. I don't give a flyin' fuck how big he is; he's gettin' under my skin."

The boy from Uncertain, Texas bragged how he was going to be the Platoon honor man and kick everyone's ass.

"Who y'all looking at, Poncho?" the kid from Uncertain said to Elijah.

"Hey, fuckhead, if bullshit was money, y'all be a rich son of a bitch," Elijah countered.

Elijah clenched his fists and rose from the bench and approached the boy.

"I'm going to enjoy this." The boy said.

A young Sergeant stepped between the two angry boys, "Save it for the fucking gooks," he said.

The Sergeant turned to the boy from Uncertain, "What's your name?" The kid had an attitude and a cheeky smile.

"Joe Buck!"

The Sergeant didn't like bragging either.

"Who do you think you are, boy? John Fucking Wayne?"

Joe Buck got his nickname. John Wayne would stick.

"Let's go," the Sergeant commanded. Seamus and Elijah picked up their brown paper bags and boarded the Southern Star.

Ofa pulled into a no-parking zone and ran toward the ticket counter.

"Where's the train to South Carolina?" she screamed to the ticket agent.

"Missy, it's the Southern Star, track eight. You'd better hurry it's about to leave."

"Sir, which cars are the Marines in?"

"The last two."

Seamus sat by the window. It would give him a better chance to see Ofa just in case she came. *Surely, she would have gotten the rose and would've come to the station*, he thought.

"Seamus, if she ain't here by now, she ain't comin'."

"But we made a blood-brother promise that we'd be friends for life," Seamus said. "We sealed it with our blood."

Seamus became pensive and realized that having a girlfriend would require an understanding of life and love that he didn't have. *Maybe it ain't right for us to be together, he thought I'd be off to war and what would become of her if I didn't make it home? Maybe it's best we don't see each other*, he thought.

"Elijah, I don't want Ofa to ever know my feelings, it just ain't right. She ain't here, and I don't want nobody feeling sorry for me."

Seamus was unable to understand the moment and the things he thought mattered didn't matter. He closed his eyes and fell into a deep sleep.

After three whistle blasts, the Southern Star began to move; Ofa ran down the length of the platform.

"Seamus! Seamus! Someone stop the train!"

But the train wouldn't stop. As the last car sped by, she saw the boy she loved sleeping in a window seat on the Southern Star.

"Seamus!" she screamed. I'm your girl! I'll always be your girl!"

The train kept moving, and she watched the Southern Star disappear down the track.

"Missy, you okay?" the ticket agent asked.

She fell into the man's arms. Ofa had a way about her; people wanted to care for the pretty girl.

"I missed him. I love him. He's goin' to the Marines. I wasn't patient with him. He just needed time to understand his feelin's."

"There, there, Missy."

He stroked her hair trying to console a girl he didn't know.

"Why on earth does a pretty girl like you have such negative thoughts?" the agent said. "Darlin', life ain't over when you join the Marines. You'll see him again."

"But sir, you don't understand. Seamus is goin' to go to Vietnam. I'm afraid for him."

"Missy – fear – it's part of life. It's not meant to keep you from livin'; you keep livin' in spite of it. Fear keeps you focused, and sometimes it causes you to appreciate what you have. But if you don't know how to deal with fear, it becomes a slow death. Have faith; he'll be okay. The way you react is the way he'll react. And if you think he won't make it back then he'll think he won't make it back. And if he thinks like that, he'll do his time lookin' over his shoulder. That's not a way for a young man to do his duty."

Ofa nodded and pretended she understood.

"Find something bigger than you, something you can pour your heart into, something meaningful. He's found meanin' by becoming a Marine. Your fellow has joined to fight for freedom. You have to respect that," the agent said.

"Sir, I respect him joinin' up. But I told him I was mad cause it wasn't what I wanted. I should have supported him. I didn't want him fighin' in this immoral war; freedom has nothin' to do with it. It's a civil war and requires a political solution; not a military solution."

"Missy, you don't have to support the war, but you have to support your man, even if he's not your guy. Keep your feelin's 'bout the war and the men who fight it separate. The country is gonna fall apart, and they're gonna blame the soldier for everything that's bad. We send these boys to fight, and you mark my word, the country will turn its back on them."

"The reason I'm here has nothing to do with the war and him joinin' the Marines. We like each other, and it's been so for a long time. But we haven't been talkin'. It was just a misunderstandin', and I'm here to tell him, I'm his girl. But he's not my man. I wish he was, but he ain't. We couldn't get together. It's complicated. I need to say bye and let him know I'm his girl."

"Missy you're upset and confused. Send him a letter. Tell him you came to see him but you were too late."

"I guess you're right, sir. I'm just a tad bit overwhelmed and I ain't thinkin' straight."

"You feelin' better?" he asked.

"Sir, thanks for carin' for me. That's what I'll do; I'll send him a letter. My name's Ophelia Hawkins, but my friends call me Ofa."

"My name is Indiana."

"Like in the state?" she asked.

"Yes, Indiana Red. Kind of funny isn't it. After 50 years you get used to it. Missy, I have a daughter; she's probably a couple of years older than you. You remind me a lot of her. She studies at Columbia University in New York City and has these views on the war but never talks to me cause I don't believe the way she does. She joined the Students for a Democratic Society. They're against the war and everything that America stands for. Don't do that Ofa, don't be against your country. Don't throw America away because of Vietnam."

"Indiana, I'm not confused 'bout the war, but I don't understand my feelin's for Seamus. I didn't think I loved him. Maybe I'm just emotional. He left me a rose on my front porch. So, I drove from Luckenbach to Austin to see him. For the past six weeks, I've ignored him. I just feel so awful. For the life of me, I don't know why I acted like that. What's gonna become of us?"

"Why do young people have to be sure 'bout everything? You have to leave something' to chance. Have faith; life will work out the way it's supposed to. Ofa — sometimes life doesn't happen the way you plan it. I suppose it's easy to say life ain't fair. But life ain't either fair or unfair. Life is life. If it doesn't work out the way it's supposed to, you accept it and move on."

Ofa smiled; she had found peace in her feelings for Seamus.

"Missy maybe the way it worked out is the way it's supposed to be. The trouble with you kids today is that you want a perfect endin'. Life ain't about that. Some stories don't have a clear-cut beginning or end. Life's 'bout not knowin'. It's takin' the moment and makin' the best of it. Not knowin' makes you work harder. But ain't that where the glory is? It doesn't matter whether you love Seamus or not. There's a reason he gave you the rose, and I think you should go with that. You know, a red rose is a sign of love. Ofa, you don't need to know how your story ends. The magic is in the not knowing."

"Indiana — you've been wonderful. I'm sure God sent you durin' my time of need."

"Well, Miss Ofa Hawkins, I'm sure I'm gonna hear great things 'bout you."

"Thank you, Sir."

"You gonna be okay drivin' home?"

"Yes, I'll be okay," she said. "I'll pray for you and ask the Lord to bring your daughter back home."

It was a long drive back to Luckenbach. The blurry white lines of the highway mixed with thoughts of a young girl in love. Indiana Red made sense. Ofa didn't have to know how her story would end.

Main and Alamo Streets – Luckenbach

Ofa stopped at the red blinking light. She looked at the general store and watched the lights reflection bounce off the window. She pictured Seamus, Elijah, and herself sitting on the steps in the moonlight, drinking Coke, and eating pulled pork sandwiches. They were laughing and they were together. The light flashed, and she saw the last four years unfold and the changes she had made. She saw the changes Seamus couldn't make. She remembered the heartbreak in his eyes. What would she do about Seamus? What would she do about Paul? She liked Paul; he was good to her, and maybe he was even good for her. He made her feel like a woman. But her feelings for Seamus were eternal, and the rose told her what she wanted to know. She would tell Paul that she loved another boy.

She eased through the intersection of Main and Alamo then made a right on Travis Street. Paul's red Corvette gleamed under a blue June moon. She dried her eyes and searched for composure.

The men saw the lights flash in the driveway. Ofa grabbed the rose lying on the passenger seat. She opened the front door. Paul's heart was exploding in his chest. He rubbed his hands nervously and stared at the beautiful young woman standing in front of him holding a single red rose. He smiled. She gave him a polite grin. His eyes focused on the rose, and he knew, and then he gazed into her eyes.

"Oh – Ophelia – I've been worried about you," Paul said. "Thank God you're okay." He smiled. "I see you found the rose I left you.

TWENTY-SEVEN

LOST HOPE

Will that light come again?

As now these tears come . . . falling hot and real!

Elizabeth Barrett Browning, *Sonnets from the Portuguese*

June 18, 1965 – 7 Travis Street, Luckenbach

"A pretty rose for a pretty girl," Paul remarked.
He looked into her green eyes hoping she would acknowledge his lie. He was betting that Ofa missed the train. She couldn't possibly have made it to Austin in time to see Seamus.

"Did I make you smile Ophelia? Hope so."

He thought it was a gallant to do such a thing and he convinced himself that it was he who left it. But there was something, which made him uneasy. It was the disappointment in her eyes. Paul was a slave to her moods. He disliked seeing her despondent. But he was a selfish man and was only concerned about the effect her feelings would have on him.

She didn't want to believe what she had heard. It was Paul who placed the rose on her doorstep.

Asa stood and smiled at their exchange. Paul Bannister was exactly what his daughter needed to forget the cowboy who ran off to the Marines and hadn't had the decency to say goodbye.

"How about a glass of sweet tea?" Asa interjected. "I made it this afternoon."

Ofa remained silent, processing what she had heard.

"I'd love a glass," Paul said.

She sat down on the red velvet Queen Victorian chair. It had been specially chosen by her mother. Her hands were gently folded lying on her lap. Her legs were together, and the ruffles of her dress hung below her knees.

She had yet another disappointment to add to a tally that began four years earlier when her mother left. Asa loved his daughter, but a girl needs a mother in matters of the heart.

Pops had told her, "To be truly happy, you need something to hope for." Her dreams gave her hope, but there were no more dreams. Her eyes were bloodshot, and her heart was heavy. Oblivions to her feelings, the two men talked about the immorality of the Vietnam War. They cared about the bleeding world but not about the needing heart that sat quietly in the room – and all Asa could do was ask if she wanted a glass of sweet tea.

"Paul, thank you for the rose. It was sweet of you."

Paul was a calculating man, and he gambled that the worst didn't happen. Instead, the best happened, and now that Seamus was out of the way, Paul would win her heart. He wanted to possess the beautiful girl wearing the purple ribbon in her hair.

Paul asked as he set his glass on the marble-topped table, "Ophelia, would you go for a ride with me?"

"I'm sorry Paul. If you don't mind, I'm not feeling well – long day. Do you mind if we go tomorrow?"

"Not at all Ophelia. I'll be up-all-night waiting for tomorrow."

Paul said what she wanted to hear. Seamus would never say such things. He obviously moved on, and so would she. And Ofa smiled at Paul.

TWENTY-EIGHT

CROSSING THE BRAZOS

The gates of hell opened, and serpents oozed from its bowels.
And Cyclops and Minotaur heralded his arrival. And there stood
Beelzebub.

19 June 1965 – Savannah, Georgia

Savannah, Georgia was the end of the line for the Southern
Star. The Texas boys were a long way from home. Some had
never crossed the Brazos River. They had entered a world where
everything that once seemed so important, no longer did. Mere
existence would soon become tentative.

"Wake up Seamus; we're in Savannah."

"Georgia?" Seamus asked, straightening himself up to peer out
the window into the night and hoping to get a glimpse of unfamiliar
territory.

He continued, "I ain't never crossed the Brazos. I think we
should get a certificate like they give sailors when they cross the
Equator and see the Southern Cross."

Seamus checked his watch. It was 10 PM, 24 hours since they'd
left Austin. An old yellow bus parked at the train depot waited for
the unsuspecting Texas boys. I'm not rightly sure how a bus could be
sad, but it was distinctly melancholy. All it did was shuttle young men
from the train station to Parris Island. The old man in the driver's
seat sat sleeping with his head slumped on his chest. After
clambering down from the train, the boys gathered beneath a light,
which cast an eerie yellow glow. The beam filtered through scores of
mosquitoes and their flapping wings were a mere indication of what
was to come. They stood in the cool salty breeze of a blackened night
waiting for Beelzebub, the angel of death. Joe Buck referred to as

John Wayne, was the only one talking. To make sure no one had jumped ship, the young Sergeant took a quick headcount.

"John Wayne shut the fuck up," the Sergeant said to Buck. "I don't want to hear another sound from you."

The Sergeant walked to the bus and gently knocked on the door. A few seconds later the engine started, and the dim lights of the bus flickered. The door opened and beckoned its passengers to an uncertain fate.

"Let's go, boys," the Sergeant said. The Texas boys boarded the bus. No one except Elijah Bravo and Joe Buck smiled. There was something about those boys. Couldn't put my finger on it, but there was just something there.

Elijah was last to board; he appeared confident. During the ride to Paris Island, there was the usual bravado. Shrugging aside their earlier fears the boys bragged about how tough they were and how they would be great Marines. Everyone seemed anxious to go to Vietnam and fight the Viet Cong. Joe Buck boasted that he would be the Platoon guide, the position of honor reserved for the Platoon's top recruit.

The Texans joined the Marines for many reasons. Some joined to prove themselves, others to become men. Some because they wanted to fight or a judge gave them the alternative, jail or the Marines. Some because they had no place to go and the Marines offered three *hots and a cot.* Others joined because they needed shoes. But they had one thing in common; they wanted to be heroes. They were the sons of the greatest generation and wanted to be like their fathers whose stories of glory in France and the South Pacific would send some to an early grave.

After a time, the chatter aboard the bus ceased. Seamus gazed into the black night, and Elijah slept as though he was napping at the South Grape Creek on a lazy summer day.

Seamus shifted in his seat and pressed his head against the chilled window of the yellow bus. Ofa had not come to see him. He thought of the words of Wilfred Owen, "Dulce Et Decorum Est." But as smart as Ofa was, Seamus was convinced she was wrong.

MCRD — Paris Island

"We're here boys. Good luck," the driver shouted to his passengers.

You could cut the silence with a knife. Even Buck had shut up.

The boys gazed into the night trying to understand what was so horrific about Parris Island. Elijah Bravo remained sleeping. The bus crept toward the gate, and the boys read the red sign with yellow letters, United States Marine Corps Recruit Depot (*MCRD*), Parris Island, South Carolina.

The bus came to a stop, and the Texans experienced their last moments of peace before hell fell upon their souls. The door of the yellow bus opened, and their lives as recruits had begun. Three Sergeants jumped on board.

"Get outside; stand at attention on the yellow footprints," they screamed. "Do you understand? they yelled. "Move! Move! Move! You're too slow! Get outside! Get the fuck outside! Get out of my bus!"

The Texas boys stood on the fabled yellow footprints and watched as the bus drove away. It was their first formation and their first semblance as a team.

No one was immune from the abuse doled out by the men wearing the Smoky Bear hats, the trademark of the drill instructor.

Elijah wore a shit-eating grin wider than the Texas prairie. A *Drill Instructor* (D.I.) grabbed him by the collar and yelled, "What's so funny you fucking puke?"

The Sergeant continued to scream.

"Get on the deck! Get on the motherfucking deck you maggot! Move! Give me 50."

"50 of what Sarge?"

It was an honest remark; Elijah didn't mean anything by it. Calling a Marine Sergeant, Sarge was tantamount to death. Sergeant Yanik would make it his personal mission to break this brash Mexican kid from Luckenbach, Texas. Elijah cranked off 50 pushups. The Sergeant had never before seen a recruit fresh from the bus do 50 perfect pushups and do them within the blink of an eye.

"What's your name boy," screamed Yanik.

"Elijah –" It was an honest reply.

He grabbed him by the collar and screamed, "What's the first word out of your mouth?"

"Sergeant!" Elijah screamed.

Yanik punched Elijah in the stomach to give him a subtle reminder what the first word should be.

"The first word out of your mouth is: Sir! Do you understand that you fuckin maggot?"

"Sir, yes Sir," he said – grinning.

Throughout the remainder of the night, the Texas boys received their uniforms, haircuts, bunks, lockers, and equipment. They were preparing for three months of hell. Trying to break Elijah, the Sergeants continued to pick on him. Regardless, he became stronger. He had *that* Elijah Bravo *'fuck you'* look on his face. On the first night of boot camp, the D.I.'s took it as their personal mission to wipe the grin off Bravo's face. *Is that all you got?* That knowing grin implied. The drill instructors threatened that the Texas boys would be punished on recruit Bravo's behalf if he continued to grin. Elijah stopped grinning, but that didn't mean the D.I.'s stopped punishing him.

The boys had been up all night, and in the morning, the recruits were standing like three rows of tall corn in front of their Quonset hut, their corrugated metal home away from home. They were waiting to meet their senior drill instructor. Throughout the evening, rumors spread that he was nine feet tall and had killed three recruits the previous series. John Wayne's leadership had impressed the screaming Sergeants. He was a brute and set the example by intimidation and making the recruits fear him. But he got the job done. The drill instructors made him the Platoon guide, the leader of Platoon 6586 and it was exactly what he said would happen.

"Platoon, A Tennnn Hut!" John Wayne screamed.

Platoon 6586 came to attention. The junior drill instructors (*JDI*), Sergeants Yanik and Poweda were all over the Texas boys finding fault with the smallest detail. After an endless onslaught of abuse, the gates of hell opened, and hordes of serpents oozed from its bowels, and Cyclops and Minotaur heralded his arrival. There stood Beelzebub, the Senior Drill Instructor.

He wasn't nine feet tall, but he looked it. He had a narrow waist, broad shoulders, and was built like a brick wall. His uniform was impeccable and pressed with well-defined creases, making him appear perfect. He was a black man standing confident and almighty under the traditional Smoky the Bear cover of the United States Marine Corps drill instructor. He made the boys wish they'd stayed home with their mommas.

"My same is Staff Sergeant B. A. D. Mothershed. You are in my Marine Corps, but you are not Marines. Most of you will never earn the title of a United States Marine because I will break you and send you home to your mama. If you do not excel under my standards, I will make you suffer, and no one will hear you scream from the Squad bay. You are fucking pukes. You maggots, the shit, has hit the fan. And the shit rolls downhill, and you're on the bottom of that hill. When I say jump, you will ask, how high. Do you understand that?"

The Texas Boys screamed, "Yes Sir."

"I can't hear you," Mothershed bellowed.

"Yes, Sir," they tried again.

"The first word out of your mouth is: Sir. Do you understand that? If you so much as displease me, I will go up your ass and come out your ear. Do you understand that?"

"Yes Sir!"

Staff Sergeant Mothershed peered into the souls of the Texas boys. His anger disguised the concern he had for the boys he would train. He loved them enough to teach them the skills that would keep them alive when they met the yellow man who waited for them in Vietnam. He gazed at the recruits, shook his head in disgust, threw his clipboard, turned, and walked off the drill field. Three months was a long time, and it would give Mothershed an opportunity to break the ones who would break. But these were Texas boys; some of their great granddaddies were at the Alamo. Mothershed might have underestimated his recruits.

August 1965

The Sergeants continued to harass Elijah Bravo for the slightest infraction. When they needed a whipping boy, they chose Elijah. Maybe it was because of his brown skin. The Marine Corps was not the most progressive of societies. Regardless of the insipid tasks they gave Elijah, he'd do them, with the little effort, and with a subtle grin. On the other hand, Seamus was the pet of the drill instructors. Everything he did was perfect. It didn't take long for the boys to look toward Seamus for example.

During the sixth week of boot camp, Staff Sergeant Mothershed held a meeting with Yanik, Poweda, and Crider.

"Staff Sergeant Mothershed, that Bravo kid is the best recruit I've seen," Yanik said. "He's an insolent motherfucker, but he's a Marine's Marine. I think we should shape him into a leader. John

151

Wayne's the meanest motherfucker in the valley, but that Bravo is our honor man, and I don't see no two ways about it."

Mothershed reflected and pulled on a Chesterfield. "Bravo doesn't want the limelight like Buck. He's a reluctant leader. You gotta give the job to the guy who wants it. But I think we're overlooking O'Grady. He doesn't have the physicality of John Wayne or Bravo but he does everything perfectly, he's our most responsible guy, and the Platoon respects him."

"O'Grady's not tough enough," Crider said. "He's too quiet. They respect him because he's a nice guy and is always helping everyone. That don't mean shit. No way he takes the guidon from John Wayne. The real fight is between Bravo and Buck. John Wayne would kill O'Grady."

"Staff Sergeant Mothershed, I'd like to see O'Grady have a crack at it," Poweda said. "Leadership isn't about being the toughest. That's Old Corps shit. The leader is the guy who knows his stuff and who the other guys respect. O'Grady is the quiet leader; he's confident and capable and doesn't shove it in everyone's face. O'Grady is the real deal. But we'll go easy on Bravo."

John Wayne continued to dominate the Platoon, but Elijah Bravo was the better man. However, in combat, the men would follow Seamus O'Grady.

*　　*　　*

"Barlow, ya dumb fuck."

The boy had screwed up for the third time that morning. The Platoon went left, and Barlow went right. Sergeant B.A.D. Mothershed had lost his patience.

The Marine Corps is unforgiving. Abuse is the foundation of the legendary relationship between the drill instructor and the recruit. The rite of passage mandates that the young Marine navigate through boot camp and surmount the unrealistic demands placed upon him by their guardians. The drill instructor demands perfection and shows no mercy until the recruit develops the wherewithal to continue the invincible ethos of his Marine Corps.

"Listen, you puke, I'm tired of you fucking up. It's your military left. Do you understand that?"

Not every recruit could distinguish the difference between left and right. Since there was only one left, the Marines called it the military left.

"Barlow fallout."

The Private dropped his weapon and ran toward Staff Sergeant Mothershed.

"No motherfucker, don't drop your weapon. Never drop your weapon."

Mothershed leaned into Barlow's ear and screamed. "Squat thrusts, forever, and ever, and ever."

Barlow replied, "Sir! Squat thrusts forever, and ever, and ever, Sir!"

Earnest Barlow was a screw-up who would not learn from his mistakes; consequently, Mothershed was determined to drive him out of his Marine Corps. Barlow lacked discipline, focus, and the will to do what was required to learn the craft of a Marine. He cared little about the team. He was first in line for chow and first to rest. The D.I.'s didn't believe he'd honor the trust of protecting his brothers in a fight. When it came to changing the attitude of a fuck-up, the Marine Corps is not creative. Therefore, there was only one solution, punishment.

Each night Staff Sergeant Mothershed made the lives of Platoon 6586 unbearable. After returning from an exhausting day in the field, they'd find their Squad-bay torn apart with wall lockers overturned and personal gear strewn throughout the barracks. The Platoon cleaned rifles until early morning and then rose at 0400 for a five-mile run.

John Wayne continued his reign as the Platoon guide. Wherever 6586 marched, he carried the guidon; it was proof that he was indeed the meanest mother in the valley. It would be up to him to square away Barlow. Until Barlow changed or was driven out of the Corps, Mothershed would continue his onslaught on the Platoon.

In the Corps, there was an old remedy that often changed the behavior of a recruit. The drill instructor would beat the recruit until his behavior changed. Barlow was punched, humiliated, and harassed by Mothershed, Yanik, and Crider. But nothing changed. Sergeant Poweda, however, would have nothing to do with such abuse.

In practice though, a Marine's peers initiated the worst punishment – a blanket party, a combination of physical abuse and humiliation used to square away recruits whose mistakes caused the displeasure of the D.I. Humiliation is the ultimate punishment. It takes away a man's dignity. In the middle of the night, the disgruntled Marines would throw a blanket over the unsuspecting recruit. The men would place a bar of soap in a sock and repeatedly beat the Marine. It was Platoon justice. Until the Marine either quit or changed, he would be beaten. John Wayne decided the Platoon would square away Barlow with a blanket party.

"We got to do something about that motherfucker, because of him, we're getting our asses kicked. I'm tired of it," John Wayne said.

John Wayne was a brute, but regardless he was a good Marine, and the men listened to him. Barlow was screwing up under his watch, and if he were to continue to hold the position of Platoon guide, it would be up to him to correct the situation.

"Listen, we're doin' it tonight," he said. "You fuckin' pukes that don't have the balls better fall in on this. If you don't join me, I'm gonna punch you out. You understand that?"

The Texas boys nodded, except Seamus O'Grady.

"John Wayne, that ain't gonna happen," Seamus said. "You're not goin' to turn the Platoon into a bunch of animals. If we do that – who are we? That Semper Fi you got tattooed on your arm ain't shit if you order that."

"Listen up Seamus O'Fuckin' O'Grady, this is my Platoon so shut the fuck up, or it's gonna be you and me, and you ain't gonna like that."

"You're gonna have to kick my ass, Joe. But as long as I'm standin' we ain't gonna do this."

Elijah got up from the footlocker and said in a calm voice, "Buck, you're gonna have to get through me first before you tangle with Seamus. I agree with him. This ain't gonna happen. You took an oath to care for your Marines. What the fuck you think Semper Fi means?"

"You're a Mexican puke, Bravo."

"Yeah, I guess I am – you're all talk Buck."

"You're a dick Bravo."

Elijah smiled. "Yeah Buck, I'm Moby Goddamn Dick, and you just swam in my water."

John Wayne swung at Elijah. He'd been waiting for this moment since the night the boys almost came to blows on platform eight at Austin Station. He swung wildly; Elijah ducked. John Wayne swung again and again he missed.

"John Wayne, I don't want to fight you. But if I have to, I'll kick your ass."

Again, John Wayne swung and missed. This time, Elijah

countered with two sharp punches to the face; he then buried his head into John Wayne's chest driving him into the wall locker. John Wayne went down hard.

"Stay down!" Elijah commanded.

Buck got up from the deck and charged again. Elijah sidestepped and with one punch to the jaw, he put Joe Buck on the floor.

"Buck, don't make me fuck you up. We'll end it right here. But Seamus is right; you ain't gonna do that to Barlow."

Buck tried to continue the fight but was bleeding from both his mouth and nose and couldn't stand straight. He had been challenged and had lost. The Platoon guide, the position of honor would now belong to Elijah Bravo.

The Texas boys didn't believe what they had seen. Elijah Bravo had toppled the giant from Uncertain, Texas.

"You okay," Elijah asked.

John Wayne said nothing. He walked over to his wall locker. On the side was the coveted guidon of Platoon 6586. He had been dethroned and was compelled by tradition to hand over the guidon to Elijah Bravo. With his eyes on the ground, he carried the Platoon flag to the new Platoon guide.

"Bravo, this is yours now; you'll be a damn good guide."

Elijah stood in front of the Texas boys holding the guidon that was rightfully his. He'd challenged John Wayne's leadership and took him down.

"Hey John Fuckin' Wayne, I didn't do that to become the guide. There are better ways to square away a man than to beat him. Listen, you've led us this far, and us Texas boys are a damn good Platoon. I don't want this guidon; it belongs to you. You're still the guide, and I think I speak for everyone, we want you to lead us."

"Elijah, I don't…"

"Don't say nothing," Elijah said. "Take the guidon and be a Marine and take care of your men, all of your men. Remember – Texas forever!" Elijah cheered.

And the boys of 6586 responded, "Living large!"

"Any ideas of how we can turn Barlow around?" John Wayne asked.

"Yeah, I think I can do it, Seamus said. Joe, assign him to me, and I'll be on top of his ass. Every time he moves, I'll be there. I'll make sure he's squared away."

"Roger that Seamus. You got 'em," John Wayne said.

Seamus' physical fitness scores were among the highest, he'd mastered drill, had the best shooting scores, passed all inspections, and was the first to lend a hand when needed. Seamus would straighten out Barlow and get Mothershed off their backs.

Seamus and Barlow did everything together. By the end of the fourth month of boot camp, Barlow began to improve. He was passing inspections, completing the runs, and had qualified on the rifle range. He could hang with the Texans boys, and for the first time in his life, he realized he had value. He began to understand that his success was dependent on the Platoon's success. Barlow realized he would wind up in Vietnam, and if he was going to survive, he had better pull his weight.

In the Marine Corps, the leader is responsible for everything that happens and everything that doesn't happen. Barlow's transformation was a credit to the Platoon guide, Joe Buck. But Mothershed, Yanik, Poweda, and Crider realized the hayseed plowboys from the Hill Country had turned the Platoon around, and 6586 was in contention for honor Platoon. The Texas boys had come together, and Staff Sergeant Mothershed had backed off, and anticipated the day he would call them Marines.

TWENTY-NINE

GIRL IN THE AUSTIN AMERICAN STATESMAN

The journey looms before me dear – I see it plain and clear.
Beasts and Mongrels will try and stop me – but girl, I'll always
come for you.

September 1965

"**Jesus H. Christ!**" **Jimmy Fields exclaimed. "Look at the tits on this peacenik.** Now that's a piece of ass. You can see her nipples cause she ain't wearing no bra."

"Let me see that. Pass the paper," Cestone asked.

"Yep, I see 'em, right through that flimsy blouse. Son of a bitch. Look what we're missing. We're cleaning these rifles, getting ready to get our asses shot up, and those fucking peaceniks are with broads like this."

"I hear those girls are easy – free love," Fields commented.

The Texas boys were disassembling the M-14, getting ready for an inspection they would inevitably fail. Nothing was good enough under the watchful eye of Staff Sergeant Mothershed.

"When I get out of the green suck, I'm joining the Students for a Democratic Society and get me one of these girls," Ashcraft said.

"Ashcraft, what makes you think a white girl is going to go for a blood?" Wood questioned.

Staff Sergeant Mothershed didn't allow pictures of women in the Platoon. However, disregarding the warnings of the drill instructors, some of the boys hid photos of girlfriends in their footlockers, or in the cavity of their helmets. When caught, and they always were, they paid a severe price. Mothershed believed pictures of women made them weak and kept them from focusing on the mission of becoming killers. What he had to teach the Texas boys would be the difference between life and death.

The Marines were passing a copy of the Austin American-Statesman around the barracks. Other than the daily misery of boot camp, the image of the beautiful girl gave the boys something to think about. A moment staring at a beautiful woman in a newspaper was a respite from their daily ordeal.

Stories about knights and their ladies spoke of love, loyalty, and courage. Knights needed a beautiful woman to be the object of their devotion. It was courtly love, a relationship between a warrior and the lady he served. A knight's love for the lady would inspire him to be brave and do great deeds in battle. Storming castles, slaying foes, and protecting the weak would make him worthy of her love.

The Marines were knights of a different era and bound by the same code of chivalry from the 12th century. They were to protect the weak, serve their Lord, be loyal, honorable, and above all have courage. Having a lady to dedicate their suffering would make their sacrifice meaningful.

The beautiful girl in the paper was their lady for the moment; The crude remarks were merely bravado. If she were in their presence, she would be their queen. Even though the girl in the paper was a hippy, the men would die for her.

The Texas boys passed the picture and, admired every curve of her body. But Seamus had no interest; he sat stoically next to Barlow helping him break down the 14 and making sure every component of his rifle was oiled and clean.

"Seamus, take a look at this girl," John Wayne yelled. "I ain't never seen a girl so damn pretty. I'm gonna marry her one day even if she's a peacenik."

"John Wayne, you're married to the Marine Corps," Barlow said. "You never even saw a girl with all her teeth."

Ignoring Barlow's remark, Buck continued. "Seamus, ain't you made of flesh and blood like the rest of us?"

Seamus was not swayed by peer pressure.

John Wayne passed the paper to Bob Wood.

He stared at her picture and said, "Son of a bitch. She's hotter than a biscuit. I love the purple ribbon in her hair."

Seamus dropped the trigger housing of Barlow's M-14. His eyes tore through Wood. He rose from his footlocker and ripped the paper from Wood's hands.

"Stop! Bob, shut your mouth 'bout her." Seamus turned and walked out of the barracks clutching the Austin American-Statesman with the picture of Ofa Hawkins on the front page.

"Elijah, what the fuck's up with Seamus?" Fields asked.

"Un-fucking-believable. Don't take it personal," Elijah said "but the girl in the paper – the Girl with the Purple Ribbon – she's from Luckenbach. She and Seamus liked each other in high school, and he ain't over her. We were friends but went in different directions. We joined the Marines, and she went to Dartmouth and became a peacenik. Her name's Ofa Hawkins."

"How did he know it was her?" Wood asked.

"It's the purple ribbon. His granddaddy said she began wearing it on graduation day and had worn it every day since. Seamus and me didn't go to graduation cause we was out fishing at the South Grape Crick. But sure 'nuff that's when she first wore it."

"I had no idea. I'm going outside to apologize." Wood said. "I feel like hell; I don't want to hurt a guy like Seamus."

"Give him a little time Bobby; he's got a lot of feelings 'bout her. It's hard for him. But he's okay. You know, Seamus can be a little righteous and sometimes he's as sensitive as a baby."

Seamus sat on the bleachers overlooking the drill field. He didn't understand his feelings, but he would battle dragons for her and carry her to his castle. He would always come for her. He starred at the picture of Ofa Hawkins holding a sign that read, "Get out of Vietnam."

THIRTY

GIRL WITH THE PURPLE RIBBON

The only way to survive in this world is by keeping alive our dream, without ever fulfilling it, since the fulfillment never measures up to what we imagine.

Fernando Pessoa

1965 – 1969

Life is like a river, and the river travels a continuous path, and yet it forever changes. Ofa Hawkins was the river and destined to follow her fate, but she wasn't ready for the changes that waited. We can try to change our fate, but it wouldn't be fate if we could change it.

Asa taught her that it was sinful to tempt the hand of fate. Fate was the Lord's will. "What's written, is written," he preached. He believed God had a plan, and if she'd listen to the Lord, He'd shine his divine light on the path she was destined to follow. "Whatever God wills," her daddy said. But she left her daddy in Luckenbach, and she had a different idea of the path she'd travel. Fate wasn't written unless she wrote it. She was a dreamer, and because she was a dreamer, she stayed on a course she had set when she first read of Dr. Tom Dooley's exploits in Southeast Asia.

But Ofa had stopped dreaming, and life had lost its color, and yet she remained true to the spiritual roots Asa taught her. That was both a blessing and a curse. "Thy will be done," she prayed. Acceptance gave her peace. She used the Lord's will to rationalize the choices she made. In her journal, she wrote a thought from Joseph Conrad's *Heart of Darkness*, "It was written I should be loyal to the nightmare of my choice." And she was that – loyal to the nightmare of her choice. She began to fear that man's potential to make the world beautiful would not materialize; thus, she fell into a dark place.

Paul transferred to Colby-Sawyer College in New London, New Hampshire. He was insecure about his relationship with Ofa; consequently, he attended a school nearby to make sure he stayed in her heart. Although he treated her like a princess, she would trade it to ride a pony through the Texas Hill Country.

She was a brilliant student, destined for medical school and had found her passion in the anti-war movement. She was determined to change the world, but it would've been better if she changed herself. But for Ofa, it was easier to change the world. The ancient Greeks would have called her a "Child of the Gods." Quixotic! She sought what humanity was incapable of – perfection. Those who attempted to achieve perfection were destined to fail. Regardless, Ofa Hawkins believed she could stop the war, and those lofty ideas became expectations. She became a symbol of the peace movement, known as Girl with the Purple Ribbon.

"When Jesus appeared before Pilot," she explained, "the Romans cloaked Him in a purple robe. Purple represents sorrow and pain, and that's what the Vietnam War will bring."

*   *   *

In February 1965, President Johnson escalated American involvement and ordered Operation Rolling Thunder, a bombing campaign against the North. Ironically, he told Secretary of Defense Robert McNamara, "I don't see anything that is going to be as bad as losing, but I don't see any way of winning." A week later he sent a Battalion of Marines to guard the airstrip in Da Nang and said, "The great trouble I'm under is that a man can fight if he can see daylight down the road. But there isn't any daylight in Vietnam. There's not a bit." In public, he portrayed confidence, "America wins the wars she undertakes. Make no mistake about it." However, in private, Vietnam became his nightmare. He told his wife, Ladybird, "I can't get out of Vietnam, and I can't finish it with what I have. I don't know what to do."

He committed the nation to war, and yet he believed the war was not winnable.

November 2, 1965 – Washington D.C.

The wind blew from the Potomac River and carried a wet chill that cut the faces of the students protesting the war in front of the Pentagon. Defying the Washington police, Ofa stood her ground. Her focus moved from the police to the crowd, and then to a suite of windows, the Pentagon office of Secretary of Defense, Robert McNamara.

"Funny," she said to Paul, she then pointed. "Why would that man standing in the street bring a baby to a peace rally?"

She watched the man hand the baby to a bystander. He then calmly walked to the center of the street, knelt on the pavement, doused himself with gasoline, and set himself ablaze. Norman Morrison, a Quaker from Baltimore sacrificed himself protesting American involvement in the Vietnam War. Morrison was a husband, a father, and he burnt himself to death under the Pentagon window of Robert McNamara. The war began to tear the country apart; Americans were questioning U.S. involvement, and opposition to the war grew. America became polarized. One either was a hawk, a dove, or part of the silent majority. Ofa Hawkins, Girl with the Purple Ribbon, would do her part for peace.

March 21, 1967 – Washington D.C.

In 1967, Ofa and 100,000 citizens demonstrated against the war in Washington D.C. The students chanted, "Ho, Ho, Ho Chi Minh, the *NFL* (National Liberation Front) is going to win." She was in the front of the melee inserting flowers into the muzzles of the soldiers' rifles. The chant became progressively louder, "Ho, Ho, Ho Chi Minh, the NLF is going to win."

The National Liberation Front, called the Viet Cong, was the political and military name of the armed insurrection, which attempted to eradicate the South Vietnamese Government.

"Stop that chant," she screamed at the students. "Stop it! What are you saying?"

"Ophelia, what's wrong?" Paul asked. "If the Viet Cong wins, the war will stop. You want that, don't you? Remember what your father said, 'To get the point across your voice must be extreme.' Look at Jesus and the apostles. They took the work of God as far as they could, and they changed the world."

"Paul, how can I want the Viet Cong to win," she cried. "We're here to stop the war. Not support a North Vietnamese victory. I'm not a traitor. Can't we love our country but hate the war? I grew up with patriotic folk. I don't want the Viet Cong to win."

The students were attempting to block traffic on the Arlington Memorial Bridge connecting the National Mall to Arlington, Virginia. *Students for a Democratic Society* (SDS) held hands, and screamed, "Death to America" and Ofa cried in the middle of a road called the Avenue of Heroes, as she stood between two monuments representing valor and sacrifice.

"Am I a traitor to my country? Let's work to stop the war but not for America to lose. If the North wins, friends will die," she pleaded.

The juxtaposition of peace and war began to take its toll on America. The anti-war movement played into the hands of the enemy and weakened American resolve to prosecute the war. Subsequently, it strengthened the will of the North. Ofa tore the flowers from her hair and ran down the Avenue of Heroes.

Paul detested the soldiers; he believed they were killing the innocent. The peace movement was a slap in the face to the boys who went to fight. Paul needed to remain in Ophelia's good graces, so he told her what she wanted to hear.

* * *

In 1968, Presidential candidate Richard Nixon spoke of a victorious peace in Vietnam. He later rephrased his position saying, "I pledge to you that we shall have an honorable end to the Vietnam War." When Nixon took office in 1969, the United States had been at war for nearly four years; more than 30,000 Americans had lost their lives. Meanwhile, the President struggled to find a way for the United States to leave Vietnam, a conflict that former President Johnson said, "Wasn't worth it and he couldn't see a way out."

The war wasn't going well for the North Vietnamese. However, on 30 January 1968, the Tet Holiday, Vietnamese Lunar New Year, the hammer fell. Enemy forces launched the Tet Offensive. More than 82,000 enemy soldiers attacked 100 cities and towns in the south. They captured Hue, the capital of the northern sector of South Vietnam and brought the war to Saigon, and to the United States Embassy. At home, Americans watched in horror as the bloody spectacle unfolded on their television screens. Although, Tet was a communist defeat, the spectacle of their effort undermined domestic support for the war. Instead of being resolute after a stunning victory, American resolve to win the war diminished.

After a fact-finding mission to Vietnam, Walter Cronkite, America's most respected journalist presented his findings in a one-hour evening broadcast. Cronkite, who had been an advocate of the war, now questioned the credibility of American politicians who saw the silver lining in the darkest clouds. On the nightly news, he read from his report:

> To say that we are closer to victory today is to believe, in the face of the evidence, the optimists who have been wrong in the past. To suggest we are on the edge of defeat is to yield to unreasonable pessimism. To say that we are mired in stalemate seems the only realistic, yet unsatisfactory, conclusion. On the off chance that military and political analysts are right, in the next few months we must test the enemy's intentions, in case, this is indeed his last big gasp before negotiations. But it seems increasingly clear to this reporter, that the only rational way out will be to negotiate, not as victors, but as honorable people, who lived up to their pledge to defend democracy and did it the best way they could.

On November 15, 1969, 500,000 demonstrators protested in Washington D.C., the Moratorium. President Nixon said:

> Now I understand that there has been and continues to be opposition to the war in Vietnam on the campuses and also in the nation. As far as this kind of activity is concerned, we expect it; however, under no circumstance will I be affected by it.

Nixon ignored 500,000 Americans protesting the war. It would take almost four years to find his peace with honor. In 1973, the terms of the Paris Peace Accords were the same terms that we could have had in 1968.

Back in Luckenbach, the old men sat around the potbelly stove staring at a picture of Ofa wearing a purple ribbon and protesting the war.

THIRTY-ONE

TOUCHING THE WORLD

At the end of the fight is a tombstone white with the name of the
late deceased and the epitaph drear: A fool lies here who tried to
hustle the East.

Rudyard Kipling, *The Naulahka a Story of West and East*

May 1967 – Today Show, New York City

"Miss Hawkins, we roll in two minutes. Dear, don't be
nervous," Barbara Walters asked.

Barbara Walters was the icon of American news and had
interviewed kings, presidents, and the Beatles. She was a cold woman
yet was sweet to the pretty girl who sat in the studio with perfect
composure.

"Why no Ma'am," Ofa commented. "I'm not the least bit
nervous; I'm actually anxious to do this. It's important for peace."

Ofa was about to appear on the Today Show, the most widely
viewed news program in the world, and wasn't the least bit frazzled.
She was a poster girl of the peace movement but didn't care much
for national attention. Whether she was speaking at a teach-in,
carrying a protest sign, or shouting down the National Guard, the
Girl with the Purple Ribbon intended to stop the Vietnam War.

The producer whispered, "Barbara, she gets one segment, let's see
if she can deliver. She looks like one of those ranting college hippies
who have no clue about life beyond the university."

"I'm not so sure," Miss Walters commented. "I can't put my
finger on it, but I think the girl has something to say. She's calm and
composed. That's unusual. You have to admit she's beautiful; a girl
like that could help our ratings. Let's hope she can deliver."

The studio lights flashed. The director motioned, "five... four... three... two... one..." He pointed to Barbara Walters.

"May I call you Ofa," Barbara asked. "I understand that's the name you used in childhood."

"Miss Walters, I now go by the name Ophelia. Ofa was a long time ago, and I hardly remember who she was. Yesterday's gone, and all we truly have is today. I appreciate if you refer to me as Ophelia."

"Very well Ophelia, but may I comment? Instead of running toward the future, you seem as though you are running from a past."

"Miss Walters, with all due respect y'all asked my permission to comment and y'all commented before I gave you permission to do so."

The producer smiled. The young woman was more than a beautiful face.

"You're right about that, and I apologize." Barbara Walters paused and moved anxiously in her seat.

"It's a pleasure to have you on the *Today Show*. You're becoming a national celebrity – Girl with the Purple Ribbon. How do you feel about that?"

Ofa became irritated. She became famous because she tried to stop men from dying. It was fame she didn't want.

"Miss Walters, celebrity – that's not important to me. I've become famous because I try to stop men from dyin'. What's important is endin' the Vietnam War. I trust you'll conduct this interview with that point in mind."

"Very well Ophelia, the Students for a Democratic Society (SDS) are calling the United States colonialists. They say we want their natural resources, markets, and military bases in Southeast Asia. Do you believe we're colonialists?"

"First of all, Miss Walters, I'm no longer a member of the Students for a Democratic Society. And no – I don't believe we're colonialists. But we have a sordid past. American was born in genocide, and we harbor the guilt of ethnic hatred. I believe we're the only nation, which attempted to exterminate its indigenous people. Much of our culture lauds the conflict between the White European and the Native American. The Native American is the true American. To understand the glorification of this conflict, y'all have to watch a John Wayne movie."

"Ophelia, do you believe we're the evil empire that groups like the SDS claim us to be?" Barbra Walters asked.

"Why no Miss Walters, I didn't say that nor did I infer it; I'm merely speakin' of the big picture and tryin' to reference my comments within the context of American history. We're not the evil empire the SDS makes us out to be. After the French defeat at Dien Bien Phu, colonialism died. The war is political, and if we're guilty of anything, we're guilty of imperialism. It's not to occupy land or impose our will but to safeguard our interests and the survival of our ideology. For sure, it's to influence our geo-political position in the world. But it's posturin' against the communists. I'm afraid our politicians have duped America."

Barbra Walters smiled. She liked the brassy young woman and was surprised by the depth of her understanding of the world.

"Ophelia, then is it your contention that imperialism promotes one's political philosophy?"

"Yes, I believe it does. But sometimes it's imperialism that ensures the nation's survival. We've bought into the absurd idea that if Vietnam falls to communism, sure 'nuff, the surroundin' countries will fall. It's the 'Domino Theory.' President Eisenhower coined the phrase domino when he suggested that the fall of French Indochina would create a domino effect, whereby other countries would become communist. Presidents Kennedy and Johnson also bought into this philosophy, and now we're involved in an immoral war. The war is unwinnable. President Johnson himself said that. This is a political war whereby North Vietnam wants to drive out all foreign intervention and unite both Vietnams. There's no military solution, only a political solution. The strategic importance of Vietnam is vastly exaggerated, and furthermore, the nationalism driving Vietnam's history and politics can't be altered by U.S. military power, no matter how great."

"Ophelia, you have parted ways with the SDS May I ask why?" Miss Walters asked?

"I am called divisive because I don't support the American political agenda to wage war in Vietnam. I have been called a traitor. I'm told I'm not a patriot. Those are harsh words for a girl from Texas. They call me a dove. A hippie!" Ofa Hawkins looked Barbra Walters straight in the eye. " I   a m   a n   A m e r i c a n p a t r i o t ! I am concerned about American life and American resources. I'm concerned about all life, even the lives of the enemy. I support the soldiers, but I don't support the war. The SDS don't support the American soldier. They want to see America lose. I want to end the war. So, Miss Walters – tell me why am I not a patriot because I have my opinions? Ma'am, is it unpatriotic to protest against policies brought forth on our behalf? No ma'am, it's most patriotic."

"Ophelia, you defend your position with considerable depth. You're not typical of students in the peace movement. What's your take on today's headlines that according to General Westmoreland, 'there's a light at the end of the tunnel?'"

"Ma'am," Ofa paused and reached for the glass of water. "Vietnam has a genius for surprise, a gift for defeatin' the slightest expectation that the war is winnable. Rudyard Kipling's verse is the antithesis of the General's summation. Kipling said, "At the end of the fight is a tombstone white with the name of the late deceased and the epitaph drear: A fool lies here who tried to hustle the East." Miss Walters the war is not winnable. Westmoreland is deceivin' the American people by constantly holdin' the carrot. Americans continue to fall for his outlandish and unfounded statements. How can anyone be silent when American boys are dyin'? Silence is indifference. Our boys bleed while Americans are preoccupied with the design of next year's Chevrolet. The administration hangs their hat on public opinion that favors the war. The administration places its rationale to wage this war on groups of Americans that are invisible to public opinion. If someone is silent and if they're indifferent, then why do they have a voice? Why then do American politicians continue this senseless war in the name of those who don't speak out? The war is not winnable because we are losin' the hearts and minds of the Vietnamese People. Westmoreland's war of attrition and his body counts will not work. The enemy is fixin' to sustain heavy losses to meet their objectives. We'll eventually lose our stomach for this war because the American public is not willin' to sacrifice like the Vietnamese."

"The Marines recently won significant victories on Hills 861, 881-North and 881-South. Don't you think that's progress? The New York Times said it was a glorious victory," Barbara Walters commented.

"Miss Walters – Please – if y'all are to assess an event, you must look at it its entirety. The paper also said 155 Marines died in the battle, and the enemy slipped away. To me, the loss of 155 American boys is not a victory. Is that progress? Y'all need to re-evaluate what you consider satisfactory progress. May I remind you, the Vietnam

War will destroy more than those who are killed. War wounds everyone. A body bag contains more than its intended corpse. When soldiers die, the livin' go with them. The nation will follow the dead. Our conscience and the image of what America was and what it stands for will also be shipped home in a body bag."

"Dear, you paint a dismal future for America. Do you think you're too pessimistic?" Walters asked.

"Ma'am, I hope y'all said that for the sake of conversation because the Vietnam War is takin' us to a new era. The decisions we're fixin' to make, and their result are not black or white. There'll not be a definitive line between who the good guys are and who the bad guys are. Sure 'nough, our vision of the world will become gray. There's no longer simple answers, no simple solutions. It's not good enough to say, send the Marines."

"Ophelia, I understand you have friends serving with the Marines in Vietnam. Don't you think it strange to be the icon of the peace movement and have them fighting this war."

Ophelia paused – she thought of Seamus and Elijah.

"Miss Walters, I don't mean any disrespect, but I find your question on the verge of sensationalism. Please excuse me, but your question is ludicrous. How can I not care 'bout the welfare of my friends? Are you tryin' to get a reaction out of me? And if you're tryin' to do that, you've succeeded. But the only reaction you'll get is me findin' foolery in your question."

The producer smiled as he watched the interview from the shadows of the studio.

"She's amazing. Her candid answers and honesty will capture the hearts of the American people," he commented. "She's pissed and just nailed Barbara Walters to the cross on national television."

"Miss Walters – Sorry – I'm not fixin' to be disrespectful, but the point I'm tryin' to make is that many of the anti-war activists are patriots. We care about Americans servin' in the war. We want to bring them home. My graduatin' class, 1965 will pay a dear price in this war. Many of those boys are there now, and will still be there next year in '69. The casualties of '67 are the highest of the war, and it's projected that things will get worse. They'll never get better Miss Walters – never."

Ofa was haunted by her premonition. The Vietnam War would be exceptionally cruel to her class. Many of the boys who joined in '65

169

reached Vietnam by '67. Their tour of duty would last through 1968. In 1967 and 1968, 28,262 Americans were killed. The graduates of the class of 1965 would bear the brunt of the Vietnam War.

"Ophelia, tell us about the funerals you attend," Walters asked.

"Miss Walters, I read the paper about the loss of our boys, and I am sick of hearin' the press rationalize their death, sayin' that they died for their country. Politicians and old men say it is sweet and fitting to die for one's country. But there ain't nothin' sweet or right in dyin'. Sure 'nough, these boys died for some misplaced notion that if we don't stop communism in Vietnam, we'll be fightin' 'em on the streets of New York City.

"Ophelia, don't you think sometimes war is necessary?"

"Miss Walters — I'm not going to answer that question. I'll not compare apples to oranges. When a nation goes to war, it must be confident that it's a just cause. Each day I read the names of soldiers killed the previous week. I place a flower on the grave of the fallen soldier; I wear the purple ribbon as a symbol of their sacrifice. I feel the pain of the mothers, fathers, wives, children, and girlfriends." Ophelia hesitated, and in a sexy Texas drawl said — "Miss Walters, I take heed of the scriptures of Genesis, 4:09, 'the Lord said to Cain. Where is your brother Able?' He replied, 'I don't know. Am I my brother's kee'pa?' — Miss Walters, I am my brother's kee'pa."

"Ophelia, you are a very impressive young woman. Tell me about your plans. Do you have a boyfriend?" Miss Walters asked.

"I'll attend medical school at Harvard and practice in Texas. At some time in my career, I'm fixin to volunteer in Southeast Asia. My childhood hero was Dr. Tom Dooley; I want to do what he did."

"Ophelia, that's very commendable of you, but do you care to answer the question about a boyfriend."

"Do I have a boyfriend? Miss Walters, that's a strange question."

"Ophelia, that's not so strange. People want to know. Please excuse me for reminding you that you are a national icon, Girl with the Purple Ribbon. America wants to know."

Ofa hesitated — she thought of Seamus O'Grady, but she had to stop living a fantasy. On national television, she'd proclaim to the world that she did have a boyfriend.

"Ophelia, you're very impressive; I'm sure you can do anything you want. But do you have a boyfriend?"

"Why yes Miss Walters, I have a boyfriend. His name is Paul Bannister, and I love 'em like all get-out."

THIRTY-TWO

A MIDNIGHT CALL

Everything that was meant happens because it was meant to happen.

Scarlett Hawkins

April 1969 – Dartmouth University, New Hampshire

It was midnight. Ofa was engrossed in a chapter of organic chemistry, and she didn't hear the phone's piercing ring. However, its persistence caught her attention. The ring was an omen that needed a resolution. She hoped it would be this, and nothing more. But she knew that a phone that rings in the middle of the night is never good.

"Hello," she said.

There was silence. She was anxious. Paul rarely called after 10 P.M., and when he did, it was to invite himself over to share her bed. It couldn't be Asa; he'd be up at five A.M. for his morning worship.

"Hello, who is this?" Ofa asked. "If this is some kind'a joke, it's not funny."

She wanted to hang up, but she didn't. The sound of someone breathing on the other end of the line frightened her.

"Who is this?" Ofa softly asked.

"Ofa, is that you?"

"Yes – It's Ofa."

It had been a long time since someone called her Ofa. Only her father and old friends called her that. Outside of Luckenbach, she really hadn't a friend.

Ofa began to shake. She dropped the book and began to cry.

"Ofa, It's your mother."

She couldn't speak. What could she say to a woman who walked out of her life, and left only a letter?

"Ofa, can you talk?"

There was no answer.

"Don't hang up on me Ofa."

"Scarlett," she answered. It was barely a whisper. That's all she could muster.

Scarlett was hardly a mother. She left her child for a man she pursued while married to her father. The woman who rejected her was on the other end of the line. It was an emotional moment, but Ofa would not succumb to sentiment.

"Ofa, if you're not going to talk, then I will."

"Well then talk – Scarlett," she said in a sarcastic tone.

Calling her mother Scarlett was a knife in the woman's heart, but Ofa wanted blood.

"I guess I deserved that," Scarlett said. "I understand."

"You understand? No – you don't understand! You left me! How could you possibly understand? Please don't insult me tellin' me you understand! So why are you callin' me Scarlett?"

"Ofa, Francois and I…"

"Don't mention that man's name, Scarlett. You cheated on my father. You left daddy, and you left me. You've missed my entire life. So now you call."

"I'm not sorry for leaving your father. I didn't love him. But I'm sorry for leaving you. It's complicated Ofa. Life is complicated, and I was selfish and confused."

"Complicated – you make it work!" she screamed. "Daddy's a good man. He gave you a good life."

Ofa didn't want passion in her life; she sold her soul for security, so she settled for Paul. She saw what passion led her mother to do. Passion didn't last.

"Ofa, imagine a world filled with people willing to apologize and others willing to accept their apology. Life wouldn't be as bitter. I am so dreadfully sorry for what I did to you; the rest is up to you." Scarlett paused, then whispered, "Ofa, I'm sorry for leaving you. I can't take back the past. Dear, everything that was meant to happen, happens, because it was meant to happen."

"Mother, stop!" she screamed.

She called the woman mother, and she continued to cry.

"Ofa, I was in Luckenbach yesterday, and I stopped in and said hello to Pops. He said you're going with a boy from Boston, Paul Bannister."

"So, after six years of not one phone call, you call to congratulate me. Is that what this is about?"

"No, it's not. Let me speak."

"I'm not stopping you, Scarlett."

"Pops said you're not in love with this boy. He said that you had feelings for his grandson, Seamus."

"How can you call me after leavin' and then tell me that? It's none of your damn business, and I do love Paul, and if he asks me to marry him, that's what I'm gonna to do.

"I saw the interview on the Today Show. I've been following you – Girl with the Purple Ribbon. I didn't have to hear it from Pops. I saw it in your eyes; I saw it in the way you spoke of him. You don't love that boy. Don't do what I did. Don't marry a man you're not in love with. I married your father, and I wasn't in love with him. And look what happened."

"Mother, I do love Paul!" She screamed."

"Darling Ofa, your understanding of love tells me that you're not in love with Paul. And frankly dear, you're very much like me."

THIRTY-THREE

THE LETTER

You'll never be happy if you search for the meaning of life. Life has no meaning. It's up to you to bring meaning to life.

Scarlett Hawkins

April 1969 – Dartmouth University

Ofa slammed the phone into the base and continued to push to keep the evil Scarlett Hawkins at bay. She hadn't done well with love, so she ran into the arms of a man who gave her the security her mother didn't. She closed her eyes, and screamed, "Mother, I hate you!" She fell into the chair and wept. Weeping is different from crying. Weeping consumes the entire body until there's nothing left. Paul was good for her; she was content. It was the will of the Lord. Asa never tempted the hand of fate; neither would she. From the Bible, she whispered, Luke, 4:12, "You should not put the Lord Thy God to the test." But Ofa was not like Scarlett who didn't accept the Will of God. Scarlett defined happiness on her terms.

Ofa searched for the letter her mother had left her. She found it hidden in the pages of *The Prophet* by Khalil Gibran

September 6, 1961
My Darling Ofa,

It's 2 AM, and you're fast asleep. I'll kiss you before I go and place this letter under your pillow. By the time you wake, I'll be gone. I don't expect you to understand why, but I hope, one day you will. Ofa, I've tried to be a good mother; there's never been a moment when you've not been the center of my world. But I've worn a mask trying to conceal an evil demon that's overtaken my soul. I can't be a good wife, and for the longest time, I'm unable to smile. I fear I'll continue to fall into depression, and will not survive — but my biggest fear is that you will be its victim. I love you, so I must leave you. Asa is a good man, and he is strong in his faith. He will be your rock and will care for you in a way that I am incapable of. I need to find joy; it's for my survival. I know it's selfish and I hate myself for it but running away is the only way I can save you and continue to live. I want to leave you with a thought that one day I hope you will follow. I believe this thought is the secret to life, and I only wish its message doesn't come too late for me. You'll never be happy if you search for the meaning of life. Life has no meaning. It's up to you to bring meaning to life. Ofa, life can be a beautiful journey. You must try to live. I will love you forever.

Your mother,
Scarlett

She thought of what her mother said – "Ofa, you don't love this man."

THIRTY-FOUR

TAPPING THE CRYSTAL STEM

...the heart has no tears to give . . . it drops only blood . . .
bleeding itself away in silence.

Harriet Beacher Stowe, *Uncle Tom's Cabin*

May 1969 – Dartmouth

"Ophelia, It's Paul, how's my girl?"
"I'm fine Paul, how are you?"

It was a polite greeting, nothing intimate. She loved him just
enough and no longer dreamed of having a man carry her to his
castle and battle her dragons. There's a difference between being in
love and loving. I think she understood, but Ofa ignored it.

"I'm missing you my darling," he said

"Me too Paul."

"Ophelia, are you busy tonight? I'd like to take you out for a
special dinner."

"Sure Paul, that would be nice. What's goin' on?"

"It's a surprise."

"Can you tell me where we're goin'? I guess that's a surprise
too," she commented. "But I need a hint, so I know what to wear."

"Can you dress sexy for me? I want to show you off."

She was annoyed by his comment. He often made her feel like a
whore whose only purpose was to satisfy his needs. Was she merely a
decoration? Ofa turned men's heads and found satisfaction in her
power over them. Paul did everything he could to make her happy,
but could not make her come out of her skin. She was a Christian
Fundamentalist who believed relationships were to create families,
but she had needs. In the evenings, she'd stare at the ceiling because

there was a passion in her Paul couldn't satisfy.

Paul bought her sexy clothes, but if she didn't meet his expectations, he became sullen until she changed into something more suitable. When she was happy, so was he. Ofa did what she could to make him smile; however, her moods made him uncomfortable, and she'd pay an emotional price. She lived a life of fake smiles and feigned organisms. But she stayed loyal to the nightmare of her choice.

Paul arrived at Ofa's apartment exactly at 8 PM.

"That dress, wow! I'm going to buy the same dress in black."

"Paul, shall we go?"

"Ophelia, tonight is special; I want to celebrate us."

Only the finest restaurant would please Paul Bannister. It was French with white tablecloths, crystal wine glasses, leather chairs and pretentious chandeliers. She didn't find such places to her liking. As she sat down, Paul held her chair.

"Here's to us," he said. He clicked her glass; he made a toast, and they drank the best Champagne. It didn't matter what Paul ordered as long as it was expensive.

"Ophelia, you're beautiful. I love you. You'd be good for me darling. I need you in my life. Would you make me a happy man and marry me?"

She placed her wine glass on the table and tapped the base with her fingernail. She was 21 and with medical school pending, and the peace movement, marriage was not what she had in mind.

She thought: *I'd be a good wife. He'll give me everything.*

"Ophelia, would you marry me? Make me happy?"

Paul couldn't read her eyes, and he couldn't see her struggle as she suppressed her mother's thoughts.

"I will marry you, Paul." That was all she said.

THIRTY-FIVE

LADY WITH A BROAD BRIM HAT

I have had to experience so much stupidity, so many vices, so
much error, so much nausea, disillusionment and sorrow, just in
order to become a child again and begin anew. I had to experience
despair, I had to sink to the greatest mental depths, to thoughts of
suicide, in order to experience grace.

Hermann Hesse, *Siddhartha*

June 1969 – Dartmouth

Ofa Hawkins would graduate **Summa Cum Laude.** But the
war and an empty soul had taken its toll. Pops taught her that if
she trusted life, it would work out. But she no longer trusted. She
talked herself out of happiness but never once into happiness. The
peace movement gave her purpose; however, she was despondent
over the war and would abandon the devotions the movement gave
her. The war, which was once insufferable, became strangely
common. She became depressed, and she hoped it was just another
obstacle on the way to higher ground.

She was the class valedictorian, the commencement speaker for
the class of 1969, accepted to Harvard Medical School, and would be
a June bride. Yet, she was aware of the void in her life.

Graduation Day

The graduates filed into the rows of white chairs aligned on the
Dartmouth Green. Ofa Hawkins waited for her cue to approach the
podium. She thought of a simpler time when she was a girl fishing
with the boys, drinking Coke, and eating Moon Pies at the South
Grape Creek. She liked who she was more than who she became, but

there was no going back, only forward.

"Miss Hawkins, are you ready?" Dean Fueling asked?

Ophelia smiled and adjusted her purple ribbon.

"Yes, I am."

She walked to the podium and tapped the microphone. The sound reverberated throughout the Green and bounced off the brick buildings. She looked at Asa; he was her rock. She knew he'd be sitting in the front row ready to give his little girl the love and assurance she needed. They made eye contact, and he smiled. Paul sat at the right hand of the father. He blew her a kiss; she nodded. Ofa acknowledged the students who wore purple ribbons. Cameras flashed and captured images of Ofa Hawkins, the girl from the Texas Hill Country.

"My Dearest Classmates:"

She took a deep breath, and a tear fell. She glanced throughout the Green and noticed the throngs of faculty, students, and parents eagerly awaiting her remarks. Her focus returned to her notes. As she glanced downward, she caught a glimpse of a tall, woman with dark sunglass and a wide brim hat standing behind the last row of chairs.

My dearest classmates, four years ago I spoke at Fredericksburg High School in the Texas Hill Country. It was the first time I wore a purple ribbon. I am saddened that I still wear this ribbon. Today, I feel your sol-li-darity as many of y'all wear a similar ribbon. I'm often asked, why I have a serious look on my face? Why I never smile? I hear I'm called the "Ice Queen." Although it's just a name; it saddens me. I'd like to believe you understand the reason why I rarely smile. There was a time when I was a child, and I ran wild and free in Texas. I was happy then, and yet I can't remember, and it's not because it was so long ago. You've never known that part of me, and that is my tragedy. It's not that I fail to see the magic that life has to offer. I see that magic – I can see it in color. But the Vietnam War extinguished any light that shines into my soul. We can live our lives in one of two ways. We can see the world as though everything's a miracle. Or as though nothin's a miracle. I'm aware of the meanin' of this thought. But how can I smile and how can I find joy?

Four years ago, I implored the U.S. to get out of Vietnam.

And yet we remain at war. Four years I've screamed, stop the war. Stop the killin'! We continue to lose soldiers and kill the innocents of Vietnam. So, I continue to wear this purple ribbon and sure 'nuff I know that what I did has been of no avail. Since I spoke at my high school graduation over 35,000 Americans, have died and countless numbers of Vietnamese. In 1965, I looked into a crystal ball and struggled to see an end to the conflict. I didn't see it. Today I refuse to look to the future because I fear what I would see. At the time, I said, the Class of '65 would bear the burden of the War. Over 28,000 American Soldiers died in 1966, 1967, and 1968. Those are the years my fellow high school graduates – and yours too would have served. I'm afraid to read the newspaper, and I certainly do not want to read the obituaries of the soldiers killed the previous week. I went to many of their funerals!"

Ophelia paused. Another tear fell. The mascara in her eyes began to run. She took a moment and tried to regain composure. She lifted her head and caught a glimpse of the woman with the broad brim hat.

I will leave Dartmouth with a strong foundation in science. The University prepared me for the academic rigors of medical school. And I trust y'all are also ready to become university professors, lawyers, artists, soldiers, teachers, businessmen and women, politicians, and citizens in a widenin' world. But what we ought to know has nothing to do with our majors, our careers, or what is found in our curriculum.

Ofa paused, stared in the souls of those who sat in front of her and they stared into hers. She continued:

We must believe in the sanctity of life. We must realize that every human bein' has value. Every man – every woman – every child. Every death is a loss. Life is precious and irreplaceable. In *Hamlet*, Shakespeare said, 'What a piece of work is a man? How noble in reason – How infinite in faculty – how like an angel – The beauty of the world – And yet, to me, what is this quintessence of dust –' My dear graduates, I have the answer to his question – W e   A r e   t h e   D i v i n e!

Ofa raised her head toward the heavens, lifted her eyes, and proclaimed:

Praise the Lord! – Oh, Jubilee! – Yes, we are!"

She paused and found refuge in the woman standing alone beyond the last row of chairs.

Ofa took a deep breath.

The world is complex, but if we adhere to the basic tenant of existence, which is love, we see that within complexity there's simplicity. When we assume intractable positions, we run the risk of a quagmire of thought and circumstance. Look at Vietnam. A different approach was needed. And oh, my dear classmates, should we not pose the question of what it means to be alive? Where does life begin? Where does it end? There is no single answer to these questions. The problem lies with those who believe there are simple answers to difficult questions. The simple answer was to stop communism at the 17th Parallel. The simple solution was to send American soldiers. With so many dead it's not such a simple solution —— is it? When we make decisions void of the sanctity of life, we see things as simple as black and white and as right and wrong. We make decisions accordingly, and thus, we find ourselves in this quagmire called Vietnam.

Who are we to make such a decision? To allow another livin' bein' – any livin' bein' – to die – when ours is the power to prevent it! Well – that's our downfall – and that will be the guilt of the class of 1969.

I wanted to be an influence that would end the Vietnam War; I wanted the perfect endin'. Four years ago, I spoke to a man whom I met one evenin' in Austin. His name was Indiana Red. He comforted me durin' a most difficult time. He said, 'Some stories don't make sense, and they don't have a clear beginnin', middle, or end. Life is 'bout not knowin'. It's changin'. It's taking a moment, and makin' the best of it, without knowing the future.' My dear graduates, life is often a delectable obscurity.

If the world were merely seductive, that would be easy. If it were merely challengin', that would be no problem. But I rise in the mornin' torn between a desire to improve the world and a desire to enjoy the world. And this makes it difficult to be in the world.

For the last four years, I've lost the frivolity of youth and decided to improve the world. But where has that gotten me? Where has this taken the world? I am in the same place that I was four years prior. But regardless! Regardless. My dearest classmates, we've gotta try. We have known each other four years, you are my dearest friends, and I want to give y'all the moon and the sky. But I have only words and one more partin' thought.

Ofa Hawkins paused, took a deep breath, and searched for the security of the strange woman with the broad brim hat. It was her swan song. There was nothing left of her, and there was nothing more to give. She could do no more. It was time to leave her idyllic world. The great devotions of purpose were gone. O f a H a w k i n s did not stop the Vietnam War.

She again stared at the heavens, raised her hands and cried:

You must proclaim far and wide that the earth is yours and the fullness thereof – Be kind and be fierce. You are needed now more than ever. Take up the mantle of change... This is your time!

She acknowledged the standing ovation. She smiled, nodded, and dried her tears. Instead of looking for Asa and Paul she turned toward the woman with the broad brim hat. The woman smiled, turned, and walked away.

Tears streamed from Ofa's eyes. "MOTHER!" She screamed.

Ofa ran down the center aisle chasing the mysterious woman, but the woman disappeared down the brick path that led toward the library. Ofa would not let her go. Scarlett followed the path that took her between the sugar maples that stood between the chapel and the library. She weaved in and out of the trees appearing and disappearing. She was a phantom ghost and Ofa frantically pursued this ghost. She wanted to drive a stake deep into the woman's heart.

"Mother! Stop!" She cried.

Attempting to evade her pursuer, the woman kept walking.

"Mother!"

Ofa stopped in the middle of the campus – sobbing. She could no longer run.

"Mother, stop! Ofa screamed. "D o n ' t l e a v e m e a g a i n ! "

The woman stopped on the red brick path and stood at a crossroad with her back to her daughter.

Scarlett Hawkins took a deep breath, turned, and faced the sobbing girl.

"Ofa!"

The women faced each other. Scarlett removed her glasses and walked toward her daughter. Ofa ran toward her mother, and the two women embraced. Ofa buried her head in her mother's breasts. Scarlett stroked her daughter's hair and whispered, "I'm sorry."

The students, and families remained in their seats watching the drama unfold. Many knew of Ofa's pain and watched it culminate on the red brick path beneath the sugar maples.

"Mother every moment of my childhood I've felt abandoned."

"Ofa, I must go!" Scarlett was unable to face her daughter. But to find redemption, she would have to face those demons.

Scarlett continued, "Darling, all I have are words to tell you how sorry I am. There's nothing more I can say. I feel your pain, and I hope you can feel mine. I will spend the rest of my life trying to fill the hole I put in your heart."

The anger Ofa carried turned her into a bitter young woman. It was her poison, but it was a double edge sword and cut both women. She had to decide if her faith was more than citing ancient scriptures penned in dusty old books? She remained motionless in front of her mother with the sugar maples of Dartmouth casting shadows obscuring Scarlett's image. Ofa thought, *we're all prodigals; we're all runners. But how are we going to treat the prodigals who come to us?*

"Mama, I forgive you!" she cried.

Ofa continued to cry, and her mother stroked her hair.

"Dear, I have to go now."

"Mother, how will I reach you," Ofa asked.

Scarlett opened her purse and pulled a linen handkerchief. She dried the tears from her daughter's eyes. "There, there, Ofa, we've shed too many tears. Look at you. You're beautiful. Seeing you speak

– I'm so proud of you. There wasn't a day I didn't think of you."

"I'll reach you, darling. We have lots to talk about. You go back to your father and Paul; I will see you soon."

Scarlett Hawkins turned and walked away.

THIRTY-SIX

ILLIGITAMUS NON CARBORUNDUM

If you are distressed by anything external, the pain is not due to the thing itself, but to your estimate of it; and this you have the power to revoke at any moment.

Marcus Aurelius, *Meditations*

January 1972 – Staff NCO Club, Da Nang

"So you're Seamus O'Grady, the guy everyone's talking about."

"Yes, Sergeant Major, what can I do for you?"

Seamus and Elijah leaned on the bar of the Staff NCO club in Da Nang. The music was loud, and the half-naked Filipina women toyed with the libido of the lonely men as they danced to the band's imitation of Creedence Clearwater Revival's *Proud Mary*. The Filipino bands did perfect renditions of Johnny Cash and Crosby, Stills Nash and Young, but typically, they couldn't' speak a word of English. It was bosses' night, and the boys invited their Company Commander, Captain Calder McGivens for drinks. McGivens had taken the boys through Khe Sanh, the Tet Offensive, and the endless search and destroy missions in *I Corps*, the northernmost sector of South Vietnam. They followed the senseless tactics of the Generals who tried to re-live American military supremacy.

The tension between command and subordinates made for an uncomfortable evening. However, that was not the case for 1st Sergeant Seamus O'Grady and Gunnery Sergeant Elijah Bravo. The Sergeants and the Captain had been together since April of '67 and had become friends.

The Sergeant Major, leaning against the bar on the opposite side of the boys was drunk, and the alcohol brought out his true nature. He had a mean disposition, and 1st Sergeant O'Grady would bear the brunt of his anger.

"Yeah, O'Grady, there's not a fucking thing you can do for me. You're the guy who lost 1/9's colors in the hill fights. And they gave you the Silver Star. In my Marine Corps, you don't get the Silver Star for being a coward."

The Sergeant Major was trying to provoke a fight. He appeared as though he had been in many and had probably won them all.

"It's disgraceful to leave the field without your colors. What the fuck were you thinking?"

"Sergeant Major, with all due respect, you weren't there, so you don't know what the fuck you're talking about. Let me buy you a drink from one Marine to another."

"O'Grady, you're a poor excuse for a Marine, and I sure wouldn't drink with a man who'd leave his Battalion's colors in possession of the enemy."

"Sergeant Major, let it go."

It was too late. The Sergeant Major stood; took off his jacket, and said, "I want a piece of you."

Elijah moved between his friend and the angry man.

"Sergeant Major you're drunk. Sit the fuck down."

Seamus put his hand on his best friend's shoulder. "Elijah, you can't fight my battles. This is on me pard, step aside."

"Sergeant Major, I don't want a fight; I'm here for a drink," Seamus said.

"O'Grady, you ain't welcome in this bar, not after what you did."

"Guys, let's go," Captain McGivens said.

Seamus turned his back on the Sergeant Major, and the men walked toward the door.

"Turn around you coward!"

Seamus kept walking. He felt a cold beer dripping down his head. Seamus continued to walk. Then he felt a glass pitcher slam into his shoulder. Seamus was a man of restraint, but he was a Texas boy. He turned and smashed into the Sergeant Major and in one motion grabbed him by the throat and threw him up against the wall.

"I didn't want this Sergeant Major."

Seamus pushed him into a chair. "We're done here. Be careful who you're calling a coward. With all due respect – you're hardly worthy of being a Marine Sergeant Major."

"Seamus, you okay?" McGivens asked. "I should've asked the Sergeant Major that. You gotta let this go. Illigitamus Non Carborundum, (Don't let the bastards grind you down). For Christ's sake, you're a hero; you got the Silver Star."

"Calder, I feel guilty. I know it's all in my head, but it gets to me. When I was a kid, I read a story 'bout the flag the Texans flew at the Alamo and how Santa Ana captured it and placed it in the Museum in Mexico City. They rubbed it in the face of the Texans. It just don't sit well with me."

"For a guy who never went to his high school graduation, how the hell do you know about that?"

"Captain, when you're from Texas you remember the Alamo. It's in your blood."

"So, to shove it up Texas' ass, legend says Santa Ana had the flag placed in the museum in Mexico City. Well, about a 130 years later, a bunch of college boys from UT Austin go down to Mexico City on Spring break. They see the flag and plan to steal it."

"So, what happened Seamus? Do they get the flag?"

"Well, shit Cap, don't know: never finished the book. It's just a story. But it doesn't matter whether it's a story or not, cause us Texas boys grew up believin' that there was a flag at the Alamo. The flag I left on the battlefield was captured by the enemy, and one day it'll be displayed in some fleabag museum in Hanoi."

"Seamus, I don't get it. Look – no one has said a thing against you. This guy was just shooting off his mouth. He was drunk. Anyone who has any wits about them knows the story. It's all in your head. Don't let the assholes go there."

"Sir, don't matter what others think. What matters is what I think."

*　　*　　*

In 1972, the boys were serving with the First Marine Regiment. Seamus was the 1st Sergeant of Captain McGivens' rifle Company; Elijah was the Company Gunnery Sergeant. They had been in the Corps for seven years. Four of the seven were spent in Vietnam. Instead of going home when the 9th Marines rotated back to the world, they became advisors to the South Vietnamese Marines. People stopped asking them why they decided to stay and those who did ask got the same answer: *that's where the men are.* They wanted to serve with like-spirited men; they were a *band of brothers.* The relationships they forged were worth the risk of death. But it was only a matter of time when their luck ran out; however, the boys didn't concern themselves with the law of averages. Ofa once said, "Angels protect fools and children – and you boys are children." They believed her. Regardless, Seamus wouldn't return home because Ofa was married to another man.

It was different for Elijah. He fell in love with the Vietnamese nurse, Nguyen Lu who cared for his wounds while he convalesced on the USS Sanctuary. War is not a time for love. But falling in love was real for Elijah Bravo. He had never believed in the possibility of love especially the possibility of finding that one woman who was the quintessence of a soul mate. He scoffed at the possibility. *Soulmates only exist in fairy tales*, he thought. And then he met Nguyen Lu and everything changed. Elijah had become a believer. He would not rotate back to the world until he found a way to get her out of Vietnam.

Before the hill fights, Elijah was a killer. He hated the Vietnamese and didn't care whether they were from the north or the south. They were just gooks. But he had changed. The night in the bunker on Hill-861 with Lieutenant Ly-Truc-Viet revealed the true soul of Elijah Bravo and the extraordinary wherewithal of a people he was supposed to hate.

"All men share the same humanity," Lieutenant Viet said. "We love. We laugh. We cry and hope for a better life for our children. How different are we? I am a simple man, and I think you are too. But we want different things. I want to be left alone, but you won't leave me alone because I am a communist. You will not let the Vietnamese people live the way they want to live. You are 10,000 miles from us and believe that what we do will affect you."

Lieutenant Viet had not mentioned world domination. The NVA officer spoke about freedom for the Vietnamese people not unlike American Patriots during the Revolutionary War. He drew a parallel between the Vietnamese soldier and the soldiers who carried the cause at Valley Forge. The pictures Elijah found in the pockets of the dead enemy soldiers: pictures of families, weddings, and children softened his heart. Maybe the Lieutenant was right – maybe all men are similar. Similar or not, the Corps taught him to hate and kill the enemy, but he no longer hated. Strange things happen in war. Nguyen Lu, the beautiful woman who cared for him on the Sanctuary, was Vietnamese.

THIRTY-SEVEN

SHE WASN'T WEARIN' BOOTING

Every woman has secret sorrows, which the world knows not; and often times we call a woman cold when she is only sad.

Henry Wadsworth Longfellow

April 1972 – Boston, Massachusetts

Ofa was in her last year of medical school and interning at Boston General Hospital. She would graduate first in her class. Paul had graduated from Harvard Law and was on the fast track to becoming a partner in his grandfather's firm, Bannister and Bannister. They had been married three years. The young couple had a good life. They were prosperous and rising stars in the city. However, the 60-hour workweek spent at the hospital and the long hours Paul spent at the law practice were not good for their marriage. That was especially true in the bedroom. Paul referred to her as the ice queen. He took her when he wanted but only for his pleasure, and after he was satisfied, she'd lay awake staring at the ceiling. She lived in denial; however, her allegiance to the institution of marriage made her emptiness bearable. Paul's good looks and charm were reasons for those late-night meetings that had nothing to do with the law. But he gave her a luxurious life, which allowed her to follow her wildest whims. Ofa gave Paul the sensation of being with a beautiful woman who would be good for his political ambitions.

She was a cold woman, and she rarely smiled. But if you're going to understand Ofa Hawkins, you need to heed the following carefully, "Every woman has secret sorrows, which the world knows not; and often times we call a woman cold when she is only sad."

Most painful were the feelings she couldn't control. She longed for the impossible: a past that never was, a longing for what could've been, a regret for not becoming another self, a dissatisfaction with the world. Her consciousness was absurd, yet it was painful, and she spiraled into her own abyss.

* * *

"Mama, I'm not unhappy. Every time you call me, you ask me if I'm happy."

"Sweetheart, when you answer such a question with the response that you're not unhappy, that can only mean that you're not happy."

"Mother, what do you want me to say? I'm not going to do what you did."

Ofa caught herself, but it was too late, and she wished she hadn't said what she said.

"Mother, I'm sorry. I just..."

"Darling, it's not you who should be sorry. It's been three years since we found each other and we're way past being sorry. I know you're frustrated. I see it in your eyes. You don't love Paul. Don't put the blame on him for you not wanting to have a baby. Don't use the excuse, there's no time. When a woman loves her man, she wants to have his child regardless of circumstance. People find a way."

"Mama, you had me, and you didn't love daddy."

"Dear, I had you because I wanted a baby. I wanted love in my life. I didn't have that with your father."

"Mama, Paul's good to me. He gives me everything I want. He's goin' to be a senator, or a governor, or even the President of the United States. That would be an amazin' life. And mom he loves me. I'm happy 'bout that."

"Darling, you love him because of the things he gives you. That's not love. He loves you because you are beautiful and bright. You make him look good. That's also not love. We accept the love we believe we deserve. You deserve more. I'd wish you'd see that."

"What happened to that cowboy you were crazy about? Molly Bone said, 'you had a crush on Seamus O'Grady.' She said, 'he's a fine boy.'"

"I haven't seen Seamus O'Grady in seven years," Ofa said. "There was never anything between us. After high school, we moved on. We never even kissed."

"Darling, I don't believe caring for someone depends on a kiss or sleeping with them. Ofa, I'm going back to Luckenbach and visit Molly. Come with me. You haven't been in a long time. Asa would love to see you."

Luckenbach

Mother and daughter traveled east from Austin to Luckenbach and into the Texas Hill Country. It was a bluebonnet spring, and the black Texas dirt with grandfather trees was the perfect frame for the endless fields of blue. Ofa searched for comfort and looked to the past, but she wasn't wearing boots and didn't see the girl she used to be.

She glanced at the bluebonnet country stretching for miles. At the sight of the Hill Country, she became sullen and shifted uncomfortably in her seat. Ofa was accustomed to living with the demons of emptiness, as though nothing in life mattered. She had lost hope and believed that her life would not change. She wanted to smile, to laugh, but instead, she saw her life endlessly stretching before her, and every day pushed her deeper into a meaningless void. She was getting older, and there was no way out. For the first time, Ofa understood her feelings. She never had time to feel; she was consumed with becoming this person, who was herself. Mother and daughter followed Highway 290 east, and Ofa remembered the evening of June 18, 1965, the night she sped toward Austin trying to find Seamus O'Grady.

She missed the endless sea of live oak, walnut, and elm trees that peppered the rolling hills and disappeared toward distant horizons. She and the boys rode the hills and swam in green rivers: the Pedernales, Guadalupe, Frito, and Medina that quietly meandered across south-central Texas. She no longer felt she belonged.

The quaint Hill Country towns had not changed, but she hardly recognized them. But she'd known nothing but change. White clouds spotted the blue sky, and she saw ghost riders flying through the heavens. One called her name. It was a premonition.

And she stared at the sky, she was frightened. And the stiff prairie wind still blew, and the grass was still bent and faced the sun all the way to Luckenbach.

Luckenbach remained a dusty town, and the old houses and barns seemed to need more paint. Scarlett drove toward Molly Bone's, and Ofa remembered sitting on the steps with the boys, eating Molly's oatmeal raisin cookies.

Ofa left Scarlett behind and drove the rental from Molly's to the intersection of Main Street and Alamo. The old post office was still there. She looked toward the general store, and the red blinking light flashed in her eyes. She saw her reflection and wondered if that person was real. She tried to remember, but for Ofa, the saddest things in life were the things she did remember. The light flashed and she couldn't help thinking of Pops and wondered if he still sat next to the potbelly stove. She saw smoke billowing from the chimney and knew someone was staying warm. There were boys and girls sitting on the store's steps, where she, Seamus, and Elijah spent much of their adolescence. They were laughing, eating pulled pork sandwiches wrapped in butcher paper, and drinking Coke. She stared at them fondly and smiled. She pulled toward the curb. The teens never saw such a woman. They examined the rental and knew she was an outsider. The ol' hitching post had stood the challenges of time and the rusty water trough held remnants of the last rain. The yellow letters that she and the boys painted in '62 spelling Ramirez's General Store were still visible. She parked across the road, and the boys watched her as she walked toward them. She wore a tight black skirt and a red blouse. Her shoes were the latest New York fashion. No one recognized the girl who wore a purple ribbon. In the store, there were pickers playing Hill Country music. She bought Coke, some Moon Pies, but didn't buy any Life Savers. She sat on the steps and popped a Coke.

One of the boys asked, "Miss, would y'all like to sit on a chair? I'll fetch one fer ya."

Ofa smiled, and in a sultry southern drawl said, "Well – that's mighty kind of you, darlin' – but I'm fine squatin' here."

The boys and girls were confused; she sounded Texas, but she wasn't wearing boots.

Being back was worse than being gone. She wanted to cry, but she smiled instead. Sometimes, smiles are tears.

Would Pops be there? She wrote him often but hadn't seen him since her marriage. She couldn't go home. There were too many regrets, but life was not lived backward. But she was a woman, and she was just passing through, and she wasn't wearing boots.

She walked across the road and into the post office. There were old men sitting in front of a potbellied stove.

"Who is this beautiful woman?" Pops whispered. He smiled and recognized the girl wearing a purple ribbon.

"Ofa darlin', my pretty girl – come. Give me a big ol' hug."

She ran to Pops as though she was a little girl running to her daddy. She threw her arms around him, and she buried her head in his chest.

"Oh, Pops – I'm so sorry!" she cried. The musty smell of old clothes, whiskey, and tobacco were soothing.

"No Ofa – no – you're here now. Nothin' to be sorry 'bout. Things just happen. Darlin', regardless how long it's been, you're still my Pretty Girl, and here you are."

"Pops, you know I've always loved you. You've always known what to say to make a girl feel like she still belongs."

"Darlin' girl, you signed it in your letters. I saved 'em. You look beautiful as ever. Are you a doctor?"

"Yes, I am Pops."

It was typical of the girl not to speak about herself. When you're unhappy about who you are, you tend to remain silent.

"Pops, tell me about you."

"Fair to middlin'. That's pretty good for an old-timer. I'm still sittin' at the same place where you said good-bye to me three years ago. Still lookin' for a mission – Any kids?"

"No."

"So, you're Mrs. Paul Bannister?"

"Well, Pops, I kept my own name, Ophelia Hawkins."

"That's kind of brazen for a woman to keep her own name. But what happened to Ofa? You're an Ofa; you ain't no Ophelia."

"Ofa left me long ago."

"Pretty Girl, I'm just gonna call you Ofa."

She liked hearing Ofa. It brought back memories, and she could almost feel the saddle and the wind as she galloped through the oaks trying to catch Seamus and Elijah.

"Pretty Girl, that's too bad Ofa's gone – just for a spell I suppose. Sure nuff, she'll be back."

"No Children – that's hard for me to believe. Why don't you have children?"

"Maybe one day Pops."

"Pretty Girl, I'm happy for you and Scarlett getting back together. She got a bum deal when she left. People said a lot of bad things 'bout her. If a woman doesn't love her man, then she's got to follow her heart. It took a lot of courage to do what your mama did. You probably don't know this, but Molly Bone wrote Scarlett once a week with news 'bout you. Your mama was sick over leavin'. Those pictures Molly took at school and around town — she sent them to your mama. Life's complicated, and not everything is as it appears."

"I followed you; I read everything 'bout you — Girl with the Purple Ribbon. My God Ofa, you tried. You weren't just talkin' 'bout makin' things better. You walked the walk. Elijah's letters said you was right about the war, — 'bout everything. Seamus never felt that way. He still believed we was there for freedom. But I'm proud of you. You stood up for what you believed."

"Pops, I just wish everything I did was for somethin'. I spent four years fightin' to bring the boys home, but it didn't happen."

"Darling no matter if you was successful or not — somethin' did happen and I think you're better for it."

"Pops, we lost so many. I went to their funerals."

"I know you did. I read 'bout it in the paper; I saw you on TV. Damn, y'all sure showed that Barbara Walters a thing or two. When you was on the *Today Show*, we brought a TV into the post office, and it seemed like the whole town was here to watch you. It didn't matter that you was against the war and the good old boys of Luckenbach wanted to nuke the entire country of Vietnam. But I have to tell ya, every time y'all said somethin', everybody cheered. Y'all one of us, Ofa darlin'. You're a Texas girl — you're Luckenbach. Just don't forget where y'all come from."

Pops was an old man, but he put life in perspective. He understood that Ofa was still 'Pretty Girl.' Maybe we're just who we are, and regardless of what we do or where we go, we're still that same person.

"How are the boys Pops? I know they were in the thick of it. I was worried sick."

Pops had a long story to tell. He told her about the battles in the hills around Khe Sanh, and how Elijah stayed behind while Seamus led what was left of the Platoon to safety. He told her that everyone gave up on Elijah, but not Seamus. The night after the Platoon escaped, Seamus saw Elijah in the North Star and knew that he was alive and Seamus went back to look for him.

"By God, if he didn't find him," Pops said.

He told her that Elijah was wounded and while recovering on the hospital ship, he fell in love with a beautiful nurse. He told her of the boys fighting at the battle of Hue City, Khe Sanh, and back into the hills along the DMZ.

"Elijah got the Navy Cross, and Seamus got the Silver Star," Pops explained.

"Pops what's happening with the girl Elijah is in love with? Are they Married?"

"No! Want to hear something funny? She's Vietnamese. Elijah's awfully worried about her though – getting her out of the country is gonna be tough. He's worried that when the Americans pull out, she won't be able to come with 'em. I suppose that's why he's still there."

"You have any pictures of the boys?" She asked.

Pops reached into his pocket and handed her a picture of Seamus and Elijah. She was afraid the war would have changed them. The boys were standing together; they weren't smiling. Seamus had the same boyish face, as handsome as ever. He seemed sad though, and his eyes appeared to be looking at something in the distance. Ofa knew the symptoms of *PTSD*. Seamus had the thousand-yard stare, reflective of how one grew old in war.

"Pops, where are they?"

"They're advisors to the Vietnamese Marines. I can understand Elijah not wanting to come home cause of that girl, but why won't Seamus come home? He says his men need him, but there's more to it than that."

"Does he know I'm married?"

"He does."

"Did he say anything when he found out," Ofa asked.

"Elijah said he didn't say a word."

She lowered her head like a disappointed child hoping for a clue Seamus cared.

"Ofa, there's was one thing I thought was strange. How long you been married?"

"Almost four years – got married in June 1969 after graduation."

"Well that's weird," Pops said; "he was supposed to come home in June of '69. But he extended his tour right around the time you got married."

"Pops, me getting married had nothing to do with Seamus not comin' home."

Ofa was defensive. She was hiding something she feared. But it was the way she said it that made Pops believe Seamus didn't come home because she was getting married.

"I'm not so sure darlin'. You weren't honest with your feelin's then, and I'm not sure that ain't still the case."

"Pops, by the time June came 'round in senior year, there was nothing between us. He moved on. He didn't want a girlfriend. I wanted him; he didn't want me."

"Ofa, that might be, but the night he left for boot camp, I remember a sad boy."

"Pops, it wasn't because of me," Ofa pleaded. "Don't say that Pops. It's not true!"

"I think it was Ofa darlin'. I think it was because of you." Her eyes filled with tears. "No Pops!"

"I always hoped you'd be together. I wanted you to be the girl for my grandson."

"But he didn't care enough to say goodbye to me!" she cried.

"Oh, Ofa – he did care."

"No, he didn't!" Ofa cried.

She buried her head on his shoulder. Pops stroked her hair. He loved the pretty girl.

"Darlin', whether he did or didn't care, is the past, but you need to know what happened that night. Do you want to know?"

Ofa Hawkins looked into the old man's eyes; she didn't want to know. She was afraid of the truth. Yet, she nodded.

"Well, he came to see me and say goodbye. He was upset. We couldn't talk cause the bus to Austin was leaving in 20 minutes. I asked him, 'What you going to do 'bout Pretty Girl?' He got sadder when I mentioned your name."

Ofa began to cry; nevertheless, Pops continued.

"Seamus told me it was too late for the both of you. That you moved on and you met someone else, some rich college boy from Boston."

"But Pops – if he cared for me why didn't he write me a note or, at least, say goodbye? He didn't even come to his graduation. He didn't want to see me."

"Darlin' girl, let me finish. I told him he needed to tell you his feelin's. I told him of the time I asked his grandmother to wait for me, the night I left for France in World War I."

Ofa was sobbing. "Pops," she whispered.

"I told him to do what I did. I told him to bring you one red rose."

"Pretty Girl, what's wrong? Why the tears?"

She fell to her knees, and her body rocked forward and backward and then she'd stop rocking and then she whimpered and then she rocked again. The worst type of sorrow is not what everyone sees. It's not the crying; it's when your soul weeps and when there's no way to find comfort from the pain.

Pops held the girl in his arms. The old man knew that knowing the truth about June 18, 1965, would eventually save her even though it would destroy her.

Ofa was the kind of girl men protected, but in doing so, they shielded her from happiness. The cycle began with her father. He dedicated his whole life to sheltering his little girl from the slightest discomfort but he kept her from finding joy. Men would care for the sweet girl. They were knights, and she was their maiden.

Pops held her, but Ofa said nothing – not a word. The man she married was a liar, but she too was a liar for marrying him.

"Pops – I have to go back to Boston."

And Ofa walked out of the post office and down the steps and onto the dusty road. The teenage boys watched her cry and then watched her drive away. There was nothing they could do. They wanted to protect the pretty woman who wasn't wearing boots.

THIRTY-EIGHT

A RECKONING

You said you loved me! You said you'd be good to me! Believe me! You said that! But you stood there – in front of me, and you lied every day.

Ofa Hawkins

Eastern Airlines, Flight 4747

From Austin to Boston, Ofa sat curled on the window seat at the rear of the plane. She realized her prince would never come, so she gazed into the blue sky and saw a graveyard of buried dreams.

The skycap carried her bag to the curb.

"Dr. Hawkins, Shall I call you a cab or will Mr. Bannister be picking you up?"

"Thank you, Thomas – a cab, please. Can you see if Mr. Lynn is available?"

The cab moved slowly down Beacon Street; she had fallen into a light sleep.

"Dr. Hawkins we're here," Mr. Lynn said.

The brownstone, on the corner of Gloucester and Beacon, had a remarkable view of the Charles River. The two-story walk up had potted red roses lining the steps and a purple ribbon tied delicately around the light post.

"Doctor, I'll carry your bag up," Mr. Lynn said.

"Mr. Lynn, please leave them in the trunk and wait for me."

He thought it strange but he opened the door of the cab and escorted Dr. Hawkins toward the building and up the steps. Ofa turned the key.

"Ophelia, you're home early. You're here to make love to me," her husband said.

She smiled, didn't say a word, and walked into the bedroom.

She grabbed her photo albums, a few assorted items, and her husband's credit cards. In the living room, she then reached for the shadow box, which displayed a red rose. Paul watched her deliberate movements. She opened the box, placed the rose gently in her bag, and then hurled the box against the wall shattering the glass.

Paul Bannister was a coward; his only emotion was fear.

"Ophelia, where are you going? What's wrong? I don't understand."

But he did understand.

She moved toward the door like a serpent. Silent! Slow! Seductive!

"Ophelia, don't leave me!" Paul screamed. You can't! You're nothing without me, you bitch!

Ofa turned and her eyes were daggers.

"You said you loved me! You said you'd be good to me! Believe me you said that. But you stood there – in front of me – you lied every day!"

She walked out the door and that was all she said.

Mr. Lynn took her hand and escorted her to the back seat of his cab.

"Mr. Lynn – Logan – Eastern Airlines Terminal."

"Yes, Dr. Hawkins."

Ofa had found her calling – a bitch.

THIRTY-NINE

FOR LOVE

And I will give you a new heart, and a new spirit I will put within you. And I will remove the heart of stone from your flesh and give you a heart of flesh.

Ezekiel, *36:26*

March 1973 – Hue City, South Vietnam

"Guns, there's no need for two of us on this mission. Go work on your tan and drink some warm Dr. Pepper."

"Listen, First Sergeant, why in the hell would I need a tan? I'm Mexican, the Brown Bomber."

"Cowboy, I've outranked your ass since '66. You remember that, don't ya? Operation Hastings! I'm used to bein' your boss."

"Well, I'll be dipped in shit, Seamus, rank between a Gunnery Sergeant and a 1st Sergeant is like honor among thieves. It only means somethin' to a limp dick like you. If the brass selected my Squad as point instead of yours, I'd be a fuckin' General by now. You may have an extra strip, but I've been carryin' your ass since we got here."

"All I got to say about that Gunny: if if's and but's were candy and nuts every day would be Christmas."

"Seamus, that don't make a damn bit of sense."

But there might have been truth to Elijah's contention. If you had to compare apples to apples then 6 out of 10 times, Elijah would be the better field Marine. But in combat, comparisons are never apples to apples; it's more like apples to oranges. When the shit goes down, there are too many variables to contend with. So, when you're determining the best combat leader, Seamus would win 6 out of 10 times. But it would be close – probably as close as a six and a half to a seven.

"Elijah, I'm pullin' rank on you; I'm goin' on the mission. You're stayin'. Take some in-country R&R, and visit your girl. All I want to hear from you is, yes First Sergeant."

"Yes, First Sergeant," Elijah said, "and you can take a flyin' leap though a rollin' donut."

"Elijah, what are you going to do about Nguyen?"

"Jesus, Seamus, don't know. I won't go home without her. As soon as we leave, sure-enough, the NVA will walk into Saigon and we ain't goin' to do nuthin' 'bout it. This peace with honor is a bunch of bullshit. My only chance to get her out is to petition the Red Cross and see if there's some'in that can be done on their end. She needs sponsorship. Maybe by American doctors. She's been savin' American lives; we owe her. If she don't get out, they'll punish her. She'll die in a Vietnamese prison just like her mother."

Elijah jumped on a chopper and headed to Da Nang to see the woman he loved.

*　　*　　*

As had been the case with Lyndon Johnson, President Nixon was determined that Vietnam would not ruin his presidency. He was the fourth American President who attempted to find a way out of the quagmire. The Nixon Doctrine called for the "de-Americanization" of the war. It was known as "Vietnamization," and involved building up the South Vietnamese Army so they could assume a greater combat role while he simultaneously withdrew U.S. forces. The plan also included a greater emphasis on winning the hearts and minds of the people by using aid and support. The U.S. role shifted from fighting to advising, and sending a massive influx of military equipment.

Ho Chi Minh said, "If America wanted to make war for 20 years, then the people of Vietnam would make war for 20 years. But if America wanted to talk peace, I would invite America to tea." We didn't understand that he meant it.

During the war, peace proposals flowed back and forth even when the fighting was at its peak. Some negotiations were public and others were conducted in secret diplomatic back channels.

The shape of the tables used by the delegates became a point of contention. The North Vietnamese favored a circular table, in which all parties, including the NLF (Viet Cong), would appear equally important. The South Vietnamese argued that only a rectangular table was acceptable since it would show two distinct sides of the conflict. Meanwhile, during the debate, Americans were dying at the rate of 350 per week. The juxtaposition of peace and war demoralized the country. In a secret message to Henry Kissinger, Nixon said, "Is it possible we're wrong from the start in Vietnam?"

By January 1972, the United States had conceded on almost every major point at the peace conference including that any cease-fire would be a cease-fire in place, which meant North Vietnamese troops would remain in the south. The North did not intend to stop fighting. Their strategy was to stall the peace process, pour forces into the South, and then strike a deal, which meant a cease-fire in place would be an NVA victory.

In March of that same year, the NVA launched the Easter Offensive. They believed a victory would give them a stronger position at the bargaining table, but because of American advisors and air power, the enemy was stopped. However, America wanted out of the war, but the president wanted to do it with honor. Nixon told the National Security Council, "We've crossed the Rubicon." He wanted to go for broke and destroy the enemy's capability to wage war and avoid the previous mistakes of letting up on the bombing that he and Johnson had previously made. "I have the will in spades," he declared. "Those bastards are going to be bombed like they've never been bombed before." Operation Linebacker brought the enemy back to the peace table. Soon, the boys would be out of a job, and the men on the ground did not want to be the last American to die in Vietnam.

Da Nang, South Vietnam

"Nguyen, let's get married. I don't care 'bout the war; I want us to be together."

"Yes – a thousand times yes; I will marry you Elijah Bravo. The world is uncertain, and I don't care. It's difficult to be away from you. But it's all we've known and it makes me love you more."

"Darlin', all we have is today," he said. "But if we dream of each other we can always be together."

The fan above the bed in the dingy hotel room blew warm air over their heated bodies. Elijah stroked her long black hair, and he kissed her. The lovers held each other tight, holding on to their moment.

"Elijah, could we have this moment one more day and one more day after that? I'm afraid to ask for that. I'll be your wife. My love, I can't find the words to tell you how much I love you."

Young lovers anticipate the future. The promise of tomorrow cultivates love and gives hope. The lovers hadn't that luxury. They had only a moment. The war was their world. Uncertainty and fear intensified their feelings, and they held each other amidst the possibility of death.

"Darlin'," Nguyen said. "Let's marry on Saturday, a week from today. We can meet in the Basilica of the Sacred Heart of Jesus. God will bring us together."

"Even if we're married it will be difficult for you to leave the country," Elijah said. "There'll be months of red tape and endless waitin'. Nguyen, the best way to get you out is through the Red Cross. Bein' married to a Marine Sergeant will have a severe penalty in the New Vietnam. Darlin' it's getting' late, I gotta catch a chopper back to Hue. I'll see you at the church – noon – Saturday. Do you have a wedding dress?"

"You're so silly Elijah Bravo. A wedding dress in Vietnam? Where would I ever find such a dress?"

Sergeant Elijah Bravo had evolved from a ruthless warrior to a man capable of the deepest love. In war, the hearts of men become hardened. Men hold on to hate and hate destroys their spirit. Love opened Elijah's heart. Loving Nguyen Lu was his greatest hope, but loving Nguyen was his greatest fear.

"Oh, Elijah, don't let me go. Hold me forever darling. I'm freighted; I won't have a life without you."

"Darlin', what's meant to be will find a way. I'll see you at the church – Saturday noon."

"And I will see you, Sergeant Bravo – Saturday noon."

Hue City

The Marine advisors lived on the razor's edge. Their mission was to lead a tired Army. But Elijah found something he could hold on to. But how could he keep from falling? If he fell, and he surely would, it wouldn't be good.

"Buckaroo, I need you to do somethin' for me this Saturday,"

Elijah said. "Nguyen and I are gettin' married; I want you to be my best man."

"Well, I'll be dipped in shit, Elijah. That's the greatest news. Married – ain't that something? You bet I'll be your best man. Through thick and thin and to the moon and back."

They read the other's mind, and they chimed.

"There are good ships, and there are the ships that sail the sea. The best ships are friendships and may they always be wood ships, and they are good ships, but the best ships of all are friendships."

"Elijah, we'll figure a way to get her out. Remember what Pops taught us: 'nothin's impossible to a valiant heart.' You gotta believe that."

Ask Captain McGivens if he'd give the bride away, Seamus said.

"But this is Viet-Fucking-Nam. Do they do that here?" Elijah remarked. Jesus Seamus, give the bride away – what you thinkin'?"

"I want Nguyen to have a real weddin'. It's crazy Seamus. Could a weddin' actually happen? How can anything be normal in Vietnam?"

"But Elijah, she's a woman; she wants a weddin'. Y'all need pictures to show your grandchildren. Cowboy, go and tell the skipper the good news. Ask him!"

29 March 1973 – Regimental Headquarters

Something was up. Choppers were coming in empty and leaving full of equipment. They were Navy choppers. The rumor was they were coming from the USS Midway, patrolling in the Gulf of Tonkin. Elijah worried that whatever was going down would not be good. In the Marine Corps, there was a saying that whatever could go wrong, would go wrong.

"Hey, Guns, call the First Sergeant, I want to talk to the both of you," Captain McGivens said.

"Aye-aye Sir."

Seamus and Elijah entered the Captain's office. It was a sandbagged hooch, not more than 10 feet by 12 on the inside. A stack of ammo crates served as a dinner table. Maps lay on another stack, while correspondence and two Pricks (radios) occupied a third. Two crates on end were seats for the Captain's frequent guests. In the back corner was a cot with a poncho liner placed neatly at the rear. Underneath the cot were loaded magazines, two M-16 rifles, two cans of ammo, 12 grenades, a *k-bar* (combat knife), and the remaining 782-gear, the field equipment issued when McGivens arrived in-country as an FNG.

"Come on in guys," Captain McGivens said. "Grab a crate – coffee?"

"What's the word Sir," Seamus asked.

Captain McGivens paused; he was pensive and not happy with the news he was about to give. He took a drag on a Lucky Strike, tilted his head backward, blew smoke into the air, and then gave it to the boys.

"We're pulling out tonight; we're leaving Vietnam. That's the end of it. That's just the mother-fricking end of it. Get your gear together; choppers will be here at 1700. It looks like we made it."

"Sir, where we goin'?" Seamus asked.

"Does it matter? – Seriously?"

"Captain it does matter. It matters a lot where we go," Elijah said.

"Jesus Christ Elijah, I'm sorry. I wasn't thinking. We'll figure a way to get Nguyen out. But for now, we leave and prepare for combat operations in case we're given the word to return."

Elijah heard the news he feared. He had found love. In three days, he was getting married and had just learned he was leaving Vietnam and Nguyen.

"Elijah," the Captain remarked, "I don't know what to say. I promise you I'll do whatever I can. You know I'll do it. I'm so sorry. I tried to get you transferred to 1st Angelico, but they're leaving too. We might be the last to leave. Guys, just do it. Just be ready, 1700 hours. There's no discussion. We're going."

"Sir, I have to get to Da Nang, if only for a moment. I have to say good-bye and tell her."

"Elijah, we're under orders," the Captain countered. "I'm sorry. You have my word that we will work this out."

Calder McGivens had been their CO since the Hill fights in '67. The men were like brothers. Shakespeare wrote, "We few, we happy few, we band of brothers..."

At 1700 hours, the Marine advisors loaded their gear on an outbound CH-53. The rotors were at a half spin, kicking up dust, and blinding the Marines as they boarded the chopper. The sound of the engine whined indicating that to clear the misery of Vietnam, the bird would fight for elevation. The pilot waited for thumbs-up from the ground crew.

The Marines stared out the window at the ARVN soldier undoing the blocks on the wheels of the chopper. What would become of him? 56,000 dead Americans – we were deserting them and all it would take to leave would be a simple thumb's up. The engine coughed, and the soldier flicked his thumb, and they dusted off. The engine struggled as they climbed higher and higher, over the ancient city of Hue.

There was no fanfare. America left the spirits of 56,000 sons and daughters. After a simple sign from a beleaguered ARVN soldier, the chopper disappeared. And that was the end of American combat operations in Vietnam.

The spin of the rotors was the only sound. Some of the men closed their eyes, and others gazed out the window at the vanishing countryside.

Life without Nguyen was worse than waiting for death on Hill-861, Elijah thought.

"This goddamn war – all it did was take," McGivens whispered.

The chopper banked and headed east toward the USS. Midway. Captain McGivens struggled to stand. Holding the webbing attached to the ceiling of the cabin, he made his way toward the cockpit. The Crew Chief yelled, "Sir, please take your seat." The Captain gave him a hard look as he ambled by.

He leaned over the pilot who was scanning the countryside looking for muzzle flashes.

"Lieutenant," the Captain yelled.

The Lieutenant shouted, "Captain – sit down. We're flying evasive – it's a rough ride."

"Lieutenant, would you to do something for me."

"What's that Sir, the Lieutenant screamed?

Captain McGivens leaned closer and explained his request.

"Captain – what did you say? You want me to divert to Da Nang?"

"Yeah," Captain McGivens screamed.

"Sir – why?"

"For love," The Captain shouted.

"Sir – hold the fuck on."

The chopper banked, changed its course, and headed for Mercy Hospital in Da Nang.

FORTY

VALIANT HEARTS

Dedicate some of your life to others. Your dedication will not be a sacrifice. It will be an exhilarating experience because it is an intense effort applied toward a meaningful end.

Dr. Tom Dooley

March 1973 – New York City

The 24-hour shifts Dr. Hawkins worked at Manhattan Veterans Hospital could not fill the hole in her heart. Regardless how life had been with Paul, she believed marriage was a sacrament. But his lie was a betrayal and destroyed any remaining hope she had. Scarlett told her that she couldn't skip the painful parts of life; yet, she held on to Pop's words – "Nothing is impossible to a valiant heart." But Ofa didn't have a valiant heart.

Her mother kept company with the most eligible men in New York. Scarlett was a socialite who previously spent four years as an artist on the West Bank of Paris; it brought her fortune and fame. Mother and daughter traveled the chic circles of the bohemian world. The women became the talk of the town. Young and handsome doctors, writers, and artists pursued Ofa, but she remained aloof and true to the name, Ice Queen. She was a renowned doctor, but that could not fill the void, but she hoped for something she couldn't define. She rummaged through old dreams, raking them over and over as though they were a heap of hot coals. She looked for a spark to ignite a flame, but there weren't any.

"Mama, I want something more than medicine. I don't know what, but I feel empty."

"Darling, find a man, someone to love and someone who loves you. You're a beautiful young woman. Why don't you go out with that handsome Dr. Bedel? He keeps calling. What do you have to lose? Eventually, those calls will stop."

"Mother, those calls haven't stopped for you. I love livin' with you mama, but please stop tryin' to get me laid. Besides, I haven't found anyone that interests me."

That wasn't the reason for Ofa's disinterest in men. She had checked out of life. Ofa's ideals were shattered into fragments, but Scarlett knew that Ofa would have to build her life on one of those broken fragments.

Scarlett believed that finding a man was the solution. But Ofa needed more. She could have any man she wanted, but emptiness kept her separate from the world.

"Have patience, Ofa. One of the most difficult tests in life is to be patient. Patience is the first step toward fulfillment. You're building who you're supposed to be, and that requires risk, and courage. If you don't take a risk, you may never find happiness."

"Mother, it's difficult to have something I know nothing about."

"Dear – when you come across one of those empty shell people, and you think, what the hell happened to them. Well, there comes a time in each one of those lives when they were standing at a crossroad – a place where they had to decide either to turn right or left – but they never make a turn and just remain standing at that crossroad. Ofa, regardless of your dreams, never ignore the chance to find love; there's nothing more important."

"Ofa, no one is saying a man is a solution. But love gives us a center. And when you have a center, it's a stepping-stone toward possibility. So, I'm not buying that you haven't found someone interesting. You're not looking. You're not looking for love, and you're not looking for fulfillment. Fulfillment doesn't fall into your lap. You won't be young forever. Why don't you write that boy Seamus, tell him what happened? Tell him you're sorry for...?"

"Mother – Stop! I can't do that. It's been eight years. It wouldn't be right. He moved on. Not even a word from him."

"But darlin' how could he. He left you the rose, proclaiming his love. And you...."

"But Paul took that from me when he lied. It's too late!" She screamed.

She turned her back and stared at the bookshelf, looking for the textbook on obstetrics. Instead, she found an old book hidden in the corner of the shelf – *Deliver us from Evil: The Story of Vietnam's Flight to Freedom*, by Dr. Tom Dooley. She remembered the day the book arrived. She and the boys had returned from the movies, and Seamus had given her a LifeSaver. A tear fell. She opened the book and saw the movie tickets pressed into the crevasse of a page.

Dr. Dooley was her hero. His life's work was caring for the people of Southeast Asia. She placed the book on the shelf and reached for the phone.

"Yes – information, please. Do you have a listing for the Dooley Foundation Intermed International? – Thank you."

She dialed the number and spoke at length to the director, Dr. Joshua Sims.

"Yes Dr. Sims, I would be willing to go to Southeast Asia," she said. "But not now, not with the war. It's too dangerous."

"Dr. Hawkins, I agree. Vietnam will soon become a very dangerous place. American soldiers are leaving, and because there are no guarantees for the safety of our medical personnel, I'm afraid our humanitarian effort there will cease," Dr. Sims added.

Vietnam

On the opposite side of the world, a rickety Navy helicopter followed the coast of where Vietnam met the Gulf of Tokin. The chopper was heading south toward Da Nang. The whine of the engine muffled any conversation.

Lieutenant Murphy screamed to Captain McGivens, "Sir, we touch down in ten."

The Captain turned to Elijah and held up ten fingers.

The chopper landed adjacent to the hospital.

"Elijah, Be back in ten."

"Yes, Sir. There are no words."

"Guns (Gunnery Sergeant), not between friends."

Crouching to minimize the blowback from the rotors, Elijah ran from the chopper. Lieutenant Murphy kept the rotors turning. If he shut the engine, he wasn't sure he could re-start it.

Elijah ran into the hospital and toward the front desk. A man with a beard peered from the top of his spectacles. He was annoyed at the Marine Sergeant's demand for attention.

"Doctor, I need to see Nurse Nguyen Lu; it's an emergency!"

The doctor shook his head. "Marine, who you want to see?"

"Nguyen Lu," Elijah said.

"She no here."

"Doctor, she's here. She's a nurse. This is where she works."

"Yes, I know. She no here. She up north, Quang Tri. Big Fight with VC. Many wounded."

Elijah shook his head and slammed the desk. "No! He screamed. He held his forehead. "Doctor, this can't be. Did she say how long she'd be there?"

"No, she no say. Big trouble with VC. She stay there."

Elijah reached into the inside pocket, pulled out a letter, and placed it in the doctor's hands. "Sir, please give this to her. Please make sure Nurse Nguyen Lu gets this. Promise me."

Elijah had lost hope and left without saying goodbye to the woman he loved.

The Vietnamese doctor whispered, "Fucking American." He tore the letter, threw it into the trash, picked up the desk phone, and called the third floor. "Nurse Lu, this is Dr. Vu. Stay on the 3rd floor and take my rounds; I'm busy at the front desk."

Elijah boarded the chopper. Captain McGivens knew he hadn't made contact. In Vietnam, there are a million sorrows. The Captain signaled Lieutenant Murphy, and the bird headed east over the South China Sea toward the USS Midway.

Three days later, at The Basilica of the Sacred Heart in Da Nang, a beautiful bride waited at the altar in a white wedding dress.

FORTY-ONE

ALWAYS ON MY MIND

It's a crazy idea – but if it works it's not a crazy idea.

Captain Calder McGivens

September 1973 – USS Midway, Gulf of Tonkin

"**Elijah, if you ain't goin' home, I ain't goin' either.** Been taking care of your ass since Christ was a Corporal. What the fuck would you do without me?"

"I can't go home as long as Nguyen's in Nam," Elijah commented, "and listen, numb-nuts, for the record, I've been taking care of your ass since we joined the Green Suck (Marine Corps)."

Hold of the U.S.S Midway

Captain McGivens brought three cans of warm Vietnamese beer. It didn't matter that Ba Moui Ba tasted like vinegar, a beer was a beer.

"It's from my stash," the Captain said. "Boys – rank has its privileges."

Elijah shook his head and grinned.

"Skipper, I'll be back," Seamus said.

Seamus returned carrying a six-pack of cold Pabst Blue Ribbon beer.

"Capt'in, an NCO has its privileges," Seamus declared.

The Marines laughed. "Texas forever," Elijah proclaimed."

"Living large," Captain McGivens replied.

The cold beer went down smooth. Life onboard ship held few amenities for the Marine Detachment. Beer was a treasure for the men who waited to return to Vietnam. The routine of sea duty was monotonous. Exercise, weapons and tactics classes, live fire, and personnel and equipment inspections caused the Marines to lose their edge. They played cards, shot the shit about home, wives, and girlfriends. Some tried sleeping on cots stacked from floor to ceiling.

Seamus and Elijah had experienced the dark side of life where soulless armies collided and rolled over the dreams of the countless dead. They had made it, but there wasn't much left of their souls, and for the rest of their lives they were condemned to live with the senselessness of Vietnam.

"I got an idea I want to bounce off of you. It's a crazy idea, but if it works, it's not a crazy idea" McGivens said. "Any of you guys ever hear from Ophelia Hawkins?" The Captain asked.

Elijah shook his head. "I haven't seen her in eight years."

"You Seamus?"

"Nothing, but my granddaddy tells me a bit 'bout her. I know she's a doctor and divorced from that rich guy."

McGivens commented, "When we were at Dartmouth, Ophelia and I had some of the same friends. As a matter of fact, one of my friends is still in touch with her. Well, for starters, she left her husband about a year ago. She's living with her mother in New York City; they've reconciled."

"That's a blessing for Ofa. She missed her mother," Elijah remarked.

McGivens continued, "I heard her breakup with her husband was also a blessing."

"I hope she's okay 'bout it. I hate to hear that she's unhappy," Seamus replied.

"Guys, your memories of her have little semblance of who she is today; it's not a good picture. Ophelia Hawkins has not fared well, and this has taken a toll on her psyche," the Captain said. My friend tells me, she suffers bouts of depression.

The boys didn't have the words to respond to what the Captain had to say.

"We should have been there for her," Seamus remarked.

Elijah said nothin', but was consumed by guilt.

"Guys," the Captain said "this is not a time for sentiment, I have an idea I want to bounce off you. I need you to focus. She's a doctor, and she just might know someone in the Red Cross. Maybe she has a friend or has a friend of a friend. There might be a way to get Nguyen out of Vietnam. It's worth a shot. For us, the war is over, and for now, we have a South Vietnam. But that's not going to last. We know what will happen when the whole frickin' NVA Army moves south. Elijah, I can make arrangements for you to call Ophelia and see if she can help."

"Seamus, how do you feel 'bout that," Elijah asked?

"You should do it, Cowboy."

"Elijah, tell her the whole story, see if there's anything she can do. My friend sent me her number. I can patch you through to Japan on the ship's radio, and from there, it's a simple call to New York. Rank has its privileges," Captain McGivens expressed.

The Captain reached into his pocket and showed the boys a paper with Ofa Hawkins' phone number. Seamus gazed at the seven digits scribbled on a crumpled piece of paper ripped from his Platoon Commander's notebook.

"Do it, Elijah," Seamus said.

New York City

Ofa was startled by the piercing ring of the phone. Since it was on her private line, it wasn't the hospital. She had fallen further into depression and lived within the confines of her own misery. She stared at the phone, yet the ringing wouldn't stop. She took a deep breath.

"Hello."

The voice on the other end of the line whispered a faint hello.

"Who is this," Ofa asked.

"It's Elijah."

"Elijah! – Is it you?" Fear overwhelmed her.

"Oh, Elijah! Elijah! It's been so long!" She began to cry. "Elijah, – tell me nothin's happened to Seamus. Please, tell me!" She continued to cry.

"Ofa, It's okay. Seamus is fine. He's fine. We're both fine. We're on a carrier; it's pretty good duty. Out of danger."

Ofa whispered, "Thank God you're both okay."

"Ofa, this is a miracle."

"E l i j a h !"

She said his name slowly and lingered over each syllable.

"I can't believe it's you. You boys are always on my mind. I pray for you every day. How are you dearest, Elijah? It's been so long; I'm at a loss for words. How's Seamus? There's so many things to say; I don't know where to begin. I hadn't seen you since before we graduated. Of course, you boys went fishin' on graduation day; they should've realized you wouldn't be there and postponed it to Saturday."

"I'm happy you and your mom are back together," Elijah said.

"Yes, mother has been remarkable; she's helped me get through some tough times. I can't tell you how blessed I am to have my mom back in my life."

"Ofa, I'm sorry about your marriage."

She paused and didn't acknowledge his thought.

"Where are you? Where's Seamus?"

"We're on a West Pac tour in the South China Sea on the USS Midway. Jesus, Ofa – so much has happened. But I can't talk for long. I need your help. I need advice. You have a minute?"

"Oh, Elijah, my dearest Elijah, anything for you."

"You okay Ofa? You're still cryin'. I hope I didn't cause that."

All Ofa ever did was cry. Crying was the only way she'd express her only emotion that remained.

"Dearest, no – no, there's many emotions and hearin' you brought them back. I have a million questions. But promise me Seamus is okay."

"He's fine Ofa."

"Does he know you're talkin' to me?"

"Yes, he does."

"Does he want to say hello?"

"Ofa, don't think he'd have the words."

"Oh – that sweet boy," she said.

"Ofa, I couldn't tell you what happened between the three of us, but it was a long time ago. We were just kids, and there was so much we didn't understand. He doesn't say it, but I know he thinks of you."

"Elijah, what happened was not what you think. One day I'll tell him."

"He sent you a letter on 25 April 1967."

"Oh, Elijah – I never got a letter from him. No!"

"Ofa, I don't think it's up to me to tell you what he said."

Thinking of the letter she never received, Ofa continued to cry.

"You must think I cry all the time. What help do you need Elijah? Anything for you."

"Seamus and I have served with Captain Calder McGivens since the hill fights in '67. That's how I have your number."

"Calder? Y'all referrin' to Calder from Dartmouth?" she asked.

"Yes, Ofa. Seamus learned about your connection when the Captain took command of the Platoon in '67."

"Calder, that's unbelievable. We were friends at Dartmouth, but we drifted apart after Paul and I got engaged."

"Ofa, you sure you're okay with your divorce?"

"Oh, Elijah now is not the time to talk 'bout the whys of the past eight years. But thank you because I know you care."

"He cares too Ofa. More than you know."

Ofa hadn't smiled for a long time. Elijah reminded her of a time when she was young and at the pinnacle of life. Knowing two old friends still cared gave her a spark and all she needed to do was fan the flame.

Elijah explained the situation with Nguyen and Ofa listened. She had no suggestions but said she would try to figure a way to get Nguyen Lu out of Vietnam.

"Help me!" Elijah pleaded. "Help me Ofa! I'm afraid I'm gonna lose her. The NVA will put her in prison, and she'll die there like her mother. I didn't know who I could turn to. It was the Captain's idea. He said that you bein' a doctor might have some connections with the Red Cross and might know someone who could smuggle her out."

"Elijah darlin', you can trust me with your life. You know that, don't you? I'll make some phone calls; whatever I can do, I will do."

She paused and took a deep breath. "Elijah," in a very sweet voice she said, "Give my best to Seamus. Would you do that for me?"

"Yes, Ofa. Of course. He loved you but didn't know how to tell you."

There was a long pause, and she continued to cry. Knowing that Seamus loved her was even more painful, but she held it together for her old friend Elijah Bravo.

"Let's get Nguyen back. Remember what Pops said when we were kids. 'What's meant to be will find a way.' I lost faith in that, but after talkin' to you, I believe it again. Call me back in a week I hope to have some answers for you," Ofa remarked.

She hung up the phone and fell to the chair. The cushions absorbed her fall, but the pain of childhood, abandonment, the war, Seamus, and Paul overwhelmed her. And she continued to cry. All the pretty girl had done was cry.

She reached for the phone and dialed the number of the Dooley Intermed International Foundation.

"Hello, Dr. Sims – This is Dr. Ophelia Hawkins. I apologize for the late call. I've decided. I want work in Vietnam. I want to go immediately. How soon can I leave?"

FORTY-TWO

WAKENING ATHENA

The rose Dawn might have found them weeping still had not
grey-eyed Athena slowed the night when night was most
profound, and held the Dawn under the Ocean of the East. That
glossy team, Firebright and Daybright, the Dawn's horses that
draw her heavenward for men – Athena stayed their harnessing.

Homer, *The Odyssey*

January 1974 – New York City, JFK International

The beautiful woman wearing dark sunglasses and a broad
brim hat hugged her mother at the terminal of Sea-Board
World Airlines at John F. Kennedy International Airport. For a
woman with no return flight, she was traveling light.

"Mama, I'll be okay, don't worry. This is something I have to do,
for Elijah. I'm going to Cho Ray Hospital; it's in the center of Saigon.
The place is a fortress and protected by thousands of soldiers, so
there's absolutely no need to worry."

"Ofa, don't tell me not to worry. I've done nothing but worry.
I'm looking forward to when your life is not such a rollercoaster, but
till then; I'll worry all I want."

"Mother, it's me who's gonna worry – you bein' all alone to fend
off all those men."

"Darling, with you being 10,000 miles away, I just might get a
date. Call me as often as you can, and let me know if you need
anything. I love you, my darling girl."

"I love you too mama. To the moon and back."

"Dr. Hawkins do you have any additional luggage?" the skycap
inquired. "You've only one bag; you're traveling light."

"Ben, you must think I'm a frilly girl and need a steama' trunk. I'm only goin' to Vietnam; it's not like I'll be walkin' the Champs-Elysées."

"Doctor, a woman like you!"

"Never you mind Ben. Y'all don't know the real me. I'm a Texas girl."

"Texas forever Dr. Hawkins."

"Living Large," she replied.

The old man had a special affinity for the doctor and loved the attention she showed him.

Ofa walked into the terminal. She was dressed in Wranglers, boots, a black hat that barely covered the top of her eyes, and a red sash tied around her waist. There was something different about Ofa Hawkins but it wasn't what she wore that made her different.

"Dr. Hawkins, your bag is cleared to Saigon. Here's your boarding pass, Gate 12-B, they'll be boarding shortly. You're in First Class; have a pleasant flight."

The ticket agent watched as she turned and observed how the jeans sculpted her body. He thought it funny that she'd wear a broad brim hat. It was an unusual outfit for women traveling to Vietnam.

A beautiful woman traveling alone is alluring. She moves through the airport and both men and women peer above their newspapers to watch as she walks by. She would soon be acting on a grander stage and would pull on the sensibilities of men to get what she wanted. Ofa Hawkins boarded flight 762 with one intention – to smuggle Nguyen Lu out of Vietnam.

The DC-8 shot across the Pacific leaving lines of chalk across its blue. Curled against the window and wrapped in a blanket, she kept to herself. She stared at the endless wine dark sea below. But she knew the risks. Finding and rescuing Nguyen Lu in a sea of millions was unfathomable. She hadn't a plan or an ally. She knew Nguyen was a nurse and in love with Elijah Bravo. Nguyen was Cowboy's Girl and that was all she needed to know. She was surprisingly calm for a girl who ventured into the heart of darkness. She accepted the fate that waited but this time, fate would be on her terms. She would follow the footsteps of Dr. Tom Dooley. She had the perfect cover: Girl with the purple ribbon, the iconic symbol of the peace movement. Of course, she would go to Vietnam.

She looked for shapes of ships. Occasionally she'd see a dark silhouette. The boys were somewhere sailing the Pacific waiting for the word to go back to Vietnam. However, Congress passed the War Powers Resolution limiting the President's ability to wage war without a Congressional Declaration. At 29,000 feet, the Pacific was a mystery and hid the answers she sought. What would become of Nguyen Lu – Elijah Bravo, and Seamus O'Grady? What would become of her?

New York City

Elijah had followed Ofa's instructions, and returned her call the following week. On the other side of the world, a strange voice answered.

"Hello."

"May I speak to Ofa, please?"

"May I ask whose calling?" Scarlett questioned.

"This is Elijah Bravo."

"Elijah, this is Ofa's mom, Scarlett. I've been waiting for your call. Are you well?

"Mrs. Hawkins, I'm doing fine. I'm happy that you and Ofa are back together."

"Yes, I love my daughter, I don't know how I lived without her. But Elijah, how is Seamus? She's been asking about him."

Scarlett remembered her promise not to speak of her daughter's feelings for Seamus. But she was a smart woman and knew that a slip of the tongue would tell Seamus she cared.

"May I call you Scarlett?"

"I would like that, Elijah."

"Scarlett, I need to speak to Ofa, please."

"She's not here Elijah. She joined Dooley Intermed International and left for Vietnam last week."

"Vietnam! What?" Elijah was startled and didn't understand. "What's Dooley Intermed International?"

"It was started in the 50's by Dr. Tom Dooley. They're physicians working throughout Southeast Asia."

"Scarlett, Ofa read his books, Dr. Tom Dooley. I remember she was excited when she got his book. Me, Ofa, and Seamus just got back from the movies. But Vietnam – I don't understand. Why she goin'?"

"Elijah darling, I'm to tell you that she went to Vietnam to find Nguyen and bring her back to Luckenbach. She's going to do it. My daughter is a very determined girl."

"Scarlett, I don't know what to say. Thank you! Thank you! Nguyen is my fiancée."

"Yes, I know Elijah. Congratulations! Ofa's told me all about you and Seamus, and I'm sure she's told you about me. Probably not very good things, but that's the past. Please don't think ill of me, Elijah."

"No Scarlett, I'm happy for you both. She never spoke bad of you."

"Elijah, I'm happy to hear; we've crossed that bridge. I don't know what else to tell you. We'll have to wait and see. She knows I'll worry, but don't think she'll call; it's just like her not to."

"Scarlett, I don't know how to thank you."

"You already did, Elijah."

After all the years, it was Ofa. It was always Ofa.

FORTY-THREE

NEW WEAPONS

Beneath the earth those hidden blessings for man, bronze, iron,
and gold – who can claim to have discovered before me? No one,
I am sure, who wants to speak to the purpose. In one short
sentence understand it all: every art of mankind comes from
Prometheus.

Aeschylus

January 1974 – Saigon

Dr. Floris DeWitt watched the passengers deplane at Tan
Son Nhat airport in Saigon. There were journalists,
photographers, businessmen, technicians, clergy, doctors, nurses, and
ranking military officials. All sent to do their part in the inevitable
downfall of South Vietnam. Dr. DeWitt thought, *there is something
peculiar about those who would come to Vietnam on the verge of a
communist victory.*

The heat shimmered off the tarmac sending undulating waves
upward making it difficult to recognize Dr. Ophelia Hawkins,
Dooley Intermed International's newest physician. All he had was a
name; he wasn't sure if she was even on the plane. Why would a
woman, who is a noted American physician, abandon her life and
travel to Vietnam? A country where everyone was trying to leave. He
saw an elegant woman with dark sunglasses and a broad brim hat
descending the steps. Although she moved slowly, there was no
hesitation in her step. The woman wore Wranglers, a maroon blouse,
and a red sash tied around a petite waist. In the middle of her
descent, she stopped to adjust her hat. He saw long blond curls fall
softly over her shoulders. He smiled when he saw a purple ribbon.

"Dr. Hawkins, welcome to Vietnam. Let me help you. I'm Dr. DeWitt. I – I didn't expect..."

Ofa interrupted. "Dr. DeWitt, you didn't expect someone like me to step off the plane? I assure you I'm not what you think."

"Excuse me Doctor, that was not my thought at all. It's just that – well, everyone is trying to leave, and when a woman like you shows up, it raises eyebrows. I'm sure you understand that – sorry."

"You're Dutch?" she questioned.

"Yes, we Dutch have a history of being in the wrong place at the wrong time, or maybe I should say trying to get whatever we can get. We disguise our sinister nature as altruism – Dutch imperialism of the 17th century. I'm here to atone for the sins of colonialism.

Ofa laughed at the glib Dutch doctor.

"But you Americans are different. For you, it's always about righteousness. But I am curious Doctor Hawkins. Maybe you are the caricature of Prometheus, and what Vietnam needs now is its hero.

Ofa smiled and thought it prudent to divert attention from her.

"Doctor, I do remember studyin' the Dutch Golden age," she said. Regardless of colonialism, the Dutch have never turned a blind eye to service."

"Yes, Dr. Hawkins, here we are trying to help the people of Vietnam, but what we really want is their rubber."

Ophelia laughed. She liked the young handsome Doctor.

He reached for her bag; Ophelia smiled and acknowledged his gesture.

"So, tell me Dr. Hawkins, why are you here and don't tell me you are here to help people."

"Dr. DeWitt, y'all must know I'm here on a secret mission. I'm America's secret weapon to win the war. You're right – I am Prometheus and I'm here to steal more than fire. But I tell everyone I'm here to help people."

Floris DeWitt entertained the thought that the beautiful woman came for some diabolical plot, some ill-conceived last-ditch effort at diplomacy trying to stop the hordes of enemy soldiers moving toward the south. Could she be the ultimate weapon? It was the way she stood with that red sash tied around her waist.

"Dr. Hawkins, I'll take you to your quarters, there's no time to waste. The North Vietnamese Army is approaching, and the number of wounded soldiers is more than we can handle. Can you come to the hospital this afternoon?"

"Give me a couple of hours to freshen up. I'm not expectin' much, but I can use a hot shower."

Dr. DeWitt smiled.

"You're lucky. Hot water is available in your quarters. I just hope it's today, and if it's today, I hope it's this afternoon, and if it's this afternoon, I hope it's working, and if it's working, I hope there's some left."

Ofa was going to like the handsome Dutch doctor.

As he drove to her quarters; he was careful to avoid the rickshaws pulled by thin old men with long gray beards. The younger men were fighting the war. The North Vietnamese Army was advancing, and without the help of the Americans, there was nothing the ARVN could do to stop them. Ophelia had to find Nguyen Lu before the NVA did. As they drove through the outlying squalor of Saigon, Ophelia noticed the sordidness caused by the war. Women squatted on the side of the road relieving themselves and men urinated along the dikes of the rice patties. The occasional garbage dump swarmed with people trying to find the next day's meal or something of value the Americans had discarded. Colonialism had destroyed the country. Whatever economic progress made under colonialism, benefited the French and the wealthy Vietnamese. The people were suffering, but America came to give them freedom.

At the Geneva Accords of 1954, the West and the Viet Minh divided the country into two separate Vietnams – North, and South. Historically, Vietnam was one sovereign nation. South Vietnam was created by the United States. In 1956, the communist North and the newly created South agreed to hold elections. Since it was certain that the North Vietnamese communists would score an easy victory, the United States disallowed any referendum. Elections were never held. America became the protector of the country they created. South Vietnam became a repressive government, and the puppets of western influence. The *National Front for the Liberation of the South* (NFL), supported by armed insurgents, called the *Viet Cong* began the destabilization of the South Vietnamese government. The people had Coca-Cola, but they had to become prostitutes to get it, and when they did get it, it was warm.

Ophelia noticed the roving eye of the handsome Doctor. She was beautiful, she was sexy, she was seductive, she was brilliant. Ofa Hawkins had amassed new weapons and she would use them.

"Please call me Floris. May I call you Ophelia?"

"Oh yes, of course, Floris. I prefer that."

"Floris, I want to find a friend, a Vietnamese nurse, who I met when I was a visiting intern at Johns Hopkins University – Nguyen Lu. I understand she's working as a nurse somewhere in Vietnam. Do you know her?"

"No, I don't believe I do. Many of the Vietnamese doctors and nurses are up North, where the fighting is. It's not safe for them. I worry about my Vietnamese colleagues. Since they helped the South, they're considered traitors."

"Do you think I can find where Nguyen Lu is?" Ofa asked.

"I don't think it would be difficult, especially if she were trained in America. Her skills would exceed a nurse trained in Vietnam, and furthermore she would speak English. She'd be noticed. Ophelia, there are four MASH units in Quang Tri Province. I bet she's in one of them. Don't think of going up there; they've been overrun, and under the control of the communists. It doesn't look good. They'll use her and then if they learn she helped the Americans they'll put her in prison or send her to a reeducation camp. It's safer to be European; it's even safer to be American as long as you're here for a purpose."

"Floris, how would I get to Quang Tri?"

Dr. DeWitt didn't believe what he heard. She was either a fool or had a peculiar motive.

"Ophelia, you can't go there. The communists hold it; there's no flights, no nothing. After the Paris Peace Accords, your government agreed to a cease-fire in place. The Northern Territories, which the NVA occupy are still under their control. Quang Tri might as well be on the other side of the moon."

"Floris, I have to see her; I have to make sure she's okay; she's my friend."

With her green eyes and a sultry glare, she gave him a look that made him think he'd have a chance.

"Would you help me, Floor-ris?"

FORTY-FOUR

IF BY LIFE OR DEATH

I can't fight for myself . . . but I can fight for Nguyen Lu . . . For others, I can kill.

Ofa Hawkins

June 1974 – Cho Ray Hospital, Saigon

"Ophelia, why are you always working? You should take time to smell the roses."

"Floor…is," she said with a wicked glare. "There're no roses in Vietnam."

"Floor…is," she hesitated. "That's not the question you're fixin' to ask me. Is it?"

She said his name with a seductive Texas drawl.

"That's what I like about you girl; you're just sooo – How do you cowboys say it? Darn intuitive."

"Darlin', cowboys use the word darn in every sentence, but I don't think I've ever heard the word intuitive spoken in Texas."

"How did a girl from Texas become so shrewd? You're more like a New Yorker."

"Is that all you like 'bout me," she blurted. "I've other assets besides the size of my brain."

Dr. DeWitt smiled and hoped he would be with this remarkable woman. Ofa had a way of leaning into a conversation and with a bat of an eye; she grabbed the doctor's attention. Under the pretext of romance, Ofa Hawkins toyed with Floris because only in love could she be pardoned for any sexual dalliances. He was reluctant to ask a question that had been on his mind since the moment they met.

"Why don't we spend time together"? the young doctor asked.

"We do, we do spend time together, we spend 16 hours every

day. I thought you'd be sick of me by now. Floor...is, you're a good friend, please don't think I don't appreciate you. I do. I really do. But my focus is on the work. It's difficult to be a woman in Vietnam. I'm attracted to you, but this place sucks the joy out of life."

He didn't hear what he had hoped, but she kept the door open. Dr. DeWitt wanted more than friendship. He wanted to love her, to hold her. But he wondered if the rumors were true. Was she as cold as ice? Was she teasing him? Regardless, he was falling through time and space and stars and sky and everything in between. Ofa Hawkins – she was a witch and cast a spell on the young Dutch doctor drawing him into an abyss that had no end. He was a man, he was her prey, and she was a black widow.

Ofa had been in Vietnam for six months and still had no idea of the whereabouts of Nguyen Lu.

* * *

In June 1974, the situation in Vietnam had deteriorated. President Nixon promised President Thieu, that if the North violated the Paris Peace accords, America would come to the aid of the South. Both sides violated the agreement before the ink on the document had dried; however, America never came. Congress refused to appropriate the necessary funds for the South's survival. Without supplies and equipment, Quang Tri, the northernmost province in the South was lost. If Nguyen was there, she was working for the communists.

At the hospital, Ofa had become a celebrity. Pictures of her circulated throughout the wards, some of which portrayed her in jeans and boots. As she made her daily rounds, her patients vied for her attention. "Doctor, check my forehead for fever." She'd lean over the men exposing the top of her breasts.

She'd touch their forehead and say, "Why do you get so hot each time I'm here?" They'd laugh.

"Dr. Hawkins, you kiss me; I feel better."

She'd bend over and give the soldier a kiss on the cheek; the men would cheer and anticipate her next visit. If she kissed one man, she would find a way to kiss them all.

"How are you feeling Lieutenant Ky?" Ofa asked.

"Much better Dr. Hawkins; I owe you my life. In my culture, you save my life; I am your servant forever. I will pray for you always. Will you take picture with me? You are a famous woman, and when I get your picture I will brag about you, then when the North comes, I will use your picture to escape."

"Lieutenant, you are such man. How will a picture of me enable you to escape? Would you trade my picture for your freedom?"

"Dr. Hawkins, I would never sell your picture. They would spare me because I am your guardian angel. Even the communists will realize you are worthy of protection."

"My dear Lieutenant, you treat me like a queen."

"You are my queen Dr. Hawkins."

Lieutenant Ky was a helicopter pilot and her favorite patient. He was severely wounded during the Easter offensive; subsequently, the chief of staff tagged him as fatal. Ophelia disregarded his diagnosis and proceeded to save the Lieutenant's life. She became irate at the European doctor and warned him never to interfere with her diagnosis.

"Doctor you're discharging me in three days; I must go back to my unit. I do not believe I will survive the next battle."

"Lieutenant, you mustn't think like that. I will pray for you."

"There's no hope for me; I will die for nothing," he said.

"Lieutenant, I don't know what's gonna happen to you or to me. But whether we live or die, the sun will rise, and the world will continue. What helps me is that I make a list in my head of all the good things that I see in this world – every little thing I can remember – it's like a game; I do it over and over. That helps me forget all the bad things that can happen. Lieutenant, I don't believe dyin' is in your future. I wouldn't write your story that way."

"Thank you, Doctor; I will hold that to my heart. May I ask how you learned Vietnamese?"

"I minored in linguistics at Dartmouth. I can speak Spanish, Italian, French, and I get by in Vietnamese. But I study every day."

"Lieutenant Ky, where did you learn to speak English?"

"I went to University in America, studied English and engineering, and then went to flight school with the Marines at Pensacola, Florida. I was in the States six years."

"What University did you attend," she asked in Vietnamese?

"I graduated from Johns Hopkins, in Baltimore."

Dr. Hawkins grabbed a chair and sat.

"Lieutenant Ky," she whispered. When you were at Johns Hopkins, did you know a Nguyen Lu?"

"Yes, I called her little sister. We were good friends. I loved her, but sometimes people are meant only to be friends. It's the way I feel about you, Dr. Hawkins. Do you know where she is?"

"I'll be right back Lieutenant."

"Nurse, would you ask Dr. DeWitt to finish my rounds?"

"Dr. Hawkins. Dr. DeWitt would do anything for you."

The nurse giggled as she walked down the ward.

"Lieutenant Ky, do you have a picture of her?"

He nodded and reached for a small box.

"This picture is of my little sister, Nguyen Lu. In my culture, we call someone little sister when they are like family."

Dr. Hawkins studied the picture and smiled. Nguyen was dressed in a white cloak, accented by long black silky hair hanging below her waist. She appeared innocent, but in the eyes of the North, she was a criminal. Her only crime was saving lives and falling in love with a Marine. Ofa realized, that the girl she was willing to die for, was real.

"Lieutenant Ky, I have something important to ask you, but I must have your trust. Your eyes will tell me if you are truthful."

"Dr. Hawkins, I have told you that I am your servant – forever. If you knew me, it would be understood what I have said is true."

"Lieutenant, I want to find Nguyen Lu, and I don't care where I have to go or what I have to do. I want to get her out of Vietnam. I can't fight for myself – but I can fight for Nguyen Lu – for others I can kill. Would you help me do that?"

"Dr. Hawkins, I would die for you." Ofa peered into his eyes and smiled.

FORTY-FIVE

AN ABSURD IDEA

An idea that is not dangerous is unworthy of being called an idea.

Oscar Wilde, *The Critic as the Artist*

June 1974 – USS Midway, Gulf of Tonkin

In the heavy rolling seas of the Gulf of Tonkin, the USS Midway bobbed like a cork. The power of the dangerous sea pushed her up and up toward the crest of a wave and then she fell and disappeared into the brink. She'd rise again, and then her 65,000 tons would drop like an anchor into the wine-dark sea. The Midway struggled in the violent depths that crashed on every side. But she kept to her course and smashed her way along the black coast of Vietnam. Meanwhile, Dr. Hawkins, one hundred miles from the Midway, plotted to rescue Nguyen Lu.

The Marines had left Vietnam with a bad feeling; they didn't get the victory they were promised. Although they had won the battles and inflicted horrendous losses on the North, they weren't permitted to reach the light at the end of the tunnel that General Westmoreland had promised. America needed a definitive victory, and the Marines wanted to return to get it. The young Marines who hadn't seen combat wanted to go ashore, but the veterans wanted to forget.

In 1973, Nixon's presidency was crumbling under the pressure of the Watergate scandal; consequently, Congress blocked any American military option. The War Powers Resolution limited the President's ability to deploy American forces without a Congressional declaration of war. Similarly, that same year, Congress passed the

Case-Church Amendment prohibiting further U.S. military activity in Vietnam, Laos, and Cambodia.

*   *   *

First Sergeant O'Grady and Gunnery Sergeant Bravo prepared their men to rescue the beleaguered ARVN forces from imminent disaster. Seamus was the good cop, and icon of Alpha Company. His meticulous attention to the details of combat would increase the odds of survival when the Marines went ashore. Gunnery Sergeant Bravo, the bad cop, could bring hell down from heaven. Bravo prosecuted the will of his best friend and earned the reputation as the meanest mother in the valley.

Life had become pensive waiting for word of Ofa Hawkins' insane attempt to rescue Nguyen Lu.

"I've no idea how Ofa's doing, Elijah commented. "She's been in Nam for nine months, and there's nothing from her. It's the not knowin' that kills me. She's riskin' her life for me. Her mom's letter said she was in Saigon trying to go north to Quang Tri. Seamus, the NVA overran Quang Tri. What's she thinkin'? I have no idea who this woman is; we haven't seen her in nine years. How would we even know her? She's riskin' her life to save a woman she never met."

"Elijah, we did her wrong," Seamus said. After she went her way, we ignored her. That don' sit well with me. I don't feel good 'bout myself for bein' mad that she never acknowledged the rose I gave her. Pops said she became depressed and neither of us had the decency to call her and try to make her feel better. She gave everything she had to try and stop the war, and what's sad is that what she did, didn't amount to a hill of beans."

Cho Ray Hospital

"Good morning Dr. Hawkins!" How is my favorite American?"

Dr. Hawkins ignored his pleasantries. "Lieutenant Ky, I'm going to release you to limited duty status with a provision that I will re-evaluate you in one month. You will be assigned to me. Since I promised to have drinks with your commandin' officer, he was amenable to my request."

"Dr. Hawkins – no. I would not want you to be alone with

Colonel Tu. He is a lecherous man."

Ofa smiled and gave the Lieutenant a sexy glance.

"Lieutenant, do not underestimate me. I can handle 100 men like Colonel Tu."

But could she handle even one?

"My lady, I'm sure you can, but allow me to be concerned."

"Lieutenant, each day you will fly me to a different village for a routine *MEDCAP* (Medical Civic Action Program). After we tend to the patients, we will offload medical supplies and store them in the village of Bien Hoa. Dr. DeWitt is preparing documents showing that you are a physician's assistant and a pilot working for Dooley Intermed International. In five days, instead of flying to our assigned MEDCAP, we will fly to Bien Hoa, pick up the supplies, and then fly to Da Nang. I have learned from the gossip of the Red Cross workers that a priest named Father Gee last saw Nguyen at the Cathedral in Da Dang, but it was more than a year ago. I will go to the church to inquire about her and then to the hospital. If we find her, we'll head out to sea and search for an American ship."

"Doctor, what is our plan if we do not find her?"

Dr. Hawkins appeared reflective. She hadn't yet told him she would give both her life and his to rescue Nguyen Lu.

"Lieutenant Ky, if we don't find her, we will head north and look for her in Quang Tri. But please know this, we will find her. Only death will prevent this."

"My dear Dr. Hawkins, with all the dangers that lie waiting for us, I join you with my hand and my heart."

Ophelia Hawkins was the most publicized anti-war activist of the Vietnam War and known as the Girl with the Purple Ribbon. She was a Doctor who traveled to the dark side of the world to help the People's Republic of Vietnam. It was the perfect cover for the young American woman.

"Lieutenant, are you ready for this?"

"Doctor, I have been fighting for five years, for nothing. You have given me something to die for: love."

"Then we have a deal," she said.

"Yes, we have a deal, Dr. Hawkins."

*   *   *

"Orderly, please prepare limited duty documents for Lieutenant Ky. He will be assigned to me. Train him in basic patient care."

For the next four days, Dr. Hawkins and Lieutenant Ky flew to adjacent villages to care for the sick. The evening before their departure, Ofa had dinner with Dr. DeWitt. He planned a romantic candlelight dinner at the Continental Palace, the showcase of French colonialism and the home of the social and political elite of the South. There were moments when the charm of the French colonial era made Vietnam beautiful.

The table was set with Irish linen, English bone china, Czechoslovakian crystal, and Japanese sterling silver cutlery. When the communists take over, there would be no elegance remaining in Saigon. They would destroy every influence of Western decadence.

Floris was pleased that Dr. Hawkins looked extraordinarily beautiful. He hoped it was a clue as to how the evening would go. Floris DeWitt was in love with the beautiful woman. She was his addiction.

"Ophelia, is there a future for us?" he asked. "I'm in love with you."

Floris leaned over the table and kissed Ophelia Hawkins on the lips. She accepted his advances. Her lips were soft and moist. It was a long and slow kiss. She bit his lip and smiled. He hoped this would be a sign there'd be a future. He grabbed her hand and pressed it to his lips.

"Floor...is..."

Her voice was sultry and deep, more like a whisper that came from deep inside and took every breath she had. When a woman says a man's name with such mystery, it could mean only one thing. But she was an actress — acting on a grand stage.

He leaned back; raised a glass of wine. "To us," he said. Her fingers were slow and seemed to crawl across the table. She grasped the crystal stem, then extended her glass. He drank. She didn't. She placed the glass on the table. Dr. DeWitt observed every move. She had told him the answer to his question.

How could I not love this man? She thought. But she had promises to keep and miles to go before she slept.

"Ophelia it's getting late. You have a big day tomorrow. You'll be in my thoughts. I want to know you forever."

"Oh, Floor...is – we'll meet again. I'm sorry."

"Shhhhh!" he whispered. "This is not goodbye."

"Yes, Floor...is, I keep my friends forever."

He wrapped a blue shawl around her shoulders and took folds of blond hair layering them gently down her back. They walked the Rue de Catinat, and they brushed against each other. He was a pragmatic man and knew she still had feelings for the cowboy.

They lingered at the door to her room.

"Ophelia, please don't worry, I'll do my part. I'll send the message. Lieutenant Ky's papers will not be a problem. He is a bright man and has learned enough skills to make him believable."

"Floor…is! Enough! Stop it! I'm not worried."

She kissed him. Soft and gentle! After the first touch of his lips, she grabbed him by the shirt and pulled him into the room. Her fingers dug into his back, and he tightened his arms around her waist. They embraced under the pale-yellow light, and the fan swirled overhead. Ofa kicked the door shut and leaned against the wall. They met violently. She wrapped her body around his. Like a hostage, he pinned her against the wall. They were eye to eye. Her lips came crashing down on his. He kissed her like he owned her. She wrapped her legs around him, and he carried her to a table. One hand held her back; the other violently brushed the table's contents onto the floor. She moved to meet his violence. Ofa moaned and placed both arms around his neck. "Take me to the bed!" she whispered. Ofa turned him on his back and ravished him until they lay exhausted. They spent the night in each other's arms.

FORTY-SIX

WAITING SNAKES

We penetrated deeper and deeper into the heart of darkness.

Joseph Conrad, *Heart of Darkness*

July 1974 – Saigon

Lieutenant Ky took a deep breath and flipped the switch, to power the Huey, and the engine began to whine. The rooters turned, and the Lieutenant held his grip on the throttle. Black smoke billowed from the rear of the chopper, and the blades moved faster and faster pushing exhaust into the cockpit and choking the travelers. He watched the ground crew kick away the chocks that secured the wheels on the tarmac. Being a helicopter pilot was simple, but he was heading into the heart of darkness on an insane mission engineered by a fanatical woman whom he vowed to protect with his life. His leg began to bounce with the rhythm of the turning blades. The Lieutenant wiped his face with the green towel that hung around his neck. Lieutenant Ky had been on many combat missions, but this time, there was more at stake. His concern was for her. He would be responsible for her for the rest of his life. He turned toward the doctor. She appeared calm and stared out the window as though she were riding the bus to school.

"Dr. Hawkins, your seatbelt please."

She smiled.

Dr. Floris DeWitt watched her sitting passively in the window, and she watched him. He was in love with her. She tried to love the handsome doctor but maybe another time and place.

Lieutenant Ky kissed the rosary hanging from the top of the cockpit. The chopper lifted off and headed north to search for

Nguyen Lu.

Floris blew her a kiss, and then she disappeared. Dr. DeWitt summoned a nurse to take his rounds for the remainder of the morning. He threw off his white coat, flagged a taxi, and left the hospital.

"Driver, take me to Cu Nhac Circle, Dooley Headquarters."

Dooley Intermed International Headquarters

"Good morning Dr. DeWitt," the receptionist said.

"Li, I have a message to send, I'll just be a minute."

"Doctor, let me send it; it would give me something to do."

"I'll do it myself. It's a lady, and I don't want you blabbering about my love life."

"Doctor, I thought you and Dr. Hawkins were lovers. That's what everyone is thinking. Last night you were seen kissing her. I don't understand you men. I hear people talking about how lucky you are to have this woman. But you tell me you are not together, and you have other woman. So, I think you are not lucky."

"We're just good friends, Li. It was just a kiss, an innocent kiss. Furthermore, you know what they say about her?"

"Yes, I know, she is the Ice Queen. But I am a woman, and I see things that men cannot. I do not think she is as cold as people say."

Floris was about to explode. He wanted to tell someone that Dr. Hawkins had broken his heart, but he would keep that pain to himself. Dr. DeWitt unfolded a piece of paper. He typed the message into the teleprinter making sure it was exactly what she had written.

01 July 74 – 07:38-USS Midway – Alpha Company-1st Battalion-9th Marine Regiment – Sergeant Elijah Bravo – Girl from South Grape Creek heading north to find Cowboy's Girl – Godspeed my Sergeants – Pretty Girl sends...

He burnt the paper.

USS Midway, Gulf of Tonkin

"Mr. Quackenbush, you better come here; take a look at this. I have no clue what this is about."

"What you got Jonesy?" Lieutenant *Junior Grade* (JG) Quackenbush inquired.

The barking teletype machines and the chatter of operators in the

Communications Center of the Midway were chaotic. The center received 1,000's of messages each day but had never received anything like the message Jonesy attempted to decipher.

"Sir, I just received a message for a Gunnery Sergeant Elijah Bravo in Alpha 1/9. Since when do we get messages addressed to Sergeants?"

"Read it Jonesy," Quackenbush said.

"It says: 'girl from the South Grape Creek going north to find Cowboy's Girl. Godspeed my Sergeants." What the heck sir? It's from Pretty Girl."

"Pretty Girl!" Quackenbush commented. "Who the hell is Pretty Girl? Must be some kind of code. Someone better not be fucking with the net. Give me that; I'll check it out with our crypto (cryptography) guys. Jonesy, do Sergeants get messages sent directly to them?"

"Sir, they get Red Cross messages but those are sent to the ship's Captain, and it's up to him to deliver the contents."

Lieutenant JG Joe Quackenbush was from rural Indiana. As a boy, he read the sea stories of William H. White who saw the sea and a ship from the viewpoint of a fo'c'sle hand. In school, he was the only student who made sense of Melville's, *Moby Dick*. It was inevitable that he would fall in love with the sea and crave a life within this watery world.

Crypto found there were no signatures with the designation, Pretty Girl.

"Jonesy, I'll go to Alpha Company and find out if there's an Elijah Bravo. Let's see if we can take care of this before it goes up the chain."

* * *

"Guns, there's a Lieutenant JG Quackenbush here to see you," Sergeant Rick MaddogMike Flynn said.

Seamus looked at Elijah and laughed, "What the fuck did you do now Cowboy?"

"I have no idea."

"Gunnery Sergeant Bravo?" Quackenbush asked.

"Yes, Sir."

"At ease Gunny. Don't get up."

Quackenbush was displeased that the Gunnery Sergeant remained seated in the presence of an Officer. Elijah wasn't about to stand for a Naval officer that had never heard a shot fired in anger. Nine years in the Marines had not changed him.

"Gunny, I know the history of 1/9. You guys have seen the shit. If I were you, I wouldn't stand for some Naval officer either. Frankly, I should get up for you."

Elijah Bravo smiled, rose from the chair, and extended his hand. "Sir, can I get you a beer?"

"You guys have beer?"

"Yes, Sir, we have cold beer."

"Gunny, I got a strange message; it's addressed to you." Sergeant Bravo shook his head and took the message. "Sir, who the fuck would send me a message?"

01 July 74 – 07:38-USS Midway – Alpha Company-1st Battalion-9th Marine Regiment – Sergeant Elijah Bravo – Girl from South Grape Creek heading north to find Cowboy's Girl – Godspeed my Sergeants – Pretty Girl sends.

"Ofa," Elijah whispered. "She's risking her life for Nguyen."

"Godspeed Pretty Girl," Seamus replied.

"Ofa's out there. She said she'd do anything," Elijah commented. "Sir, you want another beer? Have a seat; it's a long story, and I need to tell it."

Da Nang Cathedral, South Vietnam

One hundred miles from the Midway, Ofa Hawkins walked into the Catholic Church in Da Nang. She wore a western duster, boots, and a broad brim hat. A young nun greeted her.

"Tot chj em buoi sang," (good morning sister), Ofa said.

"I speak English. I practice with you," the nun replied.

"Sister, please help me. I'm Dr. Hawkins from Dooley Intermed International. I am here on a medical mission. I'm looking for a friend of mine. She's a nurse. I understand she was to be married in this church. This is her picture. Can you help me locate her?"

The young nun gazed at the picture.

"Yes, doctor, I know her, Nguyen Lu. Very good nurse."

"I be right back," the woman said.

She returned with an older man.

"Dr. Hawkins, this is Father Kee."

Ofa bowed. "Mornin' Father, do you know this woman? She's my friend, and she's missing. I am worried for her."

"Yes, Nguyen Lu," he said. "She was to be married here, maybe a year ago, but her man, a Marine, left Vietnam – very sad. I was to marry them. She came wearing a wedding dress. I thought that was unusual. Where does a woman get a wedding dress in Viet Nam? Very strange."

"Do you know where she is?" Dr. Hawkins asked.

"She was transferred north to Quang Tri to help the soldiers. But Quang Tri is communist; I don't know what happened to her. She alive or dead. If she alive she works for the communists. Her mother spied for Viet Minh, so maybe she okay. Her father American Green Beret, not good. But her big problem is that she was to marry a U.S. Marine. I don't know Dr. Hawkins; I wish I could help you. I pray for her, and if you are looking for her, I will pray for you. You too are in danger."

Ofa Hawkins bowed and left the church.

"Dr. Hawkins, seatbelt, please," Lieutenant Ky calmly requested. Ky kissed the rosary, and headed the north to Quang Tri.

FORTY-SEVEN

FOLLOWING TOM DOOLEY

The true mystery of the world is the visible, not the invisible.

Oscar Wilde

July 1974 – Quang-Tri, South Vietnam

Colonel Gee pulled on an American cigarette and blew the smoke above the forehead of his captive. He preferred Camel's but would smoke anything as long as it was American. Even the enemy understood anything American was better than anything Vietnamese. Sitting in a leather chair, a remnant of French Colonial rule, the Colonel appeared pompous. His uniform was impeccably tailored. He wore his medals signifying years of service pushing papers. As he spoke, he extended his chest to display his decorations.

Nurse Nguyen Lu was captured when the People's Army of Vietnam overran the ARVN outpost at Dong Ha in Quang Tri Province. After enemy soldiers had subdued the defenders, they moved to the hospital and demanded that she come with them. She threw the soldiers out of the tent, and her feisty nature caught their attention. Colonel Gee realized nurse Lu had valuable skills, but she had to be turned and become communist. Nguyen Lu had worked for the Americans, which was a heinous crime. She should have been executed. But being beautiful has its advantages. Regardless, her fate was not promising. The Colonel couldn't understand her desire to save lives regardless of what side they were on.

"Sister Lu," the Colonel said. "Do you admit you worked for the enemies of the People of Vietnam? If you admit your crimes, the state will show you mercy."

"Colonel Gee, I am a medical professional. I care for the sick and wounded. I don't ask whose side they're on. Man is neither friend nor foe; he is created in the image of God and if I serve man, I serve God."

"You did not answer my question Nurse Lu. You can't avoid a question by citing your Christian ideology. You must sign this paper and admit you worked for the enemies of the state. We will show you mercy. You will then work for us. We will send you North. There your skills will be better served."

"Colonel, you disregard my skills because of the party's insistence that I sign a piece of paper that is meaningless."

"Sister, that is why you should sign, so you can go on living and working. Only then will you see the error of your ways."

Nguyen thought of Elijah. She needed to find a way to go to him. There was no choice but to confess that she worked for the hated Americans. She reached for the pen.

"You did the right thing Nurse Lu. Now that you have confessed, nothing has changed. Although you have committed a criminal act, I do not see you as a criminal. Your confession is the first step toward forgiveness. Don't think we don't know that your mother was a hero of the Vietnamese People. She died for her country in a French prison. If you are wise, things will go well for you. You will be of great value to the cause."

Nguyen nodded. She hoped her complacent demeanor hid the hatred she felt for the man.

"Nurse Lu, now that you have confessed, I am sending you to Hanoi to work at Bach Mai Hospital."

"Thank you, Colonel Gee; I will bring honor to you, my mother, and myself."

She would gain their trust and live by the words of her fiancé: 'what's meant to be will find a way.'

The Colonel noted a commotion on the LZ on the opposite side of the road. He picked up the radio and demanded to know the nature of the medical helicopter that landed.

"Captain, find out the nature of that helicopter and bring the crew and passengers to me. I want them under guard."

"Nurse Lu you will leave immediately. I wish you good travels. If you do great things for the people, I will be favored, and if you do not, I will be punished but not as much as you will be punished. Good day."

Four soldiers approached the helicopter and encircled Dr. Hawkins and Lieutenant Ky. An AK-47 was pointed at Dr. Hawkins' head. The Lieutenant placed himself between the doctor and weapon.

"I am Dr. Ophelia Hawkins working for the Dooley Intermed International Foundation, and this man is my assistant, nurse Ky. We are here on a medical mission. Put those guns down," she demanded.

The guards did not expect the woman to speak fluent Vietnamese so forcefully. They lowered their weapons and ordered her to follow. Dr. Hawkins entered the bunker, and Colonel Gee, the commander of the medical unit stood.

"This American woman does not know her place," the guards complained.

Dr. Hawkins interrupted their banter and said, "Excuse me, sir, I am a doctor with Dooley Intermed International. My assistant and I are here on a medical mission. I did not appreciate the weapons pointed at our heads. You should teach these men the appropriate protocol."

"Dr. Hawkins, please accept my apology. My soldiers are too eager to please me. May I ask if you have any identification?" Colonel Gee remarked.

"Colonel, thank you for your courtesy."

"You are most welcome doctor."

Colonel Gee carefully scrutinized their credentials. He scanned their faces and then the pictures in their documents and smiled.

"I am very familiar with the Dooley Foundation; they have done great work. Everything appears to be in order doctor. But I have a question for you – why?"

"Colonel if you are familiar with the foundation you'll know the answer to that question."

"I'd like to believe I do know the answer. But Doctor, please accept my apology. If I'm to be a good servant of the people, I must check your motives and find out that you are indeed a member of the Dooley Foundation. For now, I will have you both billeted at the hospital. If you want to help as you say, become familiar with our routine. We do appreciate your willingness to assist us."

"Colonel, I regret the inconvenience I've caused you. But I go where I am needed, and I believe you need me. If you do not, then my nurse and I will beg our leave."

The Colonel nodded.

"Dr. Hawkins, do you know that the Vietnamese people believe Dr. Dooley was an American spy?"

The Colonel attempted to place the woman in a corner.

"But thank you for the medical supplies," he said. "The People of Vietnam are in debt to you. Good afternoon doctor."

The Colonel and his orderly watched her walk through the entry then down the path toward the MASH station.

Colonel Gee was a conscientious member of the communist party; his analysis of Dr. Hawkins, he would leave no stone unturned. Something didn't seem right. *Why?* He asked himself. *Why would such a beautiful and successful woman come to the aid of Vietnam? Dr. Tom Dooley? Dr. Dooley was a spy for the Americans. Maybe this woman is a spy.*

The staff of the hospital welcomed the new arrivals. Overtime, Ofa increased the competence of the hospital staff. The patients loved the extra attention she gave them. It would take a sexy American woman to win the hearts and minds of the enemy.

North Vietnamese Intelligence was not efficient. However, what they lacked in ability, they compensated by being stubborn, suspicious, and illogical. Colonel Gee took two months to investigate Dr. Hawkins and found her to be who she claimed to be. He found something else; she was the Girl with the Purple Ribbon, the symbol of the American Antiwar Movement. The People's Republic of Vietnam scored a major victory with her defection.

"Captain Lim, Dr. Hawkins claimed she came to assist our medical mission, very similar to what Dr. Tom Dooley did in the 1950's. However, she never claimed she was defecting nor did she denounce American involvement." The Colonel was not satisfied. "Maybe Dr. Hawkins came for more than humanitarian reasons, like her predecessor, Dr. Dooley."

"Colonel Gee, the investigators found the doctor to be who she says she is, shall we close the file?" Captain Lim, asked.

"Captain, there's one thing bothering me about Dr. Hawkins and Nurse Ky."

"Colonel, I respect your suspicions, but each time you question her motives, we uncover nothing. She is doing good work; we should give her the benefit of the doubt."

"Captain, isn't it odd that the day she arrived, intelligence intercepted a message from Saigon about, someone called Pretty Girl going north to find Cowboy's Girl? Dr. Hawkins is a very pretty girl.

No Captain Lim, I want you to leave her file open."

FORTY-EIGHT

A PRISSY BITCH

I'm not a prissy bitch . . . I'm just a bitch.

Ofa Hawkins

1974

It took five years for the adversaries to sign the Paris Peace Accords. In 1973, National Security Advisor, Henry Kissinger, and Vietnamese Politburo member, Le Duc Tho, the architects of the agreement received the Nobel Peace Prize for their effort in ending the War. What of the families who lost loved ones during those years? The lopsided document favoring the North was a slap in the face to the 56,000 Americans who died. President Nixon claimed he would use American power if the North Vietnamese attacked the South. However, the Watergate scandal in 1974 drove him from office. In 1975, when the North Vietnamese began their final offensive, the United States Congress refused to appropriate the funds needed to protect the South. President Thieu resigned and accused the U.S. of betrayal. He said, "At the time of the Paris Peace Accords, the United States agreed to replace equipment on a one-by-one basis; however, the United States did not keep its promise." Congress had passed the Foreign Assistance Act, which prevented any possibility of America re-entering the war; subsequently, North Vietnam began to gobble up territory, which provoked no response from the Americans.

December 1974 – NVA Mash Unit, Quang Tri

General van Minh, a high-ranking commander of the Army of the

People's Republic of Vietnam, had orchestrated much of their success. He was a brilliant tactician and a soldier's soldier. The officers and men under his command would follow him into hell. He was tall for an ethnic Vietnamese, handsome, and spoke fluent English, Russian, and Chinese. He received a BA in classical studies from the University of Moscow, and an MA in Comparative English Literature from Yale University. He was destined for major command; however, he was a womanizer and was caught sleeping with a government official's wife. Although his sexual dalliances could be forgiven, what sealed his fate was his contempt for the political elite, especially those who weren't soldiers. After the Americans had left, the NVA planned a two-year offensive to overthrow the South. The General boasted he could take Saigon in two months. A man like General van Minh would not be tolerated in the New Vietnam; subsequently, he was relieved of command and sent to the border of North and South Vietnam to commanded rear echelon troops convalescing from their wounds. There are soldiers who believe they're above the rules of the bureaucratic hierarchy because they've served their time in hell. General Minh was such a soldier.

*　　*　　*

"Colonel Gee I want to meet the new doctor. Can you arrange a formal introduction?" the General asked.

"Yes General, but you must know I do not trust her motives for coming to our assistance. We intercepted a telling message the day of her arrival. We must watch her."

"Colonel you are a man who does not trust. This is a detriment to a field commander. If you are to send men to their death, you have to trust."

It was a remark meant to belittle Colonel Gee's lack of combat experience.

"I understand General."

"No, you do not Colonel! You will never understand. I hope your reluctance is not because of my reputation as a womanizer."

"General, I mean no disrespect," the Colonel said. "I am not a field commander; I am a member of the political cadre. It is my job not to trust."

"Very well Colonel, then when I sleep with her, I will have one eye open."

Colonel Gee detested General Minh, who had no regard for rules and protocol. He was disrespectful because he believed he was a superior man. Dr. Hawkins would be his next victim.

Dr. Hawkins gained the respect of the wounded and hospital staff. Each soldier hoped he would be the lucky one to get a kiss on the cheek from the sexy American doctor. They were just boys and no longer the enemy. She loved them and gave them the best care she could.

Throughout Quang Tri Province, Dr. Hawkins had become everyone's favorite. However, Dr. Bepa Burkov, a Captain in the Russian Army, sent to Vietnam for refusing the advances of a senior Russian Officer, detested the popular and sexy American and believed that her antics were a display of American arrogance.

Although Dr. Hawkins attempted to avoid the Russian woman, it was only a matter of time before the two women clashed.

*   *   *

"Dr. Hawkins, how you walk in those jeans and boots is disgusting," Bepa Burkov said. "Are you a doctor or are you a prostitute?"

Dr. Burkov's broad shoulders, muscular arms, and cold gray eyes cut through the American. Both women faced each other, and neither broke their stare.

Ofa Hawkins was not easily intimidated, but she hadn't the wherewithal to confront the Russian woman.

"Dr. Hawkins, you're a prissy bitch," Burkov shouted."

Ofa gave the Russian woman a sexy stare.

"Excuse me Dr. Burkov, but you've seen nothing yet. Watch how I shake my ass as I walk down the ward. Every man here will dream of having a piece of me. Oh! One more thing, Dr. Burkov. Don't ever call me a prissy bitch again. I'm from Texas; I ain't never been prissy. I'm just a bitch."

Burkov moved toward the brassy American doctor, but Ofa had already turned and was sashaying down the ward. Dr. Burkov continued to follow, and as she was about to speak, Ofa turned, blew her a kiss, and continued to walk away.

Speaking over her shoulder, she said, "Oh Bepa, y'all Russians have a hard-on for everything. Yeah – I know you hate me cause you're no longer the hottest piece of ass in Quang Tri Province."

"You're wrong," Dr. Burkov shouted. "Finally, the great Dr.

Hawkins, the savior from America is wrong about something. I hate you because I've never been the hottest piece of ass in Quang Tri Province."

"Bepa you're fucked! You kidding me? When I look at you, I wish I were a lesbian."

Dr. Burkov turned and shouted, "Dr. Hawkins, you're such a fucking slut."

"You know me so well," Ofa countered.

Walking in opposite directions, the women laughed.

Later that afternoon, Ofa was feasting on a steamy bowl of Pho, a traditional Vietnamese soup with noodles and broth. Bepa pulled a chair and sat.

"Know why I hate you?" Ofa didn't answer. Burkov continued. "Because I'm always number two and the number two girl never gets the action. It's always the number one girl who gets the special room, the privileges, and gets to sit at the head table of the most powerful men."

"Yeah, the most powerful fat old men," Dr. Hawkins said. "What good is that?"

"But Dr. Hawkins, they always drink the best wine."

"Who could be hotter than you?" Ophelia asked.

"There was a girl before you. She was offered many privileges, but she refused them. She was nurse, Nguyen Lu. She worked for the Americans, so I fear for her. She went to Bach Mai Hospital in Hanoi. The three of us would make a fortune laying on our backs. Call me Bepa," Dr. Burkov said.

"Call me Ophelia."

Ofa smiled; she found what she needed to know.

"Ophelia, I never hated you. I was just testing you. I wanted to see what kind of a woman you are. Before I could trust you, I wanted to make sure you weren't just another uptight, prissy bitch. I don't trust people who are uptight. I'm happy to meet the real Dr. Hawkins. I now know you're not prissy – that must be an act – you're just a bitch."

"Bepa, come back to my room; let's have a beer."

"Vietnamese beer is shit and warm," Bepa said.

"I have an idea," Ofa said. "Why don't you spread your legs for the General and get some cold beer for us?"

"Ophelia, it's not me he wants."

FORTY-NINE

WHO IS PETER PAN

"Y'all fixin' to put me in hot water . . . or shall we dance?

Ofa Hawkins

January 1975 – MASH Unit, Quang Tri

"**Dr. Burkov, would you take my rounds? Colonel Klink requests I speak with him,**" Ofa said.

Laughing at the impertinence of her new best friend, Burkov asked, "Who's Colonel Klink? Calling the Commandant of this hospital prison a derogatory name could be punishable by having him grab your ass."

Ofa's words were provocative for a woman who was known as the Ice Queen. She attempted to appear daring to a woman who was nothing like her.

"Yes, but Dr. Burkov, what are they going to do? send us to Vietnam." The women chimed, "Oh, guess what? We're already in Vietnam."

"Bepa, Colonel Klink was a German Luftwaffe officer, a popular comical character of an American TV show. He was inept, dimwitted, cowardly, and clueless. Get it?"

The two women looked at each other and exclaimed, "Colonel Gee!"

"Yeah, Colonel Gee is Colonel Klink," Ofa said.

"Keep it up Dr. Hawkins; I'll visit you in prison. Colonel Klink has it in for you. He thinks you're a spy."

"But Bepa, I am a spy."

Dr. Hawkins entered the Colonel's office wearing a tight skirt and a loose-fitting blouse. The guard observed her long strides, which raised the hem of her skirt above her knee. Ofa knew how to please her waiting audience. Both General Minh and Colonel Gee stood.

"Gentlemen, thank you but please sit down," she said.

Ofa would take control and then watch her prey fall into her web. The powerful men sat, and she followed.

"General Minh, this is Dr. Ophelia Hawkins."

Ofa smiled, and out of respect for the former General of a battle-hardened Division she bowed. Colonel Gee had presented General Minh to Dr. Hawkins. The Colonel should have presented her to the General.

"Colonel, I understand you have a bottle of French wine that you are saving for a special occasion. Why don't you get it? Perhaps we can make a toast to peace," the General said.

The Colonel was reluctant to share his wine. He was saving the bottle for a beautiful Vietnamese journalist. The General knew of Gee's intentions but enjoyed taunting the man.

Ofa observed the General's gaze. She had grown accustomed to the eyes of men. She smiled. *I wonder if he knew what he was giving up?* She thought.

"Dr. Hawkins, it's a pleasure to meet you, and may I say your service has earned you the respect of the People's Army of Vietnam. I am not ashamed to say I was anxious to meet an American celebrity – Girl with the Purple Ribbon. Do not think that your work in the American Peace movement has gone unnoticed. We Vietnamese are grateful."

"Thank you Gen'ral, but y'all misunderstandin' my work. Promotin' peace is not why I wear the purple ribbon. My Gen'ral, do you know why I wear this ribbon?"

Ofa was acting on a grand stage and about to manipulate the handsome Vietnamese General.

"Gen'ral, I had no intention of helpin' the political ambitions of your Army. I wear the ribbon out of respect for those who lost their lives in this senseless war."

"Very well Dr. Hawkins, I appreciate you representing your intentions, and I stand corrected. If we agree on anything, it is that the war was senseless. Vietnam is a tragedy for America, but it was worse for Vietnam; however. The American War is the beginning of the New Vietnam. Dr. Hawkins, may I say you are a very forceful woman."

"Gen'ral, a woman's like a tea bag. Y'all don't know how strong she is till you put her in hot water. Is that what I'm here for? Y'all fixin' to put me in hot water? Sir, shall we dance or shall we dance?"

"Doctor, do you know who said that?"

"Which part? Y'all referrin'. How'd ya know?"

"I have a master's degree from Yale," he replied. But Doctor Hawkins what if we were to put you in hot water?"

"Well – then sir, I would say it's better to lay down some glue when a critter starts screamin' than to take a shovel to its head."

The General didn't understand but was enthralled by the sexy young doctor.

Many times, his Army had been mauled by American forces. Nevertheless, he hung on and believed that America would eventually lose their will to make war. During his studies in America, he read the exploits of George Washington, the father of the American people. Washington believed if the Continental soldier would endure, the British would eventually lose their heart for war.

"Dr. Hawkins, who's cowboy?" the General asked."

The General attempted to place her in hot water; however, she remained calm. *Is he on to me?* She wondered.

"Dr. Hawkins, I hope I have not made you uneasy by my accusation."

Colonel Gee gave her a cunning stare and commented, "Doctor, are you hoping that in your bag of tricks you'll find something to convince us that you are not, this Pretty Girl?"

"Dang Colonel," Ofa replied, "I don't need a bag of tricks. If I need to get out of the hot water you're putting me in, I'll put my trust in a witch, and frankly sir – if I can't convince you with a smile that I don't know what you're speakin' of, I'm not a Texas girl."

"Whose cowboy?" the General asked again.

"Well, spit on the fire and call the dogs, Gen'ral, you're persistent as all get-out. Sir, you're askin' the right girl. I'm from Texas, and sure 'nough I can tell y'all 'bout a cowboy."

"Bein' a cowboy is defined by a cowboy attitude. It's heart, honor, integrity, and lots of hard work."

"Doctor, I do understand the ideals of heart, honor, and integrity. As a Division commander, those virtues were my ethos."

"Gen'ral, if you understand those virtues you'll understand the essence of the American cowboy."

Dr. Hawkins uncrossed her legs and leaned forward. The hem of her skirt inched higher.

"When a cowboy gives his word, it's for life. He does the right thing. He's not afraid to take a stand. And cowboys, they're tougher than all get-out."

"I don't understand all get-out," the General replied.

"Tougher than woodpecker lips," Ofa added. "But regardless he knows how to treat a lady and when a woman walks into a room he stands and removes his hat."

"Dr. Hawkins, a woodpecker lip – your analogy – I don't understand."

Ofa smiled.

"Cowboys are patriots. Many of the boys you fought were cowboys. You may understand their cowboy-up attitude."

"I certainly do doctor," the General replied. "I appreciate the expression, 'when the going gets tough, the tough get going.' But Dr. Hawkins, I understand cowboys are ruffians."

"Gen'ral, they're just ordinary boys at heart, but they have a devil-may-care attitude. As a matter of fact, a cowboy's a lot like Peter Pan."

"Who is this Peter Pan?" the General asked.

"Oh, my Gen'ral, I have much to teach you about America."

General Minh smiled and anticipated future time spent with Doctor Hawkins.

"Cowboys need to ride. They're wild and free, just like the wind," she commented.

"Dr. Hawkins, do you know how to ride? It must be a remarkable experience to ride a horse."

"Gen'ral, it's not enough to know how to ride, you have to know how to fall."

"Dr. Hawkins, I must admit, I've never ridden a horse. Is it difficult?"

"You ever try to put socks on a rooster?" she replied.

"And Gen'ral, it's not easy for a cowboy to settle down, but when a woman loves a cowboy – it's a love unlike any other."

"Dr. Hawkins, do you know this from personal experience? A woman like you could hold any man. You explain my question very well."

Ofa was buying time – ignoring the General's assertion that she was Cowboy's Girl.

"Gen'ral this is just a start, but I think you get the idea. A cowboy attitude – it's on the inside. I admire cowboys. I've even been accused of being one myself."

"Dr. Hawkins don't you mean a cowgirl?"

"Sir, a cowboy, and a cowgirl – there's not much difference. A cowgirl is part of a landscape of promise and beauty. She doesn't only go after a loose calf or a perfect ride; she goes after a dream."

"Doctor, I do not mean to be presumptuous, but one day I would like to know your dreams."

"Sir, with the war endin' that just might be possible."

"Dr. Hawkins, you are exactly who I thought you were. You are quixotic."

"Gen'ral, I believe you understand me, and Sir, on the other hand, y'all not what I expected. Sir, there's one more thing, it's important for you to know. Us Texans are the blood of the biggest hell raisers and scoundrels in America. We're the decedents of heroes. You should never forget that."

She crossed her legs and wiggled back into the seat. The General lost this round, and he knew it.

Dr. Hawkins reached for her glass and said, "My Gen'ral I propose a toast to peace and understandin'."

"Dr. Hawkins," General Minh replied, "I love your Texas accent. You Texans have your own language. It sounds – ah – for lack of a better word – provocative."

"My Gen'ral, I only speak Texan when I'm talkin' to mama or sexy men like y'all."

They smiled, but Ofa had them twisting in their seats.

"Dr. Hawkins, you know much about the American Cowboy, so why are you looking for his girl? Are you Pretty Girl, Dr. Hawkins?"

It was now a game of chess, and she had the next move.

"Gen'ral, a lady never comments on her own beauty. But you confuse me with your suspicions."

She gave him a generous smile. "I hope you understand that the loneliest place on earth is when no one believes you. Regardless, you can't expect Pretty Girl to reveal her desires. Love is best kept a secret; don't you agree?"

General Minh leaned back in his chair. He had to have this woman. And Dr. Hawkins smiled at the powerful man, and with a slight pout on her lips she said in a slow Texas drawl, "My Gen'ral, y'all have any further questions?"

"I will have many he said."

Dr. Hawkins thought, *Checkmate*.

FIFTY

TO LOVE

What is the past? What is the present? What is the future? What magic liquid hides us and shuts us in from the things we ought most to know? We live, we breathe, and we die, in the midst of miracles.

General Tran van Minh

February 1975 – Medical Aid Station, Quang Tri

"**Ophelia, you bring the cold beer?**"

Ofa laughed at the suggestion that she had slept with General Minh.

"There's only one way to get a cold beer in the middle of Quang Tri," Bepa said. "Well, did you?"

"No Bepa, I didn't sleep with him."

"The General is a consuming man. He attempted to keep Nguyen Lu in Quang Tri. People thought he was sleeping with her, but he wasn't. He was sympathetic to her; he treated her like his daughter. Maybe that's why she's in Hanoi." Bepa said.

"What do you know about Nguyen Lu," Ofa asked?

"She was quiet and kept to herself. We were friends, and she trusted me. She told me she was in love with an American Marine, Elijah Bravo. They were to be married, but he left Vietnam, and she waited at the altar in a wedding gown. Unusual! Very sad. This fucking war has destroyed any hope for love. She believed her love affair was a secret, but the Colonel knew. The worst crime for a Vietnamese national is to love a hated American."

"Bepa, how do you know this?"

"Please don't ask how I know, I just know. She told me that the last time she saw her Marine, he said, 'What's meant to be will find a way.' Those words gave her strength. Ophelia, I need to help her. She won't survive this ordeal. I'm not your enemy. Darling, the world is an ugly place, and not everyone wants you well. But I am not afraid. I have something to fight for, something to save. But I must save Nguyen. What she and this Marine possess is the last hope that something good can come from something so bad as this war. I'm going to help her. I must go north."

Ofa began to cry.

"Dr. Hawkins, why are you crying?"

"Bepa answer me!" she demanded. "How do you know the Vietnamese are on to her?"

"Because it's the same way I know you're Pretty Girl," Dr. Burkov blurted.

"Ophelia, stop your charade. I'm not only a doctor; I'm with Russian intelligence, KGB. I know you're here to rescue her. Colonel Gee thinks you are a spy just like your beloved Dr. Tom Dooley. But General Minh could care less. The purple ribbon gives it away. The KGB watched you when you were in college; they thought you could be turned. You're a Texas girl; you grew up in Luckenbach, Texas – the South Grape Creek. The message was foolish. You left too many clues. You are a romantic. You want drama, even if it gives you away. You are driven to save her, and Vietnam is your grand stage. You have been very careless in your disguise."

"But Bepa – you keep your view of the world on the ground, and you never look up and see the possibility. What if you're wrong?"

"Stop it Ofa! All of that chivalry and romance, you've never pictured anything as disastrous as Vietnam. There's no romance here, no chivalry. And it stinks of sweat and smoke and sewage."

We Russians are good at intelligence; the Vietnamese are not. We know of your friendship with Elijah Bravo and Seamus O'Grady. When I saw you, I knew you were contacted by someone and had come for her. Your Dooley Intermed International is a front. The Colonel is convinced you are here as an assassin, but he has no proof. For now, your antiwar activities have given you a pass. But this will not last. Your only lifeline is General Minh."

"Bepa, will you help me?"

"My sweet Ophelia, it is you who will help me."

Ofa smiled, then said, "Bepa – call me Ofa."

Bepa Burkov smiled and kissed the pretty girl on the forehead. The two women had formed an unlikely alliance.

"Ofa, the Vietnamese know that Nguyen was the head nurse at the hospital ship Sanctuary. They know she was educated in America and was to marry an American Marine. For the moment, they will use her. But after the war, she will be punished for crimes against the people of Vietnam. She is a beautiful woman, and many men will want her."

"Do you have a plan?" Ofa asked.

"General Minh is a great soldier, but he is a weak man. Men like him weaken the goals of the Soviets. His weakness will give us what we want. Ofa, he wants, you and if you give him what he wants, he'll give us what we want. He could care less about the state; he is sympathetic to Nguyen. But he is a soldier. The war is over, and the government has no use for him – and he has no use for the government."

"Do the Vietnamese know about you," Ofa asked?"

"No, we Russians are arrogant. We are better than the Vietnamese. I was sent to ensure that the Vietnamese become good communists, but they are not good communists. They are peasants. Since you came, the General's attention is no longer on me. My plan was to sleep with him, so I could go north. You killed my plan." She laughed.

"Bepa, I'll get us North and if I have to sleep with him so be it. But I'm not so sure he wants me the way you think he does. His eyes reveal more than lust."

"Ofa, you are such a romantic."

Ofa found the General's, Achilles Heel. Quixotic! His attraction for her was medieval. It was courtly love, somewhere between erotic desire and spiritual attainment. He would be her knight, and she would be his lady.

The Following Morning

"Dr. Hawkins, do you mind if I accompany you on your morning rounds?" the General asked. "I've heard wonderful comments about the care you give my soldiers. I want to know what makes them love you. They forget you are American."

"My Gen'ral is being an American a crime? You were a student in my country; you must understand our nature."

"Dr. Hawkins, I respect America. The war caused much sorrow.

But my soldiers believe Marines eat babies, so I hope you will understand why they hate Americans. One day that will change."

"It's your fault they believe this," Ofa said. "We're different, but we are people. The war is over; we need compassion and understandin'. If we only see our differences – that will be our prison."

"I appreciate your philosophy," the General commented. "But please understand the words I wrote in my journal after the battle of the Hills. I want to share this with you: 'What is the past? What is the present? What is the future? What are we? What magic liquid hides us and shuts us in from the things we ought most to know? We live, we breathe, and we die, in the midst of miracles.' Don't you find that tragic Dr. Hawkins? I do. We live in miracles, and yet we make war on each other. How can we not see the tragedy we have brought to one another?"

"But Gen'ral, we understand, and that's a beginning."

"Dr. Hawkins, I'm sorry, but what we see now is the aftermath. There's no enlightenment in seeing the disaster that has already occurred. But to really see something requires forethought and if we were enlightened, this senseless war would not have occurred."

"My Gen'ral over the years, I've learned a painful lesson – we can only be responsible for ourselves, and if we want to change the world, we first must change ourselves."

General Minh followed Dr. Hawkins through the hospital. The beautiful woman received more attention than he did. He watched as she kissed his men on the cheek. They were boys, doing what they were told. They were born in the north to die in the south.

"Dr. Hawkins, would you do me the honor of having dinner with me tonight?"

Ophelia turned and gave the General a sexy glare. He was a boy who had just asked a girl for a date. He waited for her reply.

"Gen'ral, I'd love to go to dinner with you."

"Dr. Hawkins, my intentions are honorable. I seek only your friendship. I hate to think of what you have heard about my reputation. Regardless, I'd like to show you the real Vietnam."

"Thank you, sir." Ofa smiled. She tilted her head and showed just enough submission to the powerful General who could grant her anything she wished.

General Minh chose a small restaurant in Dong Ha, owned by

one of his former soldiers, wounded at Hue City. The soldier stood on one leg.

"Dr. Hawkins, tell me about the fort in San Antonio, the Alamo. I saw the John Wayne movie, the one where he is Davey Crockett."

"Gen'ral Minh, it's part history and part folklore, but I hope you understand the story is a testament to what lengths men will go for freedom."

"Then doctor you will understand the rationale for the sacrifices we Vietnamese have endured."

They spoke for hours; there was no one left in the restaurant. The soldier, leaning on a crutch waiting to serve his Commanding Officer, remained at attention throughout their meal.

"My skills are wasted here," Ofa said. "I speak for Dr. Burkov as well. With the war over, there is no need for us to be here. I can do more at a major hospital in Hanoi. Colonel Gee misuses our talents and confines us to Quang Tri."

"Dr. Hawkins, he thinks you're a spy."

She appeared confused. "I'm not a spy. But there's more than you know. Dr. Burkov and I are competent physicians; we should be at a major hospital."

"My dear doctor, if I were to send you to Hanoi, what pleasure would I have? I would not have the joy of your company."

The General and the doctor had dinner at the tiny village restaurant three nights per week. He treated her like his daughter. She told him about growing up in the Hill Country of Texas, about the boy she loved, and how she threw it away. He told her of his ambivalence to the party and the communist ideology. She told him about her marriage to Paul Bannister and the story of the red rose. He told her about his wife and child and how an American bomb killed them. She told him about her admiration for Dr. Tom Dooley. He told her about his battles and the friends he lost. She told him of the time she witnessed Norman Morrison engulf himself in flames. He told her how he was disgraced commanding the wounded. She told him about her mother leaving when she was a child.

The man sitting in front of her was not the womanizer everyone said he was. He might have been in love with her. But it was a love a father has for a daughter. It was the way she smiled and the way she called him, 'my Gen'ral.'

February 1975

"Dr. Hawkins, I wish you could trust me the way I trust you."

"Gen'ral, I'm afraid to trust – but I must, and if you break my trust, it's on you."

"My dear, the highest cliff I can fall from is trust. It's not me who has the power. It's you. When we first met, you used your beauty to seduce me to be your friend. Deception – is that what you call romance. I resented how you treated me; I didn't care. I was on to you, but I became your victim. You have changed. You accept me for who I am and not what I can do for you. I know you're Pretty Girl. The South Grape Creek runs through Luckenbach. I know you're here to find Nguyen Lu. I don't care. The Americans are gone. Vietnam will soon be one. What do you want? You're not here to hurt the Vietnamese. Tell me what you want. Maybe I can help."

"Gen'ral, why did it take so long to realize the South Grape Creek ran through Luckenbach?"

"It didn't. When you were speaking about the cowboy, you were speaking about the boy you had feelings for."

Ofa nodded. "If I trust you and if that's a mistake, everything is lost."

"Little girl, if you don't trust me, then everything is lost, and that will seal the fate of Nguyen Lu. I am only one man, but if I could change the fate of nurse Lu, I would do that. But she is considered an enemy of the state. The government wants revenge, and they will exact their pound of flesh. And since you are here to aid an enemy of the people, you too will be punished."

"Gen'ral, I'm going to trust you. I owe you that much. Yes, I'm here to bring Nguyen Lu out of Vietnam. She is in love with Elijah Bravo. She met him on the Sanctuary while he was recoverin' from the wounds he received from the hill fights. It was Hill-861."

"I was there; I was the CO of the People's Army."

"Oh, Gen'ral – so were Elijah and Seamus. The thought of you tryin' to kill each other. I owe it to Elijah – It's for love. If we can bring them together, it's a beginnin'. Help me do this."

Gen'ral, come with me," Ofa said. "Let's leave together."

General Minh smiled and raised his glass of French wine. "To love," he said.

FIFTY-ONE

GOING NORTH

Good night, good night! Parting is such sweet sorrow,

That I shall say goodnight till it be morrow.

Shakespeare, *Romeo and Juliet*

April 1975 – Field Hospital, Quang Tri

"Colonel Gee, you are wasting the talents of Doctors Hawkins and Burkov. I have decided to send them to Bach Mai hospital in Hanoi. It is unfortunate our physicians are inferior. The doctors will transform our medical system, and if you are smart, you will take credit for this."

"General Minh, that is not a good decision. Dr. Hawkins is a spy. She should be in prison. You do not have my support."

For a Vietnamese, General Minh was a large and imposing man who would intimidate anyone who didn't agree with him. He leaned toward the Colonel and slammed his fist on Gee's desk.

"Never question my judgment Colonel Gee! Never! Do you understand that? I am sending Dr. Hawkins, her assistant, and Dr. Burkov to Hanoi. That is final, and I do not want to hear one more comment. If I hear anything further from you or see the slightest displeasure in your eyes, you will be sent to fight our new enemies in Cambodia."

Two Days Later

Lieutenant Ky was cleared for take-off, yet the suspicious glares of the North Vietnamese soldiers made him uneasy. Dr. Burkov sat stoically and stared at the Vietnamese staring at her.

"Fucking communists," she whispered.

They waited for Dr. Hawkins who lingered with the General attempting to express feelings to a friend and yet an enemy who had become her father.

General Minh could only smile. He appeared unemotional; he had an image to uphold.

"My darling, I'll do what I can," the General said.

She hugged him. He kissed her gently on the forehead. My daughter, someday we'll meet again.

"My father," He put his finger to her lips.

"Shhhhh," he said. My darling girl, I will never love anyone as much as I love you. Remember – quixotic."

Ofa turned and ran to the helicopter, crying! Since coming to Vietnam, all she had done was cry.

"Let's go," she said.

Lieutenant Ky kissed the rosary beads hanging over his head; he turned toward Dr. Hawkins.

"Doctor, please fasten your seatbelt."

They lifted off and headed north. The General stood on the tarmac and watched the chopper disappear into the morning haze.

General Minh then entered the communications center at the field hospital.

"Soldier, I want to send a message to my lover" he said.

The soldier laughed and left his post.

3 April 1975 – U.S.S Midway – Alpha Company 1st Battalion 9th Marine Regiment – 1st Sergeant Elijah Bravo – Found Cowboy's Girl. Going North. Godspeed my Sergeants – Pretty Girl sends.

General Minh then walked into the office of his subordinate Colonel Gee, pulled his sidearm, shot the Colonel in the head, and disappeared into the jungle.

FIFTY-TWO

TRAI HOC TAP CAI TAO

Sure 'nough, Sir. Sheer pageantry! Loving someone till it hurts.
Pageantry... it ain't the shallow subtleties of love or the whimsical
pleasures of the moment's indulgence. But it's love that consumes
life itself. Un-dog-gone-uncontrollable! It's like a rebellion in the
heart. Yes, sir. Sheer Pageantry sir.

Gunnery Sergeant Elijah Bravo

April 1975 – USS Midway, Gulf of Tonkin

"Mr. Quackenbush, you'd better come here. Got another
message from Pretty Girl. Sir – this is getting interesting."

Rumors about the mysterious woman called Pretty Girl, intent
on rescuing Sergeant Bravo's Vietnamese lover spread throughout
the ship. Whoever she was, she was continuing the war against the
enemy. She had struck again and gave the men something to hope
for.

It was a love story between a Marine Sergeant and a beautiful
Vietnamese woman. Two people had found love in miserable war-
stricken Vietnam. Their story had the sailors and Marines believing in
miracles. The lives of the crew had become entangled with a woman
called Pretty Girl. If she survived, so would they. If she perished,
they too would perish. The Midway had learned about the young
Vietnamese woman who helped the Americans, how she fell in love
with a Marine hero, and then waited at the altar for her lover who
never came. She was now a prisoner of the North. The Marines
hoped for a chance to rescue her. They'd do it for Sergeant Bravo,
for Nguyen Lu, and the Doctor. They'd do it for love. Love would
be worth fighting for, and if it came to dying, then they would accept

their death for love. How else can one rationalize the misery and constant fear of death? Political ideology! Freedom! They are vague ideas, but everyone understood love. The story of the American doctor searching for the Vietnamese girl had become mythology.

Jonesy ripped the message from the teleprinter. "What should I do, Lieutenant?"

"Let me have it, Jonesy."

Six months had passed since the Midway received the first message from the mysterious doctor. They learned that Pretty Girl was Dr. Ophelia Hawkins, Girl with the Purple Ribbon, the renowned anti-war activist who grew up in South Central Texas and had a romantic connection to First Sergeant Seamus O'Grady. More than a year ago she set out on an impossible mission to rescue Gunnery Sergeant Bravo's girl, Cowboy's Girl. Ofa Hawkins had captured the hearts of the sailors and Marines on the Midway. As farfetched as it seemed, the crew believed the story, and if it weren't true, they'd believe it anyway.

Aft Flight Deck

Sergeant Bravo was teaching the tactical deployment of the M-60 machine gun. Ensign Quackenbush walked quickly into the center of the Platoon.

"Platoon... a tennnnn hut." The Gunnery Sergeant commanded. The Marines immediately jumped to attention. Quackenbush and the salty Sergeant had become friends. Elijah insisted that his Marines show the JG respect, even if he was a naval officer.

"Stand easy gentlemen," Quackenbush ordered.

"Sir, what can we do for you?"

Quackenbush handed Bravo the message. He raised his head, smiled, and nodded at the young officer. He then folded the message and placed it in his breast pocket.

"Sir, thank you."

"Guns, maybe you should dismiss the men; you need some time to process this," Quackenbush added.

"Sergeant Flynn, would you take over for me?" Sergeant Bravo asked.

"Gunny, I'd like to meet Dr. Hawkins one day. I don't even know her, but I think I'm in love with her," Quackenbush expressed. "She must be a remarkable woman."

"She is sir. I've a feeling you'll meet her soon," Elijah responded.

"Gunny, I have a good feeling about her. She's got – you know – chutzpah. What's she like?"

"She seems different from the way I remember her. She was always the pretty girl. Sweet! Brilliant! Opinionated! But Sir – she could ride like the wind and put a black powder ball on a quarter at 25-yards. Why there was a time when she could out-fish any boy in the Hill Country. But in senior year, that changed. I guess she growed up and became a woman. I always thought she left who she was in the hills of Texas. She was crazy about 1st Sergeant O'Grady. At the time, he was just a ranch hand and didn't have a pot to piss in. He hadn't a clue about girls, and for sure he didn't understand the pageantry of a boy and a girl. He couldn't look her in the eye and put a sentence together. But when Ofa was in jeans and boots, she could be pretty intimidating.

"Gunny, there's more to you than you reveal. You're more than the hard-ass Sergeant I pegged you for."

"Sir, that's true of all of us. But loving Nguyen has given me a new life."

"But, pageantry?" Quackenbush questioned.

"Sure 'nough, Sir. Pageantry! Loving someone till it hurts. Pageantry… it's not the superficial subtleties of love or the whimsical pleasures of the moment's indulgence. But it's love that consumes life itself. Un-dog-gone-uncontrollable! It's like a rebellion in the heart. Yes, sir. Pageantry sir."

O'Grady was in the hold of the ship teaching land navigation to the Squad leaders of Alpha Company.

"Okay gents, a back azimuth is simple. You shoot an azimuth to a given point and then reference that point back to your position. If your azimuth is more than 180 degrees, you subtract 180 from your azimuth. If it's less, you add. So, let's say your azimuth is 270 degrees, subtract 180 from 270. Your back azimuth is 50 degrees. So, from that point to your position is 50 degrees."

The men realized that what the Sergeant had to say would save their lives when they went ashore. The word around the ship was that the Marines would return to support the expected onslaught of refugees.

"Hey, Buckaroo, I need to talk to you."

"What's the word?"

"Lieutenant Quackenbush brought another message. Ofa found Nguyen. She's going north to get her. Jesus Christ Seamus, she's gonna do it. You just wait and see. It's Ofa; always been Ofa. Damn, Pops always said, 'What's meant to be will find a way.' That old man always knew everything."

"Elijah!" Seamus said, "I'm in love with Ofa."

25 April 1975 – Re-Education Camp, North Viet Nam

Colonel Ly Truc Viet inspected the documents and smiled at the humble Vietnamese girl. He placed his hand on a paper and slid it across the desk resting it in front of Nguyen Lu. The Colonel was not a pretentious man; nevertheless, he was imposing as he brushed the cigar smoke that gathered as a sinister cloud over the head of his captive. He then placed a pen on top of the paper. It was a confession of war crimes.

"Colonel, I've already signed a confession in Quang Tri. But what I did is not a war crime," she pleaded. "I am a nurse. I've taken an oath to care for the sick and wounded. There is no point signing a paper admitting to a crime when there was no crime."

"Little sister, you have aided the Americans. They are enemies of the state. That is a very serious crime against the Vietnamese People. A sin! You must become a citizen, but to do this you must confess and atone for your sins. If you do not do this, I'm afraid you'll be taking your own life."

Colonel Viet was a politician. He rose through the ranks from a Lieutenant to a field grade officer. He was a decorated hero of the People's Army and fought in the Hill Fights in 1967. Wounded by an American bomb and left for dead, he was the only surviving soldier in his Company. His story was miraculous as it was bizarre and few believed him. He had snuck through the defenses of the hated 1st Battalion 9th Marines and walked for 14 days avoiding American patrols and surviving on plants and rainwater. Delirious from putrid fever, he arrived at a North Vietnamese sanctuary in Laos. They said it was the fever that caused him to hallucinate and create such a preposterous story. Regardless, they gave him a medal. The political party said it was good for morale.

"Little sister, what do I do with you? You are a good nurse, but for eight years you helped the enemies of Vietnam. The punishment is prison. What should I do? Someone who is less forgiving than I, would sentence you to death. Maybe I can forgive some of your crimes and send you to a re-education camp. Not a happy fate, but better than prison. But you must show contrition for your crimes and to do this; you must sign this confession."

Re-education was another word for prison. The Vietnamese called it *trai hoc tap cai tao*. It was a transformation to the ideology of the communist north – revenge – a sophisticated means of repression and indoctrination. To reconcile with the new government, over one million former soldiers, religious leaders, merchants, government officials, and intellectuals from the South were incarcerated in prisons and in re-education camps. Their confinement did not last ten days or two weeks as the government originally claimed. There was no jurisprudence or charges filed and no defense. They were merely guilty. More than 165,000 people died in the Socialist Republic of Vietnam's re-education program. Thousands were tortured, raped, or abused. Some would be imprisoned for as long as 20 years. The world screamed, *Crimes against humanity!* But the communists refused to call their victims political prisoners; they called them war criminals. Their victims were treasonous and guilty of crimes punishable by death. Torture was called re-education. The communists insisted their humanitarian treatment was better than death. Nguyen Lu was guilty of the highest form of treason – helping the hated Americans.

"If you sign this paper," Colonel Viet said, you would go to level 3 re-education instead of prison."

"Colonel, whether I go to prison or re-education, it is the same thing. Let me go, Colonel. I am not an enemy. I have caused no harm in this war; I have saved lives. I can be of great value at the Bach Mi Hospital. Give me my freedom."

"Maybe I would give you your freedom, but there is one problem I am unable to overlook. You are engaged to an American Marine. That is a grievous crime. You will be in re-education; you will be the nurse of the camp."

Nguyen was guilty of loving a US Marine.

April 29 – Bach Mi Hospital, North Vietnam

In heavy rain, on an LZ adjacent to Bach Mi hospital, Lieutenant Ky landed the chopper.

"We've come a long way Lieutenant Ky. And here we are – North of where we began," Dr. Hawkins said.

"My dearest doctor, our path has been perilous, but well made.

You gave me life, and I am sorry I cannot promise you that I will be able to save you from this journey. Doctor, whatever happens, understand this: being your guardian has been the best of life."

Lieutenant Ky gave the life that Dr. Hawkins saved to her. With the lure of going to American, she saved his life twice. He jumped from the helicopter, grabbed her by her waist, and set her down on North Vietnamese soil. Dr. Burkov jumped onto the tarmac holding the luggage.

"Dr. Hawkins, these are the documents transferring you and Dr. Burkov to the hospital. Everything appears to be in order. The General is a meticulous man," Lieutenant Ky said.

"Thank you, Lieutenant; I guess we're good to go. Isn't that what you aviators say?"

"Beg your pardon Doctor, but in Vietnam, nothing is good to go. I have heard you Americans say whatever can go wrong, will go wrong. In Vietnam, if anything is good to go, it won't last long. I suggest you prepare yourself for the worst," Lieutenant Ky cautioned.

The monsoon rain poured on the weary travelers. Lieutenant Ky held a piece of plastic over Dr. Hawkins' head. Dr. Burkov stood stoically in the pouring rain, and showing no emotion, she stared into the black night.

Dr. Lam along with Captain Quan, a member of the political cadre, and two NVA soldiers armed with AK-47's approached the travelers. Captain Quan was a thorough man and examined the documents of the doctors and their assistant. His demeanor was cold. He was the type of man who'd find a problem when there was none.

"Doctors, welcome to the People's Republic of Vietnam," Captain Quan said.

He smiled. It was a cold and mistrusting smile, used only for pleasantries. Keeping the women waiting in the deluge amused the man. The rain seeped through their clothes, into their skin, and down to their bones. It was the kind of rain that made you forget there was ever a world without it. At that moment, the North Vietnamese Army was knocking on the gates of Saigon, while the Americans were frantically evacuating those Vietnamese who aided the south. The Captain's smile was a slap in their face. Quan put the doctors in an uncomfortable situation hoping they'd be less inclined to elude his questions. Although he tried to conceal his charade, Dr. Burkov understood his intentions.

"Doctors, Nurse Ky, did you kill General Minh and Colonel Gee?"

Dr. Burkov showed no emotion; she had ice in her veins. Ofa screamed and began to cry.

"General Minh, oh God no! Not my Gen'ral," she whispered.

Bepa believed the best defense was an offense. The rain was pouring, and the wind cut into the travelers. Dr. Hawkins shivered. Lieutenant Ky remained in front of her trying to provide what shelter he could.

Dr. Burkov said, "Captain Quan, what are you saying? Colonel Gee was a patriot, but he was a wretched man. He had many enemies. Someone had killed him before I had a chance to do it. General Minh's death was a tragedy. He was your best soldier, and your government treated him disgracefully. Are the Vietnamese so inept that you blame two women doctors who are here to assist? Is this how you treat those willing to risk their life to aid the People of Vietnam? I am Russian, and I will have your head for this. You Vietnamese are beggars. You're not victors."

"Yes, you are right, I'm sorry; please forgive me. I will have a driver take you to your quarters," Quan said.

"One more thing, Captain; give your raincoat to Dr. Hawkins," Bepa said.

The Captain reluctantly handed Bepa his raincoat, which she draped over Ofa's shoulders.

"Doctors, I'm sorry, I have to ask a question. Do you know what happened to General Minh, we did not find his body?"

Dr. Burkov grabbed Ofa's arm, "Get into the sedan."

"Oh, sorry – one more question Dr. Hawkins. Were you sleeping with General Minh?" the Captain asked.

Bepa turned to the inspector, "You motherfucker!" she said.

"Colonel Quan, I will not forget how you've treated us. Dr. Burkov countered. "My revenge will be a motherfucker."

FIFTY-THREE

IT'S BUT TO DO OR DIE

Once more unto the breach, dear friends, once more!

Shakespeare, *Henry V*

15 May 1975 – USS Midway, Gulf of Tonkin

"Sergeant Flynn, see that the men carry out my orders," Staff Sergeant Joe Buck commanded.

"Aye-aye, Staff Sergeant."

Buck was from the ol' breed, a hard-ass Marine from a mold broken long ago. The ol' breed defined the ethos of the men who fought against the Japanese in the second war. They earned an eternal reputation and defined esprit de corps.

"Platoon, listen up," Flynn ordered. John Wayne wants each man to carry three canteens, six grenades, bayonet, four bandoliers for the 60, E-tool, first-aid, and two days of C-rats. The Staff Sergeant said, 'no extra crap. Only fightin' gear.' Don't fuck with him; he's gonna inspect."

It was Joe Buck's turn to lead. He was tough, fearless, and fair. With his chiseled face and muscular body, he was the incarnation of Sergeant Rock. Even the new Marines referred to Buck as John Wayne, but never to his face.

"Gunnery Sergeant, Alpha Company, is ready," Buck informed Elijah Bravo.

"Thanks, Joe, I'll let O'Grady know. One more time into the breach we go," Elijah said. "I got no fuckin' idea what to expect. Stay close to your men. Seamus and McGivens will do the right thing. We need to get our ship back from those motherfuckers."

Comment [AM]:

The communist Khmer Rouge, the controlling government in Kampuchea formerly known as Cambodia, seized the container ship, S.S. Mayaguez on 12 May 1975. The ship was traveling from Saigon to Thailand when Khmer Rouge forces in a skiff fired at it when it was two miles offshore from Cambodian territory; subsequently, Khmer Rouge forces commandeered the Mayaguez. The Marines would get her back.

After we had withdrawn from Vietnam, American prestige had suffered. President Ford was intent on making a point that the United States would not tolerate the seizure of its ships. America was believed to be weak and lacking determination. At the time of the ship's capture, there was no intelligence, nor diplomatic relations with the Khmer Rouge; subsequently, negotiations went through the Chinese government. After several failing diplomatic attempts, President Ford ordered United States forces to seize the ship. Navy pilots watched from above as Khmer Rouge gunmen anchored the *Mayaguez* near Koh Tang and took the crew toward the mainland. But American officials largely ignored this intelligence and continued to plan a rescue operation on the island.

Major McGivens, the Battalion Operations Officer and First Sergeant Seamus O'Grady studied the map of Koh Tang Island where intel believed the crew was held. The island was a dense jungle with two likely places to land troops, West and East Beach. As a diversion, Gulf Company would land at West Beach. Alpha Company would land at East Beach and proceed toward the compound where it was believed the crew was held.

"Sir, I don't like it. It ain't thought out. It's the same old shit. All we do is react. We need intel and go in with force," O'Grady warned.

"The plan keeps changing," McGivens said. "I've received four different operation orders in the last two hours. I think this is it. A detachment is coming from Okinawa. They'll overpower any Cambodians on the ship and take it back."

"First Sergeant, we'll land on East Beach. Our job is to rescue the crew. Aircraft from the Coral Sea will strike targets on the mainland of Cambodia and let them know we're serious," Major McGivens said. "Charlie Company will be in reserve. Bravo will support alpha and engage any hostile forces. Alpha Company gets our guys. That's all I have. There's no intel. We could be unopposed, or there could be a Division waiting for us. We make the plan as the situation develops."

"Carry on First Sergeant. I will see you on the beach."

The 1st Battalion, 9th Marines prepared for the assault. Seamus was the senior NCO on the ground; Major McGivens was senior officer. In 1965 the 9th Marines were one of the first U.S. ground combat forces in Vietnam, and they would fight the last battle of the Vietnam War.

Koh Tang Island

While distributing LifeSavers to his Marines, the First Sergeant walked with impunity throughout the helicopter. The crew chief was not pleased, but O'Grady was an imposing figure few men wanted to confront.

He approached the pilot, "Lieutenant, give me a heads up when we're five minutes out. I wanna steady the men."

"Sure, First Sergeant. Hey, you got any more of those? I want to be chewing a LifeSaver when the shit goes down."

"You're in luck sir; got a pack left. It's yours. Good mojo."

"First Sergeant, you've seen the shit?" the pilot asked.

"Some," O'Grady replied.

"Got some vets with you, Sergeant?"

"Four Sergeants, been with me since the hill fights. The CO too. The guys are green. Not many seen the white elephant."

"The what?" the pilot questioned.

"The white elephant, sir. It's an expression from the Civil War. When you've seen the elephant, it means you've been in combat."

"I don't get it, First Sergeant. What's an elephant have to do with it? Especially a white one."

"El-tee, I'm not sure. But when the shit scares you, you look like a white elephant."

"Hey, First Sergeant," a young Marine called out. "It's gonna be like shootin' squirrels in a barrel, ain't it?"

The men laughed. It was a senseless remark. When men's nerves are tightly wound some find relief in senseless comments. They attempted to hide fear they couldn't control.

"Hey, fuck-head," O'Grady countered, "the only difference is these squirrels have weapons, and they'll be shootin' back. Listen, Marine – never take the enemy for granted; when you do that you're giving him the power to defeat you."

The men returned to the moment – where First Sergeant

O'Grady wanted them.

"Top, we're five minutes out," the pilot screamed.

"Roger that sir."

"Staff Sergeant, prepare the men," Seamus ordered.

"Aye-aye Top."

Staff Sergeant Joe Buck braced himself against the cabin.

"Easy men – steady."

Joe Buck was meant for this moment. He was destined to scream the proverbial orders to Marines about to engage the enemy. He moved to the head of the cabin to face his Marines.

"Lock and load Marines; one for Charlie and one for the road."

With one movement and with one sound the Marines jammed a magazine into the breach of their M-16 rifles.

"When I give you the word, put your weapon on safety. Do it now."

The clicking sounds of the metal switches were a warning of what approached.

"We are marksmen. Does everybody understand that? No automatic fire."

"Aye-aye Staff Sergeant," the men screamed.

The only sound was the engine and the vibrations of the cabin. Whispering silent prayers, and thinking of loved ones, the Marines were alone with their thoughts. They had lived peacefully in small towns, and farms, but now they were ready to kill and were facing the possibility of being killed.

"Listen up," Joe Buck screamed. "Get off of this fucking chopper quickly. You've trained for this. Form a 180 around the bird. At my signal, we move inland and establish a defensive position. I'll tell you where that is. We'll regroup with the rest of the Company and move toward the objective."

"Top, one minute," the pilot screamed.

John Wayne barked again, "On my command get those weapons off safe. Do it now. Squad leaders tend to your men."

The Marines converging on Koh Tang Island were unaware that the Mayaguez crew was not on the island and that more than 200 hardened Khmer Rouge fighters armed with heavy weapons waited in fortified positions. Defense officials had the intel, but no one passed this information down to the Marines who'd been ordered to attack the island. They were told to expect between 20 and 40 old men and farmers.

Following the fall of Saigon, the Vietnamese People's Army took control of islands contested by Vietnam and Cambodia. The Khmer Rouge had the responsibility for securing Koh Tang against an imminent Vietnamese attack. Regardless of who their enemy was, the Khmer Rouge was loaded for bear.

At 0607 hours on May 15, 1975, the Khmer Rouge information and propaganda minister broadcast that the Mayaguez and its crew would be released:

> Regarding the Mayaguez ship. We have no intention of detaining it permanently, and we have no desire to stage provocations. We only wanted to know the reason for its coming and to warn it against violating our waters again. This is why our coast guard seized this ship. Their goal was to examine, question, and make a report to higher authorities.

At 0612 hours eight helicopters of the Koh Tang assault task force approached East and West Beach. At West Beach, the first contingent of two CH-53 helicopters came in at 0620 hours. The first helicopter, *Knife 21*, landed safely, but while offloading the Marines, the chopper was hit. Although the chopper managed to take off, it was forced to ditch offshore. The other chopper, *Knife 22* was severely damaged and aborted the assault. *Knife 32* then came into the landing zone, and while it managed to unload its Marines, it sustained severe damage and barely made it back to the mainland. At 06:30, *Knife 23* and *31* approached the East Beach and encountered intense fire. *Knife 23* was hit and crashed on the beach, but was still able to unload 20 Marines. Two RPGs hit *Knife 31*, which ignited its left fuel tank ripping away the nose of the helicopter. It crashed fifty meters offshore. Thirteen Marines perished. One hour after the assault began, only 54 Marines were on the island – 11 had perished and would be among the last casualties of the Vietnam War.

"First Sergeant, this is a mother-fricking cluster frick!" Major McGivens screamed. "We could only land a Company, and we're fighting in three different locations. The beach is too hot, some choppers aborted."

The Sergeant pointed on the map. "We're – here – here, and here." Sir, where's Elijah?" Seamus questioned.

"He's west of East Beach. We have to link up before we push inland. Seamus, Intel fucked up. There's supposed to be 50 soldiers on this island. But with the shit they're throwing at us there must be a Battalion."

"Sir, I'm going to find him," Seamus screamed.

Of the eight choppers that brought the Marines, three were destroyed in the early stages of the raid and four were severely damaged. Only 131 men in total were able to land.

*　　*　　*

"John Wayne, where the fuck is Seamus?" Elijah screamed.

"He's pinned down 200 meters from the beach. Elijah, we got to link up before we go inland," John Wayne said.

"Joe, we can't maneuver. We'll defend this position," Elijah declared.

"Roger that, Guns," John Wayne replied.

Forward Position – Koh Tong

Gunnery Sergeant Bravo grabbed his M-16 and headed toward the tip of the perimeter.

"Guns, get the fuck down," Private Cardosa screamed.

Rounds screamed, but Bravo stood his ground. He was invincible and protected by his animal power, the Eagle.

Elijah screamed, "I'm a Gunnery Sergeant in the United States Marine Corps, and I will crawl for no Khmer Fucking Rouge Commie bastard."

*　　*　　*

Sergeant Rick MaddogMike Flynn extended the handset of the PRC-25 toward Major McGivens. "Major McGivens, Colonel Gil Robinson, wants to talk to you, says it's urgent."

The Major grabbed the hook. "Butch Cassidy here – go ahead."

"Calder, I want you to note the following – the ship's crew was released. The Mayaguez is underway toward international waters. Repeat, the crew is not on the island; they are safe and heading toward open waters. Calder, you are to disengage, return fire only if you're engaged. We're sending choppers to get you out."

"Sir, we've lost Marines. They're shooting the shit out of us. Request an air strike on the mainland . . ."

"Calder, no – somebody at the top doesn't want to make this a big international incident. I hear it's Kissinger . . ."

"Sir, with all due respect, this is more than an international incident; the enemy is engaging us in fortified positions."

"Calder, this is not the time. Get your Marines out of there. Establish a defensive position on the beach and get on those choppers... Out."

Major McGivens could no longer endure the insanity of the Vietnam War and its senseless missions. He threw his helmet and collapsed on the ground.
"Why?" he whispered. "Why? God dammit, why can't we get it right? We're Marines; we're supposed to get it right," he continued. "They died for nothing."
McGivens crouched in the tall grass trying to make sense of another useless mission.
"We didn't get the fricking word. The bastards! Send the Marines! I'm sick of it."
"Major McGivens," Sergeant Flynn screamed. "Sir, we need you. Get in the game. What are your orders?"
Calder McGivens sat in the elephant grass, weeping. He had seen more than anyone could bear; he'd been pushed to the limit.
"Major," Sergeant Flynn called.
Major Calder McGivens turned to his Sergeant and calmly said, "It don't mean nuthin'."

MaddogMikeJim Flynn assumed command of the Company and would coordinate their withdrawal. He grabbed the hook and called First Sergeant O'Grady.

"Top, get over here; the Major's lost it . . . Over . . ."

"Maddog, I can't leave this position. We're trying to move inland, but we're scattered all over the beach. What's the status with the major?"

Seamus had a presence that the Marines needed. However, not all of them were accounted for; Seamus had to remain.

"Top, the crew's been released. They were never on the island. The Mayaguez is out at sea. This was all for nothing . . . Over."

Seamus O'Grady showing no emotion calmly said, "Maddog, give me a sit-rep . . ."

"Seamus, we've lost 11 men. There are pockets of men pinned down throughout the *AO* (area of operation) . . . Over."

"Seamus, organize a tactical withdrawal toward the beach. Your orders are to cease-fire. Only engage if you're fired upon," MaddogMikeJim Flynn ordered. "Sir, what the fuck is this all about? Even the last moments of this fucking war . . . for nothing! . . . Over."

"Maddog, on whose orders?" Seamus screamed.

"Sir, I've taken command of Alpha Company . . . Over."

"Maddog, you serious? You're commanding???"

"Yes, Sir . . ." Sergeant Flynn responded.

"Jesus H. Christ Maddog, I am not a Sir. We've been together since '67, and you still can't get it right . . ."

"Sorry Seamus, that's just who you are. But now it's my turn. Just do what I say . . . Over . . ."

"Okay, Maddog, it ain't me now; it's you. Get my Marines off this beach . . ."

"Seamus, Colonel says we are to disengage . . . Over . . ."

"He did? He can go take a flying fuck . . . Out."

The NCOs were scattered throughout the area of operation (AO). Flynn had become the Commanding Officer, while Major Calder McGivens crouched in the tall grass and Seamus ran west to search for Elijah Bravo.

*   *   *

"John Wayne, where's the Gunny?" Seamus screamed.
"He's at the point, spotting targets. He's walking the perimeter, kind of like what you did. You cowpokes from Luckenbach are crazy."
Seamus reached the tip of their position.
"Gunnery Sergeant Bravo, get the fuck back to the CP, McGivens lost it; Maddog's calling the shots. Get McGivens back in the game. Buck and me will coordinate our withdrawal."
"Who's in command?" Elijah asked.
"Maddog," Seamus responded.

"Well, I'll be dipped in shit," Elijah said. "I'm okay with that, but this is a good position, if we move back we run the risk of a ground attack."

"Elijah, the crew, and the ship were released; they were never on the island. They were released before we assaulted. The Major could use you; he's shaken. Choppers are inbound to get us out of here."

"Jesus H. Christ Seamus! Released! We lost men!"

"Elijah! Get the fuck out of here!"

"Hey Buckaroo, I'm not leavin' you. Not on your life. We promised we'd never leave each other. I'm stayin'."

"Elijah, I said the same thing on 861. You made me leave. It's my turn to cover our withdrawal. Elijah, this fuckin' war has killed us. How could I have been so wrong? What the fuck was I thinkin'. Ofa was right. You go. You're goin' to be with Nguyen. Ofa will find a way to get her out. Not another word Guns. That's an order. I'll coordinate our withdrawal."

Seamus O'Grady touched his best friend's shoulder. "I'll be along shortly," he said. "Go!"

Elijah stepped toward the rear, then turned, and shouted. "Hey, fuckhead, what the fuck am I thinkin' – rank between a First Sergeant and a Gunnery Sergeant is like rank among thieves. I ain't goin', and you can go fuck yourself and the horse you rode in on."

*   *   *

On May 15, 1975, both boys crossed the line in the sand.

The Mayaguez was the last battle of the Vietnam War. It was ill planned, and a major intelligence failure. The Marines were committed piecemeal. American intelligence failed to note that the crew was not on the island and the enemy had well over 200 men manning automatic weapons in fortified defenses. The Marines would never recover their dead; they had broken their pledge. Three Marines were left behind and were mistakenly unaccounted for. The Cambodians found them and executed them. One was shot, the others were beaten to death. The insanity of the Vietnam War continued to the end. The hasty U.S. response attempted to restore some measure of prestige to the nation after the fall of Vietnam. It was ill-conceived and as a result, men died. Seamus and Elijah covered the withdrawal. They were the last Marines to abandon their position. They made it to the beach, and a CH-53 took them back to the Midway.

FIFTY-FOUR

GOOD BITCH BAD BITCH

You are a princess . . . I am a bad bitch.

Doctor Bepa Burkov

April 1975 – Bach Mai Hospital

D**r. Lam had been with Dooley Intermed International since graduating from a medical school in China.** Although he was a competent doctor, the quality of Vietnamese physicians trained in China was lacking. He was a demure man with a kind soul and had done everything he could to keep Nguyen Lu at Bach Mai Hospital. Although her skills exceeded Vietnamese and Chinese nurses, the communists would not listen to reason. They were unforgiving and would exact revenge on the people who aided their enemies. Dr. Lam despised the repressive government of the North, but he was a practical man and gave the communists what they wanted and did his best to survive.

*   *   *

"Good afternoon doctors, I trust you have had a good journey."

The women had traveled into the heart of darkness chasing the righteous indignation of Dr. Hawkins.

"Yes, doctor, we did have a good journey," Ofa replied.

"I'm Dr. Lam. I am here to assist you. If you permit me, I would like to show you the ropes. That's what you Americas say."

Dr. Burkov frowned. "I'm Russian," she said.

"Excuse me, doctor I just assumed."

Dr. Hawkins immediately responded, "Dr. Lam, no worries. Thank you for your cordial welcome and good afternoon to you. May I introduce Dr. Bepa Burkov and my assistant, Nurse Ky?"

He smiled cordially.

"You must be tired, let me show you to your quarters, I trust you will be comfortable there. Whatever you need, my staff and I are at your service. I cannot emphasize how critical the situation has become. A higher power has sent you."

"Higher power – I was under the assumption that the inference of a God is forbidden in the North."

"Dr. Hawkins, you are correct, but things that are forbidden become attractive. The forbidden fruit becomes the seeker's most strident temptation."

Dr. Lam accompanied the ladies to the professional quarters adjacent to the hospital. He chuckled and said, "Please excuse my impertinence but I heard the new doctors were competent, but I was not told how beautiful they would be."

Ophelia whispered, "I think he's sweet. Finally, someone who's not so rigid."

"I can't believe you're that starved for the attention of a man," Dr. Burkov countered. "Don't trust him. His sweetness seems too contrived. In the James Bond movies, the sweet man is always the villain. Tell him nothing. We must continue to play good bitch bad bitch."

"Bepa, you watched James Bond?"

"My girl, how do you think we KGB agents learned to be good spies?"

"Okay Bepa, you're the bad bitch. But I think there comes a time when we need to start trustin' someone. But I will listen to you even though you've been consistently wrong 'bout everything."

"Ladies, are you hungry? Dr. Lam asked. "I'll have the cook prepare something. I apologize in advance, but it won't be much, but she makes a wonderful chicken stew, and she does it without chicken."

Dr. Lam hesitated; it was as though he had something on his mind. He turned toward Ofa.

"Dr. Hawkins, please understand there is a file on you; the state does not trust you. You should worry."

"Dr. Lam, actually, I don't worry. There's been a file on me since I joined the Students for a Democratic Society. I understand President Nixon has even read reports 'bout me. It's flattering. A girl welcomes any attention she can get."

They laughed; Bepa Burkov scowled.

"It is my dream to go to America," Lam commented. "Maybe when the wounds of the war have healed, I will go. The war has been devastating to Vietnam, but the United States has lost its innocence, and there will be a scar on the soul of America. But Vietnam will not have this scar. We are born to die for the state. It is our way. We could have been friendly, but America sided with the French. We were like you during your revolution. We wanted our independence."

"Dr. Lam, Independence is not only defined by the absence of foreign intervention. Independence requires trust and morality, and I'm sorry to tell you that your country has neither," Ofa remarked.

"I can only answer that by explaining our history. After World War II, Ho Chí Minh was the proclaimed leader of the Vietminh. The father represented Catholics, Buddhists, small businessmen, communists, and farmers in the fight for Vietnam's independence from the French. He appealed to President Eisenhower for recognition. He insisted he is not communist and suggested Indochina could be good for American enterprise. He told American diplomats in Vietnam that he had no direct ties to the Soviet Union. The people believed he was a symbol of nationalism and freedom. Ho Chi Minh did not ask for economic aid, but understanding, moral support, and a voice in the forum of western democracies. But America would not recognize the government of Vietnam; the United States would not even read his mail. Your country said it was improper for the President of the United States to acknowledge such correspondence. Instead, you helped the French."

"Dr. Lam, enough of politics. I understand your history, but often history is changed by not seeing events in the greater context," Ofa countered. "It will take years to determine the truth about the war."

"Yes, I agree with you, enough of politics."

"Dr. Hawkins, you are an American celebrity," he laughed.

"Why yes, I am," she replied. "I am indeed an American celebrity."

"I hope you will find the time to tell me about that. American celebrities are very popular in Vietnam. This may be an odd question, but why are you Americans fascinated by baseball? The Yankees are my favorite baseball team."

Bepa interjected. "Dr. Lam, I beg your pardon, but I'm feeling faint from the journey. I believe I'm airsick. Would you mind? I need to take some medication."

"Yes, of course, Doctor Burkov. I will call upon you this evening, and perhaps you will be feeling better. Good day doctors."

"Bepa! Airsick! You? Let me check you for fever. You must have caught a chill in the rain. Here, lay down."

Bepa laughed. "Ofa, you're sweet to worry about me. But I am like a man. As a matter of fact, I am a man. I can put my head through that wall. Russian, you know. There's nothing wrong. I just didn't like him being so friendly."

"Bepa, don't be like one of those women who feels the need to act like they're never scared or like they're as strong as a man. That's not bein' honest with your true nature. It's okay to feel vulnerable. Beauty – it's in the fragility of your petals."

"Ofa, what would I do without you. There are so many times I want to embrace your thoughts. Just to be held! But the bible says there is a time for every season, and I've not found that season."

Ofa, did you notice that Dr. Lam led the conversation to the New York Yankees? He was leading you."

"Bepa, I don't understand."

"There's a KGB agent in Hanoi who I understand from my sources is trying to defect to America. I believe he'll try to make contact with an agent, to see if he can manipulate his way out of the North. He may or may not suspect me of being KGB, but he'll continue to pry until he finds who he's looking for. I am told by the bureau that if I find this person, I am to kill him."

"Bepa," do you think it's Dr. Lam? If it's him, he can help us."

"We must proceed with caution. We need to make contact with him and continue the conversation about New York and the Yankee baseball team. If it's him, he'll ask if either of us has seen the Broadway production, *Damn Yankees*. That's how we'll know," Bepa said.

"What do we do if it's him?"

"I don't know," Bepa said.

*   *   *

Precisely at 6 PM, Dr. Lam returned to the quarters of the doctors.

"Good evening ladies. Dr. Burkov, I trust you are well."

"Yes, I think I just caught a chill standing in the rain."

"I am sorry doctor; it should not have happened. This is one of the reasons why I am displeased with the government. It will get worse before it gets better."

"Dr. Burkov, have you been to America?"

"Why yes," many times. I studied English at Fordham University and lived near Yankee Stadium."

Dr. Lam turned toward the sexy Russian woman and commented, "Why does everyone like the New York Yankees. I understand they are the best team or maybe it's just the word Yankee. But doesn't it seem strange they are hated because they always win?"

"In America, everyone loves a winner, maybe that's why they love them," Dr. Burkov commented. "But you are right; they are a team that people love to hate."

Dr. Lam laughed then asked, "Have either of you seen the Broadway show, *Damn Yankees*?" I understand it is very telling of America's fascination to win."

Dr. Lam turned toward Ofa and waited for her response.

"I've seen it only for the music, not for the winning thing," she replied.

Trying to remain casual, Lam nodded

"Dr. Hawkins, you are the Girl with the Purple Ribbon, an American celebrity. Would you think I am silly if I asked for your autograph?"

"Dr. Lam, you flatter me."

"Dr. Hawkins, I have a favorite restaurant not far from here. It's not what you are accustomed to in Boston or New York, but I hope you'll not be disappointed. I would appreciate having dinner with you since we have much to discuss."

"Dr. Lam," Bepa interjected. "Did you forget to invite me? You failed to mention if I would be disappointed. You probably think since I'm Russian I'm accustomed to eating horse meat."

"No disrespect Dr. Burkov, I did not think that. Would you please call me An?"

"None taken. But of course, I'm not the queen that Dr. Hawkins is. You can call me Bepa."

"Dr. Lam, I'm a country girl from Luckenbach, Texas. Call me Ophelia. An, you wouldn't think I'm all that if I was jawin' on a chew."

"I'm not sure I understand what you mean by jawing a chew. Let's have dinner tonight. Maybe you can tell me. I'll send a driver for you at eight PM."

Dinner, 8 PM

The restaurant was filled with people who were celebrating the end of the war. With the hordes of refugees desperately attempting to flee the advancing communists, there was a different scene in the south.

"Ophelia, tell me about the Yankees? I also want to hear all about the musical, *Damn Yankees.*"

Bepa had neither the time nor the patience to dance between the innuendos of conversation.

"An," she said. "Why do you want to defect? You obviously know who I am."

"Dr. Burkov, I knew right away. I heard the agent was a beautiful blond woman, a doctor in love with an American. A trusted friend mentioned you are unhappy and may want to defect," Lam said.

"What troubles me," Bepa commented, "someone has become suspicious and believes I have turned. So, my good Dr. Lam, what are you supposed to do when you find this person?"

"I am to kill them," he said."

"An, I have been told to kill you as well."

Bepa's mood changed. She became serious.

"Dr. Lam, you know that as a senior KGB agent I have immunity for what I choose to do. I have a gun under the table; it is pointed at you. I have orders to find you and kill you. I have no desire to defect."

"I thought I could trust you, Dr. Lam exclaimed. Then kill me. Death is better than being here. You deserve this government. Help them slaughter the innocent. Then you will kill nurse Lu. You will have that on your conscience. Pull the damn trigger Dr. Burkov!"

"An – relax; I had to be sure of your intentions. I'm not going to kill you. I was testing you to determine if you were truthful about defecting. Understand the situation you face. To the North is China in the west Laos and Cambodia. The only way out of Vietnam is east by boat, into the South China Sea. We will need a boat. We will take Nguyen Lu out of Vietnam. You will come with us."

"Ladies, what is your plan?"

"We have no plan. Even if we had one, a plan never survives. Ophelia and I will let you know when we have an idea."

"Why Nguyen? Dr. Lam asked. "Why do you try to save her?"

"They have made her a criminal of the state."

Bepa smiled. You will not mention anything, and you will trust no one."

"Dr. Burkov, I desperately want to trust you but what assurance can you give me that you are telling the truth?"

Bepa nodded, "This is why you can trust me, An."

She took the palm of her hand and placed it on the flame of a candle; her skin sizzled. Without showing either pain or emotion, she then withdrew her hand. "It is certain because I have rendered it to be certain," she asserted.

"An, you will do everything I tell you. If you do not listen to me, you must know what I am capable of doing. Do you understand? I consider you a friend; it is important you remain that way. You may leave now."

Ofa looked at Bepa and took a deep breath.

"My God Bepa! I have to ask you a question."

Bepa read her mind.

"No Ofa, I wasn't going to kill him. I did that only to test to see if he was telling us the truth about defecting. If he were lying, he would have pleaded for his life. Then, I would have killed him."

Ofa smiled.

"Bepa, that wasn't my question. Do you really have a man you're in love with livin' in America?"

"Yes, he lives in Nebraska."

May 1975

Each evening the doctors sat at the local café on Tong Duy Street adjacent to the Temple of Literature, the oldest university in Vietnam. There, they entertained a myriad of plans on how they would rescue Nguyen Lu. Where would they get a boat? From what city would they leave? How would they get there? Supplies! How would they survive the ordeal in a sea without shores? Who would sail the boat? Where would they go? How would they get Nguyen out of the camp? But Bepa Burkov would find a way.

"Ofa, the best way to not feel hopeless is to do something. We can't wait for good things to happen to us. We have to make it happen. Let's go to the camp and plead that we need Nguyen's expertise. It can be as simple as a yes from the Colonel."

Bepa turned her head.

"Ofa, do not take your eyes off of me. Do you understand? Nod if you understand. We're being watched. The man sitting to my right by the window – I have seen him, sitting there for the past three days with his face buried behind the newspaper."

Ofa turned. "Bepa, you're too suspicious. Always drama with you. You're worse than the communists. Oh, I forgot, you are a communist. He's an old man having coffee and readin' the paper."

"I told you not to look. My dear girl, for the last three days, he's been reading the same paper. The man is tracking us."

Bepa read the headlines of the paper. "The 9th Marines slaughtered in Cambodia."

Ofa began to sob. Her head fell into her hands. "Noooo!" she screamed. "Not Seamus and Elijah! Bepa, what are we going to do? Not the 9th Marines," she cried.

Everyone in the restaurant turned toward Ofa. Everyone, except the old man. Bepa pulled her weapon, held it under the table, and pointed it in the direction of the man. The man stood then walked calmly toward the doctors. Ofa continued to cry.

"There, there, little sister. Don't believe everything you read in the paper. We, communists, tend to make things up when it suits us," he said.

"My Gen'ral! You're alive. Tell me it isn't true. Please tell me it isn't true."

General Minh smiled and said, "It isn't true. Be here tomorrow night; I have a plan."

General Minh disappeared into the café life of war-torn Hanoi.

FIFTY-FIVE

FROM THE ASHES

I have dreamt in my life, dreams that have stayed with me ever
after, and changed my ideas; they have gone through and through
me, like wine through water, and altered the color of my mind.
And this is one: I'm going to tell it – but take care not to smile at
any part of it.

Emily Brontë, *Wuthering Heights*

May 1975 – Hanoi, North Vietnam

The Phoenix, the mythological bird with the fiery plumage,
is immortal. Near the end of its life, it settles into a nest of
twigs, which burns ferociously reducing the bird and the nest to
ashes. And from those ashes, a fledgling phoenix rises – renewed and
reborn. General Minh returned from the dead, with a plan. If he
surfaced, he would be viewed a traitor and suspected for the murder
of Colonel Gee. But the general was a resourceful man.

*   *   *

"Ofa wear something sexy tonight. We want all our cards on the
table, and you my dear are the ace of diamonds."

"Bepa, the General and me – it's not what you think. He's like a
father. He needs me, and I need him."

Bepa smiled.

"Very well darling. But he treats me like a whore. Okay, let's go.
Time is no longer on our side."

General Minh sat at the same table. Ofa stared at him from the
corner of her eye. Bepa finished her soup, finished Ofa's, and then
drank three shots of Vodka. For a Wednesday evening, the restaurant

was crowded, but one never knew who was watching. There were spies everywhere in the New Vietnam.

The General left his seat, folded his newspaper, walked by the doctors, threw the paper into the trash, and left the restaurant.

"Damn it Bepa. I thought we'd finally have something."

"Darling, think."

Ofa appeared confused. "What?" she asked.

"He's written directions in the newspaper," Bepa exclaimed.

Bepa retrieved the paper from the trash. "Here it is," she said. "Trung Thien Shrine on Dai Tu Street."

It was an old shrine dedicated to Tran Hung Dao, Vietnam's greatest General. The General had written: "If you think you are followed do not come."

Before they left the restaurant, Bepa carefully observed each corner and saw no one posing a threat. Bepa hailed a public car, and the two women sped toward the Trung Thien Shrine. The shrine was dark and deserted. From the darkness, a tall figure walked slowly toward the women. He wore a long burlap coat. With his hands in his pockets, he appeared a poor man. The General smiled. Ofa ran and buried her head in his chest.

"Little Sister, we meet again. Did I not tell you we would?" His long gray beard and disheveled appearance hid the identity of a General who had commanded a North Vietnamese Division. "You remind me of my daughter Mi Lin. I have been thinking of her today. Had she lived, she would be 27 years old. That is your age?"

"Yes, I'm 27. Thank God, you're alive. We thought you were killed with Colonel Gee. What happened?"

"I killed him. He would have had you arrested. He was on to both of you. Whether you were a spy or not, it did not matter. You were intent on rescuing a Vietnamese National, who committed crimes against the state. He was convinced you were Pretty Girl. After you left, I shot him then destroyed the file he kept on you. Gee was a selfish man and refused to notify the authorities. He hoped to keep the glory of your capture for himself. But, you are beginning to raise suspicions as Girl with the Purple Ribbon. You are okay for now, but this will not last."

"How did you get this far North," Bepa asked?

"Dear, when you are a General, you have many friends, and you have many enemies. I asked my friends for help, not my enemies."

The General's calm analysis of a dangerous situation added to his charm.

"There's only one way out of Vietnam – boat. I will get us a boat and a man to pilot it. I love my country, but I am a criminal, and I must leave. The New Vietnam will purge its enemies, and I will not be part of that."

How could a man with such a noble nature be an enemy? Ofa thought.

"How much will the boat and pilot cost?" Bepa asked?

"Nothing, the man with the boat, wants to go to Montana." Regardless, I have money in Switzerland; I will be a rich American.

"How do we get to Nguyen," Bepa continued.

"Go to Yen Bai camp on Wednesday and convince the Commandant that Nurse Lu is valuable to the state. They understand there is no point imprisoning her. They are only punishing her. The Commandant of the Camp is Colonel Ly-Truc-Viet. He was one of my officers in the Hill fights – a reasonable man. He was a hero and has much influence. He could intercede. You're close, but be clever. Get her released to your custody. When you do that, drive to the café for lunch. I will have a car there waiting to take you to the boat."

The General handed Dr. Burkov a map of the boat's location. "Study the map and then burn it. When you get to the dock, we leave. Do not bring anything. Nothing – I will have things for you."

"What if it doesn't work my Gen'ral," Ofa asked.

"Have faith my girl. It will work. It's meant to be. If it does not, I will rise from the ashes and pay a visit to, Colonel Viet."

"My Gen'ral can you get a message to Seamus and Elijah. I'm worried 'bout that newspaper headline."

"Little girl, I checked with my contacts. There was a battle with a unit of the 9th Marines. They attempted to rescue an American supply ship high-jacked by the Khmer Rouge. There were minimum casualties. Seamus and Elijah were not listed on the report. Please, do not concern yourself, but I will send the message.

U.S.S Midway – Alpha Company 1st Battalion 9th Marine Regiment – Gunnery Sergeant Elijah Bravo – What's meant to be will find a way – Very close – Making contact with Cowboy's Girl – Pretty Girl sends.

"Dr. Hawkins you are a woman with an old soul. That's why I want to go to America. You Americans are dreamers. In Vietnam, there are no dreams; people are old when they are young. I want to be a dreamer too. But dreamers, often are not doers. So maybe, we are dreamers who do."

"Gen'ral, maybe that's how we found each other."

"My darling child, you are a treasure. There are many reasons we found each other and our dreams are the least of which. You risk your life for a girl you've never met. The dream of what life could become drives you. I am not as pure. I have been driven by hate. But when I met you, my life changed."

"I will send the message. When you go to the café, order lunch, then immediately exit the back of the restaurant. Make it appear you are going to the washroom. Then get into the waiting car. Maybe it will be as easy as that. I will see you on Wednesday at the boat. Good night my dear ladies."

In the cab, on the ride back to their quarters, Bepa whispered, "I'll be carrying a gun. There'll be a moment when we must decide about what we are willing to risk getting Nguyen. You know what's in my heart. But I need to know what you will risk for a girl you've never met."

Ofa placed her head on Dr. Burkov's shoulder, she closed her eyes, and whispered – "Everything."

FIFTY-SIX

JONESY SENDS

Pretty Girl . . . Coffee's perking on the burner . . . Waiting for you . . .
Come home and bring Cowboy's Girl . . . USS Midway . . . Jonesy Sends. .

Jonesy

May 1975 – Hanoi

"**O**fa, I'm still a communist."

"If you are, you're not a very good one," Ofa remarked.

"Darling, class warfare defines the history of the world – proprietor and slave, oppressor and oppressed," Dr. Burkov said. "Man has always stood in opposition to one another. Look at the war. 'Where justice is denied, where poverty is enforced, where ignorance prevails, and where any one class is made to feel that society is an organized conspiracy to oppress, rob, and degrade them, neither persons nor property will be safe.' It was your own, Frederick Douglass who said this."

"There must be justice, and if we're to be our brothers' kee'pa then we must do what we can for justice," Ofa lamented.

"Ofa, you're such an idealist. You're unhappy with the way things are, so you don't accept the world, and then you try to change it. I was born into injustice, and have brought injustice to many. And when I think about love, I never believed in it until I fell in love. I was caught in the business of the state, and that very business is blind to justice. The state could care less about idealism, yet it feeds off the world and assures its immortality. How can I love my man and love the state? The state was my god, but then I found you, and now I believe love is stronger than ideology. You have risked your life to bring two lovers together. At first, I didn't understand. But if love, as you say, defines us, then I want to be part of that. I've followed false gods all my life, and then I met Victor, so I began to change. I can no longer serve the state. I can't have two gods. I have seen the state's ugliness. This war – it's a battle of ideologies, and I don't want to be part of it. If we can bring Nguyen and Elijah together, then something good will come from this suffering. I can die for that," Bepa said.

Ofa Hawkins said nothing. She calmly sat and gazed out the window attempting to find peace in the moment.

"Ofa we have a bond that has been earned. We have been brought together by a simple Vietnamese girl. But darling, why does this mean so much to you? What drives you is beyond mere love."

Ofa smiled, and without the slightest hesitation she said, "Because I need something good to happen."

Hai Phong Harbor, North Vietnam

"Was there anything you forgot?" General Minh asked. "Captain Hong, make one more check, and I will be satisfied."

The Red Lotus was an old boat that had seen her day. Hong's grandfather built her 60 years before to fish the waters of the South China Sea. She was a strong seafarer and brought abundant harvests to hungry villagers. But the war had not been kind to her. She needed repairs, but for the past ten years, all resources went to the war effort; so, she sat, soaking up the murky sea in Ben Bin Harbor and collecting barnacles. Captain Hong assured the General that the Red Lotus had one voyage left. He would stake his life and the lives of everyone on board.

"What armaments have you procured?" General Minh asked of the old sea Captain.

"My General, we have a 50-caliber and 3,000 rounds, four AK-47s maybe three magazines each, and four RPGs (rocket-propelled grenade launchers.)"

"That will have to do," the General said, "we will have to be good shots. But is she seaworthy."
"General, everything checks out. She is seaworthy."

The weathered Captain Hong pulled on an old pipe, looked his former CO, and peered directly in the eye.

"General, I have been with you for a long time, I have always believed in you; now it is your turn to believe in me."

"Very well. Then it is good. We wait for the doctors."

May 1975 – USS Midway, South China Sea

One hundred miles off the coast of Vietnam, the USS Midway patrolled the waters of the South China Sea. While waiting for the order to send Marines ashore, the Midway was on a mission of mercy searching for the *boat people,* the indigenous Vietnamese who risked their lives on the sea fleeing the repressive communists of the New Vietnam. They were pillaged by pirates, endured overcrowded voyages, and suffered the wrath of storms. Many perished. Regardless, they left to find a dream.

On April 30, 1975, Saigon fell to communist forces. The United States initiated Operation Frequent Wind and evacuated more than 7,000 Vietnamese who helped the South and American forces.

Communications Center, USS Midway

"Jesus H. Christ sir, I got another one. Pretty Girl strikes again. The men in the communications center gathered around Jonesy as he read the latest note from the girl who had stolen their hearts.

24 May 75 – U.S.S Midway – Alpha Company, 1st Battalion, 9th Marine Regiment – Gunnery Sergeant Elijah Bravo – Close, making contact with Cowboy's Girl – Pretty Girl sends.

Jonesy ripped the message from the teleprinter. The sailors in the communications center cheered. Pretty Girl had given them hope. Pictures of Ofa Hawkins hung throughout the ship. She had become the sweetheart of the Midway and each message she sent added to her mystique.

"Jonesy, give me the message," JG Quackenbush asked. "I'm going to see Elijah and Seamus."

20 Minutes Later

"Jonesy, where's JG Quackenbush? Captain Ragsdale asked.

Petty Officer Timothy Jones jumped to attention. "Officer on deck. A-tennnnn-hut!"

"Stand at ease," the Captain said. "Where's JG Quackenbush?"

"Sir, he's speaking with Gunnery Sergeant Bravo. He should be back shortly. We got another message from Pretty Girl."

"You guys mind if I wait?" the Captain asked.

The men in the communication center couldn't believe that the Captain of the USS Midway, the largest warship in the world had asked the sailors permission to wait.

"Sir, can we get you a cup of coffee?"

"I'd love one Jonesy."

"This is damn good coffee. On the bridge, they make it with seawater. Hope you don't mind, but I ought to come down here when I need a cup. Jonesy, do me a favor; call the bridge for me, I need to speak to the XO" (Executive Officer).

Jerry Pollard, the ship's Executive Officer, answered the phone.

"Jerry, can you get down to the comm center? They make the best cup of coffee. We got another message from Pretty Girl; you need to see this. Captain Pollard, I believe it's time the U.S. Navy gets involved."

Captain Butch Ragsdale, the Commanding Officer (CO) of the Midway, Captain Jerry Pollard, the Executive Officer, Commander Steve Petit, the Navigation Officer, and Commander Dan Naremore, the Air Boss, gathered in the comm center.

"Quackenbush, I want you part of this," the Captain said. "Okay, boys, what we going to do about Pretty Girl? I'll entertain all suggestions. Before we begin, I'll tell you what I'm not going to do. I'm not going to sit out here and not help her – Jerry, talk to me."

"Well Sir, knowing what you're not going to do gives us a pretty good idea of what you're going to do. This is what we know from talking to the Gunny. She's an American doctor with Dooley Intermed International, who volunteered to assist the South Vietnamese Government."

"Yeah, Jerry but we now realize that's a smoke screen to get Nguyen Lu a Vietnamese National out of Vietnam," the Captain said.

"Yes and no Sir. Dr. Hawkins is a dedicated physician; I understand she has an altruistic nature. I think she's killing two birds with one stone. When Dr. Hawkins got to Vietnam she was hoping that Lu would still be in the south; it would've been an easy task to get her out. But Lu was sent to Quang Tri, and when the communists overran I Corps, she was captured and eventually sent to Hanoi as a political prisoner. They're punishing her cause she was a nurse on the Sanctuary. That's how she met Bravo. He was wounded in the hill fights. Dr. Hawkins apparently has gone from New York to Saigon to Da Nang, to Hue, to Quang Tri and now we believe she's in Hanoi. Dr. Hawkins is either superwoman, or she's getting help. The way I understand it – she's just a girl, and to do what she's done – I just don't know. Someone who's pretty capable is helping her."

"In the last message from the doctor, she said she's making contact with Lu," the Captain stated. "That has to mean she's in Hanoi."

"Sir, if Dr. Hawkins gets her out of prison, I expect we'll get a message and another when they leave country," Quackenbush commented.

"The only way out is by sea," Jonesy interrupted. "Excuse me, Captain, I don't mean to interrupt, but I feel like she's sending these messages to me. It's personal to me sir."

"Jonesy, that's what I like about you. You're a thinking man. You join us. Maybe we need to see Pretty Girl up close and personal. Might give us a different perspective of how we're looking at this. I'm confused why she hasn't asked the U.S. Navy to help her."

"Captain, I don't believe she thinks that's an option," Jonesy answered.

Captain Ragsdale knew exactly what he wanted to do, but Congress prohibited any offensive actions in Southeast Asia. Regardless of the wishes of Congress, Ragsdale would commit the Midway to rescue Nguyen Lu, the fiancée of one of his Marines. It had become personal.

"Captain, hear me out, I have an idea," Captain Pollard interjected. "We need to explore Lu's release through diplomatic channels. Right now, our hands are tied. Perhaps we can negotiate something with the Vietnamese."

"Gentlemen may I say something?" Jonesy asked.

"Shoot," Pollard remarked.

"Sir," Jonesy said. "With all due respect, I don't think that's a good idea. I majored in Asian Studies at Northwestern. We've no hook with which to negotiate. We've nothing they want. How do you justify buying a Vietnamese citizen from Vietnam? The Asians believe Lu's involvement helping the enemies of the state is a most grievous crime. They must punish her. It's the only way they can save face. If we try to negotiate, we will destroy any chance Dr. Hawkins has to rescue her. We'll also destroy the Doctor's cover. She'll then be picked up as a spy for interfering with their justice, and we'll never get either woman out. This is not a matter of diplomacy. Look at it like they would. Lu is an enemy, and so is Pretty Girl for trying to help her. But I'd bet my life they haven't figured Dr. Hawkins out yet, but her luck will run out soon. Her messages are careless. She's either a great actress or she has the luck of the Irish. We can't go in and get her; it'd be like trying to find a needle in a haystack. She'll come to us."

"Jerry, I think we got it," Ragsdale said.

Their heads turned toward the Captain.

"This is what we're going to do. Right now, it's up to the doctor to make contact and get out. Let's wait till we hear from her. When we do, we'll react based on our interpretation of the situation. We'll scramble a Squadron of Intruders and see if we can find her on the open sea. We'll keep an eye out. The only way out of Vietnam is towards us. Draft an operations order Jerry."

"Sir, May I interrupt," Jonesy said?

"We need to send her a message," Jonesy said. "Let her know we're waiting. It'll give her hope and whoever she's in cahoots with."

"Jonesy how on earth can that work?" Commander Pollard questioned.

"Sir, we'll put it on the same frequency that she's been using. The message will float on the channel and with a little luck whoever sent the last message will get it. Request permission to draft the message. This might sound crazy, but I feel close to her. I want her to know I'm here for her. I'll sign my name. Make it personal. She'll realize what she means to us."

"Jonesy, I think Pretty Girl has become personal to all of us. Shouldn't we tell her where we are?" Ragsdale asked.

"Sir, I don't think so. She's been three steps ahead of us; she knows we'll be south of the 17th parallel. If we send her a message, she'll think we're heading north."

"Draft the message Jonesy," the Captain said. "We'll float it out there and let's hope whoever sent her message will get ours. One more thing," the Captain said, "Change course, head toward the coast, and let's start pushing north."

Jonesy grabbed the pencil lodged behind his ear.

"Pretty Girl – Coffee on the burner – Waiting for you – Come home and bring Cowboy's Girl – USS Midway – Jonesy Sends.

FIFTY-SEVEN

A WHITE WEDDING DRESS

The most critical part of a mission is like blowing out candles on a birthday cake – Don't over-think it.

Dr. Bepa Burkov

24 May – Bach Mai Hospital

Dressed in traditional white medical cloaks, the doctors left their quarters precisely at 7 AM. But Ofa wore boots, wranglers, and a broad brim hat. Whatever she had to do, she'd do it as a Texan.

"Ofa, this is it. You okay?" Bepa asked.

Dr. Hawkins attempted to speak, but couldn't. She could only manage a smile.

"Darling," Dr. Burkov said. "Remember, what we do today is worthy of any sacrifice we may be called upon to make. Ofa, you're shaking."

There was nothing Bepa Burkov could do for her friend. She wanted to assure her that everything would be fine, but she couldn't.

"Ofa – bad things will happen or they won't."

The women waited in front of the hospital for the public car to arrive. From the shadows of an adjacent alley, an old man in a disheveled burlap overcoat appeared. He opened the door of the car for the women and expecting a tip he extended his hand. He placed a note in Dr. Burkov's hand and then disappeared. The doctors entered the car and Bepa handed Ofa the note.

"It's for to you," Dr. Burkov said. "You'd think since I'm the brains of this insanity, it would be for me."

Ofa unfolded the paper; her hand continued to shake.

"So, what's it say, Ofa?"

Ofa gazed at the message. She appeared delighted by its sentiment.

"Just read the fucking thing," Dr. Burkov gruffly demanded.

Pretty Girl – Coffee is perking on the burner – Waiting for you – Come home – bring Cowboy's Girl – USS Midway – Jonesy Sends.

Ofa handed the note to Dr. Burkov and smiled.

"I wonder who Jonesy is? He sounds sweet. I like him."

"Oh Please," Bepa said.

She scanned the message. "This is good. They'll be looking for us."

She crumbled the paper, placed it in her mouth, and swallowed.

"Can you imagine what Seamus and Elijah must be thinking," Ofa said.

"Darling, don't get sentimental on me. I need you to focus. Sentiment will make you weak."

Yen Bai Re-Education Camp, North Vietnam

The car arrived at the camp at 7:30 AM. Bepa insisted on an early meeting. As the car moved through the barbwire gate, she held Ofa's trembling hand trying to comfort the girl from Texas. Ofa had never prepared for anything like this.

"My KGB training officer said, 'the most critical part of a mission is like blowing out candles on a birthday cake,'" Bepa said.

"I don't get it?" Ofa questioned.

"Don't overthink it," Bepa added.

Two soldiers carrying AK-47's met the car, one opened the door and greeted the Doctors.

"Good morning Dr. Burkov, Dr. Hawkins. Colonel Viet will see you shortly."

The women exited. The guards were cold and abrupt; their sinister eyes made Ofa anxious. She despised the guards and knew their game. But Burkov had ice in her veins, and she gave the soldiers what they attempted to give her. Dr. Bepa Burkov had the look of death on her face, but it wasn't her death.

"We must get the upper hand and not have them think we are pushovers. We will get a lot more from them if they respect us." Bepa said.

Scolding the guards, she shouted, "We are doctors working for the state; we do not have time to be kept waiting. Please tell Colonel Viet that if he does not see us immediately, we will leave," Dr. Burkov asserted. "I will report this up the chain to the highest level of the party."

The soldiers remained silent holding their weapons at high port and blocking the entrance to what appeared to be the administration building.

"Come, Dr. Hawkins," Bepa said. "We'll not be treated as enemies. These men are peasants, not soldiers. They do not know how to treat women."

From a side doorway of the building, a voice bellowed.

"Doctors, please forgive my rudeness, I was tending to other matters. Please come. Enjoy some tea with me. I am Colonel Viet."

Bepa whispered. "He's full of shit with that sweet stuff. He was watching. They're going to search us."

Ofa noticed a loose brick on the walkway and fell backward. The Colonel was a stoic man but couldn't resist a glimpse of Ophelia Hawkins. The Colonel attended to Dr. Hawkins, which gave Bepa time to stash a pistol in the bushes.

"Dr. Hawkins, are you okay?" the Colonel asked.

"Yes, thank you. How did you know I was Dr. Hawkins?"

"Girl with the purple ribbon. You are very famous, and the People of Vietnam are grateful to you for your service."

The Colonel extended his hand and Ofa extended hers.

"Colonel Viet, I'm pleased you recognize my work, but I want to assure you that as much as I wanted the war to end, I wanted your side to lose."

"Very well Dr. Hawkins, I respect your honesty. But you got your wish; we did lose. More than one million Vietnamese are dead. Our country is in ruin. There's poverty everywhere. America will continue to prosper, and we will beg for bread. Reasonable men would have stopped the war."

"Colonel Viet, the war is over, and I hope our countries will agree not to repeat the horrors of the past. But I'm afraid that ideologies are fickle and have the proclivity for self-destruction."

"Colonel, I understand you are a fair man. General Minh mentioned you were one of his most trusted and heroic officers and said that you might grant my request," Ofa asserted.

"I am saddened by what happened to General Minh," Colonel Viet said. "He was a great man. Ladies, please follow me inside, and we will sit, have tea, and speak. But please, I beg your forgiveness, I must have you searched. It is our policy to do so, and I am unable to make any exceptions."

"Colonel Viet," Ofa remarked, "by the way, your men leered when we exited the car, I hope they're not doin' the searchin'."

Ofa would interject the lure of sexuality into circumstance. It was the only weapon she had.

"No, of course not, I will have one of the women caretakers of our female boarders."

"Colonel Viet, thank you – but please – the people you're holdin' are prisoners, not boarders. You've taken their rights; they've not been charged or tried by a jury," Ofa asserted. They are not boarders."

"Dr. Hawkins, let's say we agree to disagree. But we see the world through different eyes. We are people no different from you. But we have a different ideology and we are fearful of dissent. In America, everyone is free. Freedom is a worthy idea, and that is your strength. But freedom will be your demise because the people who speak against America will eventually change America and then you will be like us with a political ideology that few will speak against for fear of speaking against what most people expect. You will not be free. Your political freedom will become political repression."

"We have caused each other such misery. Doctor Hawkins, finding the truth was difficult. We couldn't accept a possibility that either one of us was wrong. I am saddened. But you Dr. Hawkins, you spoke against the war. You played into our hands. If America were united, you would have destroyed us. But when your Walter Cronkite said that the Vietnam War is unwinnable we knew we would outlast you. You beat us militarily. I was there. But we won because we lost. Your country gave up. You were Girl with the Purple Ribbon, and you fought for us, and you didn't know it. I am sorry to say that especially when you are here to help us."

"Colonel, I didn't fight for you. I fought for peace to end the killin' on both sides. In America, it's our right to believe different from the government even if this causes us to lose the war. If we lose the right to express our ideas, we lose who we are as a people. And that's when we'll become like you."

"Doctor, I too want peace. I have lost too many men, taken many lives; I have ghosts that haunt me. Would you allow an old soldier his peace and not discuss this further? I am no match for your wit. If you pardon me, I will leave the room, and the guard will search you."

Several minutes later, the Colonel re-entered.

"I am glad this is done. It is our way, and I do apologize."

"Colonel Viet," Dr. Burkov said. "You understand the reason for our visit. We work 16 hours each day. Every day we tend to the sick and the injured. I do not mean to insult you, but your physicians are inferior. We need Nguyen Lu at the hospital. I worked with her in Quang Tri. She is a competent nurse and will save many lives. She cannot help your people by being locked up in this prison. Release her to us."

"Dr. Burkov, I realize her value. We are not as cold-hearted as you think. Although I am tempted to release her, I am fearful to do so because I do not trust you. You have come to Hanoi very mysteriously. The state calls you suspicious characters. Two high ranking officers were killed in Quan Tri Province the day you left. You were there. There have been unusual messages about a 'Pretty Girl' looking for a 'Cowboy's Girl!' Our intelligence believes there is a plot to kill one of our leaders, and we think Pretty Girl is the one who is charged to do this."

"Dr. Hawkins – are you Pretty Girl?"

"Colonel Viet, I am a medical doctor on a humanitarian mission. I've given your country service that your medical personnel are incapable of," Ofa angrily asserted.

"Doctor, maybe you are as you say you are and I hope that is so. If I am wrong, and you are not this Pretty Girl, you will never understand how sorry I am to ask that question. But we are a suspicious people."

"Dr. Hawkins," – the Colonel hesitated; he was about to make an uncomfortable request.

"May I have your white cloak, please?"

"Colonel, I have already been searched."

"Doctor – please."

Ofa met Colonel Viet's gaze with indignation. He was on to her.

"Dr. Hawkins, please forgive my impertinence. I am trying to protect the state. We have laws."

"Colonel Viet, when a government is most corrupt, its laws are more numerous. That will be the demise of the New Vietnam," she responded angrily.

Ofa had shown her cards, and her anger exposed the secrets she carried.

The Colonel took the jacket, excused himself, and left the room. Ofa turned toward Bepa. Ofa was shaken but decided not to fall apart; there'd be no more tears. Dr. Burkov reached underneath her dress for her pistol.

"Ofa," she calmly said. "If things go bad we take him hostage. Trust my instincts. He's a climber and will not want to lose his life over a prisoner, even if that prisoner is Nguyen Lu. Darling, I will not let anything happen to you."

Moments later, the Colonel returned with a sealed envelope, and the white cloak torn at the seam.

"Dr. Hawkins, I will give you one chance to tell me what is in this envelope and then you will tell me why you are here."

Bepa fingered the pistol strapped to her thigh. The Colonel thought it strange that both women had remained calm.

Ofa looked toward the Colonel; there was fire in her eyes. "Colonel just open the fuckin' envelope; I'll explain. And then you will give me what I want, or you will be killed."

As he opened the letter, the Colonel stared at the doctors. He reached into the envelope and pulled out a picture of Sergeant Elijah Bravo. He stared at the picture then shook his head. Bepa cocked the pistol. The Colonel didn't speak. There were tears in his eyes.

"No – this can't be Sergeant Bravo!" Colonel Viet said.

"Speak Dr. Hawkins! You better have a good story. Goddam you! Speak!"

"Colonel, how do you know this man?"

Colonel Viet responded, "Tell me, why do you have this man's picture? Talk to me. Now!"

"His name is Elijah Bravo. We grew up together in Texas. His best friend is Seamus O'Grady. They joined the Marines in 1965; I went to college and then medical school. The last time I saw them was June 18, of that year. About 18 months ago I received a call from Sergeant Bravo; he was on a ship patrollin' your coast. He told me that in 1967, he was wounded durin' the battle of Hill-861 and taken to the hospital ship, Sanctuary. He fell in love with Nguyen Lu, a nurse on the ship. They were to marry in Da Nang, but the Marines left Vietnam the day before their weddin'. Sergeant Bravo called to ask if I knew anyone in the Red Cross who might be able to get her out of the South. I volunteered for Dooley Intermed International and came with the sole purpose of findin' this woman and get her out. I must do this."

Colonel, you must release her to me. For God sakes, do it for love! We've killed each other for many years. The love between a Vietnamese and an American can be the first step toward healin' the hatred existing between us. Colonel, I will not go home without her. We accept our death and if it comes to that, then so be it. But you too will die."

The Colonel said nothing but stared at the picture – and a tear fell.

"Colonel, it's your turn to talk."

He cleared his throat. "This man, Sergeant Bravo saved my life on Hill-861. I was wounded, and I was his prisoner. We were hiding in a bunker. He was waiting for Sergeant O'Grady to find him. Your Elijah was a great hero; he saved his friend and the Marines. That evening we spoke; he cared for my wounds. In the morning when the Marines returned, he hid me, and then he let me go."

He looked at Ofa as though what he had expressed was a story she wouldn't believe. He rang for the guards.

"Guards, I will not need you. Dr. Burkov, please come with me."

The Colonel, along with Bepa Burkov, left the office for the infirmary. Nguyen saw Bepa, and she ran into the arms of her friend.

"Dear, no time for words. I've come for you," the doctor said.

"Nurse Lu, come with me. Do you have any important belongings?" Colonel Viet asked.

"Yes, Colonel. Should I get them?"

"Do it quickly," he said.

Nguyen was an obedient servant. In her quarters, she pulled a board from the floor and retrieved a picture of both she and Elijah. She grabbed an envelope containing pictures of her mother, father, and the sister she never knew. She then pulled a wrapped package from the floor's interior. It was a white wedding dress. The Colonel smiled.

"Nurse Lu, where did you find a white wedding dress in Vietnam?" the Colonel asked."

"My Colonel I will wear it to marry my man," Nguyen said.

"Is that all you have little sister?" the Colonel Asked. She nodded and immediately followed the Colonel.

"Little Sister, from this point I do not want you to ask any questions, do not speak. Do what you are told; do you understand?"

"Yes, Colonel Viet."

The Colonel opened the door to his office; he, Dr. Burkov, and Nguyen entered.

"Dr. Hawkins, you are getting what you want; it is what we both want. Do not say another word to me. Although I can understand your insolent and threatening behavior, I do not appreciate it."

Nguyen continued to cry. Her emotions had not died. Bepa wiped her tears. "It's okay darling," she said.

"Nurse Lu, you will go with Dr. Hawkins and Burkov. I will accompany you," Colonel Viet said.

Nguyen bowed and said, "Dr. Hawkins, it is a pleasure to know you." Ofa thought she was more beautiful than Bepa described.

"Doctors, I will walk in front of you. Please, one more thing Dr. Burkov. Do not think I did not see the pistol. Maybe if your dress weren't short, I wouldn't have been looking. You KGB agents could learn from a Vietnamese soldier."

"Colonel," Ofa said. I need to beg one more favor from you. Please send this message."

The Colonel scowled at the insolent women.

USS Midway – 9th Marines – Got Cowboy's Girl – Jonesy, put coffee on the burner – Coming home – Pretty Girl sends.

"Dr. Burkov, would you really have killed me?" Colonel Viet asked.

Bepa smiled and walked into the prison courtyard and met the sunlight.

FIFTY-EIGHT

TO THE BROKLYN BRIDGE

What did the man say when he fell off the horse? I was going to get off anyhow.

Joe Alexander

24 May 1975 – USS Midway, Gulf of Tonkin

"**J**erry!"

"Sir!"

"Scramble four Intruders and two 46's. I want all vectors out of Hai Phong covered. Aircraft are authorized to engage any suspicious boats interfering with outbound vessels. I'll be on the bridge monitoring comm."

"Captain, you're aware Congress placed us under orders to avoid all confrontations. U.S. Forces will not conduct hostilities throughout Southeast Asia."

"Yeah Jerry, Congress isn't here, and I don't give a damn. Whoever interferes with the Doctor, our assets have my permission to kill 'em. If Dr. Hawkins is out there, we're going to get her. Saving the Doctor will be the Midway's greatest mission."

Re-Education Center, Hanoi

Nguyen walked into exploding sunlight that impaled the prison courtyard. The rays penetrated her body and found their way deep into her core. She stared at the blue sky and saw shapes of billowy clouds. The warm light gave assurance that life was indeed beautiful and maybe what's meant to be would find a way.

She approached the black sedan.

"Ky Chien, my dearest friend, you have come for me. I am

blessed," she whispered. Her old friend smiled and nodded.

"I would always come for you," he asserted. The loyal Lieutenant opened the car door, grasped her hand, and gave her the reassurance she needed.

Dr. Burkov entered the North Vietnamese staff car and sat in the front seat with Colonel Viet.

Ofa and Nguyen entered the rear seat in the second car driven by Lieutenant Ky.

The drive to the restaurant in Hanoi was 20 kilometers and from there an additional 100 to Hai Phong. Riding in Politburo staff cars ensured their journey would be expedient and unencumbered by nosey officials. Nguyen sat silently next to Ofa. She bowed her head and placed her hands reverently on her lap.

"Dr. Hawkins, I must ask you a question, I know the Colonel asked me not to say a word, but please, may I speak?"

In a soft Texan drawl, Ofa responded. "My darlin' girl – y'all may speak. Y'all may speak anytime you like. You're no longer in prison."

Nguyen stared at Dr. Hawkins, and her eyes were wide. She struggled to find the right words for the question that plagued her.

"Dr. Hawkins, are you Ofa from Luckenbach?"

Ofa smiled, leaned toward the beautiful Vietnamese girl and kissed her on the forehead.

"Why yes darlin' – I am – I'm fixin' to take you home."

Colonel Viet and Lieutenant Ky pulled in front of the restaurant. The passengers were silent as they entered the café. They spotted Dr. Lam having lunch. Dr. Burkov sensed danger and orders Lieutenant Ky to escort the women through the rear door. From the corner of her eye, she sees three anxious men. One reaches into a bag for an automatic weapon. Dr. Burkov steps in front of Ofa, pulls her pistol, and puts two rounds between the man's eyes. The others raise their hands and beg the woman in the white doctor's cloak for mercy. One was Captain Quan, the man who had insulted Dr. Hawkins at the prison.

"Dr. Burkov – it's Captain Quan – please, don't shoot me."

Ofa turned to Dr. Burkov. "Bepa, God created such moments so we can understand his mercy."

Pleading for his life, Quan raised his hands above his head. Bepa remembered his insults, yet signaled she'd spare his life thus acknowledging Ofa's sentiment.

"Captain Quan – revenge is a motherfucker."

Dr. Bepa Burkov shot him in the head and turned toward the third man and shot him as well. Burkov scanned each corner of the restaurant. No one moved.

Dr. Lam pulled a pistol and shouted, "Dr. Burkov, leave, I will cover your withdrawal. I'll take the extra car."

Bepa gave a casual nod. "Let's go," she commanded. The cars sped from Hanoi and headed toward the Red Lotus waiting in Hai Phong harbor.

"Are you sure you are a doctor?" Colonel Viet asked "Bepa Burkov, you are very sexy when you are violent. I have a notion to run away with you."

"My dear Colonel, that was not violence. If you want violence, you should see what I would have done to you if you did not give us Nguyen Lu. And Colonel, I have a man in Nebraska. But I can't believe you do not have a woman. You are a remarkable man, very charming and confident. And, may I add, you are very handsome."

"You are a most provocative woman. It's all clear to me. Pretty Girl looking for Cowboy's Girl." But intelligence is not intelligence when you learn the plot after it happens. My dear doctor, I pray we survive this. But if we die we, at least, died for what Dr. Hawkins said – love."

"Colonel, come with us. Let's try our luck on the open seas and hope for a better life in America. Come with us," Bepa asked.

"Dr. Burkov, your invitation is tempting; I would love to see Sergeant Bravo again, but I love my country. If I can pull this off, I will have a great position in the New Vietnam. I love power more than freedom. But doctor, you are doing this for what?"

"For Nguyen," she said. It's why I'm risking my life. I too want to be with my man. I will risk everything for that chance."

"Dr. Burkov, I am doing this for the Marine Sergeant who saved my life. I told him I would kill him if I had the chance. But when we parted, I said, I would be his slave forever. Sergeant Bravo gave me my life, and now I serve the state in glory."

Bepa laughed. "Always loyal to the state. That's exactly our problem, Colonel. The state tells us how to choose our allegiances. The state takes our body, mind, and soul. We are not human, but become automatons of an evil that we perpetuate."

What did Sergeant Bravo say when you said, you would kill him?" she asked.

"I remember, but I don't understand," the Colonel Answered.

He asked, 'what did the man say when he fell off the horse?' I have no idea what he was talking about. He then said, 'I was going to get off anyway.' It was probably some stupid American expression that probably has no meaning."

Bepa interjected, "Colonel Viet, you must know your enemy. You must not have read, *The Art of War*. I'll tell you what Sergeant Bravo meant: I can kick your ass from here to the Brooklyn Bridge."

Colonel Viet sped down the highway heading toward the Red Lotus waiting in the harbor at Hai Phong.

"If you did not have a man I would go to America with you. By the way, Dr. Burkov, what does the Brooklyn Bridge have to do with anything?"

FIFTY-NINE

GOT COWBOY'S GIRL

For the first time in my career, I know what's at stake. It has
nothing to do with ideology. It's for one woman and one man.
The mission is clear. We gotta help the Doctor.

Captain Butch Ragsdale

24 May 1975 – Gulf of Tonkin

"**B**ig Papa, this is Eagle One . . . Over . . ."
The A-6 Intruder dropped below the clouds, and the pilot
scanned the obscure blue sea looking for the doctor.

"Go ahead Eagle One . . ."

"Sir, there's nothing out here. I'm far from shore, got to get a
little closer . . ."

The Captain's philosophy was not to ask permission but to ask
forgiveness. That was a bold move for the Commanding Officer of
the largest aircraft carrier in the world. Ragsdale had a storied career,
and fortunately, the things he did without asking permission didn't
need forgiveness. However, in the Gulf of Tonkin, the stakes were
different. Pretty Girl had raised the ante, and to save her the Captain
would have to defy the mandates of Congress.

"Eagle One, I don't care if you buzz their beaches, we can't
protect Pretty Girl from a hundred miles offshore . . ."

Eagle One, piloted by Commander James Messerschmitt turned
the aircraft 45 degrees and headed into the airspace of the People's
Republic of Vietnam.

"Jerry, we have no idea if they even made it to Hai Phong.

They'll have to get beyond the swift boats patrolling the harbor. I want aircraft on station. If they're out there, we'll give them all the cover they need."

"Sir, as your Executive Officer, may I speak freely?"

"Yeah Jer, I'd like to think you've always felt you could speak freely. Even if I disagree with you, I expect you to speak your mind."

"Sir, you're risking your career on this Ofa Hawkins predicament. Is this even happening? Are we chasing a ghost? This not only goes against naval protocol but with our aircraft patrolling the coast — we're defying Congress. Captain, I don't get it. You have an agenda that neither of us can see. You're willing to create a major international incident for this Doctor."

"Jerry, we've sent men to their death, and for what? For nothing. We have to live with that. For the first time in my career, I know exactly what's at stake. It has nothing to do with ideology, revenge, or the war. But it's for one woman and one man. For the first time in my career, the mission is clear. We gotta help the Doctor. If I get relieved, you'll take the Midway, but right now I'm the skipper of this ship, the most powerful fighting force in the world, and we're going to do everything in our power to help the Doctor rescue Cowboy's Girl."

Hai Phong, North Vietnam

The cars sped through the streets of Hai Phong toward the harbor, turning a corner, and then another; they were almost there. Nguyen rested her head on Dr. Hawkins' shoulder. Her breathing was shallow; it was unusual for one whose life was dependent on a precarious fate.

"Ofa, I have no words to thank you for what you have done. I am humbled. But I am hopeful for us both."

"Darlin," you're my sister; I've known you a lifetime. No words are needed."

Ofa was a Texas girl who grew up in the shadow of the Alamo. She understood what crossing the line in the sand meant. She had done all she could to save Nguyen Lu. She was at peace; she could do no more. She gave her heart and soul to the peace movement, yet the war continued, and more men died. But at that moment, sitting in the car with Cowboy's Girl she found meaning in every disappointment she experienced.

Ofa stroked Nguyen's hair and said, "You are my dear friend's true love."

"Ofa, Elijah spoke of you often. He said Seamus loves you and he always did. Elijah told me his heart broke when you didn't acknowledge the rose he gave you. He stopped hoping. He was young and didn't understand that love takes time to bloom; just like a rose. Can you ever fall in love with him again?"

"Nguyen," Ofa whispered, "how can I fall back in love with Seamus when I never stopped lovin' him?"

"Can I ask you a personal question, Ofa?"

"You may ask me darlin', but I don't know if I will answer it."

"Why did your marriage end?" Nguyen asks Ofa.

"It's a long story, but Paul, the man I married, lied to me the night that Seamus left for the Marine Corp. He said that he was the one who left me the rose. When I learned the truth, I left him."

"Oh God," Nguyen said. "Seamus doesn't know that, does he?"

"No, he doesn't."

Four soldiers pursued the fugitives in a captured American jeep with a mounted 50-caliber machine-gun. The doctors had kidnapped a Colonel, freed an enemy of the state, and murdered three government agents. The North was convinced that the doctors also murdered Colonel Gee and General Minh. The pursuers raced down the highway and were closing in on Dr. Lam. Shots were fired. Dr. Lam pulled to the side of the road, made a U-turn, and faced his pursuers. As they converged, he gunned the engine and drove his car toward them colliding in a fiery explosion.

Colonel Viet pulled alongside the Red Lotus. A man with a beard emerged from the ship. Bepa was the first out of the car.

"Lieutenant Ky," Burkov said, "get Dr. Hawkins and Nguyen on that boat."

The engine of the Red Lotus sputtered as she idled and bopped like a cork, straining the lines holding her to the dilapidated pier. She didn't appear seaworthy, but regardless, she was a boat, and she would have to do.

Bepa shouted. "We're being followed. That explosion – Dr. Lam must have given his life for us."

It had been seven years since Colonel Viet had seen his CO. The Colonel faced the General and saluted and the two men embraced.

"General, I'm happy you are alive," the Colonel said.

"Ky, can't believe you'd think the rumor of my demise was true."

The bonds of war form a connection that only those who've

experienced battle can understand. It would be both a reunion and a farewell for the old soldiers who embraced in front of the Red Lotus.

"Ly, come with us. Leave this country. The New Vietnam will bring sorrow. The Doctor paints a beautiful picture of America. Maybe there's something about this freedom she speaks of. Ly, I need my officer; we can start a new life. After what you have done, they will execute you."

"My General, I would've come if that Russian woman did not have a man in Nebraska. But she has a plan. My life is here, General. I love my country. You of all people should know how we sacrificed for Vietnam. I want to build the New Vietnam. Maybe I can do some good and become an influence in the direction Vietnam will take. I have to believe in something."

General Minh nodded. "I hope you are right Ky; Dr. Burkov's plan had better be good."

"We shall see General. But how can I not believe such a bewitching woman?"

Nguyen reverently approached the Colonel; she knelt and bowed. Colonel Viet extended his hand and placed it on her head.

"My Colonel, I can only say thank you," she said.

"Little sister, thank you is the perfect prayer. You tell Sergeant Bravo I will see him in the North Star. He will understand. One more thing – tell him I understand about the man falling off the horse, and we shall see about that."

"Colonel," Hawkins interjected. "Sorry, but there's no other way to approach you. I've come a long way, and you were in the way."

"Dr. Hawkins, you appear as though you are a demure woman, but you are not what you appear. I mistook your passion for insolence. This is not goodbye Dr. Hawkins," he said.

Ofa took Nguyen's hand and followed the General on board.

"General Minh," Colonel Viet shouted. "You are the greatest officer I have served with." He stood at attention and saluted. The General smiled, returned the salute.

"Bepa screamed, "Get on the goddamn boat! I'll untie the lines."

After she undid the last line, Bepa turned toward the Colonel, pulled a 45-caliber pistol, and shot Colonel Viet. She jumped onto the ship, and the Red Lotus limped into the Gulf of Tonkin.

Bepa commanded, "General Minh, "Send a message."

SIXTY

THE LINE IN THE SAND

Do all the good you can, by all the means you can, in all the ways you can, in all the places you can, at all the times you can, to all the people you can, as long as ever you can.

John Wesley

24 May 1975 – USS Midway, Gulf of Tonkin

The sounds of a steady hammer erupted in the communications center on the USS Midway. Jonesy watched the message spew from the printer. As he reached to tear it from the spindle, he saw two the words he waited for – Pretty Girl.

"It's here!" Jonesy shouts. He ripped the message from the Teletype. "Lieutenant, call the Skipper. She's underway. Pretty Girl's coming! Let's fucking get her."

"Skipper, it's Pretty Girl. Dr. Hawkins got Nguyen. She's underway sir," Quackenbush said.

"Okay, read me the exact message," Ragsdale asked.

"Yes, Sir."

USS Midway – Jonesy – Got Cowboy's Girl. Running – Look for us – Pretty Girl sends.

"Quackenbush send a reply. Have Jonesy send it."

Jonesy sat behind the keys of the Teletype and pulled on a Chesterfield. The cigarette hung from the side of his mouth, and the smoke drifted into his eyes as he punched small divots into the tape.

Pretty Girl – Draw a line in the sand – never surrender – Give us a sign – Jonesy sends.

The Captain turned toward the XO and quietly ordered. "Jer, launch four more birds. Put two Sea-Sprites in the air; I want Marine assault teams on the choppers. Fixed wing is cleared to patrol the coast. Keep the choppers in international waters."

"Sir, what's the sign?"

"I have no idea. We're gonna have to get lucky. Aircraft are to buzz all swift boats."

"You sure? Skipper, I'm not going to remind you of the Congressional Order cause you're the Royal Admiral of the High Seas, and you're gonna do what you damn well please."

"Hey XO, that's what they called Columbus."

The word spread throughout the Midway that Dr. Hawkins was somewhere in the Gulf of Tonkin and that she had rescued Nguyen Lu. The crew began to line the deck and peered into the misty blue-green sea straining to see as far as they could in the direction of the New Vietnam.

The Captain turned to the navigation officer. "Lieutenant Commander Petit, maintain heading 365 degrees."

"Sir, that's heading straight for Hainan Island."

*   *   *

Ofa continued to cry on the bow of the Red Lotus, and Nguyen Lu collapsed in her arms. Witnessing Colonel Viet's death was more than they could bear. General Minh's face had turned white, and he stared out to sea.

Lieutenant Ky screamed, "Dr. Burkov, why did you shoot Colonel Viet?"

The Red Lotus cut through the ocean swells. The only sound other than the rumbling of the engine was the lament of the crying women.

Bepa's face was stern; her eyes were black as coal. She stood on the small bridge of the ship.

"Give me your attention," she commanded. "Everybody! What I did on the dock was a plan to vindicate Colonel Viet; it was staged. He has a flesh wound on his shoulder. The impact of a 45 caliber round knocked him down. He will be fine. I promise. I had the highest pistol score in my KGB class. He will say we abducted him and Nguyen at gunpoint. By now the Vietnamese have learned I have turned. The story will be that I shot the Colonel while he was trying to prevent us from leaving. I will send messages to KGB officials explaining how he fought to stop us. My contacts go to the heart of the political party. The Colonel will be a hero, and Vietnam loves its heroes."

The Vietnamese learned of the escape and scrambled cars to pursue the fugitives. After analyzing the message traffic between Pretty Girl and the Midway, they launched four swift boats to patrol the waters of Hai Phong. Nguyen Lu was guilty of high treason, and they would make an example of her. Two women using seduction and wit had bested North Vietnam, something the most powerful country in the world could not accomplish.

At sixteen knots the Red Lotus plunged into the Gulf. She took on as much water as she displaced. She was an old vessel, and the seawater seeped into her hold making everything wet and salty, but the pumps kept her afloat. Nguyen sat at the ship's bow. It was a clear day, and the eastern sky appeared promising.

The Red Lotus moved further and further from the oppressive world of the New Vietnam. The country that Nguyen Lu helped during the war did not desert her. Regardless, she couldn't smile. She had known only hardship and disappointment and believed a story rarely ended well. The boat moved further into the unknown, and Dr. Burkov scanned the heavens and the waters surrounding them.

"Captain, do you have any paint, any brushes, any large pieces of canvas," Bepa asked.

The Captain peered over the helm, his eyes barely cleared the wheel. "What a demanding woman," he whispered to General Minh. "Fucking Russians, their women do not know their place. But she is very handsome."

"Maybe below," the Captain called out.

"General Minh go below and check for supplies. We must identify ourselves as they requested," Burkov ordered.

The Captain looked at his former CO as if to apologize for her impertinence.

The General laughed, "Montana women are not as bitchy."

Instead of taking the Qiongzhou Strait, the quickest and likeliest route out of the Gulf of Tonkin, the Captain hugged the Coast of Hainan Island, following it south then around into the South China Sea. He hoped the Vietnamese patrol boats would assume they would take the shortest route straight into the South China Sea.

USS Midway, South China Sea

"Big Papa . . . this is Eagle One . . . Over . . ."

The CO clicked the receiver, "Go ahead Eagle One . . ."

"Sir, there's nothing out here. The lanes coming out of Hai Phong are empty. Just fishing boats. Two Swift Boats are patrolling . . ."

"They're there," the Captain, said. "Keep looking . . . Out."

Ragsdale turned toward the XO, and by the look on the Captain's face, the XO knew Ragsdale was about to do something outside of operational protocol.

"Someone, other than Dr. Hawkins is calling the shots," the Captain remarked. "Whoever it is, they know their shit. There're too many variables. Doesn't make sense. How did she get the girl out of prison? Jesus Christ, how did she get this far? Too many maybes."

"Captain Ragsdale, what if they head toward Hainan and follow the coast instead of taking the straight? It's longer, but maybe they think they'll fool the Vietnamese patrols. That's the last place the Vietnamese might expect them to try. Sir, you ain't thinking what I think you're thinking?"

"XO, get Eagle One on the hook."

"Sir, you're going to provoke an international incident with the Chinese, and get us both relieved."

"Jer, sign a paper saying you're carrying out my orders under protest. They'll relieve me; you'll be okay. I've got 30 years in – I'm ready to buy that cabin in New Hampshire."

"Captain, no-can-do sir. If you go down; I'm going with you," the XO answered.

"Yeah! We're both pretty stupid," the Captain commented.

"Eagle One this is Big Papa . . . Come in Eagle . . .Over . . ."

"This is Eagle . . . Go ahead Big Papa . . ."

"Eagle, extend your patrol to the territorial waters of China – Hainan Island. Circle it and patrol the Gulf. Keep the same rules of engagement. I think Dr. Hawkins is headed south around the island then straight to open waters . . ."

"Big Papa . . . Did I hear you correctly? You want us to patrol toward the tip of China?"

"You got it . . . Out."

"Jer – why do I have to repeat every order?"

"Sir, you're kidding me. With all due respect, maybe because the orders are illegal."

The A-6 Intruders broke off their heading and turned 180 degrees south into Chinese waters off Hainan Island.

Red Lotus, Gulf of Tonkin

"Dr. Burkov, we've found paint," Lieutenant Ky said.

"General, paint 'Pretty Girl' in the largest letters possible."

"Where?" the General asked.

"On the goddamn canvass! Where do you think?"

"Dr. Burkov I am a Field General in the Vietnamese Army, and I never thought I'd take orders from a woman."

"My General, with all due respect," Bepa said. "If we are lucky, we'll be going to America. In America, women control everything. I'm getting you used to it."

Hai Phong Harbor

When the Vietnamese jeep reached the pier, Colonel Viet was laying on the ground feigning unconsciousness. His arm was bloody, and he had smeared as much on his face.

"Colonel, are you okay?" the North Vietnamese officer asked.

"I tried to stop them," The Colonel said; I did my best, but they beat me and shot me."

"We are sorry we came late. The guards saw you walking from the camp with Dr. Burkov. She is a KGB agent who has turned against us. We have been tracking both her and Dr. Hawkins who is responsible for sending the messages about Cowboy's Girl. They killed Colonel Gee. We are certain of this. She is trying to get Nguyen Lu out of Vietnam and has the help of General Minh. He was not killed. We must get them, or this will be a terrible embarrassment. Colonel Gee discovered the doctors are spies and were trying to get to Lu. And General Minh was sleeping with Dr. Hawkins. Our boats are in pursuit. We will get them. Colonel, do you have any idea of the direction they are taking?"

"They must be taking the quickest way out of the Gulf. Due east, through the straight."

"Colonel, that is the obvious thought. We think they are heading south and following the coast of Hainan Island and into the sea. I'm

315

GIRL WITH THE PURPLE RIBBON

sure of it. We are following the thought process of the Russian. She is very clever. I am sending our patrol boats to the south. We will get them; if they resist, kill them."

"Traitors," Colonel Viet said.

"Colonel, you were very brave trying to stop them; they almost killed you. I will recommend a citation for your bravery."

The Colonel smiled and nodded. He thought of the beautiful Russian woman. There was nothing more he could do for Sergeant Bravo, the man who saved his life on Hill 861. It would be very difficult for them to escape but he remembered the words of his Marine friend, 'what's meant to be would find a way.'

SIXTY-ONE

CLARERE! AUDERE! GAUDERE!

The wind is rising – We must try to live!

Paul Valéry, *The Graveyard by the Sea*

24 May 1975 – Gulf of Tonkin

The Red Lotus traveled south toward Hainan Island and into the territorial waters of China. She had to enter the heart of darkness to leave it. Although they had seen no sign of swift boats, Bepa Burkov refused to rest. During the night, she remained vigilant yet continued to check on the welfare of the women.

USS Midway, South China Sea

"Eagle One . . . this is Big Papa . . . Over . . ."

"Go ahead Big Papa . . ."

"What's your fuel status?" Captain Ragsdale asked.

"Sir, enough to get home . . ."

"Eagle, return to mama. It's getting dark. We'll keep an aircraft on station in case the Red Lotus surfaces. I'll scramble Striker Squadron and two choppers at 0500 hours . . ."

"Roger that Sir . . . Out."

Red Lotus

"General Minh, it's dark; we'll be okay till dawn," Bepa said. "Keep a heading of 108 degrees; that should get us close to Hainan Island. We'll hug the coast and blend in with the fishing boats. I

Don't think the swift boats will follow. They'll take the obvious route and head through the straight. It's common sense."

"Dr. Burkov," General Minh said, "The only problem with common sense is that it is too common. They're not heading toward the straight. I am sure of it. They are following us. You Russians are narrow in your thinking. You lack imagination, and you believe this defines the practical man. But being clever is an Asian trait. You are powerful, so you make the obvious choice. Whatever you think is true, must be true. But we Vietnamese do not think the obvious; we think of possibilities and assume that because you think the obvious is to head for the straight, then, that is where the Vietnamese will go. But they won't."

Bepa nodded and contemplated the General's warning.

"I'm afraid you are right, General," she said.

"Dr. Burkov is it possible you made a mistake?"

The General's assertion did not amuse Dr. Bepa Burkov.

"I have a plan," she said. "Let's send a distress message to the Midway. Tell them our engine has died, and we're taking on water."

"But we are taking on water. Going full throttle with these choppy seas have taken its toll on the Red Lotus," the General said.

"General, hear me out. The enemy will be monitoring the net," Dr. Burkov asserted. If they think we're in trouble, they'll slow their pursuit and search for a disabled boat. We can buy some time."

"But we need to inform the Midway that this is a smoke screen?" the General asserted.

Bepa went to the hold of the ship and woke Dr. Hawkins. "Dear, I need you topside." Ofa fixed the blanket over Nguyen and followed Bepa.

Dr. Burkov explained their predicament.

"I got it," Ofa said. "Let's send this."

USS Midway – Jonesy- engine dead – taking on water – sinking – have my fingers crossed. Clarere! Audere! Gaudere!" Pretty Girl sends.

"I don't get it," Bepa replied.

"In American Folklore, when you make a statement, and your fingers are crossed, then sure 'nough whatever y'all said means the opposite," Ofa asserted.

Bepa appeared confused.

"Ofa, no wonder we were first in space. You Americas are very confusing. What makes you think they'll get it?"

"That Jonesy, he's been getting our messages. He's sharp. *Clarere, Audere, Gaudere – be bright – daring – and joyful.* He'll get it," Ofa said. "My dearest friends, those three words tell of our journey. We'll never forget and whatever happens; let's remember how we came together and how we sacrificed."

Dr. Burkov, the General, and the ship's Captain continued to study the charts trying to determine the best route around Hainan Island. They realized they couldn't outrun the swift boats; subsequently, their best chance was to hide among the junks fishing the waters off the island. Once they entered the open seas, they would make a run but would be the prey of the North Vietnamese swift boats.

"General, we should prepare based on your estimate of the situation, Burkov said."

"Dr. Burkov, what would we do without you? You are not only a beautiful KGB agent; you are superbly trained. Is there anything you cannot do?"

Appearing to be deep in thought, Bepa asserted, "Why no General, I don't believe there is."

USS Midway, Communications Center

"Captain Ragsdale, you need to come and see this. Got another message from Pretty Girl," Jonesy said.

The Skipper, Captain Pollard, Commanders Petit, and Naremore, and JG Quackenbush studied the message.

"By the time stamp, the message was sent within the last 15 minutes," the Captain said. "Gentlemen, I'm afraid this is a game changer. Her boat is inoperable. I want choppers launched immediately. They'll need fixed wing support."

"Skipper that's a big footprint," Commander Pollard said.

"Jer, we're too committed; we have no choice but to escalate."

"Captain, with choppers and fixed wing on station we're running the risk of a confrontation. But if you want to start a world war, I'll draft an operations order."

"I don't know what else to do, Jerry. There's no time for an operations order. Just get birds in the air and have them fly toward Hainan and maybe we'll get lucky."

Jonesy interrupted. "Captain – something's bothering me about that message. Sir, may I?"

"Go," Captain Ragsdale replied.

"Sir, it's a diversion. Meant to buy some time. She's trying to send a false message to the Vietnamese."

"What makes you think that Jonesy?"

"Look how she ends the message. She's saying, I have my fingers crossed. When we were kids, we could say something isn't true as long as we had our fingers crossed. That's what she's telling us. She's saying that her message isn't true and she's crossed her fingers. Sir, I know the Doctor, she didn't get this far without being clever."

The Captain glared at the message.

"Jonesy, I think you're right. Okay, if we're lucky, we'll find her near Hainan Island."

"Captain, look how she ends the message, Clarere, Audere, Gaudere. It's Latin – be bright – be daring – be joyful. She wouldn't be saying that if she were in trouble. Sir – it's who she is – it's clear – those three words – that's Dr. Hawkins."

26 May – USS Midway: 0330 Hours

"Sergeant O'Grady," Major McGivens said, "Captain Ragsdale wants a boarding party in case the Red Lotus needs some muscle. Seamus, you're not going, neither is Elijah."

"Sir request permission."

"Seamus, I know what you are going to ask."

"Sir, I want in."

"No, you're too emotional. That's final. Get me a reinforced Squad."

"Sir, everyone is emotional." The Major refused to negotiate. "Very well sir," Seamus added.

"Elijah," Seamus said, "Give the job to Joe Buck and have him take Maddog. There's nobody I trust more than John Wayne. Maddog – he's our good luck charm."

*　　*　　*

James Messerschmitt, the Commanding Officer of Striker Squadron, badgered the skipper to allow his aircraft a role in bringing Ofa Hawkins out of Vietnam.

At 0455 hours, the night was unforgivingly black. The few stars that dotted the sky would soon move to the other side of the world. Messerschmitt strapped into the cockpit and waited for the pageantry of the launch. In the adjacent seat, Matt Durney, the *B/N* (bombardier-navigator) checked the controls, one last time. Men wearing the purple shirts pulled fuel lines and gave the A-6 enough gas to complete a mission that each man on the Midway anticipated. To rescue the Doctor! The red shirts loaded maverick missiles, 500 hundred pound bombs, and 20mm ammunition into the gun pods. Commander Messerschmitt then gave him the signal to break down the chains. Once the chains were clear, a yellow shirt removed the chocks and with slight head turns he signaled Messerschmitt to taxi forward toward the catapult (cat). Messerschmitt aligned the aircraft. Men wearing green shirts checked the mechanics of the cat and using hand movements the aircraft moved forward, and a green shirt assured the cat's connection to the front wheel. A yellow shirt ordered the green shirt to take up the tension. Messerschmitt verified the hook-up. With the cat attached to the front wheel, a yellow shirt then tuned control of the aircraft to the shooter. The shooter raised his arm and began waving his hand for the pilot to increase power to 100 percent. Commander Messerschmitt saluted the shooter giving his okay and requesting permission to leave the Midway. The shooter continued to signal power-up, which would send Messerschmitt hurling over the bow of the Midway. If something went wrong, he would have a second to decide either to power-up or eject. The shooter pointed throughout the area of the launch making sure every component of the ballet was secure and ready. He returned the salute and knelt on the tarmac. Commander Messerschmitt studied his movements; both were ready. The shooter then touched the deck and a green shirt put steam into the cat. Then the shooter pointed to the vast emptiness of sea. The engine screamed, and the Intruder instantly accelerated. With flaps down, Commander Messerschmitt disappeared into a dark morning.

"Striker One . . . Striker One . . . this is Big Papa . . . how do you read me . . .? Over . . ."

"Big Papa . . . Striker One . . . I read you five-by . . ."

"Striker, you have your orders; go get the Doctor . . .Out."

Commander Messerschmitt lifted into the black morning. Ragsdale, Pollard, Petit, and Naremore watched the red flames from the engines and then the aircraft disappeared.

The sun promised it would rise and when it did, the men of the Midway would line the side of the ship facing the Vietnam Coast. They anticipated the same miracle as the dawn.

The elevator aft carrying a rescue helicopter slowly moved toward the main deck where a reinforced Squad of Marines waited to board.

"Godspeed Joe," Seamus said. "Wish I was going with you."

"You sit this one out Seamus; don't you worry, if she's out there, we'll get her."

Elijah stood off to the side and touched each man as they boarded. He'd been trained by the Shamans of the Comanche nation, and his touch would give them power. He wanted to say something, but he couldn't, yet Joe Buck understood. As Sergeant Buck boarded, Elijah touched him, and neither smiled, and their eyes met, and Elijah knew that Buck would die for the Doctor and Cowboy's girl.

Red Lotus, South China Sea

At 0500 the Red Lotus turned east, left the safety of the Hainan coast, and headed into the open waters of the South China Sea.

"Captain, please — the engine, full throttle. We have a good sea, and we should be out of Chinese waters shortly," Bepa said.

"Dr. Burkov, there are no good seas. My people, they will follow us to California. Dr. Burkov would you get some rest; you have been up all night. We need a clear head," General Minh replied.

"General, I have a clear head. Please assemble everyone on deck. I no longer feel comfortable making all the decisions; I need to know what we're going to do if we're overtaken. Lieutenant Ky, would you please wake Dr. Hawkins and Nguyen."

Bepa stood at the stern of the ship. She appeared somber and unusually hesitant. Since she and Ofa had entered the prison camp, Dr. Burkov had been their rock. Now, it was different. She was afraid for the women; their fate would be worse than death.

"I was going to say, comrades," Dr. Burkov said, "but since we're going to America, I have to watch myself. We'll have to make many changes. My friends, I don't know whether the Vietnamese swift boats will find us, but they're searching. The General is sure of this, and if he says this is so, we must listen. If they find us, they'll board us. We can either fight or surrender. I do not mean to scare you, but the risks to the women are severe. They will punish us and not treat us with dignity, which means they will rape us. General Minh will be executed immediately for shooting Colonel Gee. They will shoot the Captain and Lieutenant Ky. I need to know how you will choose to die."

Nguyen was the first to speak. "I will fight them; I will fight them even after they have killed me."

Dr. Hawkins spoke next, "Bepa, I've already crossed that line."

There wasn't much left to say. But Bepa, being Russian did not linger on Ofa's sentiment.

Looking for reassurance, Bepa turned toward General Minh.

"Dr. Burkov, I am the ranking officer among the men, and they are soldiers; they will fight with me. And, Dr. Burkov, everyone on this ship knows what you will do."

Bepa smiled and said, "I will protect Dr. Hawkins and Nguyen. What do the Americans say? I'm going to kick ass and take names."

"Okay, that's it." General Minh said. "Dr. Burkov, Lieutenant Ky and I will hide in the fish netting. We will each have an *RPG* (Rocket Propelled Grenade Launcher). We will engage on my signal. When they come at us, they will try to surround us. They will want to take us alive so they can enjoy the process of killing us. Their boats will be on either side of us. That's our best chance to destroy them. Ofa, after we fire, you will bring additional launchers to me, and ammunition to the Captain manning the 50-caliber. Nguyen, you will be down in the hold of the ship."

"General, with all respect, I cannot do that, I can fight too. You have risked your life for me; I choose to fight with you."

"Very well Nguyen," the General said, you will assist the Captain with the automatic weapon. God bless us all."

Bepa said with a surprised look, "General – God Bless us? That sounds funny coming from a communist."

"The General answered, "My dear Doctor, we are no longer communists, we are Americans."

Bepa Burkov, Ghin Ky, the old Captain and Nguyen Lu stared at each other, and they smiled. It was the first time they thought themselves American.

The swift boats were moving at full throttle pushing the engines to 35 knots. They had been traveling south on a hunch that the unobvious was too obvious.

Striker Squadron, South China Sea

Striker Squadron pushed into Chinese airspace then banked south toward the open waters of the South China Sea. They flew at 1,000 feet, high enough to view vast stretches of water. When they sighted a vessel, Striker Squadron would swoop from the sky for a closer look.

"Big Papa . . . This is Striker One . . . come in . . . Over . . ."

"Big Papa here . . . go head Striker . . ."

"Big Papa, Got some blimps on the radar. I think the Chinese are scrambling. Waiting for orders . . ."

"Striker, you will not engage unless it's to protect the Red Lotus. Let them chase you; you'll outrun em. When they disengage, return to the A.O . . ."

"Roger that Sir . . ."

"Captain, there are 100's of fishing junks; they all look the same. Whoever's calling the shots on the Red Lotus, is smart enough to hide among the traffic. But I think they've turned the corner on the island and are heading to the South China Sea. That's where things will get rough. The NVA will know who she is. Sir, we're leaving the Gulf. We'll look for her in open waters..."

"Jimmy, it's a crapshoot," Captain Ragsdale said. "She's out there; we're her only chance. I can't call it Jimmy. Just follow your gut . . ."

"Yes Sir," Commander Messerschmitt responded . . . Out."

Red Lotus, South China Sea

"Dr. Burkov, there are two dots on the horizon, and they are closing. At that speed, I believe they're swift boats. Prepare the weapons," General Minh ordered.

"Yes, my General, I am ready to fight. In the battle, I will defer to your leadership."

"Very well," the General nodded.

Bepa jumped into the hold of the boat. "Ofa, Nguyen, my darlings – the time has come. There are boats approaching fast. They should be on us in 15 minutes. Let us go meet them and send them to hell."

North Vietnamese Swift Boat

"Fire!" the swift boat commander ordered.

It was a warning telling the Red Lotus she was doomed.

The North Vietnamese Commander said, "The enemy ship is slowing down. They will surrender. Prepare to board."

"Yes, Captain.

Red Lotus

General Minh peered over the railing. "They have slowed, he said, "keep moving but cut your speed. It is good that one of the boats is far ahead. Captain – as soon as we fire, full throttle. I'll nail that fucker."

"General, you are beginning to sound American," Dr. Burkov said.

The swift boat cautiously approached.

The North Vietnamese Captain commanded, "Go to the stern of your boat; place your hands over your head." Ofa, Nguyen, and the Captain proceeded to the rear of the Red Lotus. The swift boat pulled alongside.

"Dr. Burkov, now!" the General ordered.

The General and Bepa Burkov emerged and fired two RPG rounds into the boat; one of the rounds hit the gasoline tank of the ship sending flames and smoke billowing into the sky. The Captain and Nguyen ran to the gun and riddled the ship with machine gunfire. Ofa Hawkins carried two additional RPGs to the General. The Captain hit full throttle, and the Red Lotus raced into the empty sea.

"One down, one to go" Bepa said. "The second boat will take us on with cannon."

1,000 Feet Over the South China Sea

"Big Papa, this is Striker One . . . Over . . ."

"Go ahead, Striker. . ."

"Sir gaining altitude. There's smoke and what appears to be fire on the horizon. Need to take a better look. I pray that's not Pretty Girl . . ."

"Striker, after all we've been through, it's not going to end like this. I have faith; we're gonna get her. Take a look . . . Out."

Heading for the speck of smoke in the distance, Commander Messerschmitt powered-up.

Red Lotus

"My General, listen." Bepa scanned the skies "That's aircraft; they're either Chinese or American."

Striker Squadron

"Big Papa . . . this is Striker One . . . Over . . ."

"Go ahead, Striker . . ."

"I got the Red Lotus. I see one swift boat closing and firing. I'm going down for a closer look. Sir, I have the green light . . ."

"Affirmative Striker . . ."

The Captain picked up the phone and called the Comm Center, "Jonesy – we got Pretty Girl!"

Jonesy screamed, "We got her! We got Pretty Girl!"

The comm center erupted. Men were hugging, some were dancing on the tables, and JG Quackenbush broke out his stash of Kentucky Bourbon. The Midway had not seen such joy.

The Captain keyed the ship's intercom. "Attention on deck: Just received confirmation that Striker Squadron has secured Pretty Girl. We got her. They're about 70 miles out; we'll pick 'em up in three hours."

The ship erupted.

The A6 dropped from the sky and flew over the Red Lotus.

"Striker One . . . this is Striker Two . . . Over . . ."

"Go ahead Two . . ."

"You get that name on the canvass?"

"No sir, chopper coming in for a visual."

Captain Burns brought the Seasprite over the Red Lotus. The blowback of the rooters stretched the canvass tied to the outrigger, and its tip fluttered in the wind exposing a name painted in red on the old canvass: Pretty Girl. The Marines on board prepared to repel onto the boat

"Sergeant Buck," Captain Burns called, "have your men stand down. Striker Squadron has secured the AO. Looks like John Wayne ain't going to be the hero today."

"Sir, coming for a look-see. I wanna see this, Buck asserted."

"Captain Burns you patched into the Midway? Buck asked.

"Affirmative! Need to make a positive confirmation — make sure they're okay. Have one of your Marines repel down."

"Big Papa... this is Rescue-One Over..."

"Go ahead Rescue-One...

"It's Pretty Girl. Big red letters on canvass. We got our girl. There's six people aboard five are waving, and one is just staring at us. Three women, one is Vietnamese, one tall striking woman with weapons slung over her back, and one blond woman and Sir — there's a purple ribbon in her hair. That's Pretty Girl. I saw her! Son of a bitch Captain! Pretty Girl's real."

Striker Squadron flew over the Red Lotus pushing 560 knots heading for the swift boat. Commander Messerschmitt took the lead, pulled up, did a barrel roll, looped around and came in for another pass."

"Striker Two, give them a warning shot across the bow," Messerschmitt ordered. "There's been enough killing; if they continue to pursue, blow them the fuck out of the water . . . Out."

Striker Two dropped to 50 feet above the water and buzzed the Vietnamese boat firing across the bow. The A-6 then climbed, did a barrel roll, and exploded out of the sun coming in for the kill.

"Big Papa . . . This is Striker One . . . They're running . . ."

"Striker Two and Three you are to escort the swift boat toward Vietnamese waters. Striker One and Four, bring Pretty Girl home." Captain Ragsdale commanded.

"Aye-aye Sir . . . Out."

Bepa, Ofa, and Nguyen embraced.

"My darlings, we're going to make it, Bepa said. "Ofa, you were right. What's meant to be will find a way."

USS Midway

"Jer, we've some explaining to do, but we got our girl, didn't go to war with China, and didn't kill the swift boat. We came out of this pretty good," Captain Ragsdale said. "Captain Pollard, I want every man who's not piloting this boat on deck. I want this to be something to remember. I want the deck lined with sailors in their Class A uniforms. I want everything. Get the band. Damn, Jerry! We won the last battle of the Vietnam War."

Red Lotus

"General Minh our escorts are gone. We're close to a ship. What will you do in America?" Lieutenant Ky asked.

"Lieutenant, I will be a movie star. I want to play the evil oriental in James Bond movies. How about you Lieutenant Ky?"

"I will study to be a doctor. Dr. Hawkins will sponsor me."

Ofa leaned on the railing of the boat's bow. Arm and arm, Ofa Hawkins, Bepa Burkov, and Nguyen Lu embraced.

"That's her. That's our ship, Bepa said. "Ofa, what are you going to do about that boy Seamus?"

"I don't know. It's been ten years, a lifetime ago; it's frightening. What's more frightening than an ending, is a beginning.

"But aren't they the same?" Nguyen replied. "Ofa, there won't be many people you'll love in this life."

Ofa Hawkins closed her eyes and remembered herself a girl fishing the South Grape Creek.

"Ofa, you can't go back, what matters is today," Nguyen remarked. "When love is gone, only then you'll know what a gift it was. Go back and fight to keep it."

Ofa opened her eyes, and the women stared into the wine-dark sea. The Red Lotus taking on more water than she displaced floated at 12 knots.

TO BE CONTINUED

Book Reviews

"Anyone who reads Joe Puglia's *Girl with the Purple Ribbon* will never regret it. This compelling novel presents an incredibly poignant and relevant story of the love, adventure, and courage of three lifelong friends struggling with the inevitable consequences of war during the turbulent decade of 1965 to 1975. Puglia — a Marine Corps officer during the Vietnam War, who describes himself as "a cross between Genghis Khan and Saint Francis" — artfully paints a canvas that stretches from the rolling countryside of the Texas Hill Country to the battle-scarred hills of Vietnam. The result is a nuanced tour de force — that in Puglia's own words — 'is a novel not meant to change life but instead — add to life.' It does just that in spades."

Michael Wallis, Bestselling author: *Route 66: The Mother Road, Billy the Kid: The Endless Ride, The Best Land Under Heaven: The Donner Party in the Age of Manifest Destiny.* **Three time Pulitzer Nominee.**

"Sweeping in scope and totally engrossing, *Girl with the Purple Ribbon* is a moving testimonial of the American experience from the Vietnam War. Simultaneously haunting and heartbreaking, Dr. Puglia's novel combines the author's experience as a Marine Lieutenant with an in-depth analysis of what war does to men and women who wage war and who are touched by the experience. *Girl with the Purple Ribbon* is historical fiction at its best, an instant classic."

Colonel Cole C. Kingseed, USA-Retired, co-author of New York Times best-seller Beyond Band of Brothers: The War Memoirs of Major Dick Winters and Conversation with Major Dick Winters.

Girl with the Purple Ribbon is a sweeping tale of love, loyalty, friendship, and redemption amidst the turbulence of the Vietnam War. Author, Joe Puglia captures the essence of the historical period but reveals the emotions of three friends caught up in a struggle to bring humanity to the horrors of war."

Jack Sacco, best-selling author and Pulitzer Prize nominee: *Where the Birds Never Sing.* **Best-seller,** *Above the Treetops* **and** *Resurrection Sequence.*

Biography

I'm called, *the mechanic of the soul*. As a teacher, I've quelled the waters of troubled souls. Before, I worked the docks, boxed, counseled street gangs, hustled beer at Yankee Stadium, fought a war, fell in love, been a dad, failed a bunch, been a friend and a sinner, hopped an eastbound freight, and raised some holy hell. I just didn't fall off the

vegetable truck. As a street gang worker in the East Bronx, I kept the gangs from killing each other. There, I developed an "Outward Bound" program taking bad-asses to the mountains teaching them how to survive off the land. Thoreau said, "Wilderness is the preservation of the world," I still believe that. I have a Bachelor's in the classics and a quixotic heart; subsequently, I've a penchant for a story. As a columnist for the La Canada Valley Sun, I've written 800 stories, and have three books in my computer looking for a believer. I enjoy writing, philosophy, history, and biography. I'm an adventurer, *on the loose*, hoboing though the *blue highways of America*. Shakespeare asks, "what piece of work is man?" I travel and write my stories to answer this question. Although I've graduated from umpteen universities with assorted degrees lost in drawers, my best education is a Ph.D. from the college of hard-knocks. I've a Master's in Counseling and a Doctorate in Education. I've taught English, history, philosophy, psychology, social science, and wilderness studies. Since I liked the smell of gunpowder, I joined the Marines, became an officer, and served in the Vietnam War. I have two beautiful daughters: Sabine, a junior at the University of Illinois and Simone, a sophomore at the University of Texas. I became father a bit late, but damn the torpedoes, full steam ahead. Send me a note. doctorjoe@ymail.com

Made in the USA
San Bernardino, CA
19 January 2019